Three Corner Fire

K. Hamilton

THREE CORNER FIRE
Copyright © 2021 by K. Hamilton Hutchison

All rights reserved. No part of this book may be reproduced in any form or by any electronic or mechanical means, including information storage and retrieval systems without permission in writing from the publisher, except by a reviewer who may quote brief passages in a review.

ISBN: 9798746052766

Front cover photo by K. Vogee
Book design services by Manuscripts To Go
www.ManuscriptsToGo.com

This is a work of fiction. Names, characters, businesses, places, events, and incidents are either the products of the author's imagination or used in a fictitious manner. Any resemblance to actual persons, living or dead, or actual events is purely coincidental.

This book is dedicated to my best friend, my husband, John Vogee. Summoning the motivation to write while the cancer consumed him, and simultaneously enduring a pandemic shutdown, was incredibly difficult…yet he always had my back and never stopped encouraging me to persevere.

December 10, 1959 - September 19, 2020

"Letting go is not easy, letting go is necessary, and you have to let me go."

I miss you….

ACKNOWLEDGMENTS

To the remarkable Cris Wanzer, you make me look way smarter than I am! This is our second book together and I am so fortunate that the best editor, mentor, and friend loves my work. You never cease to see in me what I miss. During the last few years, when I thought I couldn't, you motivated me to keep going. Thank you for believing in the story and me.

To Debbie Lewis, thank you for knowing what was coming and standing by me when it came. You saw the future because you lived it and I couldn't have made it through everything without you. Love you.

To friends and family who helped us during the most difficult time in our lives…there are so many of you, please forgive any glaring omissions. Thanks to Gary Sello, the Wyckoffs, Ann Felldin, and the Tobins. Thanks also to our extensive Bend, Oregon family, Yvette Blount, the Williams family, the Indian Valley neighborhood, and hospice.

To his beloved dance community, you all made a huge difference in John's life. Thank you to Cheryl Baldovi for making the trip to visit him, to Larry Wilke for being his friend, Robert Royston (who called every day), Connie Bartlett for her constant support, our Bonnie Aby, Bob Fugle, Diane Micheli, and Carlos Contreras.

Above-and-beyond credit: Nancy Thomas, Angela, Ryan, Mad Cowboy, and the team that keeps the lab and the ranch the best they can be.

To the very patient fans of *Three Corner Rustlers*, thank you for waiting! To John Pirhalla for narrating both audio books, and Lorin Rowan for his amazing songs "Three Corner Blues" *(Three Corner Rustlers)* and "Phoenix Rising" *(Three Corner Fire).*

Finally, special thanks to Tommy, for changing a life and helping me realize that the hardest part of healing after losing someone you love is recovering the "me" that went away with "him."

Have you rode the Three Corner country,

in the bunch grass where the free cattle graze?

Have you searched for something you lost,
and learned the high desert's ways?

Trails of the world be countless
and most of the trails be tried.

You tread on the hoof beats of many,
till you come where the hoofprints divide.

Kim Vogee
Bend, Oregon
7/2015

PROLOGUE

The Malheur was primed to burn.
Before it happened, it seemed impossible.
After it happened, it seemed inevitable.

Rancher Boden Criswell couldn't sleep and the weather forecasts did nothing to help his nagging feeling that something bad was about to happen. He heard the distant electrical storm before dawn and with the sun not yet over the hills, a burst of hot, dry air blew into his face as he set off on his four-wheeler to look for "smokes"—those telltale, thin columns of smoke signaling the start of a fire.

Boden headed northwest up a track to a ridge above his grazing pasturelands. He saw his herd there, ambling along the north boundary fence, and noted how healthy the calves looked despite the dry conditions. A team of flankers—wranglers responsible for keeping the calves restrained—would meet him there in a few hours to brand and doctor them. With the conditions being so dry, Boden began to reconsider the branding.

He drove across Pleasant Flats to the high bluffs and stopped when he reached the top. Boden scanned the clear sky and saw no sign of smokes. Relieved, yet still uneasy, he headed back to the ranch for coffee and maybe some breakfast.

He got the call on his cell shortly after he sat down to eat.

It was a neighbor and fellow rancher.

"Did you know you've got smoke up in Adler's Divide?" he said, referring to the spot Boden had just checked, and Boden told him so. "Well, there's something there now," his neighbor informed him.

With one arm in his jacket, Boden switched phone hands and slid his arm into the other sleeve, then adjusted the jacket over his shoulder holster while keeping his phone to his ear.

"I didn't go as far as Three Trails," he said, wondering if he should have. "I'm on it." He was already across the porch and leaping down the steps at a run.

Adrenaline pumping, Boden jumped onto the quad and spun his worn baseball cap around backward. Dirt and gravel sprayed from the rear tires as they grabbed for traction, splattering the porch as he accelerated. He raced down the main road to the ranch and headed for a better vantage point near the highway.

Boden's attention swiveled from the road to the ridgeline off to his left. He slammed on the brakes, skidded sideways to a stop, and faced up to a thin column of smoke drifting into the sky from behind a ridge. He did not need the binoculars but his right hand went to the leather case, freed the clasp, and pulled them out. An untrained eye might have thought it was smoke from a chimney on a calm day...but Boden knew better.

He immediately called dispatch. They had heard about the fire but did not have an exact location. He gave them that and the name of the road that passed close below it.

"If a crew meets me at the ranch," Criswell told the dispatcher, "I can drive them to within a short hike of the fire start." He figured that would be about a thirty-minute trip from their nearby Fire Service compound.

Next, he made a call to the flankers and set them to

rounding up the herd and driving them closer to the ranch.

Later, records showed the call to the dispatcher but the message about the fire was not passed on. No hand crews were available so an aerial assault was scheduled. Crews and resources were misdirected as the number of fires in the area increased. Hours passed and valuable time was lost. Each time they thought they had the fire moving the way they wanted, a freakish gust of wind stole it. The fire flared past them into a draw, up the steep sides, and away. It was one of hundreds of fires that were underestimated…until it was too late.

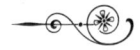

A small team of firefighters arrived at the Criswell Ranch and Boden drove the four men up the road to the base of the ridge, where they still had an hour's hike to the fire. Temperatures were rising and the humidity falling. Overhead, tankers dropped fire retardant. Before the day was half done, high, erratic winds grounded the air assault.

At the quad, Boden watched a young firefighter pull a psychrometer from his belt weather kit to measure the relative humidity in the atmosphere. The firefighter explained that the instrument operated on the principle that dry air enhanced evaporation. "This will help me calculate the likelihood that flying embers will start a new fire," he explained.

The firefighter fell silent as he stared at the device's calculations. Boden asked him what the readings indicated.

"I'm not sure what to say…I've never seen this level

before."

"What does that mean?" Criswell asked.

The firefighter looked around with deep concern and more than a touch of fear across his furrowed brow. He removed his hat and wiped his forehead with his sleeve. "If you throw ten matches on the ground, eight or nine will start a fire."

At that moment, a gust of wind swirled hard around them. Both shielded their eyes as bits of debris pelted and stung. The firefighter shook it off but looked more worried as dust devils spun away from them. He glanced at Boden. "We don't have enough men."

Chapter 1

Life on the McDermitt Indian Reservation on the far northern border of Nevada was a constant struggle. The area, once supported by mining, ranching, and farming, was now sparsely populated and the last silver mining operation had closed in 1990. The community called the "Dugout" had been established as support for Fort McDermitt, which was five miles outside the current township, and the old stage road was the military's most important transportation route to southeast Oregon.

Things had improved some with the arrival of the rescued Three Bit herd. Carson, daughter of rancher Kitzie Collins, had the administrative skills to secure grant money for economic development for the native tribal members. The idea that the herd should stay at Uncle's at the Dugout had coalesced in conversations after the rustled herd had been recovered a few weeks earlier. Harper Lee—undercover government agent and resident of the Dugout with his aunt and uncle—thought it was progressive of Uncle, who tended to avoid bureaucracy, to consider the notion. But Auntie had convinced him to trust Harper and Carson. After all, wasn't that why Harper had been sent off to get an education? With everyone in agreement, the details of the cattle cooperative were worked out and the papers were signed without objection.

Harper Lee sat on the front steps of his aunt and uncle's

tiny, worn-out house. He pushed a strand of long black hair away from his tattooed cheek, then swirled the remains of his coffee in a chipped mug. He watched the odd bits moving around in the bottom, grimaced, and finished it. He thought about the coffee place near campus when he was at college and wished he had never been exposed to really good coffee. On the bright side, his coffee consumption had drastically reduced after returning to the reservation.

He set the mug aside, dusted off his jeans, then rested his elbows on his knees and watched the cattle as they grazed. He could hear his aunt as she cleaned dishes in the kitchen following the waves of breakfast she had made for all the kids. The kitchen was tiny and the table could hold four at most. And since CJ Burke—the athletic, tattooed ex-con from Australia—had been bunking in Will Wyker's trailer and helping out, the kids had been practically living at the Lee homestead.

Harper looked up as one of the older boys, Ely, brought his bowl of cold cereal outside and sat next to him on the step. Ely tucked his long black hair into the collar of his worn T-shirt to keep it out of his bowl. He adjusted the baggy pants that sagged around his thin, teenaged frame and began to eat.

Harper sighed as his gaze returned to the pasture and the outbuildings around Uncle's place. So many things needed attention. CJ had started with the fencing, though he could have pointed himself at the barn and shed rows just as easily. Uncle's place had decades of "deferred maintenance." When Wyker called it that, Harper had stifled himself, as the term was relatable to the entire reservation. Aside from a couple of government buildings made of cinder block and the "historical points of interest" near the highway, the entire Dugout needed maintenance.

William Wyker—Will to his close friends—had been traveling with his border collie, Tammy, in his big truck back and forth between the Three Bit Ranch and the Dugout to set things up. He had left his horse at Uncle's along with his fifth-wheel, which he had offered to CJ. The arrangement was working out well but Wyker wasn't surprised. CJ had few personal possessions and prison had made him a neat person accustomed to small spaces.

Harper listened to Ely crunch his cereal. The boy was a natural storyteller whose favorite tale was about the time Rio, CJ's big, red-roan mustang, was loose in the large field and stole CJ's shirt.

It went something like this: CJ was fixing a section of fence and had removed his shirt to keep it clean. Ely always interjected comments here and there about the intricate, elaborate tattoos that decorated CJ's arms and how strong CJ was, then told how Rio curiously sniffed around CJ's toolbox. The horse picked something out of it and walked off with it in his mouth. CJ said something and Rio dropped it. CJ retrieved it, then Rio took something else as soon as CJ's attention went back to pounding posts. This went on until CJ set down the post pounder, closed the lid of the toolbox, and wagged his finger at his horse, who stood four-square close and seemed to listen.

When CJ bent down to pick up the pounder, Rio trotted up behind him with a mouthful of rabbit grass. He nuzzled CJ's backside, then took ahold of his belt with his teeth and yanked. Some of the slobbery grass dropped down the back of CJ's pants.

"Ugh! Rio!" CJ barked.

Rio took off at a lope with a hump in his back. He dropped his head and swung it from side to side, sending a mass of reddish mane to flop up over his neck. He stopped short, worked his mouth a couple of times, and extra bits of dirt-laden roots and grass fell to the ground.

CJ brushed the grass off his jeans and shook his leg to get out the bits from inside his pants, which jostled them into one of his cowboy boots. He balanced on one foot, pulled off the boot, and dumped it out. Rio sensed an opportunity and trotted straight at CJ. As CJ scrambled to get his boot back on, the bottom of his jeans got hung up in the top of the boot, but he made it, then crouched low and played cow. Rio slid to a stop and they played cutting horse for a few seconds before Rio trotted past CJ toward the kids, who sat on the fence watching. CJ returned to work and tried to ignore them.

Ely embellished the tale in true storyteller fashion when he described Rio's casual amble in the general direction of where CJ had hung his shirt. Rio snatched it off the fence and trotted off. CJ turned just in time to see Rio running away with it, playing with it and swinging it around in the air. Rio half reared and the breeze caught it like a flag. It held momentarily, stretched full, then draped over Rio's face, covering his eyes. The horse stopped short, face covered in the Pendleton shirt, and froze. The kids held their sides, laughing.

CJ dropped the pounder again and ran after Rio. Rio shook the shirt from one eye and bolted off with it, CJ in hot pursuit. Rio dodged, weaved, and swung the shirt tantalizingly close, then trotted off out of reach. The bottom edge of it trailed in the rabbit grass as CJ moaned, "Not another shirt."

Rio eventually surrendered his prize and Ely would always finish with, "And Rio didn't even tear it! Good horse, huh?"

Three Corner Fire

CJ and Rio had been brought together in the Wild Mustang Prison Program—a horsemanship program run by Wyker where inmates helped train wild mustangs. CJ and Rio were his favorites. Fresh to his memory was the day that CJ had his first—and at the time, only—ride on Rio, just before he was paroled. After CJ left that day on the prison bus, Wyker stopped a pair of crafty kill buyers from taking Rio, and the horse became a special project for him. Wyker handled him daily, solidifying his groundwork and manners.

There would always be a streak in Rio that was more stud than gelding but he was whip-smart, athletic, and he never forgot a thing. In a pen with over a hundred horses, Rio would catch your attention by the way he carried himself—how he moved, the shake of his head, that red-devil hair, and the sparkle of the sun on his well-set neck. There was a strong character inside that big-boned red roan and Wyker understood that he needed to be very clear with this one. But Rio was a quick study and he couldn't have been in better hands.

Without CJ's knowledge, Wyker arranged work for him at the Three Bit Ranch, owned by the widowed Kitzie Collins. It took some convincing for the indomitable ranch owner to agree to hire an ex-con, but Wyker asked her to trust him. And she did.

"Tuff trusted you," she said, referring to her deceased husband. "And if he were here, I believe he would agree."

CJ arrived at the Three Bit in the middle of a crisis and was flung into action. He handled things as best he could, though it was a bit like being tossed into the deep end of a pool without water wings. Much to his surprise, not only was his mentor, Wyker, there, but Wyker had brought Rio with him. Rio was Wyker's gift to CJ—one that CJ struggled to accept. Good things happening to him was not how things usually worked in his life and he didn't know how to handle it. But Wyker had a way of stating things simply and honestly, and he didn't care how CJ took it, just as long as he did. It wasn't long before CJ was proving his mettle and the adventure to find the stolen Three Bit cattle began.

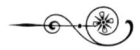

Uncle joined Harper Lee and settled into his favorite chair, which barely fit on the small front porch. The antique barber's chair had a well-worn leather cushion, which was smooth and shiny in places where it had hardened to a patina. In the winter, the snow blew drifts around the armrests and the sun melted it unevenly, leaving permanent, slender shadows on the seat. The mechanics of the chair were long frozen. Somewhat preserved were the carved wooden sides and wrought-iron hardware that were unwilling to surrender their past. The screen door hit the arm of the chair, wearing a spot on both. Stubbornly reluctant to disintegrate, the chair's old-time elegance still shone through, out of place on Uncle's unrailed porch. It didn't matter what was going on, Uncle loved to sit out there. He told Harper that if he sat still long enough, he could feel the earth moving.

As Harper Lee sat on the stoop, his elbows still on his knees, he found himself reflecting on how things were working out. He liked it that a routine had quickly settled into place. The midmorning sun dappled the ground and played shadows on the worn wood of the porch. Wide, weathered planks that once felt solid were warped from use and time. Out of the corner of his eye, Harper studied Uncle's face—deep crevices and leathery skin over proud cheekbones that curved up to eyes that missed very little. Harper had come to know this from personal experience. Nothing of consequence got past Uncle and if it did, it was because he let it.

"Uncle, this side of the porch is failing. I'll fix it," he offered.

"It's fine," Uncle answered without looking at his nephew, his long, graying hair shadowing his face slightly. His focus was on young Ely, who had left the porch and was standing with CJ, perfecting a rope trick.

Harper watched Uncle's face, not the trick. It was a rope trick Uncle had taught them and when he thought the trick was getting away from Ely, he squinted. His right hand lifted off the chair arm and his fingers moved as if willing the rope to make the pattern. The tiny lines on his face eased as the trick pulled back together and gained momentum to a clean finish. The result brought a small *harrumph* from deep in Uncle's throat, a straight-lipped smile, and a sip of coffee from his old mug.

The screen door creaked a brief protest and Auntie's soft footfalls padded the few feet across the porch. The stitching on the toes of her handmade moccasins was even and neat, the beading delicate and colorful. Auntie liked color in her art but her personal clothing style leaned toward the predictable. She always wore loose-fitting dark pants that stopped at the ankle, and she favored a man's navy-blue buttoned shirt, rolled up to the elbows. Cinching the shirt at her waist was her father's leather belt, adorned with stamped sterling silver slide conchos that he had collected throughout his life. But the most remarkable part was the sterling silver and Paiute turquoise belt buckle, with its gorgeous electric-blue color and black spiderweb matrix. Paiute turquoise was uncommon and of extraordinarily high quality, and Harper's eye was always drawn to it. Auntie's gray-streaked black hair was as shiny as a young girl's and she wore it in two long, perfect plaits.

Auntie touched Uncle's shoulder. The coffee pot tilted and tepid coffee arced into Uncle's cup. He looked up at Auntie and in their silent language, said thank you. She poured the rest in Harper's cup and retreated as quietly as she had come.

Then, possessed of a thought, Uncle softly said, "CJ's come a long way in a short time."

Harper mused, "You think?"

"It's good he stayed. The kids are good for him."

Harper sipped the coffee, made a face, and threw the rest onto the ground. Uncle cast him a disparaging look as if he'd thrown away gold.

Harper laughed and shook his head. "I don't know how you drink that all day."

Uncle sipped some more, then said, "A man may run from his nature but the world finds him out."

Harper, incredulous, piped back, "That I've become a coffee snob?"

Uncle just nodded. Harper knew a philosophical mood on Uncle when he saw it. Best not to distract him when he was trying to say something. Some real gems spilled out if he let him roll.

Uncle tipped his chin up at the clouds that scudded overhead. "Sometimes pain sits so quietly, he thinks it may be gone, but then the clouds gather and he's not so sure."

Harper stood up, cup in hand, and tapped his uncle's knee. As he opened the screen door, he turned and watched CJ and Ely rope. Some of his long black hair slid past his left shoulder and a mischievous twinkle appeared in his eye. He looked down at Uncle and teased, "Where do you get that shit?"

Uncle gave him the look he'd given Harper his whole life. Harper grinned and went inside. He smiled at Auntie, his heart full as he walked into the kitchen and set his mug in the sink. That's how it was at Uncle's on the Rez. There wasn't much money but there was an abundance of something solid and enduring. Something to be counted on.

Harper Lee went back to the screen door and looked at the ropers. Though hard ground between Harper and CJ still existed, Harper had started to see a glimmer of CJ's dry sense of humor. Harper surmised that completely relaxing his guard around a government agent was still a walk too far for CJ, but he felt some progress. There were unguarded moments when CJ's defenses showed signs of fracture, especially around the kids—when joy and simple pleasures just happened. When CJ was around the kids, his eyes smiled.

Later that day, his chores done, CJ sat atop Rio and leaned on the horn of his saddle. He squinted at the approaching kids, who had gathered and were staging an "attack." He sat up, pulled off his hat, and ran a hand through his long brown hair. His hand-me-down shirt strained against the honed muscles of his upper arms. Replacing the hat, he wondered if Auntie was any good at haircuts. He could use a shave too. The days-old grizzle on his face completed the picture of "the bad guy" and his mouth set in a firm line as the kids stalked and hunted him from the brush.

After the short hunting game with the kids, CJ and Rio approached the Dugout. Carson and Wyker had returned from the Three Bit. They were readying for the upcoming ride to retrieve two pack horses, one of them injured, that they had left behind at Sanctuary—a safe, hidden canyon with shade, feed, and ample water—after rescuing the Three Bit herd. He saw Wyker and Carson in the field by the barn. Carson was on Wyker's horse, Johnny, polishing up on her roping skills, and Tammy ran back and forth along the fence. CJ's eyes met Carson's for a second as he rode past, then he looked away.

Carson, unreadable from under her flat-brimmed Buckaroo hat, did a clean rollback on Johnny and her long, auburn braid swung freely down the back of her vest. She carried a knife on her belt—her father's favorite, single-blade folding knife that she'd found in the drawer of his desk in the barn. He liked it because it held an edge and the years hadn't dulled it. She kind of hoped the same was true of her. The rest of her "kit" consisted of her thick leather chaps (the ones that turned the brush well), a neckerchief, and gloves, all of which were in Wyker's truck. She was ready to go.

In the tight quarters of Auntie's kitchen that night, dinner was a rowdy affair. The excitement was palpable and the kids crowded close to hear everything. The conversation revolved around the ride. Wyker and Harper felt that they needed to get going before the Sanctuary grasses were depleted. Ely made an impassioned plea to go, and the floodgates opened when four of the other boys wanted in too. It was hard to deny them a day's adventure as they got excited and talked of finding the rustlers that had gotten away. Wyker assured the boys, and

Auntie, that they were long gone. The younger boys asked Uncle if he would paint their faces to look like Harper's facial tattoos, and he said he'd think about it.

Wyker asked if they had any hay nets and Auntie sent the kids to the barn to retrieve a bucketful of strings pulled from the hay bales. When they returned, Auntie sat cross-legged on the floor with a handful of string and began to straighten the pieces. In quick succession, she weaved together two bags and attached them so that when they were filled with hay, they'd sit balanced on either side of a saddle. The kids surrounded her, fascinated. Carson stood and watched too, equally intrigued by Auntie's resourcefulness.

Afterward, Auntie sent the kids to bed. They were stoked about the next day's adventure and hoped it would turn into an overnight campout. Dampening their expectations was all but impossible. None of them would sleep a wink that night.

CJ disappeared into the fifth-wheel. Everyone else bunked where they could find space.

Carson stayed in what felt like a closet with a tiny window and a daybed. She should have been tired, but like the children, it took her a while to fall asleep. She was surrounded by Auntie's Native American art projects in various stages of progress. The upside was that Auntie's art was marvelous; the downside was the room was next to the only bathroom, and the habits of the household were well known to Carson by morning.

Chapter 2

A strong wind sent dust devils down the street and a gust struck the window of the restaurant with a sharp blow. Sheriff Spence was about to take a sip of coffee from his white porcelain mug when he stopped and looked.

"That was a strong one," Lyle remarked.

Spence was having an early breakfast at the Pine Tavern with Lyle Martin. Lyle's family had founded the town and he owned and operated the local hardware and ranch supply store, Martin Ranch Supply. A cattleman himself, he was the spine of the community, a leveling force, the calm-in-the-face-of-chaos guy, and a natural leader everyone appreciated.

The town of Martin was part of Spence's beat and it was generally a quiet shift. It had been a while since he and Lyle had had time to catch up—not since the deaths of two of the town's citizens under suspicious circumstances.

That had been a very stressful time for Lyle and extremely difficult for the small, tight-knit community. The deaths were connected to the cattle rustling that had been going on in the Three Corner (ION) country of Idaho, Oregon, and Nevada. The rustling had stopped right around the time an old cattleman, Hank Larsen, was found murdered along with his dog, Sonny, and the mysterious death of a local loser by the name of Del Riggs. The cash theft by the tavern's only waitress, Shiloh Taylor, followed by her disappearance, had capped off that tumultuous week.

Lyle was relieved the rustling had stopped. It had caused longtime friends and neighbors to become suspicious of each other. Lyle saw the damage firsthand and it saddened him. He had hoped that once the general facts became known, a kind of healing would take place, but the once dearest of friends never got beyond casual politeness afterward and Lyle knew there was nothing that could be done.

He confessed to Spence, "Gawd, I don't miss all that." He shook his head. "Got so I had to watch who was in the store, those awkward silences between longtime friends...or worse, I had to step in occasionally to see that a bump or shove didn't come to blows."

Trina, the new waitress at the Tavern, walked the tables holding two coffee pots. Spence nodded a thank you for topping up his caffeine. Lyle had decaf. He enjoyed his eggs overmedium with bacon. He left some of the whole wheat toast on the plate, wiped his hands with his napkin, and watched Trina help another customer.

Toby, who ran the tavern, cooked breakfast and lunch, and silently mourned the loss of Shiloh. She had been very popular with the customers, especially the men. Hearts were broken when the attractive, shapely blond disappeared.

Trina was a quiet, efficient waitress who set a different tone than Shiloh did and the customers adapted to the change faster than Toby did. With black hair and dark eyes, Trina was built like a pre-pubescent boy. Fluently bilingual, Goth style, piercings, tattoos, and shiny black lipstick, she was the antithesis of Shiloh.

Spence swallowed a bite of his fried-egg sandwich. Damn, he loved those. He decided that Toby had outdone himself.

This one was perfect. The cheese melted into the slightly soft egg-yolk center. He hurried another bite so it wouldn't drip onto the plate.

Lyle leaned in and quietly asked, "Any sign of the girl?"

Spence swallowed. "Nope. Off the radar completely. As if she didn't exist. Darnedest thing. No signs and it's all gone stale now." He sipped some orange juice and continued in a lower voice, "Toby's either forgotten all about it or he's resigned himself to the fact that she's really gone."

Lyle's voice was low too as he asked, "Was there any truth to the rumor that Del beat her up?"

"Or worse…" A shadow crossed Spence's face. He abhorred violence of any kind against a woman. "She got beat up, that's for sure…and something bad happened that night and it was bad all the way around."

Lyle lifted his mug and drained it, then turned his gaze to the bits of tumbleweed blowing down the main street in town. A large piece of uprooted grassy stuff swirled into the air and got stuck in the roof lights of Spence's patrol car. It lingered and shook until a sideways blast of air freed it and it flew away.

"I was thinking about Hank this morning," Spence said. "Think I'll drive over there and check on the place." He wiped a bit of yolk up with the corner of his sandwich. "That place bank-owned still?" He popped the morsel into his mouth.

"Yeah, and I haven't heard of any activity on it," Lyle said. "Why? You interested?"

"No. You?" Spence replied.

Lyle shook his head and placed his napkin next to his finished plate. "I was holding out hope that one of his boys would come back. Those bank deals are just paperwork. There's no love for the history of a place. No understanding of the generations that loved and worked the ground they called home. I'd like to see it run again."

"Don't hold your breath on that family. No one ever claimed the body," Spence said, shaking his head.

Lyle sighed, slid to the edge of the vinyl bench seat, and pivoted to look at Spence. "Really? I didn't know that." He pulled some money from his pocket.

Spence stopped him, said that he had it this time, and they rose together. Lyle smiled. They shook hands and parted.

The wind tugged at Spence's cap as he stepped onto the sidewalk. He grabbed it and pressed it more firmly to his head. A couple of birds flew overhead, tumbling in the wind as Spence got into his cruiser. The engine came alive with a throaty roar and he waved at Lyle as he cruised down the street.

On his way to Larsen Ranch, Spence slowed when he saw a group of buckaroos heading and heeling calves in a pen near the road, readying them for branding. He pulled over and watched the men work. Some outfits heeled and dragged, others headed and heeled. The goal was to bring the calves to the fire with minimal stress to the animal. Spence admired how smooth and quick they were. They knew their jobs and so did their horses. They had a man on the propane fire this day—more of a contained heater that looked handcrafted and efficient. In this dry air and wind, any open fire would be unwise. One of the buckaroos rode his horse closer to the road and spoke to Spence. He said they didn't like the way the wind felt and that they were quitting. He turned his horse and rejoined the crew.

Spence waved to the others, who waved in return, and he moved on until he came to the dirt road that led to Hank Larsen's old place. The bank's For Sale sign had gotten shot up by someone and one post had been hit by something, then the wind must have blown it flat.

    Dust roiled behind the patrol car and Spence closed his window. The road and everything else vanished from the rearview mirror as he made his way up the driveway carefully. Gravel and rock bits pinged and sang against the undercarriage. Brush and sedges had taken hold on both sides of the road and were reclaiming what had been theirs decades ago. There were some nasty ruts and Spence braked to a crawl and maneuvered the cruiser to navigate the worst of them. His mind flashed briefly to his truck sitting back at the station but he liked his patrol car. It wasn't the latest model, which was fine by him. It reminded him of the old Crown Victoria. He had a history with the Vic. It made him think of his dad.

    He passed the place where he'd found Del's body. He slowed to a stop near a boulder and let the dust blow past, then rolled down his window as details of that awful night flooded back. Del had crashed his piece-of-shit car into that big rock there as he fled the scene of his crime.

    Spence looked at the spot and remembered odd bits, like how he didn't initially understand the wetness around Del's head. The coroner later answered the question—there was urine in Del's mouth, which begged more questions. Spence pressed him for his best guess and recalled the sound of the coroner snapping off his latex gloves as he headed to the sink and washed his hands. He turned toward Spence as he grabbed a towel and dried them. "Specifically, it wasn't human urine, it was animal. And, if I were to hazard a guess, canine."

    Spence eased his foot off the brake and the car coasted forward. The rocks and gravel crunched beneath his tires. The road was narrow and bent before it went up a small bluff. The long hood momentarily obscured his vision and crested the rise to reveal a large, flat area that served as parking for the house, the barn, several outbuildings, and lean-to sheds. He stopped there and surveyed the sight. Not much had changed aside from weeds and brush busily reasserting themselves. The outbuildings, ahead and off to the right, were undamaged by the fire that had destroyed the house. The old truck was still there, as were other farm and ranch tools, and the tractor. A shame, that. The chimney, a lone sentry, stood tall, its bricks intact but blackened. The concrete foundation, front stoop, and frame of the front door remained.

Spence turned off the engine. He heard the sound of the wind whistling and it whipped up another small dust devil, which spun itself onto the stoop and through the doorframe. He got out and walked over to the spot where he'd found Hank and Sonny. He turned, went to the stoop by the remains of the door, and saw it—that butt-ugly porcelain frog thing. It was still there—the thing he'd accidentally overturned that night and found the cell phone inside.

Hank had been obsessed with finding out who had stolen the last of his cows, and he had zeroed-in on Del. Near as Spence could figure, Hank had followed a hunch and lifted Del's phone from his car, probably when it was parked behind the tavern that night. Witness statements from the bar said that Del was in a sour mood and had been drinking heavily. Though Spence would never know Hank's full story, he suspected that Hank had figured out who was responsible for the cattle rustling.

Spence's mind rewound to that day when he had walked up to Hank as he sat in his truck, parked on the main street of Martin. Hank was staring straight ahead, his colorless hands gripping the steering wheel of the only thing he owned. Sonny's white-flecked muzzle rested on his master's thigh. Spence hated being the one who had to deliver the bank's eviction order. Though rage and hatred consumed Hank, he did not blame Spence. Somehow, Spence found the words to encourage Hank to go back to the house. He was pretty busy and said he didn't have time to check on the place for the bank, nor did anyone else for that matter. He remembered that was when Hank finally looked at him and there was a kind of gratitude in his tired eyes. After that difficult conversation, the two of them walked to the Pine Tavern and had breakfast together.

Spence regretted that he hadn't paid more attention. He wished Hank had trusted him enough to tell him what he knew or suspected. Spence figured Hank had acted on his own and that the stolen cell phone was the catalyst for his murder.

Spence walked carefully around the spot where he'd found Hank's broken body with his beloved Sonny lying on him, dead too. Hank had probably fought back when Del came to get his phone. Someone at the bar told him Hank had it but Del wouldn't have thought to look in that porcelain frog on the front step. Clever of Hank to hide it there.

Spence reasoned that when Del was unable to find the phone, in a rage, he'd struck down the frail old man. The coroner's report mentioned that Del had been bitten on his legs repeatedly.

Good boy, Sonny, Spence thought.

He felt that tickle in his nose and the moistness in his eyes. He removed his cap, held it in front of him, bowed his head, and said a prayer as heartfelt as if he was standing at his father's grave.

Sheriff Spence had kept track of what happened to Hank's

remains. He'd admired Old Man Larsen since he was a kid in short pants. He was more than dismayed to learn that Hank's family was either too cheap or too heartless to claim the body. They'd abandoned the family homestead as soon as they could and abandoned the old rancher just as thoroughly.

Hank's body lay unclaimed in the morgue. Both the coroner's calls to the family and Spence's went unanswered, their messages unreturned. At the scene, the coroner had taken Hank's body but left Sonny's. In a moment of...Spence didn't know what to call it...he'd scooped up Sonny, wrapped him in a blanket, and put him gently in the trunk of his patrol car. He contacted the local veterinarian and was able to store Sonny's body in his freezer. When no one made arrangements for Hank, Spence decided to tap his retirement account and the coroner made the arrangements for Hank's cremation. Spence also asked for a favor. The coroner gave Spence directions and said someone would meet him when he got to the mortuary.

"Where is he?" the attendant asked.

"In the trunk of my car."

"Jeez, for how long?"

"Long enough," Spence answered with a shrug. "He's been on ice at the local vet's."

"I see. Um...this is a little unusual. Please go around to the double doors in the back." The attendant pointed the way. "I'll meet you there." He turned and disappeared down a long passageway.

Spence drove around the building and saw two huge doors swing open slowly. They seemed to open automatically and held until a button was pressed inside.

"Damn, why such big doors?" Spence asked as he put his key into the lock and the trunk lid popped open.

The attendant approached wearing a pressed blue, smock-style lab coat over his day suit, his red tie peeking through the top, and he had thick, black rubber gloves on. "Some of the clients are, shall we say, more…*substantial*…than others."

"Oh?" Spence said, his eyebrows arching.

"Yeah, the old doors were too small and there was a…situation. I had nightmares for weeks."

Spence's trunk was neat and organized. He had wrapped Sonny in a blanket and then in a large plastic bag. Among the things you'd expect to see in the trunk of a patrol car, there was a small pile of neatly folded blankets, half a case of bottled water, and a couple of brand-new stuffed animals. The man picked one up and gave Spence an amused look.

"For when there's a wreck and if there are kids, or sometimes it's a DUI… One time this idiot had his kid in the car. It got ugly, the kid was crying, he wouldn't stop. Anyway, after that, I carry those and I keep a supply of soft blankets that I can wrap a frightened child in." Spence bent down and picked up Sonny's body.

"Or an old man's dog," the attendant added in a softer voice.

"Or an old man's dog," Spence repeated, then said, "This is Sonny."

A week later, he returned and collected two plastic containers, Sonny's the smaller of the two. The size and weight of Hank's ashes surprised him. Spence realized he'd never held a box of human ashes before. He placed them on the seat next to him. Sonny and Hank.

He fastened his seat belt and looked at the boxes.

"Buckle up, boys," Spence said to them.

Now, there he was, back at the Larsen Ranch. The weather

had been dry and the forecast warned of high fire danger. The wind tugged at his cap and he removed it and placed it on the seat of the car. Unbidden, memories of his father welled up, as if he could hear his words telling him he had done the right thing.

He set the containers on the roof of his car, rearranged his sidearm, straightened his heavy belt, took a moment, and leaned his back against the door. He desperately wanted to replace the memory of Sonny and Hank lying on the bloody ground.

The morning light stretched long and made the mundane extraordinarily beautiful. The light played across the vertical boards of the barn's weathered siding. Partially extruded nail heads cast horizontal lines scattered between shades of brown and gray and the dotted tufts of vibrant, greenish-yellow lichen.

Spence turned, sighed deeply, and picked up the two plastic receptacles. He stepped away from the car and turned in a circle as if giving both spirits another look at the land that they'd once held so dear. Then he faced what was left of the house. Between teeth held tight against upwelling emotions, he sucked in a soft whistle. The sun shone perfectly through the portal of what remained of the Larsen homestead. The skeletal casing of the front door framed the rising sun as it cast its tongue-like beams around Spence's patrol boots. It was as if he was being shown sacred ground. His vision blurred for a moment.

Spence crouched and worked the tight-fitting lids free. The ash looked like any other ash. Setting the plastic lids aside, he balanced the boxes together in his hands, Hank in his right hand and Sonny in his left. With streams of golden light all around him, he poured them out together on the spot where their lives had ended. Oddly, the strong wind stopped long enough for the ashes to fuse in a steady stream that fell softly to the earth. There they lay together peacefully.

This ending would be Spence's new memory—the violence not forgotten, but the old vision replaced with a fresher, less painful one. It placed the experience in a form he could accept and move on from.

He held the empty vessels in his hands, closed his eyes to the warmth of the sun, and recited the Lord's Prayer. This light was his way forward. When he was done, the wind returned and blew a lock of his hair free. It had given grace just long enough for this ceremony, then blustered its intrusion as he finished.

Spence placed the containers in his car, wiped his eyes on his sleeve, and knew that he'd done his best there. He reached for his seatbelt and looked over at the spot. The ashes were gone.

Chapter 3

Six weeks after the assault, Shiloh Taylor noticed the changes and they dismayed her. She bought a pregnancy test at a drug store and pointed her motorhome toward the nearest Planned Parenthood to get checked out.

A stiff breeze bent the trees where she parked and it was strong enough that she didn't put the awnings out. She'd chosen the location because it was within walking distance to the clinic. In the laundry room of the motorhome park, she found a payphone and erring on the side of caution, used it to make an appointment.

The voice at the other end was kind and professional, though edgy at first. The woman asked questions that Shiloh felt were meant to screen callers. Shiloh reassured her that she legitimately needed women's health services.

"I'm sorry, dear," the woman said. "There are protesters outside and they try to get in here by faking who they are." She paused as she buzzed someone in. "We have security," she reassured her, "but these people are very aggressive. Would you like me to have someone escort you into the building?"

Shiloh assured her that she could handle it on her own.

The next morning, she donned an oversized shirt, a baseball cap, and put on sunglasses. She wanted to be anonymous. She locked her real identification in the safe, made note of who was around her unit in the park, and locked it up tight before she left.

As she neared the clinic, she heard the chanting protesters before she saw them. One of them pointed at Shiloh and another trotted toward her, brochure in hand, quoting bible scripture. She was middle-aged, heavy in the wrong places, and her face was flushed from the exertion. In raspy, urgent breaths, she urged Shiloh to "join" them and stop the slaughter of innocent babies.

Shiloh shook her head and politely said, "No, thank you, please let me pass."

But the woman was pushy and refused to be denied a few moments of Shiloh's time. Shiloh was determined too and in her breathy "baby" voice, she declined the woman's impassioned entreaty again and attempted to walk around her.

Then the woman grabbed Shiloh's arm. "But they're killing babies! Don't you care?"

Shiloh stopped and stared at the hand on her arm, and her mind swirled. Her eyes tracked a path up from that hand to the woman's face, and in slow motion, she twisted her arm free and walked purposefully ahead.

The woman chased after Shiloh, calling out to her companions, defying a court-ordered limit of how close to the clinic they were allowed to be. They formed a barrier on the sidewalk. Shiloh didn't want a bunch of drama and tried to calmly move around them. But they persisted and pawed at her. Behind her dark glasses, Shiloh's eyes hardened and something snapped inside.

The woman caught her by the arm again. Shiloh faced her and her hand slowly encircled the woman's exposed wrist. Her grip tightened and she began to dig her nails into the woman's flesh. The woman's stream of rhetoric stalled, then she croaked, "That hurts…"

Shiloh's nails dug deep and the woman winced and tried to curl away from her.

Shiloh leaned in close to the woman's face, her voice hard. "Yeah, try to get away. That's what I tried to do when he attacked me." And she squeezed harder, her nails carving deeper into the woman's skin.

The woman cried out that she was being assaulted.

"Grabbing me twice is assault," Shiloh said. She didn't let go.

One of the other women tried to intervene and Shiloh hissed, "Back off, bitch, or I take you next." Shiloh straightened, released the woman's wrist, and saw that her nails had broken the skin. Her voice instantly reverted to that sugary tone, all feathery, and she sweetly said, "Oh, dear…you'd better get something on that. Don't want it to get infected."

The woman recoiled, rubbed her wrist, and mumbled something about how Shiloh should love the child herself. Looking a little ashamed, she tried to spout more propaganda. Her cheeks were flushed as she turned to her two shocked friends and they consoled her. One yelled at Shiloh's back.

"Murderer! That was assault!" she screamed.

Not turning back, Shiloh flipped her the bird and said in a loud voice, "Sue me."

The guard reached Shiloh and motioned that he would escort her inside. Shiloh raised her hand and sweetly said thank you, but she was all right. With a calm that belied the turmoil she felt inside, she walked to the entrance as the guard caught up and held the door for her. She continued the façade of calm as she approached the reception area, though her heart pounded in her chest and her head throbbed.

The demeanor inside the clinic was opposite of what she'd encountered outside and the receptionist was very kind. Shiloh used a false name and claimed she didn't have any identification after being robbed and raped. Her cash spoke for her.

She was handed a clipboard with forms to fill out. She certainly had no intention of being truthful but there were spaces to fill in with something. Her head swam and she felt nauseated. Shiloh found that the adrenaline rush had turned her thighs to jelly and she was more upset by the confrontation than she wanted to admit. She felt dizzy for a moment and sat down harder than she meant to. The chair jarred against the wall with a thud. The receptionist looked up over the high counter with a questioning glance and Shiloh tried to act normal. She mouthed, *Sorry*, but the room still spun. The receptionist disappeared and reappeared in front of Shiloh with a cup of water, which Shiloh gratefully accepted.

Shiloh nodded her appreciation and the woman retreated to her post. As Shiloh held the cup in her hands, the pounding in her head didn't recede. She looked at a brochure on the side table and the message at the top read, "Rape doesn't ask for permission, always resorts to violence and fear, and is assault and spiritual theft."

Shiloh nodded. She had been robbed. Robbed of everything about herself that she had tried to like. Now she was a host. The hate was growing inside of her and she wanted it gone.

Then the pounding drained like water out of a tub and she felt the blood rush from her head. Tunnel vision filled her sight. *What an odd sensation*, she thought. She set the cup aside and put her head between her knees, hoping it would pass. The clipboard fell from her hands and made no sound as it clattered to the floor. She thought she was reaching for it...she thought that was where her hand was going...but her body followed and she slid to the floor and passed out.

When she awoke, she was on a gurney. She felt cold and clammy. A nurse's voice close to her head explained that she'd had a miscarriage and had been transferred to a hospital. She let the nurse fill out the form she hadn't completed fully and signed an illegible scrawl across the page.

Shiloh was treated with respect and kindness. As things worked out, during the procedure, they caught something—an early diagnosis of cervical cancer. The days that followed were a blur and Shiloh remained a calm and trusting patient. She wasn't exactly sure where she was or at what hospital, but whoever they were, they were efficient and caring.

When Shiloh met the doctor afterward, the physician was clear and specific. She explained that she felt they had gotten all the cancerous cells, that she had experience with cases just like hers, and that Shiloh would need to seek other measures to have children if she chose to have a family.

They offered her referrals for further treatments and Shiloh dutifully took them but she had no intention of pursuing them. For a few weeks, she stayed close by in the motorhome and recuperated from the surgery without incident. She felt she had been successfully treated and got what she considered to be a clean bill of health.

While she rested, she read, watched some of the movies that had come with the coach, and stayed out of sight from anyone in the park. She'd set aside that blasted box she'd found in the motorhome, cleverly hidden in the depths of a storage compartment, and though curious, she wasn't in any particular hurry to open it. It was so cleverly constructed that her admiration for the stranger who had provided the motorhome for her grew. *One step at a time*, she told herself.

When she was stronger and no longer sleeping most of the day away, Shiloh set small, daily goals for herself. One challenge that remained a constant was the box. So, one day she pulled it out and set it on the kitchen table by the window, where it taunted her and held fast to its secrets.

Chapter 4

A documentary film crew was at the state fairgrounds to film a slick promotional video for the American Quarter Horse Association to highlight the sport of Cowboy Mounted Shooting—a fast-growing sport that combined target shooting, barrel racing, and pure adrenaline.

At the production house, an editor watched the live feeds from his cameramen on one monitor, and routed clips to his editing screen on another. One of the cameras slowly panned to the polished smoothness of a stainless-steel Colt 45 set on a table in the armory—the only place competitors were allowed to load. Later, they would add the narrator's country-tinged baritone explaining that the gun was single-action and the hammer was pulled back after each shot. Embers from the black powder blanks went no more than twenty feet to explode balloons set on the ends of five-foot-tall poles.

The next scene focused on one of the premier competitors, Rae Royston, who waited calmly for her turn on her horse, Docket. The crisp close-up captured the line of her cheek, then her hands as she inserted her earplugs. Docket's earplugs were already in place as shots reverberated in the arena while the competitor before her finished up his pattern.

Docket was one of those outwardly unremarkable Quarter Horses, solidly built, with a good eye and expression, deceptively fast, and wickedly agile. Inside that bay body was the heart of a champion who only needed the right partner to make him shine. He was one of those rare, once-in-a lifetime horses who was lucky enough to have a perfect match in his human. He and Rae thought and moved as one entity, seamlessly, their respect for each other undeniable and permanent. He was her priority and she his.

Gun smoke hung low in the arena, wisping and curling in the air currents. The editor liked the look of it and isolated a clip. He messed with the film speed, rewinding and replaying it until he had something he really liked. Distant thunder rolled somewhere in the background and there was something cool about the mix of sounds and the natural echo in the arena. He made more adjustments and replayed the sequence again. Unaware that the sound he was creatively manipulating was part of an electrical storm—the herald of dangerous events unfolding—he paused his edits and returned his attention to the live feeds.

Nearby, one of many lightning strikes landed and similar wisps of smoke curled against the leaf litter. It faded red to black and lay unborn. Wind whipped a power line overhead. It bounced and swayed erratically, contact came close, missed, and came close again.

Rae and Docket jogged into the arena, circled, and picked up an easy lope until Rae turned her head and Docket hit the gas. At normal speed, the scene would have been over too quickly. The editor resumed editing and manipulated the speed of the footage to capture the flash of the gun muzzle in slow motion, the burst of smoke arcing and curling away, and the balloon bursting with the rider setting up the next shot and moving slightly out of focus.

At the same time, off in the distance, a moderate breeze

kicked into stronger gusts that violently banked the branches of the trees. A cascade of sparks showered tinder-dry vegetation below high power lines that met the wind and failed to resist it. Bursts of hot air found ground where glowing embers crawled. Tufts of smoke rose; minute flames multiplied and caught hold of leaf litter and dead debris. One smoldering leaf caught the chaotic wind and was joined by many more.

Docket and Rae made excellent time through the first part of the pattern and the camera effectively captured the horse's chest muscles as he powerfully carved the arena's footing. Bits of dirt splashed up and away, accentuating the action despite the reduced film speed. Docket's face reflected years of experience and skill as he maneuvered for maximum torque as they cleanly rounded a barrel. The editor highlighted the clip on his screen and played with it a bit. He found that returning the action to normal made the burst of speed coming out of the tight turn more dramatic.

A perfectly timed gust of wind mirrored his edit as it howled down to the smoking strike and the ground exploded into flames. Nearby brush caught and embers fanned out in all directions.

Docket's steadiness at speed was his special gift. Rae dropped the reins onto his neck as she drew her rifle at the height of the gravitational pull, cocked, and fired. Docket stretched out, his powerful legs pulling the planet beneath his body.

As if driven by an invisible force, the wind whipped the fire into a frenzy, and like a swarm of angry bees, red-hot embers ran unhindered through rugged terrain and consumed dry, grassy hills connected to the mountains beyond. A tree, engulfed in flames, bent over in the wind and was gone.

Superheated air rose in tornadic columns, broke at the apex, and shot ahead to breed. The devil's only friend took an acre a second, the unburnable burned, and the unconsumable was consumed.

After Rae's winning run, the editor went back to slow motion and captured her as she rotated in her saddle, fired, and completed the pattern. The last balloon exploded. He gasped at the artistry of what he had just seen, stopped the film, and replayed it. The action rocked. The angles were great, the lighting perfect, and he was stoked. He again looked at the live feeds, anxious to see what his cameramen were going to catch next.

And then the lights went out in the arena and the feeds went dead. The editor tapped on his monitor, then sat back and looked at the frozen image of MacRae Royston and Docket on his editing screen, wondering what had happened.

Chapter 5

Shiloh had vanished down the road once again. She followed a route that eventually took her out into the desert. It was the wrong time of year if you loathed the heat but most resorts were empty and she had her pick of places—really nice ones. Top-drawer hook-ups and she didn't care if the AC ran all the time.

She found a space under an elaborate cover that provided protection from the sun and kept the units cooler for the year-rounders It was nicer than the big, pitch-dark warehouse she'd found the coach in, which was private and hidden from everything but was like living in a pocket. She had no desire for that.

During her recovery, Shiloh had had plenty of time to discover most of the motorhome's secrets. She found an old pair of cowboy boots in a storage bay. Her guess was that the owner was average-sized man and she almost gave them away, but changed her mind. Now, as she set the levelers, she had an idea. She pulled the old cowboy boots from the bay and set them neatly, just so, by the doormat but decided it looked too contrived. She picked them up and dropped them. They flopped down and landed toe to heel, as though they'd been kicked off, one upright and one lying on its side. She considered what kind of message one might get from used footwear. What kind of man was the wearer? And most importantly, what kind of message was she trying to silently send? Satisfied for the moment, she left them on the mat. She studied her effort, considered leaving her shoes out there too, but decided against it. Before she closed and locked the door, she decided that finding an enormous, truly hideous pair of used men's shoes that might dissuade strangers from bothering her was something to do at a Goodwill somewhere. But for now, these would do.

Shiloh sat down at the table, where she had left a manila envelope she'd recently found in the coach. She felt like an archeologist after unearthing something rare. A detective of the past, contemplating how to examine the find, then interpret its meaning, its place in history. Whose artifact had she found? What realities would its history reveal? She glanced at the mysterious box, which she still hadn't figured out how to open, then turned her attention back to the envelope.

Shiloh opened the thick envelope. Inside was a series of documents and the first one she looked at was a birth certificate. *Hers.* She held it in her hands and read it carefully. She'd never seen it before. When her mother was dying, Shiloh wasn't around. She never got along very well with her mother. She read the name of her father. *Lawrence. Lawrence Michael Stiles.* It didn't mean anything to her and she set it aside. There was a marriage certificate and she learned that, contrary to what her mother said when she was drunk, Shiloh was not a "bastard's bastard."

Shiloh took a sip of white wine and looked out the open side door into the desert. It was late afternoon, almost dusk, and a little cooler. Her favorite time of day. Though seeing the beauty through the screen door cast fuzzy little lines across the desert landscape, she still felt the warm breeze and loved where she was. Perhaps now she could love *who* she was, she thought wanly.

She found the divorce paperwork and some old letters. It seemed that Lawrence wrote letters. The writing was crude but legible enough. She thumbed through them and realized that a few of them were meant for her mother but never sent. Some were letters from his family that he'd saved. And then a fair amount of letters he'd written to a daughter he'd never known. She opened the oldest one and read the first page. It seemed that the marriage had failed after a very short time and he didn't know about her at first. He'd found out by accident the last time he'd seen her mother and saw that she was pregnant. Then she disappeared and there was no finding her. He said he'd hoped to hear something and stayed as long as he could, hoping for word of her. But eventually, time and circumstances took him away.

Shiloh cast her heavily edited memory back to garbled conversations she'd had, or tried to have, with her mother. She'd been raised by a smattering of well-meaning individuals, distant relatives mostly, and she'd been passed around. Literally. There was a hazy memory of something bad that had happened with a much older cousin. There was talk that he'd abused her sexually and her mother referred to her as "damaged goods." Shiloh found that ironic considering what her mother had been up to. As far as Shiloh was concerned, her mother had few redeeming qualities.

By the time she was fifteen, Shiloh was pretty much done with her mother and it was almost a relief when she heard that she'd died. She didn't make any effort to go to the memorial. Unbeknownst to her, had she gone, she would have met her father. He found out about the service by word of mouth and went to a great deal of trouble to return. Though paying his respects was an excuse, he'd really gone to retrieve whatever personal papers her mother held. He came away with only a few records and scraps of information, given to him by a relative he tracked down with the help of the local sheriff, who hoped it was in Shiloh's best interests for him to have it.

It turned out that Shiloh's mother was buried in the equivalent of a potter's field at county expense. Only a couple of drinking buddies attended the five-minute, graveside ceremony and Stiles got little useful information from them about her child. He did learn that he had a daughter and that her name was Shiloh. There were five possibilities for a last name. But Shiloh would never know unless he could find her. And he did find her. Eventually.

The mysterious calls on her cell phone back when she had worked at the Pine Tavern had been him—the voice of her father. In a strange way, he may have been trying to make it up to her, to atone. Since he could not be like a normal father, his sense of how to be one was, at this late stage of life, crooked, his perspective bent and twisted with the passage of time. Yet he still held a sliver of hope that what he had tried to do, what he wanted her to feel, was that someone had wanted to somehow reach out and help her.

And in a way, that's exactly what Shiloh was doing, helping herself—betting on the kind of luck she'd never had. Driving around with all that cash she'd found in the motorhome felt great at first...but then she began to grow paranoid. One accident and she was toast. A rollover and fire would wipe her out. It had never occurred to her how complicated it was to have money. For years, she was like everyone else with nothing, envying those that had when she didn't. But as having settled over her, keeping and growing it started to dawn on her. She'd never had to think about that and she needed a teacher.

Chapter 6

The second Dale heard her voice, the muscles in his jaw tensed. That the call was a surprise was an understatement. This woman had out-maneuvered him on their first meeting and he was determined not to let that happen again. She had left him stuck in a pouring rainstorm, and the permanent water stains that marred the then-brand-new perfection of his leather briefcase still rankled him, serving as a constant reminder of her forceful personality. He wondered how her husband had managed it.

Kitzie Collins apologized that she hadn't called sooner with a report regarding the status of one of his charges, CJ Burke. She expanded on the performance and contributions he'd made at the ranch and finished with his active involvement in the recovery of a herd of stolen Three Bit cattle.

Dale's internal manner went from mild annoyance to intense interest in a flash. His posture in his big office chair changed as the story unfolded and his eyebrows arched at the details. CJ had been in on the rustled cattle thing? Christ!

He lost track of the conversation as his mind raced to piece things together. He asked her to repeat what she'd just said. He modulated his tone to hold some suspense and acted busy and distracted. But he was laser-focused inside. She repeated that she was calling to let him know that CJ was no longer at the Three Bit and had moved with the herd to the McDermitt.

CJ's file was a hand-off and Dale had forgotten about it after he had delivered him to the middle of nowhere, figuring that was the end of the story. Dale's heart pounded when he heard Kitzie Collins describe the current location of his parolee, if he was still on parole. He stood up, walked to a map on the wall, and pressed a finger to the exact spot she was describing. "Yes, I know exactly where that is," he said into the phone.

Dale bought some time with some gobbledygook about issues of CJ being just over the border in Nevada and that there may have to be a transfer of his file. Kitzie pointed out that Harper's family was at the edge of Oregon and she was not sure he'd left the state. If it was a condition, she said they could make sure he knew that he'd have to stay on the right side of the line.

But Dale had no intention of letting this case go to anyone else. He wanted control of it and instead, he played the good-old-boy bureaucrat card. He said maybe, just maybe he could pull a few strings and allow the temporary situation as described. He said he'd get back to her and hung up.

Kitzie looked at the phone for a second, then down at the faces of her miniature Schnauzers, Wyatt and Lulu. "That seemed to have gone well..." Her leg was propped up on a pillow on a chair. She touched the brace on her knee. Her knee ached. Hopefully, that meant healing. She rubbed her eyes. "Maybe a little too easy..."

Dale placed the phone back in its cradle and said out loud, "CJ Burke on the McDermitt. Well, whaddya know."

He placed his fingertips together, his mouth pursed in a lipless grimace and his brow furrowed in concentration. It had seemed so innocuous, CJ getting assigned to him. It was ironic that his parolee had been involved peripherally in Dale's rustling operation, and now he was sitting smack on top of another of Dale's projects, Cedar Wara. In another frame of mind, Dale might have laughed at the coincidence.

He slid open his desk drawer and extracted a manila folder. It was a thick file marked "Cedar Wara, LLC investment." It didn't mean anything and that's why he liked the name. No one would connect it to what it really was. It was like a password that had no association—it was just a password.

The file contained the documents that granted his LLC rights to the oil and mineral rights underneath part of the McDermitt. Through his connections with the land bureau that regulated activities ranging from livestock grazing and recreation to mining and oil extraction, he'd discovered the specific locations of gallium—a rare mineral used in high-tech applications—and the Dugout was sitting on top of his future. High levels of gallium, in fact.

Dale's effective exploitation of the livestock angle had run its course and he had invested considerable energy and resources toward the current administration's drive to loosen environmental restrictions for oil and gas drilling, and other development, on public and private land. He had a close, leveraged relationship with the leading steward of public lands, who was an unconfirmed nomination. It was therefore prudent that he moved quickly and with finesse. Being an expert himself in disinformation campaigns, Dale felt uneasy with the chaos being generated from Washington. Was it enough to keep the public attention on the "show" part of the "shit-show" and not the actual shit that was going on while they were looking the other way?

There were competing interests and there were current

development activities that would result in the renewed mining of gold, silver, and uranium throughout that area. Dale knew which multinational companies were already into the permitting process in the Malheur. With the administration that was in power, the West would open up to all kinds of exploitation, and he was in on the ground floor. Open-pit mines would dot the area within a decade. Unemployment would be a thing of the past for those living out there.

Dale also knew that most Paiute and minority Shoshone stakeholders were hammering out their differences as they moved forward on the formation of the FMPC—the Fort McDermitt Production Company. It would only be a matter of time before they instituted operating procedures and created the same thing the Colorado tribes had created. It was no surprise that the lawyers who worked on that would be involved in streamlining their process. Then there would be a Guidance Manual for E&P—exploration and production—and for which operators, tribal or non-tribal. Dale's frown deepened. When he'd had those lawyers investigated, one turned out to be in Noah's office—Rae Royston's name popped up as a consultant.

Cedar Wara, LLC was the Dugout. The Dugout was on the McDermitt. And Dale's gallium was directly under Uncle's lodge.

Chapter 7

The woman sitting in the chair in front of Assistant District Attorney MacRae Royston's large desk had eyes that had cried a thousand tears. She picked up the engraved nameplate on Rae's desk, put it back, and ran a finger over the engraving. She seemed to be buying time to compose herself and asked the opening question—the one Rae had heard a thousand times.

"MacRae?" she said, looking at the nameplate.

"Rae is fine," Rae said, and the woman nodded, the question answered in her eyes. Rae continued, "My mother was a dancer and she taught my father how to dance. It was how they met. She passed away giving birth to me. It's her family name and my father liked it. He said it would give me good timing. He thought good timing was better than luck."

"Is he gone too?" the woman asked delicately.

"Oh, no, he's with the Oregon Agriculture Department, law enforcement and investigations," Rae replied.

"I'm sorry. There are no words for what I have in my heart now."

The woman looked exhausted and defeated, her expensive-looking clothes were a bit disheveled, her hair slightly unkempt, and her pale cheeks streaked with tears. Rae didn't know how she could help but she decided she would at least try.

Rae opened the file the woman had clutched when she first arrived, then slid across Rae's shiny desktop. She had been on a hunt—a search for someone she loved. Rae was the only one who would agree to make time for her and the woman was grateful between jags of tears. Rae knew this heartbroken woman deserved a chance to feel heard because she was not giving up, wouldn't take no for an answer, and had worked her way up the hierarchy of authorities. She had been to every agency she could think of, used all manner of social media, and written scads of letters. It had been a year and she hadn't given up on finding her black gelding, Nairobi, a hunter-jumper who had been taken from the pasture right in front of her house.

She pleaded her case once more and her questions came at staccato speed. "But he was micro-chipped and tattooed. What is the enforcement? What can I do? I've tried everything! Please tell me where to go. There must be records. They're not supposed to let horses go to slaughter without checking…are they?"

Rae had heard these words before, years ago, from her own mouth as she spoke to local authorities. For the then-teenaged Rae, it was her brown Quarter Horse mare. Though that was twenty years ago, the grief and pain were as fresh as if it had happened yesterday. She listened to this woman's pain and struggled with a choking feeling and the tears so close underneath. She wanted to get up from behind her desk, cast off her officious bearing, and hold this heartbroken person in her arms. She wanted to have an answer for her, a solution. But the only words she had for the woman seemed grossly inadequate.

Rae glanced down at her own folded hands, her nails trimmed neatly and unpolished. She wore no jewelry. In this moment, she wished she looked a little less professional. Her pantsuit, an effective armor in most situations, was immediately uncomfortable, too bureaucratic, for this. Even the color screamed "I don't care!" But she did.

A short while later, Rae walked the woman out past the doors that had closed discreetly when she arrived. Light filtered down from a massive skylight that illuminated the open, airy foyer. A large sculpture hung in the center, made of prismatic glass and lightweight metal of some kind. Rae guided the woman carefully to the top of the broad, gray-carpeted stairs.

Suddenly, the woman stopped and stood stock-still. She stared, eyes unfocused, out the wall of glass at the brilliantly sun-filled day. She turned her head slowly toward Rae.

"He's really gone, isn't he?"

Rae's eyes betrayed her before she could utter a word. She started to speak, then stopped herself mid-breath. *Speak things into existence. Believe it...* It was a mantra she could not reach for and grab in this instant.

The woman's eyes lowered and her shoulders sagged. And when those eyes came up and met Rae's, they were full again. "Oh, God, I'll never get to say good-bye..." She said it quietly, and then, with each word, her control slipped away. "He'll never know how hard I tried to save him. He'll never know how much I love him..."

Then she rushed down the stairs, sobbing. She stumbled blindly to a set of large glass doors and almost knocked over a man in a business suit carrying a briefcase. She barely uttered an apology before she was gone. She vanished in the glare as if transported.

Rae gripped the edge of the rail and stared at her white knuckles, trying to will the awful tightness in her throat to back down. She dared not blink. She held her breath, then raised her head and closed her eyes. Rae released her grip on the rail and wiped the moisture from beneath her mascaraed lashes, then looked at her fingers for the telltale black. She wiped her palms together, made prayer hands, pressed the edges of her compressed fingertips to her mouth, and focused on the pressure of them resting against the center of her nose. *Focus. Refocus...*

Rae needed to pull herself together. She released her hands, squeezed them into separate little balls, then unclenched them. She ran her hands through her short brown hair and pulled it into a stubby, thin ponytail. She used to pull her hair back that way when it was longer, and she twirled the end bit before letting the little tail go. Rae liked the ease of her shorter hair yet the habit remained.

Rae looked down into the echoing marble foyer of the office building. Everything was smooth, fine, clean, and shiny, like a major center of governance should be. And then she noticed the man with the briefcase staring up at her. It was Noah.

He said nothing as he disappeared beneath her toward the bank of elevators that would speed him to his top-floor office. She knew he would probably not ask. He was a compartmentalized man and one who could not waste time on tawdry emotion. The woman had run out of the building and for that, Rae knew he was relieved.

Noah Bainbridge was movie-star handsome with perfect hair, well-spoken, appealing, and destined for a political future. While his legal acumen had been a fraction above marginal, he had surrounded himself with betters. He made sure those under his leadership amassed an impressive and successful record. He counted on people only seeing the surface of a person—people who were easily convinced of his competence.

Those he kept. Those that outshined, he discarded.

Quietly, he had assembled an "exploratory" team complete with a fundraising effort. Rae was suspicious of how successful he had been at both, keeping it quiet and raising that much money, though she had to admit, Noah and his wife looked great for the parts they were aligning themselves to play. They donated time and money to the right causes, appeared together as the perfect power couple at the right events, and best of all, they were genuinely fond of each other. They were an effective team with a charming and growing family. Someone had chosen them to be groomed for public office and it was being accomplished under the thinnest of radars.

Pundits fueled speculation about which office Noah had set his sights on. That question was always answered in vague terms with a careful eye on the rise and fall of political friends and enemies. Who was vulnerable and who was not? Things changed quickly, timing was everything, and Noah hated to lose.

While it became clear to Rae that Noah's true personality was flawed when it came to ethics and principles—that for him and his like, it was all about power and winning—Rae's parallel pain was a gnawing feeling that her thwarted investigation overlapped his political ambitions in some way. She could not be sure of the proximity or whether the link was remote, like one of fate's twisted little ironies or a shadow you can't see. It was a feeling...something her boss disparaged at every turn. He swore it was only the facts that mattered, not feelings. But the shadow that had fallen over her team, her work, was more than a feeling. It was fact.

Noah had assigned the case to Rae. When he'd hired her, she struck him as almost androgynous. Her face was beautiful—full lips, dark eyes, and short-cropped, styled dark hair. She had pierced ears and the clever earring on the upper part of her ear had initially caused some stir as not being professional. She reminded him more than a little of the television commentator, Rachel Maddow.

Rae was very smart, a total professional, and completely dogged with whatever Noah put in front of her. She had quickly worked her way up to getting assigned important cases and managed them beautifully. She never muddied the waters with idle gossip or tittle-tattle, and she did not "piss in her own pond." No one had any details about her private life. In fact, by the way she worked herself, Noah was certain she did not have one. Work was her life. Work and her horses. They were her constants. Her Mounted Shooting trophies were the only decoration in her office. Otherwise, she kept the walls bare.

He had given her carte blanche to manage her department. Rae assembled a capable team and he saw to it that she was assigned an important investigation. And for almost three years, they had worked in collaboration with the Office of Inspector General of the US Department of the Interior. But about halfway into the case, it became clear to Rae that top-down directives coming from inside the beltway had interfered. Their investigations had revealed ominous connections between the rancher and livestock hauler, Don Thomas, and the former Secretary of the Interior. And they had found conclusive proof of a conspiracy. Thomas admitted to investigators that he had illegally bought wild horses with cleverly obscured taxpayer money, and that close to all of them were resold for slaughter with Thomas pocketing the proceeds. He had figured out how to use the system coming and going with a triple-dip scheme.

"There was only one place to go...the kill plant," he had said. He also pointed out that, "Tax dollars were used to pay me to do it."

In fact, the scheme had worked out so well that he was paid two or three times for the same animals. And yes, it was fraud, approved by the government. It was a fact—Noah's precious currency until it was not.

The erosion began shortly after a conference with Noah, where Rae had laid out the connections to the Secretary of the Interior. What was once his unwavering enthusiasm for her and her team's work melted away like an ice cube in summer.

This case, this long investigation, had unbalanced her in ways she had not anticipated. Her dream of earning Noah's top job when he inevitably went on into politics had fueled her ambition and she wanted to be in a position to make powerful, sweeping changes. That only came from embracing politics.

But embracing politics and being good at politics was another matter. Rae was uncomfortable with the "politics of the personal," or so she called it. If you didn't excel at understanding and manipulating what people wanted, and how to get them what they wanted while you got more of what you wanted, it would be a steep and fruitless climb up that ladder. And then there was the cutthroat, take-no-prisoners kind of politics. Rae found that she despised the phonies who were proficient at it...and there seemed to be a lot more of them.

It was what her father had warned her against, her better nature. He believed only friendly sociopaths did well in politics. And in part of her being, she was too soft, so she committed herself to a different kind of politics—one where the gains, accomplishments, and wealth of others grew as her own did. She didn't want to succeed on the broken dreams of others—

dreams she'd helped break. She believed there was a way that America, the greatest country on earth, would only continue to be so if all boats rose on an incoming tide.

During the past year, Rae had felt her dreams brush past her like strangers in a crowd. Her usual deft read of office inner workings had faltered...or someone was faltering it for her. Information was being routed around her and she had no idea who was doing it or why. She felt influence coming from somewhere. And then, mysterious, generous offers began to disassemble her team. She was not sure exactly when that had begun.

Rae tried subtle methods to get to the bottom of why her team was being systematically gutted and when that failed, she became more direct. And still, she was thwarted, as if being held in check on a gameboard while other pieces were being moved without her knowing why. She was not used to this and it undermined her standing in her once-solid team of truly close friends and colleagues. And Rae deeply resented the loss of control.

Chapter 8

Good intentions for an early start might have been effective had it been only four riders going out, but the group's size made that impossible. Finally, it all came together. The horses were fresh, anxious to get going, and the kids—Ely, Slides, and five of the younger ones—were excited. Before long, everyone was riding at ease, chatting among themselves, the sounds of their voices mixed with the four-beat footfalls of hooves on the ground. Carson rode near Wyker with CJ and Harper riding out ahead of the group. She hadn't forgotten how good it felt to be out. Tammy happily trotted next to them.

It had been some time since Carson had been around her "Uncle" Will and she still held childhood impressions of him. He was tall with deep-brown, almost midnight-black eyes that were warm and friendly. He had an even, broad smile, and his tanned face had the well-placed lines of a man who laughed often. He dressed in a rancher's functional comfort with a favorite pair of boots and chinks that he wore like a uniform. Now, as then, he found peace in the company of horses and his dog.

After a while, he casually asked her what had happened, why she had left for the big-city life, and she mumbled something about not being on the best of terms with her dad.

"What does that mean?" he asked in a tone with no

judgment attached.

She shot a sidelong glance at him. He sounded like her father and she was too eager to take it as a criticism. She felt judged and became instantly defensive. It wasn't Wyker doing that to her. She was doing it to herself. Emotions ran up her spine and into her throat. They grabbed at her neck like an invisible hand, depriving her of air, constricting her answer. Carson went silent. She wanted to open up and share but felt trapped—and the feeling annoyed her.

Wyker rode easily beside her, content on Johnny. His calm hung about him like a cloak. After the boiling in her head abated a little, Carson looked over at him again. The frame of her father's dear friend was outlined clearly against the backdrop of the Oregon sky and mountains. A brush of wind lifted the edge of his neckerchief. She inhaled several deep breaths.

Wyker said, "He told me about the last time you two spoke. Mentioned it over drinks at the Running Horse, in the Deer Club. As I recall, we were drinking with Buckets. He's the ranch foreman."

"I know Buckets," Carson said, glad to feel less in the spotlight. "Those aren't hands at the end of his arms, those are paws."

Wyker smiled at the apt description. "Yeah, Buckets. Well, he had to bring us both upstairs to the bunk section and deposit us on two of the beds."

"Dad? Drunk?" Carson stared.

Wyker laughed. "He was alligator mouthed!" He shook his head and covered his eyes.

Carson had never seen either of her parents drunk. They were moderate and careful. She knew that her behavior when she'd made her big return to the ranch would have been met with one of her dad's stern talks. She was grateful her mom hadn't taken up the practice.

"Oh yeah, we both were. Felt it the next morning too. Our eyes looked like piss holes in the snow." Wyker laughed. "Buckets was there with the best damn coffee and the greasiest breakfast he could whip together. He has the perfect recipe for a hangover, that's for sure." He looked at Carson.

"Wish I'd known that when I arrived," she said but did not elaborate.

"We weren't alone. Half the crews of wranglers and buckaroos were hung-over at those bench tables…and there was a day's work to get to," Wyker added.

Carson saw that the memory was perhaps one of his favorites of her dad. And she knew that she had run away from her father's plans for her in a fit of selfish anger that she could never take back.

They pushed into an extended jog on a flat section as they approached a split at the foothill trail that led toward Sanctuary. The hay bags bounced on the kids' horses, bits falling out and catching in the wind.

Carson didn't carry hay on the ranch horse she'd been given. She had other supplies they would need and it helped that her mount had a smooth jog. The gelding surprised her. There wasn't much to distinguish him and she had no complaints. Slides had chosen that horse especially for Carson—a fact he took pains to remind her of frequently.

Wherever Slides was in the string, his neck was usually craned, hand on the rump of his thick ride, riding bareback, half the time hands-free and the tandem hay net full of hay sticking out on either side. He cushioned it with his bedroll and for whatever reason, it all stayed put, even when they moved faster than a walk. It was impressive, Carson had to admit.

Carson said as much to Slides as he rode up next to her. "You really got that, don't you?"

He smiled broadly back at her. "I don't much like saddles," he laughed as he trotted up to join the others near CJ. "You'll see."

Slides was the kind of kid who always had a smile, benefitted from a healthy appetite, and like the rest of his family, was solidly built. His physique did not dim his enthusiasm or curb his prodigious energy. He was curious about everything and moved like a boy half his size. He had a gift with horses and could ride anything. He had no fear and no use for any, as he claimed he "bounced" if he ever came off.

The trail seemed easy enough to follow. A worn path went down a steep draw and up the other side, where it opened up.

Carson trotted up next to Ely and asked, "When was the last time you were at Sanctuary?"

Ely's horse pinned his ears at her mount when he inched ahead of him by a nose. She smiled and he put a little leg on him to create space.

Nodding toward Harper, Ely said, "He took me out here last summer and taught me about the place. He showed me the drawings, taught me what they meant, trained me to read 'sign.'"

"What kind?"

"Any kind."

"Really..." Carson looked around on the ground for something that he could read...and he laughed at her attempt.

For someone so young, he had a good laugh and kind eyes.

"What?" Carson said.

Ely smiled. "It's everywhere. The rabbit we just passed

knows that three coyotes were traversing that part of the creek bed," he pointed, "following scent."

Carson turned and looked back. "Huh. I missed the rabbit."

"She's moving slow, cautious-like, watching everything and listening," he explained. "See those longer depressions behind the small ones?" He pointed down as they rode by the faintest of marks in the soft ground. "She's good-sized. Would make a nice dinner."

Slides came alongside Carson and it seemed their two horses were familiar and got along. Ely's horse was not pleased but it didn't matter. Carson commented on the sling bag that Slides wore. The handmade strap came across his chest, and back in Silicon Valley, the bag might have been called a "murse." Carson asked if he had made it himself. He had, from the skins of the rabbits his family raised, sold, and ate. Carson learned more about subsistence rabbit farming than she ever wanted to know but his enthusiasm was hard to crush, and he relished telling her how he'd prepared the hides, picked the right ones, and made the pouch with his own hands. Maybe a little help from his dad but mostly it was him, he assured her. At the end of his story, he offered her a piece of something shriveled and dried from the pouch. She thanked him but declined. He shrugged, popped it in his mouth, grinned, and jogged up the line to ride near CJ.

Carson dropped back next to Wyker and Harper joined them for a time. Carson hadn't gotten all the details about the Three Bit herd event and asked Harper how he'd met up with CJ and Wyker.

"When I first watched them, they were four; they had two other riders and one had two exceptionally good dogs. When I saw those two break off and leave, I was relieved," Harper said. He looked across Carson to Wyker.

Wyker smiled. "I'll bet." For Carson's benefit and the chronology of the tale, he added, "Your mom had gotten hurt. I think you were with her?"

Carson nodded.

"Right. So, at that point, Luis, Jorge, and the dogs headed back to the Three Bit." He leaned forward toward Harper. "You saw CJ lose control of the packhorses, huh? When I was up on that bluff scouting for the herd?"

Harper's lips were tight as he smiled. The tattooed lines on his cheekbones moved with the memory. His long black hair fanned up his back with a light breeze. He was serious-faced with the iconic looks of a man of his heritage—full lips and deep-set eyes under dark brows. Though it didn't happen often, it was quite marvelous when he smiled and his laugh was deep. He recounted his observations when the two packhorses got tangled up and they broncked off, scattering supplies as they went. "I watched you two pilgrims follow their trail."

CJ overheard a bit of that, turned his head, and shot a look back at them. From under the brim of his hat, a narrow smile touched one corner of his mouth, then he looked ahead.

"Yeah, after that I figured you really needed my help," Harper replied. The creases next to his eyes deepened as he said it loud enough for CJ to hear.

Without turning back, CJ's left arm rose, bent at the elbow, and he flipped the bird.

Carson laughed. "Riding up like that, on strangers in the backcountry...I mean, you didn't know who they were out there."

Harper's smile closed some. "I knew. I'd been watching.

I'd been watching for those rustlers. They drove stolen cows through our land like they owned it."

Wyker added, "I knew we were being watched, I just couldn't spot him."

Harper added, "You tried."

"Yeah, you were too good for me."

"I know my country and I had an idea about you," Harper said.

Carson enjoyed the story and it filled in what she didn't know, how it all had gone down. Then she asked, "How were they when you approached them?"

"This one," Harper's thumb pointed to Wyker, "I was fairly confident how he would react." Harper nodded toward CJ. "He was not pleased at all, huh?"

Wyker laughed and agreed.

Where CJ was civil to Carson, he was different with the kids, engaged in a way that Carson did not expect. She didn't know anything about him, what he had done afoul of the law. Was he a murderer? She discreetly asked Wyker if he had done something heinous and if it was OK for him to be around children.

Wyker said no, nothing like that, no murder, mostly general mayhem. Repeatedly unlucky. He'd attached himself to the wrong people too many times, and once he had a record, just getting pulled over with an expired tag by the wrong cop got him time.

Harper added an observation, not his own. "Uncle says sometimes the journey from a familiar place to an unfamiliar place takes surprising turns." He shrugged. "This has been that."

Carson looked at him and studied his tattoos with

momentary curiosity. She asked about the horizontal lines on his cheekbones.

"Uncle did them for me, said it marked my passage," Harper explained.

"Passage from what?" she asked.

"He didn't say," he replied.

Harper looked down between them and saw Tammy's face looking up at him—her tongue out, eyes glistening, a happy expression on her face as she trotted with them. He moved his horse over a bit to give her more room.

Ely dropped back and joined Harper, who moved forward. Everyone's positions changed up again with different conversations. It was clear that Ely had great respect for his cousin, showed him deference, and listened to him intently.

Carson swung back to her previous conversation with Wyker. She pressed her lips together as if she felt a spasm of pain. "I made a terrible mistake, Uncle Will. I don't even remember what the fight was about. We never spoke again." She stared ahead and watched the kids as they flanked CJ and Rio. Her mind let the painful memories emerge from the surface. She distracted herself from more honesty and focused on CJ's back. He perplexed her.

Maybe her curiosity was too obvious. The kids had his attention. They were just being themselves. She was awkward and uncomfortable. She longed to be that open-hearted kid again...to be free enough to trot over there and be a part of something—not *apart* from something.

Carson rolled that thinking around in her head and wondered if that was the core of it. She wasn't sure where she belonged. She stroked the neck of her horse, felt the pleasant footfalls of his feet, the motion of her body in the saddle, and heard the gentle panting of Tammy just below. She looked down at the dog and as if Tammy knew, she turned her head up and "smiled" at Carson.

Carson realized she had not quite come back yet. She was there, comfortable on a horse, and breathing the air she hadn't known she'd missed—but was it temporary? She hadn't thought much about the future. She just went along with the present. Maybe she was hoping for a sign, a reason to know she was staying. She longed to disappear into the happy days full of horses on a busy ranch.

"You're entitled to be young," Wyker said after a long pause. "And stupid and selfish, for that matter."

It was spoken truthfully and brought Carson out of her thoughts. She gave him a quizzical look as she caught back up to the moment.

Wyker continued, "He always loved you. Loved you very much. Which brings us to what now?"

The answer percolated as they came to a draw with steep sides and no clear trail down the fifteen-foot drop into a bone-dry creek bed. The water had flowed through with such violence that it had chewed up the banks and flattened what vegetation was there. The kids and CJ plowed through in a crazy-assed way, laughing as the horse Slides rode stumbled and he came off. He made a half-decent landing, recovered, and scrambled back aboard without losing his gear and hay nets.

Carson was more cautious. She looked downstream for a cleaner, less-steep way down. She found one that didn't have scrub ripping at her as she guided her horse through, then fell back in step with Wyker, who had waited for her on the other side.

Her words tumbled out. "I lost everything, Uncle Will, and

believe it or not, I'd done very well for a few years. I fell far and I fell fast." Carson heard the words and realized that they didn't sting as much as when she'd first arrived.

She didn't elaborate that she had dribbled into town on her last dime and had drunk herself silly at the Pine Tavern until Lyle Martin frog-marched her to the ranch supply store, where he left her to sleep it off. Yeah, she chose to skip that part for sure.

Typical of Wyker, he rode in patient silence next to her.

"Trouble rained on me like a drain. I'm bankrupt." She spat it out and it was like vinegar in her mouth. "There, I've said it. I think that's the first time I've said it out loud."

Wyker showed no judgment at her statement.

Carson continued, "I'm an outlaw hiding out till some financial posse finds me."

"Like the IRS?" Wyker asked.

"Oh, God…" she groaned. "You coulda gone all day without saying that. I don't even know the last time I filed my…" She put her hand over her eyes. "Ugh…" She dropped her hand to rest it on the gently rocking horn of the saddle. The cool, smooth leather soothed her palm and the fear that had risen.

In the wide-open country that held her now, no reality could penetrate and find her. This landscape was all she saw and all she wanted to see. Her gaze found CJ's back again and the proportioned width of his shoulders. Brown hair drifted from beneath the brim of his hat and into the collar of his jacket. He was talking to Slides, the one who had tumbled, his back dusted with bits of debris. A piece of something was stuck in his hair and she watched CJ point to it. The kid brushed it off with his left hand.

"What's his *real* story?" she asked Wyker, changing the

subject.

"CJ's complicated. I believe he's a good guy but complicated. His story is not mine to tell," Wyker said matter-of-factly. Then, quietly, he added, "He's found a spot to be safe, I think."

"Safe?" Carson asked.

"I dunno, safe with Rio. Safe is a day when you don't mess up." Wyker wasn't sure either and added, "Safe from himself maybe..."

Carson nodded. It was safe out here. And she felt safe. Safe from herself.

Chapter 9

There is nothing more wonderful to discover than a good secondhand store, and when Shiloh ran across a really big one, it was like Christmas—or as close to a gift as she was likely to get. This find reminded her a little of the one in Bend, which was terrific, and she had gotten lucky when she found a place to park the motorhome on an empty lot next to this mega-sized Goodwill store.

Fortunately, the size of her rig and its limited storage encouraged restraint. She looked at her clothes and chose some things she could let go of, and bagged them to donate. It was interesting to have all the money she could want, and that fate would give her a small home.

Shiloh had a mission. Those "boats"—the biggest, ugliest men's shoes she could find to set out on the mat instead of the cowboy boots she had found in the rig. If the shoes looked especially nasty, it might be surmised that the owner was too—a subtle suggestion that the "nosies" should stay away.

Shiloh felt good, her health restored, and she took her time browsing. It fascinated her how the things in this type of store reflected the affluence of the area it was located in. At a long rack of shirts, she thumbed through many that had seen no wear and still had their original tags. Lots and lots, in fact, and her mind wandered to the stories behind them. Did someone just not like what they had bought and gave it away? What were the backstories on the things that found their way into this store?

Shiloh stopped browsing and looked up over the low racks at the people in the different sections of the store. A couple browsed through the coats and the man averted his eyes as she looked over at them. The woman was oblivious. Two heavy ladies looked at unmatched curtains and household goods. In fact, as Shiloh scanned the large space, she noticed that everyone was on the heavier side. She restrained a piquant judgmental thought for another time and briefly wondered why it had come to her at all. She was there to buy enormous shoes. What did it matter if enormous people shopped there?

She continued to thumb through the shirts and stopped on a buttoned number that had a pattern she was almost sure she liked. It was in her size and she set it aside. But lately, with the means at her disposal, Shiloh had discovered that her wants had mysteriously shrunken to a pittance. When she could afford nothing, she'd had urgent desires for everything she couldn't have. Now that she had money, all the things that once sparkled for her seemed dull and unimportant. In a way, she fought harder, struggled more, and worked more seriously than when she had nothing. What was that about? It was as if the thought of a fine, expensive meal, once served, had the same bland flavors as the food she had already eaten dozens of times. What was so special about that?

A silence preceded her through the aisles as she shopped. A wave of energy radiated from her and was hard to ignore. Finally successful in her hunt for the biggest pair of men's shoes she could find, she also hoped to find a cap with either a military or law enforcement appearance. And maybe a man's flannel jacket with a camo design. None of these items would adorn the perfect body she had been blessed with. They were just for appearances, to give the casual observer an impression.

The ripple effect of her presence in the store was more felt than shared verbally—the brief cessation of movement, the coughs, the clearing of a throat, the lifting of heads. The slide of hangers on metal poles stopped. The general urge was to look around and see who was in the store that caused this.

Shiloh moved along as if nothing was happening. The electricity she generated was more pronounced in the male occupants of the store and caused an annoyed tightening of facial muscles on the females in the building. The older women resumed their pursuits almost immediately. They had seen fine ass distract their menfolk before and undoubtedly would again. The middle-aged women stood up straighter and inhaled, silently willing gravity to please suspend effect, and if possible, reverse it, if only for a few moments. Men were too slack-jawed to attempt the transformation. They simply turned the corner, picked up the pace, and held that retreating vision as long as a firm memory could be uploaded into the numbness that was between their collective ears. The older men stared, unashamed, as if they were immune to the scrutiny of others.

Ultimately, Shiloh picked out a few things for herself and carried her items to the counter, where a nervous young man was operating the check-out. Several people became intolerably warm and removed a jacket or loosened a collar. Her blond hair fell perfectly about her shoulders. It was clear she didn't need any support from an undergarment and that the room was not warm. The entire structure seemed to exhale after she paid for her purchase and left.

The man who had taken care of her at the counter blinked as he followed perfect jeans out through the glass doors. He used a forefinger to push his glasses up the bridge of his nose and looked over the top of the rims as Shiloh walked provocatively through the parking area to the open space where she had parked her huge bus motor coach.

He turned to the next customers, an older man and his wife. She was busy pulling things from her cart—things that looked like they had been shopping for the grandkids, so there were lots of socks and small items. The husband's help was not required and his eyes traced the same path as the clerk's. Then they returned and a silent message of agreement passed between the two men, and they smiled at each other knowingly. From the wife's thickened fingers tumbled some towels and bedding as she said, without looking, "Pull your tongues back in and get it together, you two."

The clerk cleared his throat and promptly entered the customers' purchase incorrectly and had to call for the manager's assistance.

Inside the coach, Shiloh dropped the package on the floor behind the passenger's seat, started the big rig, and drove off. An hour later, she was parked in the farthest spot she could find behind the Elks Lodge. She had made a point of joining the Elks for the privilege, though if they checked her information, they would find salient details fabricated or missing. She set the levelers and the unit auto leveled, and she dry camped for the night. Hook-ups were more for the long term and she did not intend to stay there a moment more than necessary.

The slider on the inside screen door was open and she fingered the locking mechanism. It wasn't exactly fussy, just particular. If she unlocked it correctly, it was smooth and easy but if she reached for it from a different angle, it would not open.

It was a habit thing, she told herself. She would get into the habit, then it would be smooth and easy every time.

She opened the door and the step automatically slid out from underneath. Shiloh looked around, noticed how many vehicles and RVs were there, and stepped out. She lifted the lid to one of the undercarriage bays and found the carefully rolled-up doormat, pulled it out, and closed the bay securely. She decided not to put the awning out as she felt it was not worth it for an overnight stay. She unrolled the mat and centered it under the steps. Shiloh made like she was talking to someone inside, and opened the door and stuck her head in as if answering someone.

From behind the passenger's seat, she grabbed the men's shoes she had just purchased and placed them neatly on the mat outside, as if their ginormous owner could open the door and step right into them. Anyone even considering messing with her would look at those big, ugly shoes and hopefully make the wise decision to not knock on the door. Confident that the ugly boats would do most of the guard duty, she locked the door behind her and closed the front window curtain.

Shiloh watched a couple pull in and set up camp with almost military precision. They had it down, all the gimmicks and gizmos, and had drinks in hand and the outside TV on in twenty minutes flat. And like moths to a flame, a little gathering happened by dusk.

Despite the boats on the doormat, one or two tried to pry her out and she made excuses behind her closed door and put forth the impression that the male counterpart inside was immune to the social graces. She nicely demurred the invitations to cocktails or a barbecue. She muttered something about PTSD and the hapless friendlies skittered away. And that was how she liked it.

Shiloh packed up and resumed her travels the next day. She was on holiday, she told herself. The only reason she'd needed anybody before was for things—money, food, a place to stay, and whatever her needs happened to be. Did she miss the open male adulation of the café and tavern? It flattered her for sure and the power she wielded to manipulate was entertaining in some ways, but since the attack in the parking lot, she found that even thinking about attracting the attention of a suitable man didn't interest her. The effort felt too tiresome and nothing interesting had caught her eye for a while.

Shiloh's thoughts drifted to the box sitting on the kitchen table, still unopened and taunting her. She'd found it in a hidden compartment when she was vacuuming one day. The coach was tidy and spotless, as her passion was complete order since she had been assaulted. She wanted total control over her environment, and she found vacuuming—lots of vacuuming—very soothing to her once-frayed nerves. She had already burned a motor out and had to buy a better one. She wondered if she might be hurting the carpet by keeping it so clean.

Solving the mystery of how all this had come about—the motorhome, the money, and the man who had set it all up—became her mission. She explored the motor coach and kept finding cleverly concealed places. Once she realized that she should look for the obvious, it dawned on her that looking for the unobvious was important too.

For a few weeks, Shiloh had tried to convince herself that there was nothing more to be found, yet she kept poking around. Not familiar with luxury on wheels, she'd assumed there weren't many places to hide things. She had never lived in a place that was so nice. This coach was extraordinarily well appointed and there was so much to learn about running it. The manuals filled large binders and she committed herself to reading a little every night to learn how to operate the systems aboard her land yacht.

Shiloh learned how to correctly deploy the three pop-outs and how to be sure she didn't overextend them. There were hinges beneath the headboard part of the queen-sized bed, and there was a neat system that helped her lift it. This revealed a large storage area, where she discovered four slender compartments expertly carpeted over with the same carpet as the bedroom. They looked like the inside edges of the frame under the bed. Shiloh accidentally bumped one, she didn't remember how, but it was a press-release latch and a click drew her attention. She gingerly fingered the carpeted edge and a small door opened. It was there that she'd found the handgun—a rather nice one, by the looks of it—in a case. She found more than one box of ammunition for the gun and she read the label on it. Shiloh was unfamiliar with guns and made a mental note to look up what kind it was and perhaps find someplace to learn how to use it. She had watched enough crime dramas to know that she should have a license or something and she would check the papers for such a thing.

Shiloh found exploring and hunting through things strangely calming. She found it interesting, the time and effort he had put into it all. The planning must have taken years. She held little or no sympathy or consideration for how that person might be feeling at that moment. Her needs simply took precedence, that's all, and it was her needs over his. License or not, she put the weapon and some of the ammo where she might easily reach them if need be.

Just when Shiloh thought she had a good bead on things,

she'd find something else—a compartment or concealed cubby she'd missed before. It was like a scavenger hunt with its own twists and challenges. Point in fact was a flat compartment on the far side of the bed, near the sliding glass doors of the closet, where she'd found the box. It was a tight space between the bed and the slight lip up to the mirrored closet doors. She'd missed it for months so when she found it, she felt particularly accomplished. And curious. What the hell was in there that was so important that someone had gone to these lengths to hide it? Shiloh thought the money was valuable so whatever was in there, he must have felt was even more valuable. And then it became a challenge to discover the mystery of it all. The man who had set this bolt hole up for her...for *them*...he'd had a plan. In the back of her mind, Shiloh was wary. Most men's "plans" for her she wanted no part of, and the plain fact was that she had taken his motor coach and all the money hidden in it.

The box was not unlike a small safety deposit box—solid, brushed aluminum, smooth on all sides. Once she had extricated it from the compartment, Shiloh shook it gently from side to side and heard its contents move. She felt the weight of it—nothing like gold bars, it wasn't that heavy—but maybe some papers and information. The box was so meticulously made that finding the seams took careful examination under decent light with a magnifier. This box meant something to him. She had to figure it out.

Shiloh's efforts were futile the first time she tried to get into the box. Frustrated, she put the box back where she had found it. She considered the possibility that to cut into it with something was the only way. She let it be for weeks as she traveled and enjoyed her new home on wheels. Shiloh was making her way as she pleased and was determined to experience Yellowstone, which she did. She spent time in various locations and saw some of the country.

She decided to stay in Indio for a few days at a super-nice motorhome park, where she rented a very private space at the end of a lane in a posh community of time-shared spaces. It was the edge of the off-season so the sunbirds had flown. The space had a built-in outdoor kitchen, landscaping, and a little parking shed for the owner's custom golf cart. A gurgling water feature played lovely, soothing sounds through the bedroom window.

The next morning, after a good night's sleep, Shiloh lay on her side in bed and watched the desert awaken. The sky changed from starlit to brighter edged, then to the long light that played off the desert plants and colors. She loved the desert. She couldn't imagine why she'd stayed so long in the Jordan Valley. Shiloh rested her head on her hand and gazed outside. It was so nice not having to set the alarm and wonder if it was time to go to work. She rolled over onto her back, left hand underneath her head, and looked at the ceiling of the coach's bedroom. Shiloh heard a bird start to chirp. It calmed her, listening to it. She wondered what he was saying. Was it just to say something and hope it would be heard by another? Or was it just that it was alive and happy?

The sun's rays slanted low and long, casting shadows and filling the coach with a lovely warm glow. During the night, the sheet had worked its way down. Fine points dented the fabric and a taught ridge of material concealed the valley between them. Shiloh elongated her arms in a languid stretch, yawned, smiled, then rolled out of bed.

As she leaned against the countertop, sipping a glass of

juice, she noticed something. The sun was shining on the box at just the right angle that it revealed an imperfection she'd neither seen nor felt previously. It was so obvious to her in that light, and she wondered how she'd missed it. Without dressing it up too much, she'd simply overthought things and within minutes, the box was open.

Over the next few days, Shiloh began to go through the contents and it was quite an education. The first thing she saw was a handwritten scrawl on a slip of paper that read, "Good girl." Shiloh raised her eyebrows. It was an interesting thing to see first off and she set the paper on the kitchen table. She felt as if she were Cleopatra and hesitated to put her hand inside the box, as if a viper might lurk in its depths. But her curiosity got the better of her, and she thrust her hand inside. Instead of a poisonous reptile, she felt paper.

With a respect she was not sure it deserved, Shiloh gingerly pulled out an envelope and felt its weight in her hands. Possibly pictures? She was intrigued. Setting it aside for the moment, she retrieved all the box's contents and arranged them on the table in front of her. She slid the top papers to one side and peeked inside the envelope. The edges of the pictures inside were tired and frayed, as if someone had looked at them repeatedly.

Shiloh sat back against the bench of the kitchen table, one hand covering her mouth thoughtfully, the other resting on the coolness of the Corian countertop. What to open first? She reached for a packet and pulled out a beige vellum envelope, unsealed it, and turned it over to the front, where "Keep" was written in a woman's script. She set it aside when she recognized her mother's writing.

One business-sized envelope was labeled CRYPTO. Inside

was information on something she was not sure she had ever heard of, so she moved on.

She pried the lip of the legal-sized envelope apart and saw that the papers were bound along the top. No staples. It was a prepared document—finished and perhaps legally filed. Shiloh set it aside as well. There was another envelope and on the outside was the address of a county recorder. She felt the weight of it, many layers, thrice folded and with the weight of "property" to it. That made her heart pinwheel.

Shiloh lifted the shade and slid open the bottom part of the window so she could hear the desert. It held its own sounds of birds and other creatures, their chirps and noises emanating from underneath thorny bushes with thin, waxy leaves.

She looked around the motor home at the clean wooden cupboards and myriad storage compartments. Hidden in soup cans and boxed dried goods was a fortune. Shiloh was secure and a thief, but a secure thief as long as she was smart about it. Then, paranoia crept in at the edges of her reality. She'd been parked there for too long.

Chapter 10

Dale paced in his office, lingered briefly near a wall of photographs (mostly of himself) and paced some more. He thought better when he was in motion. He was a tall man, deceptively fit, with a penchant—no, a raging habit—for expensive Western boots and hats. His expensive tastes extended to his big truck and no one seemed to question how he could afford it. His walls were tiled with pictures of him mugging with the rich, the powerful, and the political from all the public stages, state and national. Dale dominated most conversations and had a good-old-boy homily for just about every social situation. He had piercing, hard eyes that his jovial act and broad smile struggled to balance.

He returned to the desk, guided the wireless mouse, and scrolled to the computer files to find CJ's paperwork. He had given it a cursory review when it had first fallen into his lap. Now it was time he looked at it more thoroughly.

Dale's interests were far-reaching and many overlapped. He had a vast network of influence he'd spent years cultivating and each strand of his web produced predictable benefits. Much of his "business" was in a gray area and a serious slice of it was completely black—and had to be that way or he would be in jail. There was a smattering of insider trading in the commodities markets, political lobbying for favorite people, and, of course, blackmail. He was privy to the details of wide-ranging fraud, more than a few conspiracies, sexual cover-ups, and set-ups, all of which involved people in high places. Some manipulations he derived minimal monetary benefit from; it was more the ability to influence matters toward things that he was deeply involved in that held his interest. Dale's military experience had blessed him with a variety of skills he was not afraid to use. Though he disdained "wet work," he had handled "situations" in the past—most recently, a messy bit of business for Tiny, one of his business partners.

There were details that led to what had happened that Dale didn't know and couldn't have known. He hadn't forgotten about the disaster at the rendezvous near the McDermitt. He simply didn't want to think about it. Stiles had come in ahead of the Mex, took his horse in a rig, and completely vanished. That crazy Mex, Stiles' riding partner, arrived later and went nuts with a knife because he thought he was being cheated. When Dale arrived to clean up, the Mex was gone but the mess he made was not. It was a long night.

That agent—the native, the one who worked with Hy Royston...what was his name? He was in a report Dale had seen after the rustling thing had blown up. He had access to the Oregon State Database and a back door into files he wasn't necessarily allowed to see, and he dug deeper until he found what he was looking for. Hyland Royston—an Oregon Ag Agent with extensive law enforcement credentials—and his partner, Dave Clancy—a retired cop—had connected with a native and used him in certain undercover operations. Royston had good stats and was highly regarded.

The lucrative rustling deal Dale had going with his partner, Tiny Bellamy, had run into bad luck because some eager-beaver agent named Miranda got curious with a microchip scanner and Royston and Clancy got there before Tiny could fix it. They had him dead-to-rights with stolen cattle in one of his own stockyards. Tiny was beset with bad news for a while after that, lost some lucrative contracts from his legitimate avenues of income, and he was not a happy guy. He had been crawling through legal challenges for months. But Dale was working on it from another angle and he assured Tiny that it would all go away. "Be patient," he told him.

There was more on Royston. Dale got lucky and found the name of the undercover agent Royston was working with and saw he was on an indefinite leave of absence. "Really?" Dale mused out loud. His eyes bulged when he found that the agent had a direct connection to the McDermitt.

Dale sat at his desk, thinking. He rotated around in his big, leather swivel chair and reached up to remove his clip-on tie. He always wore clip-ons—a habit from his bouncer days. He knew that in a fight, it was best not to give your opponent a way to strangle you.

Chapter 11

At the Three Bit, Jorge and his horse loped out ahead of his cattle dogs, Tucker and Dusty. They were the serious kind of working dogs, not only true to their breeding but exquisitely well trained by Jorge. They were the envy of the local cattlemen and were often invited to help out on other ranches. Jorge almost regretted bringing them today as the wind blew dust and debris into their faces and eyes as they did their work. They had moved the cows as quickly as possible and were now headed home to get out of it.

A blast of hot, dry air hit him and he brought his hand up to the side of his face to shield the dust from pelting his eyes. He hunched his back against a stronger gust that pushed him sideways in his saddle. As he rounded a small, spring-fed pond, Jorge saw deep bovine footprints along the shallow edge. He could almost hear the mud sucking at legs as the cattle retreated from drinking their fill. There were a couple of seasonal ponds on the Three Bit but this one managed to have water in it year-round. High above, barn swallows defied the wind with their fluid bursts of straight speed, making quick, tight turns and dives as they fed on the wing—a process made more difficult by the wind.

Jorge's thoughts went to the sharp memory of a "conversation" he'd had with his father, Luis, earlier. Luis was not pleased that Jorge's friendship with the new waitress at the Pine

Tavern seemed to be getting more serious. Luis did not hide his disdain for Trina and told Jorge so. He said she was not good for him.

When they were just passing acquaintances, Trina had served Jorge and Luis breakfast a couple of times and Jorge hardly cared about her. But over time, there was an attraction and then they were on the phone at all hours. Luis felt she was that certain kind of distraction his son did not need. He objected to the pierced nose, the heavy black eye make-up, the dark-themed tattoos, and she favored the style of apparel and jewelry that involved leather and spikes. Luis had taken to avoiding eating anything at the tavern but Jorge seemed to find a way to slip over there if they were anywhere close to town. When he came home one night with a purplish hickey on his neck, the torrent of Spanish cussing and hollering could be heard well beyond the walls of their cottage. Luis pleaded with his son to slow down and they fought about it to a stony silence that lasted for days.

Of course, that made Jorge want her more. Jorge was slightly built but strong and had an olive complexion. His hair was on the longish side and his father chided him about it. Trina was a bit taller than he was and at first, it bothered him—especially when she wore her heeled boots. When he had his cowboy boots on and she was in her work shoes or sneakers, he was just shy of eye level with her. But in her regular shoes, she almost towered over him.

So, like any teenager, Jorge struggled with his newfound feelings and the exploration of a whole lot of other things. And besides, women—for him, anyway—were not exactly crawling out of the woodwork out there. He recalled the moment he'd said that to his father, and it stopped him cold. Because it was true.

Jorge looked around at the country and at his two dogs. It was desolate, dry, and harsh, but he had grown up to it so it was beautiful to him. Jorge was born at the Three Bit and he and Luis had been there for a very long time. He had no past anywhere else and because his father was undocumented, they stayed where they were for security.

With Trina, he felt like he had a foothold in both of his worlds. She was half and half, spoke Spanish and perfect English, and was the color that passed for either. She was legal, born in the United States like he was, and when they went to the tavern, they were welcomed. When Jorge was with her, he felt like he'd never felt before. Jorge had always belonged at the Three Bit. He was family.

When Shiloh worked at the tavern, before all the trouble, Jorge had taken the lead from his father and hardly spoke above a murmur. They kept to themselves and only went into town for specific ranch reasons. Lyle always treated them with equanimity. He was a man who judged the character of a person and nothing else. But there were more conservatives in ION country than open-minded progressives, and Luis and Jorge knew when they stepped off the Three Bit that it was potentially dangerous for Luis.

Their contact with the outside world was limited as well. The TV they had in the cottage was a very old black-and-white and received the barest of programs the antenna could pull in. Kitzie had helped Jorge get a cell phone and that was how most people got in touch with Luis when they needed him. Jorge was a message conduit. The phone plan was limited, so he did not surf the internet much. Trina had a better one and she showed him all kinds of things on it.

His father had shown him the old metal cigar box that contained his birth certificate and family papers. Much of the family stuff was in Spanish—things Luis had carried with him when he crossed the border nineteen years ago with Jorge's mother, Blanca. She knew she was pregnant at the time but Luis didn't. She was afraid he would leave her behind if she told him and the pregnancy was very early at the time, so she didn't show. The coyotes ditched them in the dark and it was up to Luis to guide the group. He took the lead and in his calm, unflappable way, instilled in the others faith that he would succeed. Blanca never wavered but she knew he did not have a clue and was counting on some old astronomy he'd learned from his uncle and the strength of the group.

Dehydration was the enemy and Blanca shared her water ration more than she should have. With her strength fading, she and Luis separated from the others and took shelter in an abandoned homestead. Luis ventured to a gas station for water and food, and raised suspicions with his filthy appearance. When questioned by the cashier, the man behind him in line stood up for him and paid for his goods, telling the cashier that Luis was with him.

The man motioned for Luis to follow him and they got into his rig. The huge horse trailer had some horses in it and Luis heard a whinny as they drove off. It seemed the big man was alone—there was no one in the living quarters. When the man pulled over so Luis could get Blanca, Luis looked at the food and water on the seat, then at the man.

The man's eyes were firm and all he said was, "Trust me."

Miles and hours later, Luis looked in the back of the crew cab and saw Blanca fast asleep. The man had put his coat over her and made sure she felt safe, and she had fallen asleep quickly. Luis was good with people and told the man he worked hard, and offered him their services. And that is how they made it to the Three Bit. That man was Tuff Collins.

Luis told Jorge the story over and over. He taught him the value of looking someone in the eye and how to shake a hand. None of the soft, squishy stuff—no, his father had told him that a limp, clammy hand was not a sign that a man could be trusted. "Always mean it when you shake someone's hand and look them square. They should know you can be trusted and that your marrow is deep."

Jorge shook his head at the whole marrow-deep thing. That his father was well-read and self-taught was off-putting where he had come from. Blanca left them when Jorge was very small. She missed her family, and the politics of America's immigration policies alarmed her more than the poverty of her home. She left without a word, just a note saying she wasn't suited for this horse-ranch life. Luis lost track of her but a rumor drifted back to them that she had died in Mexico.

Kitzie once told Jorge that when Blanca was around, the cottage was neat, their clothes were clean and mended, and she held Luis's hoarding tendencies in check. After she was gone, Kitzie and Tuff had to constantly pressure him to clean up the clutter of parts and vehicles, tires, engines, and anything that remotely smacked of "useful someday" in his book.

"I can't fathom a half-bald tire being useful but he just looks at you and smiles. It's a constant with him. He comes back from town with something he's found on the highway in the back of the truck," Kitzie had mentioned and she shook her head as she said it. "Drove Tuff crazy. But Luis is such a hard worker, and a decent man in every other regard, that Tuff set up a yard of sorts with a clear perimeter in the back of that shop." She laughed. "Your father has managed to not only fill every inch of that but he creatively stacked. He went vertical and Tuff had to rein him in as he pretty much ignored my entreaties."

Luis liked making things mechanical work. He'd do some riding and cattle work with his son but he was not as suited to it as he was fixing broken things. Repairs on a ranch were constant and he was a decent carpenter as well as a mechanic. It gave him satisfaction and he was always busy in that shop of his. People brought him things to fix, so there was always the smell of oil and gasoline in the shop and the fumes hung around him like cologne.

To Jorge, it was a mess and he didn't like stepping in and around all the junk his father kept. It was a miracle he could get in there at all. The old cigar box's place on a shelf along the back wall required a contortionist's skill to navigate around the engine blocks and oil, parts everywhere, bits of radiators, and welding torches, all of it either rusting or too precious to haul away.

Kitzie allowed it as long as it stayed in the confines of his shop, hence the crammed-in feeling. The growth filled shelves he'd put up and bumpers rested on the cross-members of the roof. The sliding doors allowed a small measure of ventilation in the three-quarter, sloped roof shed, which was as deep as it was long. Luis managed to have a couple of parked vehicles behind the shop but Kitzie held a tight rein on him and he did not cross her. Well, almost… It was like mold. It just…*crept*.

And now, when Jorge wanted to hang on to something—or in this case, someone—his father was telling him to lose it. Jorge was more than half in love with Trina now. The more he was convinced he loved her, the more he was afraid. It was very confusing.

As he came into the Three Bit, he sidestepped his horse and leaned down to open the gate. Without releasing it from his hand, he maneuvered his horse around and closed it. His dogs had run ahead into the big arena, where they met up with Wyatt, Kitzie's miniature Schnauzer, whose gait was comical and his enthusiasm sincere. Kitzie's other Schnauzer, the much older Lulu, lay at her feet.

Kitzie sat with her left forearm resting on the pipe rail, her chin on top of her hand. She turned her head and watched Jorge ride up. Her shoulder-length hair had been graying by subtle degrees and she let it. Longer strands seemed determined to work themselves free of her baseball cap and a slender finger found them and tucked them back. Though the years hadn't accumulated on her face, time had carved fine lines that were the map of every life. Slim and athletic, Kitzie possessed those indefinable qualities of durable beauty. And though she had forgotten that about herself, it was obvious to even the most casual observer.

Jorge stopped his horse near Kitzie, who smiled up at him. The wind whistled through the long steel rafters of the arena. The pitch of the whistle fluctuated with the intensity and direction. The birds who made the rafter complex their home soared and wove their way around them, pushed off course by the erratic directions the wind chose.

"Jesus," Kitzie said. "This wind. It's supernatural."

They discussed the cows and Kitzie pulled her cell phone out of her back pocket to check for any notifications. The screen was scraped and dusty, and Jorge wondered how she could see anything on it.

"Why don't you get one of those protector things?" he

asked…again.

    She didn't look up and mumbled something about how she meant to, and shoved the phone into her back pocket. She did little to hide her annoyance, her mouth a straight line and her silence voluminous. Kitzie was easily frustrated by technology. Tuff was at ease with every newfangled improvement, update, and upload, and she had zero patience for most of it. She still wrote more letters by hand and actually sent them the old-fashioned way than communicated by e mail. She did not treat her phone well and she knew it. She would have preferred carrier pigeons to a cell phone.

Chapter 12

Rae had court on Friday and it was her favorite judge, Francis K. Remington. Judge Remington, Frank to his friends, was a tall man, over six feet. His wife, Carolyn, was well shy of five feet tall. It was said that she never "walked" a day in their married life. In fact, Carolyn—known as May—and her twin sister, June, were diminutive twin ladies who had married men of great stature. Rae adored them and found it amusing that they called her by her given name, MacRae.

Friday ended up being a day in court Rae would never forget. Judge Remington had called a break for lunch and the court was returning to session. All rose dutifully when the judge entered the courtroom, stepped up onto the dais, lowered himself into the chair...and disappeared.

When the chair broke, the court bailiff froze in shock and a collective gasp ran through the room. It felt like an eternity before a large hand rose dramatically over the edge of the bench, fingers outstretched, palm down, and grabbed the smooth wood surface. With equal presentation, the other joined it and slowly, the rest of the tall judge elevated from the depths. The expression on his face was stoic. He straightened his robe, patiently waited as a new chair was brought for him, then took his seat, and in his signature baritone, said, "Must've been the weight of the evidence."

The statement brought laughter to the court, broke the

tension, and court proceeded. It would become a story of legend, oft-repeated, and Rae found herself still smiling about it when she went into the office on Saturday afternoon.

She'd ridden in the morning and had some things she wanted to catch up on. Rae often worked alone in her office. She liked the quiet.

Hours later, hunger gnawed and convinced her to take it up early the next morning. She looked at her watch and saw that it was almost eight. *No wonder I'm hungry as hell*, she thought. She shut down her computer, packed some files into her briefcase, and took her coat off the back of her chair. Mentally, she went down the list of restaurants between her office and home. What was she in the mood for? Something easy with quick access from the highway.

She turned the lights off and stood in the quiet darkness. It was peaceful in the building with no one there. Rae thoughtfully prepared her coat. In a ritualized way, she slid her arm into one sleeve, then repeated the motion with the other. As she did up the buttons, she heard a door open somewhere down the hall. The sound of footfalls neared her office, and shadows passed by the window in the door as the footsteps continued down the hall. Rae felt that childlike superpower stealth come over her and she silently took the doorknob in hand, rotated it slowly, and opened the door a crack. She peered down the hall with one eye to see the back of a tall, thickly built man. He had a nice cowboy hat on and was dressed Western to the core. Nice boots too, silent on the smooth floor. Rubber-soled? He paused at Noah's door, and when she realized he was checking the hall behind him, she slivered her view with her door. He stared, then looked the other way.

Cautious fellow, Rae mused, and that curiosity turned to hairs standing on end on the back of her neck. Rae knew her boss's after-hours meetings were none of her business—she didn't even know he was in the building—yet she found her loyalties were more frayed than she realized.

Rae stood at her closed door and considered what she was feeling. The man didn't knock on the door to Noah's office, he just walked in. She looked down at her briefcase. Inside it was a brief she'd been meaning to get to Noah's desk for a couple of days. It could easily wait until morning, but Rae set the case on the chair and retrieved it. She opened the folder to double-check that it was the right one, then gathered her briefcase and her purse, locked the door, and made her way to Noah's office.

Rae entered the waiting area—a large, lushly appointed suite where a personal assistant screened visitors and oversaw Noah's calendar. To the right was another sectioned-off area for a legal assistant who usually accompanied Noah when he appeared in court. Legal briefs were piled high on that desk and Rae didn't envy the job that poor soul had.

The doors to Noah's suite of offices were just beyond and Rae made her way straight through. She raised her hand to tap on the door but hesitated. She thought she heard muted voices inside. Noah's office lights glowed through the lovely, etched windows on either side of the massive doors. The building had a fancy, energy-saving system so hall and atrium lights were halved after a certain time to save money.

Rae knocked politely. The voices stopped and she heard movement. Noah came to the door and opened it a crack.

"Oh, hey," Rae said. "Saw your light on and I meant to…"

She craned her head to see through the crack. The big man

was settled into a chair at Noah's desk, his hat upside down on the desk's smooth, polished surface. The back of the man's head and his broad shoulders, smooth in a well-tailored, beige, Western-cut jacket, were all that was visible and he didn't turn around.

Noah looked caught and a little uncomfortable. Rae couldn't tell whether that was because of her or the man.

"Oh, sorry, here," she said and slid him the file through the crack. "That report you wanted, on the oil and gas leases."

Noah recovered somewhat and said he'd review it and talk to her later. He shut the door without any further pleasantries.

Jesus, Rae thought as she turned to walk down the hall. *That was weird.*

She glanced over her shoulder to see the door open a crack and Noah's eye on her. He quickly closed the door again. Rae kept going, muttering under her breath, "And cagey, and as deep as a birdbath."

Rae proceeded down the hall and took the elevator to the main entrance. The night guard was at the desk and he rose to let her out of the building. He was a regular fixture and they knew each other from Rae's many late nights. She always asked after his family, listened with interest to his answers, and was genuinely concerned about his well-being. She knew that he was smart, even if others thought he was just a glorified mall cop. She knew of his dedication and his years of fine service in law enforcement, and that he didn't miss a thing. If there was a situation—and there had been some hairy close calls—he had a pretty good bead on keeping all of them safe.

This night was no different, and he had a young, new hire he was showing the ropes to. He instructed him to monitor the closed-circuit, high-definition cameras while he walked Rae to her car. Rae demurred, then thought otherwise when he insisted. He put on his cap and coat and his hand went to his holster to make sure it was secure…a cop's habit. He once walked a beat and had his routine. Rae liked his chivalry. He was the kind of gentleman so rare these days. It was important to him and she respected him.

As they left the building, he locked the door behind them and clicked on his powerful flashlight. He played it around the darker corners of the parking lot and looked at the few vehicles that were still there.

She asked after his mother, who'd had an operation recently. He seemed relieved to talk to someone who cared. This allowed Rae to listen and look. There was Noah's car, in its reserved spot. The guard shone the light at the trunk and swept the beam underneath. As he escorted her to her reserved spot, he played his light over a big, very clean truck that took up two spots in the visitor's parking section.

It's OK, Rae thought. *There's no one really in the building…*

But she heard the guard blow a breath between his lips and she knew that in his OCD-ordered world, the least the guy could do was park it straight. He let the light hang on the license plate for a few long seconds and she figured he was memorizing it.

After Noah brushed Rae off, he closed the door and locked it. Dale had that poker face with unreadable eyes, which always made Noah wary. Noah loosened his tie as he returned to his desk.

"Who was that?" Dale asked.

Noah envied Dale's control and was simultaneously a little afraid of him. Noah felt like a supplicant to a visitor in his own office. He knew what he owed Dale and he knew a lot about Dale's myriad "legitimate" businesses, some of which he'd privately advised him on. And he had benefitted from Dale's hand on the political scales. There were times that Noah was sure Dale had seen his own files and was more knowledgeable about the department's work than Noah.

Hell, he knew it was Dale's advice and strategic craftsmanship that had positioned him where he was, and now Noah found himself on the very edge of real political power. He would be a broker and have a seat at the table Dale obviously didn't need himself, as long as he had people like Noah.

Noah gave himself a minute and moved a sheet of paper across his desk, put it in a file, closed it, and placed it neatly on top of another set of files. He made sure the edges lined up and lifted his eyes to meet Dale's. If Dale's look could possibly harden, Noah felt its granite now.

"She's one of my district attorneys." He tried to sound casual about it.

Dale's look bore down on him. "The one who's been working on that case—and she's *yours*, you said?"

Noah nodded, then waffled. "No, she's—she's not, not that way..."

"Is that business under control?"

Noah shifted. "It wasn't possible." He met Dale's gaze and continued, "Priorities shifted and I reassigned most of her team away. The case on this end is completely stalled."

"It will stay that way?"

"Yes."

"And did you look into the Tiny business as I asked?" Dale

added.

Noah leaned forward and put his elbows on the desk. "That is a bit more complicated. I didn't know the scale and scope of the operation he was running. You failed to mention that he was the goddamn godfather of stolen cattle."

"You have all you need to know. Redirecting is what we do. What *you* do. Just do what I ask and it will be fine," Dale told him.

Noah put on a game face, leaned back, and said, "I made sure, indirectly, that his taxes are unavailable because of an audit."

Dale looked at one of his fingernails and added without looking up, "Seems like a tactic that's been successful of late for a lot of people."

"That business, or whatever went on, is a mire of untraceable. By the time the investigators had access to any records, most of the evidence was gone."

"Really?" Dale said, his face softening into one of previous knowledge.

Noah had suspected, and now confirmed, that Dale probably knew more about Tiny and his organization than the authorities ever would.

Dale narrowed his eyes. "And you've been seeing all of her files on that case and there's no mention of Tiny?"

"None," Noah replied.

"Good. Make sure it stays that way. Oh, and there's something I need you to check on for me. It has to do with mineral rights on some land. Don't let *her*..." He tipped his head in the direction of the door. "...around this." He slid a thin file across the desk to Noah. Across the top were the words "Strictly Confidential."

"What do you want me to do?" Noah asked, a little confused.

"Just be sure she has no interest in that," Dale repeated for extra emphasis.

Noah opened the file and scanned the top sheet without going further. "This is way out of my lane," he said, and closed the folder.

"Nothing is out of your lane...*Senator.*" Dale's icy eyes shifted. "Now, let's talk about the next steps in your campaign."

Dale and Noah talked well into the night and Noah Bainbridge saw his entire political career laid out neatly before him. By the end of the meeting, Noah visualized himself in Washington in a few years, being respectfully referred to as Senator Bainbridge. It had a good ring to it.

The next afternoon, after a quiet Sunday morning at the office, Rae waved at the security guard and headed to the parking lot. With coffee in one hand and the handle to her rolling briefcase in the other, Rae checked her stride well before she got to her truck. Out of an abundance of caution, she had peripherally done a mental look around her immediate environment and noted nothing unusual. The envelope was slid under the driver's side windshield wiper blade and when she saw it, she automatically rescanned the entire parking area. Rae visually located all the cameras and noted that they were not damaged or defaced. She knelt, rested a knee on the pavement, and looked low under the surrounding vehicles. Clear. She cautiously approached hers, knelt again, and examined the undercarriage more carefully, then the pavement underneath. No telltale signs of tampering, nothing hanging, no odd little dollops of fluid from anything punctured.

Still wary, she looked around the entire circumference again, and when nothing gave her pause, she leaned over to the envelope for a closer examination. It was an ordinary-looking manila envelope, thickened by what seemed to be paper. No lumps or oddities.

Rae unzipped the outside pocket on her briefcase and her fingers withdrew a single latex glove—the kind used in a medical office. She had a friend who got them by the crate. Handy. With a gloved hand, she slid the envelope out from under the wiper blade that held it fast.

Once she was home, Rae read the dossier and found it disturbing on several levels. That someone had sent it to her anonymously was one. That it seemed to be thorough, professional, and carefully researched meant it was compiled by someone with access. Access from where and to whom? Ideas and suppositions meandered in her imagination as she scanned and then read with increasing dismay.

The gist of the document was a somewhat clinical account of how a group of wild mustangs, rounded up by the BLM and turned over to haulers for transport, had ended up all shot and buried in a shallow grave. There were photographs attached and Rae saw mares and foals in the carnage. There was an approximate location noted and the words, *They do it for fun, and they will do it again...* scrawled across the bottom of the report.

Rae shook her head. Who would do this? Since an uncomfortable amount of attention had been placed on the fact that taxpayer dollars were going to a buyer just for receiving horses, perhaps the money was harder to come by. Perhaps someone had found another way to earn revenue from herds they were supposed to haul.

She looked up horses getting shot on the internet and was astonished at the number. Most were just bored-stupid people doing drive-by shootings from the road, but she managed to find one other case of a mass shooting that wasn't all that dissimilar from the anonymous tipster's information. It was near the Steens in Oregon. It made her think of the standoff between the cattlemen holding public property hostage to protest overreach by the government. That they had refused to abide by their leases never entered their conscience, or that the land was not theirs alone by any right. It belonged to the rest of America too.

Chapter 13

An easy quiet enveloped the riders as they headed for Sanctuary, all absorbed in their own thoughts or no thoughts at all. It was the way of the country. It took you out of your head and made the world's problems seem small and insignificant. It was easy to imagine that this time could be any time in history, how it might have been when the country was in its infancy, and being on the back of a horse was the main mode of transportation.

The ground stretched evenly for a couple of miles, then rose into the bluffs and canyons beyond. Sanctuary was guarded by strange-looking, stony hills. The way in was hidden from obvious view and there was a moment when it felt as if the ghosts of the past rode with them. It was not unlike the ground Wyker, Harper, and CJ had traversed while chasing the herd, though it had gone unappreciated at the time with so many other things to think about.

Buzzards wheeled high on the drafts above the man. One caught a strong thermal and soared up to clear the lip of a cliff face as if propelled from a cannon. Its black wings sheared the edge directly in front of a pair of deep-set eyes in a weathered face. Startled, the bird rolled back and away from the precipice.

The man grunted as he felt the heavy leather sheath dig into his upper leg. He readjusted it to the side of his hip as he belly-crawled back to his vantage point. The high bluff bowed out, forming a half-ring of sorts that allowed him to see for miles in every direction. But there was only one section that caught his attention—the trail of dust the group made as they approached.

His dark eyes squinted from a lined face that had been beaten by weather and hard living to a texture that bore a resemblance to a dry creek bed. His clothes were ragged and filthy, blending into his surroundings perfectly. He looked over his shoulder down a short slope to where he had tied the horse. It had settled some, though it had cried when he'd separated it from the injured one. He had tied it well out of sight. The last thing he wanted was for it to see the other horses and call to them.

He watched the group and counted how many there were. When they drew closer, he saw a red horse he recognized immediately. It was impossible to miss that crafty bastard and his rider, and he scowled. He felt the knife dig in again at his side, as if to remind him that it had missed its mark…once.

When he had seen enough, he slithered away from the edge of the cliff.

Wyker looked around and took his bearings. His memory said they had come near here after they'd encountered the rustlers and taken back the herd. He looked over at Harper to see if they were close, and he nodded that they were.

Harper stopped and let the others pass. He encouraged the

younger kids to take the lead to find Sanctuary. It was a good exercise. The kids knew the place only from stories and an elder's curled finger on a map. Wyker stayed close and followed them as they turned onto a narrow track and the group thinned to single file.

Wyker continued to check the ridges and bluffs. He had grown to count on Harper and when Harper did that thing he did, there was always a reason. Maybe it was a learned habit from Uncle or just a gift that Harper was born with, but when his sixth sense, his third eye, bade him to look, he did. His hawk-like vision extended outward, often misconstrued as "edgy," and he gave Ely a knowing glance. Ely responded with a minute nod of his head. He pushed his horse off laterally to their position to check flank, then returned shortly and shook his head at Harper. If someone was out there, they were staying low.

They maneuvered through tangled boulders on a twisting trail until they came upon a sharp turn between the rocks. One by one, the riders disappeared into what looked like a dead-end. It was narrow and tight, and legs rubbed hard against the sides in places.

Carson watched Slides, who rode ahead of her, as he prepared to go through. He lifted both his legs onto the neck of his horse and pulled the hay nets up, holding them to his knees and blocking his view forward. In this tight space, words carried and echoed. His voice bounced off the walls of the sand-colored rock as he said, "Bareback is pretty smart, huh?"

Carson mimicked his style, her knees over the swell of her saddle, heels aligned with the shoulder blades of her horse as she squeezed through the same spot. Though it wasn't her saddle, it was Carson's nature to care for it. The rocks scored the leather and threatened to pull the fenders and stirrups off until a stubborn stirrup reluctantly spun flat and slipped through. She groaned at the scars the rocks left.

Slides unfolded himself as the path widened, dropping the hay nets back on either side of his horse and letting his legs down. Tufts of white and black hair fell to the ground behind Slide's and his horse as they navigated the tight bends. It reminded Carson of the Peanuts cartoon character, Pigpen. The horse apparently didn't mind getting a firm currying from the rocks.

The narrow passage widened into three hard turns before it opened into the spot where the bramble gate was. They heard a horse's shrill call bounce off the canyon walls—a herald of their arrival to Sanctuary.

Behind Carson, Wyker frowned. Only one horse called out. An uneasy silence descended over the group as the lead rider slid off his horse, worked to unhook the bramble gate, and held it open for the others to go through, then secured it behind them.

Slides slid off his horse and pulled the hay nets and his bedroll with him. In one fluid motion, he removed the bridle and let his horse loose. Soon, several mounts were similarly freed.

The lame horse attempted to jog a few paces toward them, nickering at the sight of companions. He stopped and waited for the new horses to meet him. They sniffed noses, sharing breath in that greeting horses do with each other as a way of introduction. He was thinner than Carson had hoped. Though she had no prior experience with him, his weight still seemed light and she hoped his injuries weren't too serious.

Slides' horse did not waste time with greetings. He was

thirsty. The gelding went straight to the water that dribbled from a crack high up in the rock into a carved, bowl-shaped divot in the stone, creating a trough that held ten inches of water at its deepest. From there, the water found its way out over a natural lip and vanished into the ground. The dirt around that spot glowed fluorescent green where grass and lichen had claimed a stronghold of survival in an otherwise barren landscape.

The other horses parted respectfully when Rio approached to drink. After long moments, he lifted his head, water dribbling from his soft mouth. He swallowed, working his lips as he stared into the half cave that formed a low shelter beneath the cliffs. A few more drops found the earth as they dripped from his long muzzle hairs and he looked completely relaxed. Rio took some more water, then stepped away, and the horses behind him moved aside to let him pass. He flattened his ears at one that hadn't cleared out of his way quickly enough. It was a sign, nothing more, and the offender gave ground.

The damp sweat mark on Rio's back from the saddle pad was edged with white, salty sweat from the long ride. He found a soft spot in the dirt, circled several times, then folded his legs and rolled. He grunted in satisfaction as he rubbed his back into the sand. With his legs in the air, Rio twisted his body to properly scratch all the right places. He balanced midline for a split second, then kicked his legs to roll himself over to the other side, where the same twisting motions ensued before he rose from the dusty bath. He shook his entire body and a cloud of dust vibrated off, yet stuck to the perfect saddle-pad-shaped pattern on his back. Rio ambled off, checking to see if any tender grass shoots remained in Sanctuary. But the ground was thoroughly shorn and the hungry, lame horse stared at the hay bags with laser focus.

The horse who stepped up to the water next patiently waited for the spring to refill the bowl. The sucking sounds he made as he drank bounced off the cliff walls and sounded like a kid going after the last dregs of a soda through a straw.

As the injured packhorse hobbled around the others, Wyker and CJ exchanged glances. CJ's mouth was tight and two furrows creased between his eyebrows. Both wondered how the second horse had gotten out, yet this one had not. Certainly, with the gate closed and secured, it had help.

Carson was the last to dismount. She dallied her reins around the saddle horn so they wouldn't drag, then approached the injured animal. There was pronounced swelling on a front leg and some of the cuts had festered under scabs, trapping discharge and probably a mild infection. The gelding stood calmly and when she rested a hand near the swelling to check for heat, he laid his ears back and swished his tail in pain, but didn't move away.

Wyker said, "Looks kinda ugly."

Carson nodded but seemed unconcerned. She'd seen worse.

Harper looked over at the kids. "They should've stayed saddled up. They should start back right now to get to Uncle's by nightfall."

The moans of protest were instantaneous. The kids wanted to stay—which was probably why they'd all pulled their saddles so quickly.

Ely waited to see which way the wind blew on it, ready to take them home if asked. There was more discussion. Initially, Wyker seemed to think it was a good idea for them to head out but as they talked about it, they concluded that they'd be riding in the dark at some point, so it was agreed that the group should stay together for the night. There were smiles all around as everyone busied themselves setting up camp.

CJ took Johnny from Wyker and Slides took Carson's horse. She said he didn't have to but he was eager to help. All the kids were. Wyker approached the injured gelding and gently slid a rope halter on him. While Carson had brought some supplies with her, Wyker described where she might find more in the packs they had left behind in the cave under the cliffs.

Carson crouched low at the entrance and saw a pack tucked up against the back edge. The second pack had been opened, and its contents tossed about and ravaged by someone. She stepped on bits of debris and wondered aloud whether the horse had caused the damage.

"I doubt it," CJ, behind her, said.

She craned her neck to look up at his back-lit form. "You seem sure of that."

CJ replied, "I am."

He saw the torn-up pack and recognized it as the one that the injured horse had on when he'd fallen off the edge of the cliff trail. Unconsciously, he touched the thigh of his jeans. The bruise from that rope, where it had pinched his leg, had taken its sweet time healing and if it hadn't been for Rio's quick moves, the packhorse would have taken them down the cliff too.

CJ ducked to avoid the rock outcropping as he stepped away from the cave, then stopped in midstride and crouched when his eyes caught sight of the faint drawings on the canyon walls. His gaze followed a fire scar that went up the rock face and curled around the edge. He rose stiffly and walked a few feet to where Harper stood.

Carson inventoried what they had to work with. What was scattered about in the cave looked as if someone had emptied the packs and sussed out what they wanted, then left the rest behind. She gathered what was usable, then joined Wyker and the gelding.

"You're getting old," Harper teased as CJ gimped up to him.

In Aussie, CJ replied, "It ain't the years, mate, it's the mileage."

Harper told two of the boys to go out and look for something to make a fire. CJ started to speak but Harper held up a hand. A younger boy joined them and Harper pointed to a certain size of rock and set him to looking around for more inside Sanctuary. The horses wandered about freely, some taking turns to roll near the spot Rio had chosen. A low cloud of dust hung in the air as each took a turn.

CJ waited as Harper spoke to Ely. The boy nodded, went to his bow, strung it, and swung it up over his shoulder. CJ had noticed the detail and craftsmanship on the bow during the ride. Though he spent a great deal of time roping with Ely, he had never seen his bow.

Ely straightened and saw CJ staring. He smiled before setting off at a jog to catch up to the two boys. He was gone from view after he passed the second bend in the narrow canyon.

CJ wanted to talk about the rock drawings but stopped when Harper pointed to the supplies scattered on the ground. "Do you see that?" He bent down and picked up a piece of leather rigging. "Someone got in here. And they were sloppy about it." He rolled the bit of leather in his hand and looked at it in the fading light, then handed it to CJ.

CJ stared. "Bloody hell." He glanced down at the solid oak

forks of the sawbuck saddle pack that had been hastily cast aside, its kiln-dried, hand-shaped smoothness immune to just about everything. The counter-sunk hardware was packed with soft dirt and the adjustable, single rigging was tangled. CJ noticed the heavy harness leather rigging straps, a full inch wide, with hand-beveled edges to reduce chafing.

"Know of a knife that could make short work of that?" Harper asked.

CJ nodded. He could still feel the blow to his back and how lucky he had been. The Mex's rustler's knife had sliced through the back of CJ's thick coat like butter that day. Fortunately, the coat was its only victim.

CJ frowned and spun toward the opening to Sanctuary, thinking of the kids out gathering wood by themselves. Harper's voice stopped him.

"Ely's with them and watching. He's aware. He'll keep them close." Harper walked toward Carson and Wyker. He called over his shoulder, "He'll figure out which way that other horse went."

CJ nodded and turned the piece of leather over in his palm, impressed by how clean the cut was. Then, to Harper's back, he said, "It's the Mex."

Harper stopped. "I think the white guy split."

"Could be," CJ said as he tossed the bit of leather back toward the cave.

The younger boys needed some help with the rocks to make the fire ring and they were being way too picky about size. Harper laughed at their process and let it be until he got his bedroll and old military saddle set down. He wasn't too particular about the saddle and he set it up to be his pillow. The tree of that old saddle was tough and it didn't seem to hurt it if it was laid flat.

CJ noticed that Carson had set her saddle horn-down, with the back skirt pointing skyward, the bridle carefully hung off the edge, and the reins and mecate neatly looped. Her parents had taught her that laying the saddle flat-side down would get the sheepskin lining dirty and that it was bad for the tree—the hard resin frame that made the bones of the saddle.

CJ considered the Three Bit and felt like he'd thrived there with the organization he'd seen and the methods used to manage it. It was a cool set-up and spoke to the kind of man Tuff Collins must have been—man enough and good friend enough for Wyker to drop his work at the correctional facility. He looked over to where Rio stood, and his horse stared at him as if he knew CJ was thinking about him. Rio blinked and shook his head. His red mane fanned and resettled, then he closed his eyes.

Wyker and Carson decided to hold their small supply of Banamine for the journey back, hoping that the stronger painkiller would get the injured horse moving better, and that the stiffness and lameness might ease up with movement until then.

"I hope the injury on that front leg will go down some by him walking tomorrow," Carson said to Wyker as she moved in to begin the clean-up of his more festered wounds, then stopped before she started. "You got him?"

Wyker stood on the right side with Carson and tipped the gelding's head toward her so he would have a harder time cow-kicking her with his back foot. His right knee was stocked up and swollen about halfway down his leg, though the pastern area and hoof looked remarkably good.

"I wish we could run a hose on that swelling," Carson said.

She knew that once they got him back to Uncle's, treating him would be much easier.

Carson pried the dried and dirty bits off the wound above the worst of the swelling, where the legs came into the chest. "Sorry, buddy, that stung." She had the scissors and was freeing a flap of skin that had scabbed over. As she did so, white pus oozed from underneath. There were only a couple of pairs of exam gloves in the kit from the pack and she was being careful, though she would have done without had there been none. They did the best they could with what they had.

Harper sat on a rock and watched the boys as they fussed with their fire ring. CJ walked over to Wyker. He watched Carson's auburn hair tumble over her shoulders as she knelt in the dirt and squirted some dark-magenta liquid onto cotton and dabbed the ooze that still emanated from one of the punctures.

CJ spoke to Wyker about the theory that it was the Mex who had found Sanctuary and taken the other horse. Wyker considered it. While CJ and Wyker watched her work, Carson focused on what she was doing, though she wanted to look up.

Wyker said, "That's uneasy news."

CJ said, "Right is. You don't think they'd try for the cows at Uncle's, do you?" He frowned. "Bloody hell if they do."

The horse shifted his feet. Carson jumped up and stood back in case he moved into her. "They'd be crazy to go there and try," she stated with more certainty than she felt, then looked to Wyker hopefully. "Right?"

Wyker shrugged. He couldn't say for sure. "I'd like to think the rustlers gave up on the herd and lit outta here."

"Then I'll bet the cattle don't concern them anymore," she said. She looked at CJ, who glanced at her, then her eyes locked on Wyker.

"If Harper isn't concerned, I don't think we should be," Wyker said.

Carson stayed standing. "I've done about all I can for now."

A small pile of wood and burnable bits soon grew into a rather sizeable mound, and Harper kept the kids busy by sending them out for more. Ely talked quietly with Harper in between, and Carson watched them. Harper nodded in agreement to something Ely said, then Ely, his bow in hand, followed the kids back through the entrance to Sanctuary.

Carson crouched by a pack and organized dinner. Harper walked over and knelt beside her and watched as she set out the supplies.

Carson looked up. "What did Ely say?"

Harper brought one knee up and rested his elbow on it. He looked around the makeshift camp. The light was going fast and he pulled a flint out of his pocket.

"I have a lighter," Carson offered.

Harper smiled. "Kids learn to make a fire better when they have nothing."

Carson's eyebrows went up and she snorfed a nasal laugh. Why hadn't she thought of that?

Harper reassured her before he rose. "Ely said the horse—and the Mex, if he's the one—made straight away from here. He feels that he did not loop back. He's making sure."

Ely and the kids returned and it looked like they had enough wood for that night's fire. Most of the kids carried pouches of jerked meat—either deer, beef, or lord knows what, as they all hunted and experimented drying what they killed. While a couple of them set to finishing the perfect fire ring and put the small bits of wood in a conical shape with some dried tufts of grass, Carson watched Harper hand the flint to one of the older boys. Within a few minutes, a wisp of smoke had started in the cone. One of the boys bent low and blew on it.

Slides and a few of the younger boys surrounded CJ. Carson saw Slides dig something out of the pouch around his waist and hand it to CJ. CJ thanked him and held it to his nose. Slides motioned for him to taste it, and politely, CJ complied and wrinkled his nose. A couple of the younger boys laughed, poked each other, then went to see their fire grow.

Carson looked at Wyker, who wasn't paying attention, and then at Ely, who was close by. She caught his eye and gave him a questioning look, eyebrows raised.

He moved closer and said, "He likes snakes. We are not sure what he catches exactly, but we call him something that would translate to 'Slides in Rocks' at home."

"But isn't snake, like rattlesnake, good eating?" Carson asked, holding her bedroll in her arms.

"Like I said, we aren't sure what he catches. Sometimes he gets what the snake hunts and not the snake."

Carson nodded. She inspected her saddle and the saddlebags and noted the fresh scratches and hard rubs from the stone. Her fingers traced the new scars. She chose to see them as a memory, a story only the leather could tell. She set her bedroll down. Slides said he would save her a place next to him. She smiled indulgently at him and said she would unroll it a bit later, after dinner.

She pulled out the Ziploc bags of refried beans that Auntie had given them along with folded aluminum foil, the thick kind, and had one of the kids make a vessel out of it to set them to heat near the fire. Depending on the fire, they would be lukewarm or bubbling hot. Wyker carried the bread, a kind of native flatbread that Auntie was talented at making, along with baggies full of butter and one of a hummus-type of concoction. Dinner would consist of bread and beans and storytelling.

They all sat together around a more decent fire than Carson had expected. After a hard day's ride, the bread and beans tasted as good as a filet mignon at a San Francisco steakhouse. The kids told stories that their parents and grandparents had told them, native myths and legends. Some of the boys were better than others at storytelling. One of the older boys held everyone rapt with his tale, his delivery one of style and ease that made him a natural at it.

Carson observed that CJ, as was his custom, sat back and a little apart from the others. But he was close enough to the fire to feel its warmth and watch the firelight trace the shape of Carson's cheeks, eyelashes, and lips.

Slides looked over his shoulder at CJ and asked him to tell them a story. CJ shook his head. He had no stories. Slides persisted and asked about prison. Wasn't there a story about prison?

"I don't know how to tell a story," CJ said.

One of the kids reminded him that he had told them some aboriginal stories.

CJ swallowed and stared into the fire. "I've told you all the stories I know," he mumbled.

The kid persisted that he wanted to hear about something CJ had done. After all, he said, everybody had a funny story about themselves.

If CJ could have put a wall around himself, he would have. But he was there. He had nowhere to go, no place to hide, so he retreated to an effective silence.

The stars above shone brilliantly in the dark sky. The crackle of the fire became the only sound as conversation checked for a heartbeat or three.

Slides in Rocks asked, "Why won't you tell us about yourself?" He said it softly, gently, then lowered his eyes as if confronting a wounded beast he wanted to help.

CJ shifted and found a pebble near his boot. He rubbed it between his thumb and forefinger. "Because it's never all of it," he replied.

"All of what?" Slides persisted.

"All of the story." CJ's Aussie accent became more pronounced the more he spoke.

"Please? We want to know..."

Slides wasn't backing off despite the steely stare CJ gave him. Ely nudged him in the ribs and Slides protested.

Wyker broke the tension and the silence. "Good luck, guys. That's a wall you will not scale." And he threw out a different topic, in part to rescue CJ, and partly because uncomfortable was contagious. But mostly, he found the conversation tiresome. The boys didn't know when a subject had been turned—they were too young to understand.

Slides looked at Wyker, then to Carson. She said nothing but her eyes didn't exactly discourage. She was curious to learn more about CJ and Slides was a persistent young man.

"Come on, tell us. Please?" he added with just enough conviction.

CJ put his hand to his chin and scratched an itch he didn't have. His hand swept up to his mouth in thought before he replied, "If I do, will you promise to never offer me anything from that pouch of yours again?"

Everyone laughed. The boy next to Slides shoved him on

the shoulder and he tipped over.

Slides nodded to CJ, who dropped his hand and folded his arms firmly across his chest, nodding thoughtfully.

"All of the story…" he started.

The silence deepened as all eyes were on him.

CJ stared into the embers. "Where is my truth?" He paused. "What I hear when you ask is, what happened? What did I do?" He looked away. "I don't know where to start…"

The Aussie's words hung in the still night air. Some of the boys, along with Carson, looked away, as if the second he had said it they knew they didn't want to know. A tiny space into CJ had opened, and it was so vulnerable that it no longer mattered. It was as if you had made a wrong turn, took an exit too soon, then slid right back onto the freeway. Those faces wanted to hit the gas and regain the other path, not stay on this one.

CJ continued, maybe sensing the shift. "And the why is all that matters now, and hell, I don't know." He paused as all eyes fell on him once again. The eyes that mattered most were Wyker's, and CJ lifted his own eyes from the fire to meet them straight on. "Truth is, mates, I don't remember why…and I was there." He shrugged. Then he frowned, looked at the eager, fire-lit faces, and added, "There is one thing I'll never forget. The gates with steel bars clanging shut behind me."

Carson found sleep fitful and thought it might not come at all. At Sanctuary, the stars seemed to burn twice as big and she watched them wheel past the opening between the boulder walls—the movement of the earth captured by snapshots of the heavens. She tried a different position on her side, her arm resting under her head, and saw that the fire still glowed in the ring of stones. Her eyes adjusted to the night and the sounds of breathing bodies, each in its own world of dreams. A coal settled and a tiny flame leaped like a heartbeat. Her eyes refocused beyond the stones. In the dimness, she saw the shine of CJ's eyes watching her. Without speaking, he turned over, his broad back facing her, and his breathing drifted to sleep.

Chapter 14

Two masked gunmen burst into Gem Jewelers in Redmond wearing bulletproof vests and waving guns. The thieves ordered the owner and a terrified customer to the floor, then smashed a long, glass jewelry case and grabbed thousands of dollars' worth of custom-made jewelry. Then they took whatever cash was on hand from the cash register and fired a warning shot inside the store. Thankfully, no one was hurt.

Detectives were aware of who the men were—"persons of interest" in pending Redmond criminal investigations. Both suspects could have been wanted on outstanding felony warrants but there was a glitch in the system and that was not known at the time. One of the men was a double convict who had spent most of his forty-three years in prison and had only been out for six months.

During the investigation following the robbery, court records revealed that the police had been following them. They had been observed as they cased the jewelry store and five others. Then, two days before the robbery, the police lost track of them.

Those facts did little to calm the nerves of the owner of Gem and he couldn't sleep for weeks following the heist while the thieves were at large. His paranoia was such that he refitted his Main Street store with bulletproof glass and a secure, electronically activated line-of-sight visual entry system on the door. He also added a state-of-the-art alarm system. He acquired a weapon and took gun safety classes to be adept at using it if the need arose. Customers now had to call ahead to make an appointment.

All these frenetic measures were modestly reassuring but if someone wanted to get in, there would always be a way. He had managed to keep his insurance company from canceling him, though his premium went up, but at least it kept him insured against future losses. Almost simultaneously, he was in a pitched battle with the same company regarding the existing policy and what exactly his coverage was. He had begun to realize he was under, if not at all properly insured, to begin with.

While that part alone would have distracted and angered most, it was not the thing that kept him lying awake at night. What the owner could not un-see, could not forget, were the eyes. The lead guy, the one obviously in charge, had blue-gray, steely eyes that looked right through you—not at you or to you. They were like lifeless doll's eyes. Empty. There was no whisper of conscience there. He imagined the terrible things a man with eyes like those was capable of...and that terrified him.

The investigation proceeded quickly and two weeks later, there was a standoff where the suspected thieves had holed up in a house east of Redmond. One was captured and one escaped. This did not do much to assuage the fears of the victims but at least one of the suspects had been caught. The other, a known felon, had all-points bulletins across the state.

The escaped thief, Malcom "Denny" Denison, was later captured after an extended foot chase in Portland. The capture of the suspects did not lead the police to the jewels, the guns, or the bulletproof vests the men had worn during the heist and the suspects were not forthcoming with this information in interviews with investigators. The owner of the jewelry store had suffered a near-catastrophic loss and all his entreaties to the detectives and the district attorney's office failed to recover any of the stolen property or money.

After the suspects were apprehended, the case moved forward in the courts and the victims were assured of a conviction. The investigators felt confident that the thieves would give up the location of the stolen property in exchange for sentence modification. In other words, they believed the DA would deal and the property would be found. What was very clear to the jeweler during the pre-trial meetings he had with the DA was that this DA was terrified of one of the suspects—Dennison, the sociopath with the haunting, cold eyes. Tiny beads of sweat pebbled the DA's forehead just talking about the case. He feared retaliation and he feared everything about Denny. For this man, his only solution to never seeing that face or those eyes again was to negotiate a sweet plea deal.

To the jeweler's profound dismay, the district attorney pleaded them down from armed robbery to robbery when he elicited a promise from Dennison to return the unrecovered jewelry. They got four years and were supposed to return the stolen goods. But somehow, they were sentenced without divulging the whereabouts of their plunder. The jeweler called the district attorney's office constantly and messages went unreturned. One time, he managed to get through and the voice on the other end of the line said he would follow up and file something or other as it was a violation of the plea agreement. But that never happened. Nothing was ever recovered. It seemed the criminals had done a deal that benefitted primarily themselves.

To add insult to injury, there was a ridiculous meeting with the young district attorney. The victim managed to finally corner him and forced him to talk. His name was Noah Bainbridge and he sat across the table from the jeweler and blithely assured him that he would get restitution from the criminals. He told him not to worry, that he could garnish their wages and the jeweler would be made whole. The earnestness with which he painted that rosy, all-will-be-well scenario was laughable.

The owner of the jewelry store turned to stone in the chair, stunned. The words he heard rendered him speechless. The horrifying vision of receiving anything of value from that monster spun in his mind. Did the DA honestly believe that Dennison would make restitution when he got out? The way the district attorney sold it as justice, that he should be feeling grateful that the perpetrators had been caught and punished, was proof that the system worked. He even quipped some drivel about "your tax dollars at work."

This was the best the legal system could do? The jewelry store owner was outraged. Where was the inventory? Hadn't the return of that been part of the plea? After he had lost over one hundred thousand in inventory and cash, along with his peace of mind, all this pathetic wimp offered was some promise of restitution. He never wanted to set eyes on that cretin again, let alone go after him for repayment. Ironically, for a time, the owner did receive some compensation from Dennison through the state of Oregon. Fourteen dollars a month appeared in his account for six months and the state took out a processing fee and taxes from that.

Noah Bainbridge's success relied heavily on connections. His ascent to higher office began later that year and he left Oregon and landed the plum top spot in Boise. The owner of Gem Jewelry never tired of calling him ridiculous and openly mocked the news when he heard a rumor that Noah was destined for higher office.

Four years later, the owner of Gem was contacted by the Victim's Notification Service about Dennison's impending release date. His accomplice was not being released. This news did little to ease the anxiety he felt but he was grateful for the heads-up.

Later the same week, one of his "irregular" customers appeared at the door and he buzzed her in. She had the same dress and overcoat she always wore and had a scarf over her hair in a style reminiscent of an eastern European babushka. Generally, she was kind, benignly odd, and he suspected she was regularly homeless. He was not sure how old she was and she hadn't taken the best care of herself, but she did seem more solid on this visit. Her hair was clean and she looked better, and she beamed when he complimented her.

Her annual visit was to drop off her necklace for a clasp repair. It was the same clasp repair he did for her every year. He would fix it and it would sit there for months until she resurfaced. The repair was always twenty-five dollars. The storage was free.

She was feeling good and was more talkative when she arrived to pick up her necklace. She was effusive in her praise of his work and made a point to say that he was the only jeweler she used. She paid him in cash. During her visit, she recounted a story she had heard. She was foggy about where she had overheard this "ruffian" bragging.

"Skinny runt, and ugh, the hair on these young people…awful," she said. And she leaned in when she said it. Her fingers slid around on the glass and left unsightly smudges on the glass.

He was polite, though not really listening, and was about to tell her he was terribly busy. His hand reached for the glass cleaner and a towel when she continued about what the kid had said. His old man was a felon, a repeat offender. A real tough guy doing four years for armed…something.

The jeweler stopped in mid-motion, interested. "Robbery?" he asked, encouraging her story.

She beamed with self-importance, then put her finger to her upper lip and muttered a question to herself. "How did he put it?" She wrinkled her brow in concentration and didn't notice that the jeweler held his breath as she searched her memory. "He bragged this to just about anyone…" She brightened. "…that his old man was getting out and that they'd be rich." She smiled up at him. "Said they were going to go out and get something or other and be rich."

The owner of Gem Jewelers already felt a heightened state of anxiety, and that mixed with a burning anger he could barely contain. He couldn't believe what he was hearing. As soon as he shuffled her out of the store, he locked up, went into the back, and got on the phone.

He found the investigating detective and recounted the story he had just heard. He could not sit for the call—he talked animatedly and paced around his small office.

The detective revealed what he knew some of the criminals did with their plunder and evidence. "They drive out into the high desert with those big, five-gallon buckets—you know, the ones with the lids. Then they pick a spot and start digging. The stash from the robbery—the jewelry, the gun, the bulletproof vest, and anything else he didn't want anyone to tamper with—he probably buried somewhere in the Three Corner country."

Someone interrupted the detective, asking a question about

something, and it seemed that he had to go. So, he finished up quickly. "Then he goes to trial and jail with the knowledge that it's waiting for him when he gets out."

The jeweler felt that at least the detective was being honest, though not much help. What he gleaned from the conversation was that the whole plea deal was shit. "Well...can't you follow him or something?" he asked hopefully.

"We don't have the manpower or the budget for that. Dennison's partner got out and was then sent to Pendleton on another charge and he's up for years." His parting words to the owner were that the jeweler would never see them or his merchandise again.

Chapter 15

Criswell jumped back on the quad as the wind increased. He dodged ruts in the track and raced back home as fast as he could. As he neared a fork, he saw his cattle and thought he saw rain. But it wasn't rain. It was swirling ash mixed with flame-red embers. He realized that the wind had increased exponentially and that the fire was running. No, not *running*...that was too slow. It raced and flew. It was behind him, next to him, and ahead of him in an instant.

Criswell had some experience with fires and knew the wind would ground air support. He also knew the bright-red liquid couldn't stop the fire. When it dried, a fire could burn right through it. It bought the firefighters time to dig a line that could hold back low, crawling flames but these flames would not be crawling.

He talked to a reporter later and recounted the horror. "Fire jumped the road and we had twenty minutes to get out. We had already loaded ten horses into two trailers, grabbed our six dogs, and went to safety. The horses were by the house and easy to get to, and we had an escape route. There was no time to cut fences for the cattle."

Criswell's story continued. They had ten more horses in a five-hundred-acre pasture and there was no way to gather them. In a faltering voice, he said, "Five of them died and three had to be put down later. If we woulda gone to get 'em, we woulda burned too."

Criswell, born of generations of a tough ranching family, had hands like shovels and the strain showed clearly on his face. "This fire was scary, burned so hot, never seen anything move so fast. And if I had it to do over, I'd have gone to get those horses earlier and moved 'em close, but I had no idea…" His voice trailed off and his wife took up where he could not.

"We had ten steers that kept to the far west side and miracle of miracles, they made it. We've lost so many we don't have a count yet." Her voice faltered. "But the horses…" She wiped her eyes with the back of her hand. "Basically retired, but our best and we loved them. That is heartbreaking and we may never get over losin' them." She burst into tears.

The fire had too many names, until the whole region had one—the Three Corner Fire.

Fifty-mile-an-hour winds fanned embers like fireworks streaming along the pavement. The ground glowed and towering flames burned skyward. It was unlike anything anyone had ever seen. Nothing could outrun the speed of it. Huge, twirling columns of fire grew up and bred. The entwined, undulating arms flew upward violently, combustion erupting like volcanic matter pressing to be free of earthly bonds. Large sections of flames at the top broke free as if spat from the fuel below. The wind caught this and exploded it into a million tiny, hot bits that ran ahead of it and started new fires. In the darkness, the hills glowed.

Wildfire managers were forced to let fires burn unchecked, and in some circles, a renewed debate raged about whether it was better to fight them or let them burn out. The loss of life made the argument more strident as families mourned. Red-orange, black-red, burning, hellish flames created gusts, adding to the hurricane-force winds that did nothing to blow a fire out, and instead helped the fire grow faster than any in collective memory. Many wondered, with the lingering droughts and global warming, if this fire season would be the new normal. And since the fire was ignoring the designation of "season," some argued there was no longer a "normal."

Baked under a toxic sky, the large fire jumped the lines. Firefighters were concerned about explosive growth and each hour their predictions changed. Infrared mapping showed that the fires had burned thousands more acres overnight and the hectic winds skipped the fire over larger swaths of ground, making containment minimal. In many places, the crews were staffed by volunteers throughout the night. Emergency radio traffic reflected the struggle.

The land itself was transformed by flames into a gruesome, alien world. When the unnatural wind event occurred, born from a hurricane, its effect was not initially thought about...but it made its strength known thousands of miles away.

A blessed piece of heaven called Churn Creek lay squarely in the paths of many of the out-of-control wildfires. The fires developed tentacle-like arms, and divided and grew in ways that cut off escape.

When the devil's only friend took possession of the Churn Creek Ranch, it was perfect. This magnificent property sat in escrow, awaiting the .com mega-millionaire and his extended family to come from their palatial Rocky Mountain vacation home, where they'd spent an idyllic two-month getaway while the ranch was readied. The Churn Creek Ranch had been on the market for a while, waiting for the right buyer with deep pockets and a demand for utmost quality and privacy. This property offered both in abundance. Real estate agents loved showing it because it was stunning and listed with Sotheby's International. Besides its prime location and private airstrip, it had its own water rights, good crop rotation for feed hay, sheds, a huge indoor and outdoor arena, barns, and a spacious, upgraded ten-thousand-square-foot home. There was a thousand-bottle, temperature-controlled wine cellar, custom pool, a swim-through cave, and a lavish waterfall beside the hot tub next to the pool house. A twenty-five-hundred-square-foot, two-bedroom guest house sat near a two-thousand-square-foot caretakers' home. The remodeled bunkhouse was the envy of other big operations, along with level acreage, much of it irrigated. It was stunningly landscaped, had well-lit walkways and paths throughout, a pond with a one-bedroom artist's cottage, and a tiny dock from which guests fished a stocked pond.

The long, winding asphalt drive wound past the covered arena, and was heated to melt any ice it might accumulate in winter. There were three electric-gated entries to the property, designed so that, in case of emergency, there was a path of evacuation for livestock. The shed row that housed the livestock trailers and the various horse trailers (to be sold with the property) were lined up along a path that allowed two routes of emergency escape.

There was an on-site caretaker, a young man and his dog. The main gated entry to the house was custom made, took three years to complete, and featured a waterfall theme that the artist had "churned" in the form of a metal sculpture from either side's twelve-foot stone posts so that when the electric gates opened, the waters parted. It had solar power and was alternately on the electrical grid. Whatever power the occupants needed was easily available and it was the only connection not upgraded over the past ten years.

They had shaped defensible space in the landscape that reflected the nature of the property and its structures. Where buildings were constructed of combustible materials, they had increased defensible space to compensate. The series of management zones had been thoughtfully considered and the builders had gone to great expense with the plan.

The scene was vivid when they got back in. It was as if the fire had folded around and eliminated every last trace that anyone or anything had been there. They found some wine bottles that were in the cellar, now mere molten blobs of glass. The granite counters in the kitchen were gone. Maybe they were buried in the ash…no one knew…but how does stone burn? None of it mattered. The devil didn't care.

Even parts of the gate mechanism had melted, though the gate itself stood as a lonely testament to what once had been. Several horses were found days later, barely alive, standing on the asphalt driveway, their horseshoes melted firmly to the pavement. They were euthanized where they stood. The caretaker and the dog survived by taking shelter in the swim-through cave for several hours.

It was later surmised that one part of the Churn Creek Ranch Fire was started by power lines blown down in a freakish windstorm that was the result of a surprise weather "event." It was the first of thousands of properties destroyed, and the firestorm spread from there. The hundreds of fires behaved as though they were possessed. An entire region was burning, and the flames crossed boundaries that no one thought would ever burn.

On a nearby ranch, a single-cylinder John Deere had been lovingly restored by a father and son. They had soaked each rusted piece in gas, scraped and polished them to near perfect condition, then put it all back together and started it up. The rhythmic thud of the engine brought smiles to both. They parked it next to the pumphouse under the dry, high-desert sky, and admired their work.

"That's the way I remember it," the father had said as he smiled at his son.

Mirror images of one another, they stood together, shoulder to shoulder, and, despite the father's age, his posture successfully fought gravity. He ruffled his grown son's hair as if he were still a boy, and smiled at him without words, until his son almost blushed.

"Let's go get a cold one," the father said.

"We deserve it," the son replied.

Of all the memories they shared, the son would say, "He'd look you in the eye with a sparkling willingness to be your friend."

The fire took the John Deere, the pumphouse, and the father.

Chapter 16

Hy Royston stepped out from one of the four-wheel-drive trucks while his partner, Dave Clancy, leaped from the back seat of a quad cab and tackled one of the drunk shooters. His years of policework served him well as the pot-bellied man tried to wobble away, clutching a cumbersome AR15. Dave was careful and when the man's arms flung wide from stumbling, Dave seized the weapon in one swift movement. He laid it carefully on the ground, the business end pointed away from everyone, then did a leg sweep that tripped the fat boy into the dirt. For a man who hadn't seen his own dick in years, the guy skittered and flailed on the ground like a jittery lizard in a pathetic attempt to crawl away. Dave planted a boot in the center of his back, smushed him into the dirt, pulled the handcuffs off his belt, and cuffed him. He retrieved the weapon with gloved hands and secured it safely.

During the melee, Hy lost track of his team but as the dust settled, they caught a few and confiscated some of the vehicles that hadn't hightailed it out the back tracks into the high desert, their lights disconnected so their taillights weren't visible.

Dave appeared out of the semi-dark between the lights and the black of the high desert with another perp—a cattleman, in cuffs and puking, who was dirty and barely registered that he knew anyone. But Hy recognized him. Dave swung him to their right, sending bile away from them. The guy hollered that he had been attacked and there was some bruising on the side of his head and face. A lip was bleeding rather profusely.

Dave's forehead glistened with sweat. "This one fell as I caught him," he said. "The ground attacked him. He's too drunk to run in the dark."

"Happens," was all Hy replied as he straightened his bulletproof vest—a gift from his daughter, MacRae, as she did not like their standard issue. His badge was just visible, clipped to the top edge near his neck. "Weapons?" he asked his partner.

Dave sounded a little breathless. "More than I thought. Shit, Hy, it's impressive. We're lucky they were so busy with it that they didn't hear us. These drunken idiots would've shot us and themselves."

Hy nodded, already thinking about his outline for the morning's debriefing. "That rig that went by us, the one that got away, did anyone get a partial?"

Dave shrugged.

Hy shook his head. There needed to be a coordination of tactics or people would get killed. Hopefully, they had a partial plate on the truck and trailer they had passed as they came in, and there was the damage on the front left of the trailer that might help identify the owner. "The game coulda been blown if they'd been closer to the road," he said.

"Yeah, that bit was a surprise," Dave replied as they looked to where a lonely pair of halogens still illuminated the death zone. "What a god-awful mess…" He wiped a dirty hand over his eyes as if to rub the image from his mind, then turned away.

But as team lead, Royston didn't have the choice to look away. He held his Nikon camera up and the shutter clicked furiously at the vehicles, lights, contents of the trucks, and the horrific carnage between the trucks and the berm.

He left the rest of his small team to load up the prisoners as Dave called for a tow for the vehicles to be impounded, certain that a number of them would be reported stolen.

Hy walked over to the pit. The vehicles formed one edge of the ring and an earthen berm had been created using heavy equipment in preparation for that night's "party." Several sites like this had been found. The berm was later used to cover up the bodies and the evidence.

These ranchers were occupying federal land and dispensing their own form of range management. This was another new wrinkle in their revolt against the government that involved armed occupations and violent stand-offs in the Malheur region and the West. A judge had dismissed a big case after severely criticizing the prosecutors for willfully violating the due-process rights of the defendants. Several gunmen were among protesters who had assault-style weapons and they had been acquitted of criminal charges in two trials not too long ago. Hy didn't doubt that he'd discover matching names from those legal prosecutions among this bunch. And as he did the inventory of the arsenal they had confiscated, he made sure the evidentiary chain was followed to the letter.

He looked at the dead bodies shredded by automatic weapons and could barely recognize what he was looking at. As his agents went to each of the vehicles at the site to gather data on make, model, and registration, he heard one call to the next one that the registration was missing on the beat-up truck he was examining.

There were no survivors in the pit and Hy was uncomfortably grateful. Dealing with the survivors was just too hard on him. When he got to the far end and found the dead stallion and the destroyed gate panel, he shone his light on the ground beyond and saw disturbed earth and hoofprints. *Maybe some got away...* he thought. He turned around and surveyed the scene of total horror and could only hope that somehow, a few had managed to survive.

Chapter 17

The lame horse had improved a little by morning, but it was a very slow start ponying him out of Sanctuary, and a long, minced trip back to the Rez. But they finally made it and enjoyed a few days of rest after their trip. The packhorse was tended to by Carson and was healing up well under her diligent care.

Breakfast was over and Carson and Wyker were set to leave for the Three Bit. Wyker remained at Auntie's table and Uncle sat out on the porch with his cup of coffee. Carson wandered out to take a last look around. She saw CJ in one of the pens, bent over and working on a broken waterer. She looked for Rio, who was at the far end of the pasture, leg cocked, head low, taking a nap. The kids were nowhere to be seen.

"Where's your posse?" she asked CJ as she approached the pen.

"Don't know," CJ answered without looking up. "You ready to go?" It was more of a statement than a question.

"Just about." Carson turned around, then turned back and added, "Nice riding with ya."

She walked away. Dust puffed out from beneath her boots and she looked down at a memory. Time warped and she was ten years old, eyes filled with tears over some imagined slight at the barn. Now, inside her heart, Carson felt that same pain of somehow not measuring up or being grown-up enough, and that turmoil was as fresh in this moment as it was then.

CJ made busy until her footfalls faded. He thought he felt her look back once and turned to look at the spot where she'd just stood. He looked at the back of her—her long auburn hair, those jeans—and wiped his hands on a rag and stared at the open country. He breathed in deeply, then let out a long sigh and told himself not to dwell on things he shouldn't. He couldn't allow himself the luxury. It wasn't her, she was fine. *More* than fine. It was him.

CJ was clear about very few things, but the fact that he screwed up everything he touched was one thing he was certain of. Then he heard Rio blow and turned to look at the only thing he truly had not.

As he knelt to gather his tools and sort things out, CJ looked at the ground beneath his feet and felt the history there. Not his history...but he felt something as he stood on it. He was there through a set of circumstances he never could have predicted, and he had a horse the likes of which he never could have imagined. He hadn't seen any of it coming. He was acutely aware that he'd been given a second chance. He closed his eyes and felt the breeze dry the sweat on his face.

CJ hadn't seriously considered a woman in a long while. Most of the ones he had known were nothing but the bad side of trouble, as were most of the people he had chosen to be around. He'd made a habit of attaching himself to troubled people for so long, he decided he knew nothing different. The pattern was set and he didn't want to mess up something else. If it meant being a bit of an ass to convince people—to convince *her*—to stay away, then so be it.

Yet...there was something about her and it frustrated him to think about it. He'd pissed in his own pond before and it never worked out.

"So, do something different this time. Don't muck this up," he said to no one.

He was startled by Rio, who was now awake and had moved closer to him. The horse sneezed and blew. CJ brushed the dirt from his jeans. "Ah, c'mon, don't look at me like that…I'm being careful, for both of us."

Rio cocked an ear and bent his head low.

CJ looked up at him and added, "Trust me."

Another sneezy snort showered CJ with a fine mist of snot.

CJ leaped to his feet. "Ugh! Thanks, mate," he said, wiping himself off with his shirt sleeve. He ran a hand down Rio's face and Rio leaned into his touch and closed his eyes. CJ pressed his forehead against Rio's, and they stood together for a moment. The guarded CJ melted away and the hardness around his mouth and eyes softened.

When CJ straightened, Rio looked at him, craned his neck to watch the distantly retreating Carson, then looked back at CJ. He shook his head and neck vigorously, gave the eye to CJ, and wandered off.

CJ looked at Rio and felt like his horse had made a statement. Maybe Rio knew CJ was only one twist of fate away from disaster. CJ was chill with it. It was the nature of an animal adapting to change. *Perhaps faster than we do*, CJ thought as he watched the red roan's rump saunter along the fence line.

The horse sniffed the ground and turned a couple of circles, then his legs started to buckle and he dropped to roll in the soft, dusty earth. He wiggled on his side and back for an extra measure of scratching, sending hair and dust billowing into the air. Rio stood, shook himself off, then looked out over the fence and the cattle that grazed nearby.

The whole scene filled CJ with a calm he hadn't known before. He had no idea where he stood with his parole and all he wanted was to stay with Rio. He looked at his filthy hands—fingers with a good kind of dirt on them—and he looked over to where Wyker's rig was parked near Uncle's lodge. He saw Uncle sitting, as usual, in his antique barber's chair on the small front porch.

CJ watched Carson open the trailer door and a sleepy Tammy stepped out. She yawned, stretched downward, legs straight in front of her, and then the other way, nose high and eyes closed. She walked a few paces and nosed unseen scents, then squatted to pee as Carson walked over to Uncle.

CJ watched her and admired the straightness of her, the way she moved in an effortless, smooth stride as a dancer would move. He squinted and the fine lines deepened at the corners of his hazel-blue eyes. CJ set his hat on a nearby post, flushed dirty water through the newly repaired waterer until it was replaced with clean, cupped a handful, and splashed his face. He felt the stubble on his chin and cheeks and ran his hand over the front of his face. It felt cool and clean and he repeated the motion with both hands.

The warm wind swept ragged clouds across the sky. He heard two mourning doves cooing. The beating of their wings made music of the motion. It looked as though the male dove was courting and he was working hard at it. CJ silently hoped the female hadn't lost interest in him as she started to wander off. He rooted for the male's success and willed her to make the jerky little strut back toward him. And he smiled when she did.

He murmured to the oblivious suitor, "You're welcome, mate."

Wet drops peppered his collar and the front of his T-shirt. The shirt was borrowed and the muscles of his chest and back pushed against the fabric. CJ plucked his denim jacket off the fence nearby, collected his gear, and started for the shed row barn.

Carson rested a boot on the first of the two porch steps and her hand on the post, its surface gray and rough, weathered to the touch. Uncle nodded his silent greeting, as was his way. His marbled hands rested on the wooden arms of the chair. Carson easily imagined it in the barbershop of a dusty Western town with a red-and-white striped pole near the door. The chair's thick, leather padded parts had aged to ossification and it had oodles of character, like the man sitting in it. His jeans were on the short side, and they hiked up on his nondescript leather boots, which were round-toed and worn. She noticed one of the heels had wear that sloped and guessed it needed a new one.

Carson made small talk and thanked Uncle for everything they had done. They both glanced up when Wyker called Tammy and hoisted her into the back seat of his truck. Carson stepped away and turned to go with a wave and a smile.

"He'll be OK here," Uncle said after she had taken just a few steps.

Carson stopped and looked at him.

"They'll all be OK here."

Carson hesitated and looked into Uncle's wise face. She wasn't sure who he was referring to and followed his gaze. He looked at some of the herd that roamed near a fence not far from the house, then at a grazing Rio, and finally settled his eyes on CJ. They both watched CJ walk to the barn. Carson watched longer than Uncle did, and felt his eyes on her. She hoped her face didn't betray her thoughts.

"I know it's gonna be fine. I'm happy that you have them here. It's a good thing for all of us," she said.

Uncle didn't speak but his eyes did, and with a slight lift of his hand off the arm of the chair, Carson felt as though he had hugged her. She nodded with a smile that lit up her face, and with another wave, she again turned to go. As she began to walk to Wyker's rig, she watched CJ in the distance, his jeans jacket tossed casually over his shoulder. Rio watched him too.

Auntie's voice stopped her. She'd quietly appeared behind the dusted gray of the screen door and Carson put a hand up to shield her eyes to focus on her. Auntie came out of the door and down the steps with a small bundle in her hands. It was a cloth folded over a hunk of bread and some fruit.

"For your journey," she said.

Carson thanked her. She looked more closely at the cloth and saw that it had marks on it that were unfamiliar. She looked back at Auntie, who held up a Sharpie marker. Carson smiled quizzically.

"It's a prayer of my people for you. Be well," Auntie said. She took a step back and added, "He likes you."

Carson felt like a teen in front of her parents pretending that she didn't like a boy when it was obvious she did. Her smile revealed that she knew what Auntie meant and she nodded as she walked away.

Carson was almost to the truck when she said to Wyker, "I looked at the gelding."

"I saw that," Wyker replied. "He seems to be on the mend."

The gelding was sore after the long walk back to the Rez and had been dead lame afterward. Harper consulted with a vet over the phone. The swelling was about the same now, and the kids would take over the care and recovery of the injured horse. It was their sacred mission, they told Carson. Harper and Uncle would supervise, and the gelding was in good hands. Kitzie had no issue with him staying there. They didn't need him on the Three Bit.

Wyker climbed into the truck and rested his hands on the top of the wheel as Carson got to the door. He looked in the rearview mirror to see that Tammy had fallen asleep. Wyker started up the diesel and put it in gear. Carson waved to Uncle, who nodded his good-bye.

The road was rough. The truck's suspension did its job to smooth the ride and Carson edged the seat back a little to better stretch her legs. As they made their way north, they passed several livestock trailers going south. Wyker's head followed them as they passed. He frowned. Carson noticed them too and asked him what was up. The change in his mood was palpable.

"We're inside a removal boundary area. There's a trap site off to the east and a main holding corral south of the McDermitt. It's a huge area and it hurts my heart knowing the fear and confusion inside those trailers. Broken-up family units and injured animals that I cannot help," he said.

Carson frowned, then stared ahead with unseeing eyes. What was the reluctance she felt at leaving the Dugout? She dissected her mixed feelings in the silence of the drive. Wyker had thoughts of his own and amiably let her be.

Carson contemplated her future. She wished for an "ear worm"—something with repetitive, meaningless lyrics so she could skip this part of her mind's processor and go to a less serious place. She reached for the radio dial, then thought it presumptuous, and pulled her hand back.

In the back seat, cleverly wedged between bags and a larger duffle, Tammy had worked out a comfortable position. Carson glanced over her shoulder and was charmed by the soft white eyelashes, the line of her black muzzle against the sturdy canvas fabric of the duffle, and her deep sigh of contentment to the vibration and sounds of the truck on the highway. She blended, incongruent puzzle pieces that fit together perfectly. Carson considered that metaphor, that life was like a puzzle without the box to see what the picture would ultimately be. What pieces fit where…and how the ones that looked like they should be together ended up not fitting, no matter how hard you tried. She mulled over that thought and resigned herself to watching the landscape blur by like time.

Once back at the Three Bit, Carson put her things in her room and headed to the barn, which never failed to fill her being with calm. The smell of hay, horses, a tinge of leather, and the fresh shavings mixed with barn wood always created something indefinable yet as powerful as a bouquet of the most fragrant flowers.

Carson grabbed a broom and began to sweep. The sound and repetitive motion of the corn bristles on the rubber matted sections that bordered the stalls became the beat to a song that only the horses and the owl in the cupola could hear. She paused to look at the light that filtered down from the beamed ceiling and cupola to the dirt floor in the center of the barn.

After she had fled the disintegration of her once-successful life in Silicon Valley and had run through the last of her money, Carson had settled back into her family home after turning her back on it many years before. She had unpacked her guilt and shattered dreams and placed herself at the mercy of a mother she hadn't spoken to since she'd left. With Kitzie's gentle encouragement, her old skills replaced the shiny new ones that had failed her. Within a matter of days, Carson found her feel and her seat again riding horses. She could still throw a rope and be handy in the herd. Her groundwork was more than passable and she quietly longed for some colts to start. Her skills, perfected in childhood, returned easily enough. She had felt empty and lost when she arrived, and time with the horses, cattle, and open country seemed to help her find herself again.

Carson smiled as she swept and inhaled the air around her. She had enjoyed the trip in Wyker's rig and the adventure they'd all had together to rescue the injured gelding. The story of how CJ, Wyker, and Harper had caught up to the stolen cattle, had a run-in with the rustlers, drove them off, and returned the cattle was fast turning into a Three Bit family legend.

Chapter 18

Entire communities went from normal to a conflagration in minutes. Animals—farm and domestic—were caught in panic and ran blindly in every direction as avenues of escape were cut off. The swirling, high-pressure dome stalled and downslope winds flowed from the high mountains, plateaus, and hills to the valleys and plains below. A high-pressure whorl, created by fires so hot they made their own weather, moved in all directions.

The extraordinary number of fires made them impossible to fight. They were everywhere and the list grew. One report had a fire about ten miles southwest of the Jordan Valley, then another, and another, and then the reports simply made things more confusing.

The media and emergency services put out what evacuation information they could. The news reported zero-percent containment. In the southeastern central area near Redmond, Oregon, fire managers recorded three thousand lightning strikes in a span of days. The Jordan Valley reported a thousand of their own. And the reports continued up into John Day, Idaho, and parts of Nevada.

It took but a moment for a spark to take off and the scattered reports piled up like autumn leaves. The fires burned in every direction. Some combined and lasers of red embers spawned more fires. Many people didn't know where the fire was until it got them. There were simply not enough resources or a coordinated state, county, or regional system to keep track of what was happening. Talk of containment percentages became impossible because of the number of fires and how fast they were moving.

The wind kept tankers on the ground and aerial assaults neutered. From space, the smoke looked like a hurricane on land, and it created fast-moving walls of incendiary disaster. The wind did things forecasters had not conceived to predict. In an era where climate change was creating more intense fire seasons, the crisis was only expected to worsen in Oregon and across the country. The lightning storms started some of the fires, downed power lines and blown transformers caused others, and the hurricane-force winds drove them, scattering flames in all directions and creating fire tornadoes from the perfect combination of wind and fire, with vortices that could lift cars.

Walls of fire a hundred miles in either direction traveled at wicked speed over open ground. Chunks of ash and hot coals rained from the sky in every direction, starting more blazes. While that alone was impossible to fight, there was an intensity to each not recalled in living memory. A blanket of flames cloaked the earth.

Massive smoke plumes rose into the atmosphere, gathering heat and energy from the flames below along with water vapor from the vegetation the fires consumed. The unstable air column—a pyro cumulous cloud—could collapse at any time, resulting in devastating shifts in wind direction. This posed a major danger for several teams of firefighters throughout the Three Corner region. The fire was no longer dependent on local weather, it was changing it—something only observed during massive wildfires and volcanic events.

Columns of angry smoke rode the atmosphere and made monstrous bruises in the sky. Illegal fireworks started one and on the second day, pushed by hellish winds, the fire jumped a riverbed and headed west. When it crossed the highway, folks had to evacuate immediately.

During that same time in the Three Corner region, seventy-mile-per-hour winds propelled thousands of fires in search of fuel. The firestorm pulled the fuel into its greedy mouth and spit embers like artillery that ran along the ground, consuming oxygen faster than a horse could run.

Chapter 19

With his long arms resting on the top rail of the corral, a relaxed Buckets stood with fellow ranch hand, Green Eyes, and watched a recent hire, Bodie Ransom, work with the crew. Neither spoke.

Buckets was tall—very tall—and thin, with smooth black skin over even features that made him look younger than his years. He had hands like shovels and a code of ethics as firm as his handshake. He was given the nickname "Buckets" in high school. He liked it. It fit. He'd played basketball in college and some professionally. Though a better assistant coach than player, he was an educated sort, a student of history, one of his passions being the American West—specifically, the history of the black cowboy, and he knew a few personally in Compton. Though most Westerns told tales from a biased point of view, he watched every one and loved them anyway. If Buckets could not make the trip to the National Finals Rodeo, he watched it on TV. He loved cowboy boots and hats and always wore them.

Buckets was self-taught in many areas. He read prolifically, studied marketing and finance and the psychology of leadership, and none of it satisfied his desire to live and work on a cattle ranch. He studied agricultural business management—specifically, ranch management and the livestock business—and he'd been on the Running Horse long enough that his previous careers and pastimes were a distant memory.

He had made significant contributions early in his stint at the Running Horse, and the boss—aptly called Boss by his employees—had promoted Buckets based on results. Buckets made a convincing argument to develop a uniform herd and produce uniform calves. He believed in consistency of product and because it was the management's job to understand the shifts in supply and demand, he pressed the ranch's owner to hear him out. The boss, surprised by Buckets' ambition, was an open-minded fellow who encouraged innovation and good ideas when he thought he saw them. So, he gave Buckets an opportunity—a decision he did not regret. Buckets' uniform herd practices reduced the need to separate animals by size for winter feeding and resulted in a calf crop that consistently received premiums at the marketplace.

Buckets loved the ranch as if it were his own. There was a timeless quality to ranch life. He found it easy to lose himself in the cycle of seasons, comings and goings, and the devotion of energy the work required.

Whenever Buckets came around, everyone knew what he would say. "Are you doing something useful?" It got so the ranch hands knew it would be the first thing out of his mouth. Buckets did not suffer fools at all and almost never called a person stupid—he was more inclined to describe someone who came up short as "suffering from a lack of intellectual rigor." Nothing tired Buckets out more than explaining things to people who should already know their job.

He knew the vagaries of cowboy life...wranglers all. They came and went. They drifted by nature. Half of them liked the change and impermanence. They brought little and left with the same. Buckets tried to take the time to find the right man for the right job and to understand what he needed to know to keep the ranch running.

It was Buckets' job to keep everything running smoothly. He liked his "second in command," Green Eyes, because he was as good at spotting things with those translucent emerald eyes of his as Buckets was.

Green Eyes was in charge of the "cavy"—short for "caviada" or saddle horses used daily on the ranch. His job was to evaluate the horses, measuring the performance and attitude of each. He was the liaison between management, the wranglers, the horses, and the cows.

Cow and calf operations were traditionally more profitable than stocker operations, and Green Eyes was keenly aware that a horse that had completed his usefulness on the ranch was worth a lot of money on the outside market. He had a small operation on the ranch focused on the business of raising and making nice horses. He had a good working relationship with a broker and childhood friend, Charlie, in California, and the ranch horse business had been steadily growing.

Green Eyes' given name was Rustin Dillard—a name supposedly from a long line of Dillards, much revered in his family lore, and he was never fond of it. It begged a diminutive, like Rusty—old, nail-like—and Dillard sounded too much like *dullard*, both of which he'd had to bear all through grade school. He'd enjoyed high school rodeo and was half-decent at it. He got his nickname, Green Eyes, in high school and as he grew older, it stuck. When he turned eighteen, he left his hometown, rodeoed for a while, and got lucky, ending up at a premier ranching operation. Buckets had spotted him and asked the boss to hire him on.

Green Eyes had been at the Running Horse for years. He

knew his skill set and he knew his place and was comfortable with both.

Buckets had some reservations about the newest guy, Bodie Ransom. And while his job was to notice small improvements and make mention of them when appropriate, he was struggling. Green Eyes was struggling with it as well. It was their joint responsibility to protect the integrity of the crew by culling inferior cows, horses, and wranglers. Most used the ranch life as a pit stop. Some made it a way of life because they loved it—they loved the hard work, tolerated the rough life, and some even rolled with the tough weather. A good crew would thank the man who was not afraid to send a bad one down the road. Bodie was smooth—a master of spin and spin's close cousin, dissembling. He didn't get caught outright lying but used that behavior to deliberately conceal his true motives and beliefs.

When Bodie first showed up, many were taken in by his charm. By all appearances, he was a solid, upstanding guy, too good-looking for this life, and he tried enough so that everyone liked him. It was easy to be a little jealous of his looks. His one failing was that he was morally challenged where women were concerned. Women loved him to the point that he could pick and choose. He made them feel special and beautiful, even the ones who had no chance at all with him. It was his special gift. And both Buckets and Green Eyes were sure he used it more for evil than for good. It was a trust thing.

Bodie knew how to work a room, politics. And that is what Bodie was born to be, a politician. Someone who could lie convincingly to your face and take your money. He believed the honeyed words that spilled from his tongue. It was a skill that was wasted on the Running Horse. Buckets looked at his crew as a team, and even though he could not put a firm finger on it, he knew in his cells that Bodie should not be there. Bodie was clever enough to up his game to do what jobs were put to him, but he always needed supervision or he'd slack off.

The question that nagged Buckets was, what was Bodie doing there? His performance was better than good enough and he had the stamina, but Bodie was the kind who was looking for an easy way out, a way that would benefit him. Buckets shook his head. Good help that stayed at a ranch was an asset, and this situation would have to be resolved.

The day's shadows grew long and the crew began heading in for dinner. The Running Horse Bunkhouse Bar, also referred to by the old-timers as the Deer Club, was an institution. The ranch was miles from civilization, and keeping the crew well fed and "watered" helped with morale. There was a ping pong table in a back room, a pool table, skittle ball, tables that hosted card games, a couple of computers with internet access, a decent kitchen, and extra bunks in an upstairs loft. Two dartboards were along the wall to the left of the passage to the restrooms and a wide entry to the kitchen. The kitchen was run by Cook, his assistant, his daughter, and an extra if it was an event. The Deer Club was host to monthly, large gatherings, and sometimes dancing, especially after Boss bought an old-style jukebox. The tables could be pushed aside and there'd be enough room for twenty or so to dance. Neighbors, fellow ranchers, and hunters were welcome, and there were times when the Running Horse's Deer Club had as many people in it as the Pine Tavern in Martin.

The bar was an L shape in the corner immediately left of the main doors. Large windows encompassed a striking view behind the bar. The working buildings and homes were constructed on a bluff that lent itself to a commanding vista. There was a strip of mirrors behind the double-glass shelves that rose from the counter to the sill of the large windows on the wall behind the bar. An electric shade could be lowered to shield the glare and protect the lined-up bottles.

In the center of the great room were the two rows of tables—a farmhouse seating arrangement that encouraged everyone to eat together. Buckets noted that the sounds of the kitchen had changed from preparation and service to clean up. Dinner was about through and some of the men gravitated toward the darts. A few gathered at the pool table and the skittle ball (Buckets' favorite) was already in use.

Boss liked to tend bar as it allowed him to really see and judge a man. Buckets rarely sat at a desk to take in Boss's ideas and orders for the day or week. That was usually done there, at the bar. The sensitive or important stuff was discussed behind a closed door.

Boss and Buckets didn't talk about the fires much. Some of their buckaroos had left to help family. Boss was distraught about those that had lost everything—homes, equipment, and most of their livestock. Buckets knew that they would be checking damage to the range and making assessments about food availability. The fires would undoubtedly disrupt normal market behavior and there would be a conversation about that very soon.

Bodie approached the bar and leaned in with drink in hand. There were times that he fit in and didn't "play" a note off. And then he would behave in a way that made the sharper tacks in the box hold their cards a little closer. It was certain mannerisms he displayed like he had practiced in a mirror. It gave the impression that he was on the inside, the inner circle, and he said the right things. He cracked appropriate jokes and had a quick and entertaining wit.

Bodie said something clever and maneuvered himself in on one of Boss's conversations.

Smooth, thought Buckets as he lifted his coat from the hook by the door. He caught Green Eyes looking toward the bar from a nearby table. It was a casual glance, but it was his skill to look without looking. He had felt the energy change at the bar as the after-dinner moods and places shifted. Green Eyes looked at Buckets, then at Bodie making his move. Buckets shook his shoulders into his jacket.

Green Eyes turned real easy to the right and sipped his beer as Bodie leaned in to laugh at something Boss was saying. Green Eyes set his mug down and lifted the cowboy hat off his head with his right hand, held it aloft, ran his left hand through his hair, and replaced the hat with a nod at Buckets.

Yeah, Buckets thought, *I can go. He's got his eye on that bugger.* He waved to a couple of guys, patted the shoulder of another, and made his exit as he had done a hundred times and would a hundred times more.

Bodie Ransom's most recent problem was the girl who worked in the kitchen. She also functioned as one of the ranch's go-to people—a cook, maid, office girl...whatever needed doing. She thought she was in love. It was disastrous and an error he had made before, though he didn't see it that way. Bodie told himself that there just happened to be women making their own choices wherever he was. None of their pain was his fault and he felt no guilt about them—*any* of them.

Buckets and Green Eyes knew she was vulnerable, sweet, and a bit naive about people. They liked her. Everyone looked out for her like a little sister, and they had watched the slow-motion train wreck unfold. They knew they needed to get rid of Bodie. The moment was coming. It just didn't come soon enough. Then the fires happened.

Green Eyes had met the Collins women once at the Deer Club, shortly after Kitzie's knee injury. Boss had taken him aside and asked him a favor, to show them every courtesy, which he did. Green Eyes valued his position at the ranch more than a casual temptation, so he was very respectful. Carson, then recently returned to the family ranch after a long absence, had been more than a little uncomfortable the whole evening but Green Eyes had been a bright spot and he thought she had enjoyed herself. It was refreshing to see.

Buckets knew that Carson was tough and that she'd been gone for a long time. Some wounds don't appear obvious to the casual observer, but he easily felt that she was wounded and not eager to line herself up for more from anyone. He appreciated Boss extending his most gracious hospitality to them. Boss had a canny way of understanding people, which Buckets both admired and tried to emulate.

Chapter 20

Carson felt she was beginning to heal. The monetary stuff was real but would wait. All that mess would wait. It would demand resolution at some point but for now, she felt relieved of that struggle.

Carson had felt like a snail crawling across a hot griddle as she went through the process of losing it all and being stripped bare of who she thought she had become. She'd massaged her wounded pride with wine and she didn't miss that part of her self-destruction. Though she'd been welcomed home and forgiven, Carson hadn't quite made it to a place to forgive herself. Since her world had unraveled, she didn't yet feel that old strength and confidence when she looked in the mirror. Some days, she was a walking mess of insecurity and felt she had nothing inside.

She shook her head as she thought about the huge amount of fiscal debris she had left behind—most of which she hadn't even looked at. Yes, there was the mess of a jettisoned financial life that might eventually catch up to her. It was as if she had disappeared from her old life. She wondered if anyone missed her…or even noticed she was gone.

Carson was most susceptible to waves of reflection when she wasn't riding a horse, and she did her best to immerse herself in that pursuit. The horses benefitted from the attention yet when the girths were loosened, the damp saddle pads slid off and hung to dry, and when the body brush was applied to sweat-encrusted hair, the mind movies played.

She didn't really want to relive the memories but there had been many a pleasant encounter with her married lover. He had charmed and seduced her and given her little things...pillow-talk gifts and NSO (no special occasion) presents. Nothing obvious that would have gotten them caught. But there were other things...things he told her in the quiet, things he could give her, odd bits he told her to put away and forget. Carson had forgotten that he'd said, "Someday you'll thank me." She was in love with him and she didn't care what he could give her. Time was the gift. She had gotten pieces of him, which she had taken and treasured.

In hindsight, she wasn't sure what the hell she had been doing with him for...what was it, three-and-a-half years? Had she used him for a distraction...and had he done the same with her? She had quietly closed that door in her memory and lost the key.

Kitzie tried to bolster Carson's mood by reminding her that she had been noticed at the Deer Club dinner at the Running Horse Ranch. Carson admitted that she had enjoyed the respectful attention that "very handsome Green Eyes" (Kitzie's description) had shown. But how impressed was she? Carson didn't even remember his name.

Kitzie and Carson sat at the kitchen table, a room little changed from Carson's childhood. She had done homework at that table, loved her mother's cooking there, and loved the noisy meals when there were not enough chairs but plenty of everything else.

Carson's sleeves had been rolled up to the elbows all day, and she unrolled them as she and her mother sat and enjoyed a beer together. Hay bits fell out of her clothes onto the chair and floor. Carson tried to scoop them up and toss them into the can. Her mother teased her and Carson tried to lighten up.

At the Dugout with Wyker, Harper, and his extended family, Carson had felt similarly happy. It was there that she recognized she was content in her element, even if it was all about an injured horse. Bits of things rolled up and then freed, and Carson's mind dropped into another confusing chasm.

She thought about the recent ride to Sanctuary, and how the kids—CJ's posse and fans of the Aussie and his horse—had worked tirelessly at thawing the chilly and remote CJ. The more reserved CJ was, the more attractive he was to them. Carson mused that maybe that was why she found him intriguing too.

She recalled how she had enjoyed sitting on Uncle's funky porch and watching the kids pepper CJ with questions. They told him their tall tales and during the ride, CJ was constantly surrounded. Carson loved that she reconnected with Wyker, and she shared this with her mother. She told her that she had opened up more than she thought she would and it was cathartic. She was happy she had gotten to know Harper, though she never did muster up the courage to ask him about the two lines tattooed over his cheekbones.

Carson shared with Kitzie the kids' version of getting the Three Bit cattle back, and how the tale grew taller by the day, at least when told by CJ's posse. Their favorite part was when Uncle Harper had faced-off, unarmed, with the gun-bearing cattle rustler. Storytelling around the campfire made for a late night with lots of laughter.

Kitzie recognized that these were Carson's new memories. It was as if her life had bifurcated somewhere and along the way, blended. She was back at her new reality at the Three Bit. Carson grew more introspective when the subject of CJ came up. According to Harper, he had begun to relax a little and laugh more, but there was a wariness there. And although he was polite to Carson, it did seem that he was more guarded than she was. That was it—they were both guarded, as if to open up to their feelings would destroy them.

Protective. That is what Wyker had said about CJ, that he was protective, walled up, and he might stay that way. It was a survival skill and to abandon it meant death. CJ had given Carson no cause to think he thought of her at all. He was deferential, no more. They had circled each other as if both were enveloped in individual bubbles. They had walls around themselves, impenetrable walls—a seemingly natural response to each other. Carson thought maybe her new wisdom was to be careful and that her choices of late begged her to be so.

As Carson helped Kitzie prepare dinner, she shared these observations with her mother. Kitzie looked over at her and smiled. Even she had learned to say less and mean more. They now had a bond the likes Carson never thought she'd be comfortable with. And there she was, not wanting to be gone, not looking to find fault in herself or her mother.

Carson pulled the salad fixings out of the fridge and grabbed a large wooden bowl. She rooted around in a drawer, looking for something to toss the salad with, and asked, "Where are they?"

"They're in there," her mom replied, her back to her as she stirred something on the stove.

"You're not even looking. How do you know what I want?"

"The salad tong thingys," Kitzie said and looked over her

shoulder. "See that paper towel tube, the cardboard thing? Look in there."

"Ahhh, clever," Carson said as she slid the compressed tongs out of the tube. Then out of the blue, she asked, "What happened to Dad?"

There was a pause in the stirring and for a second, Carson felt she had gone where she shouldn't have. But she had never asked what had happened. She'd just heard that he had died and didn't know the details.

Kitzie didn't turn around. "It was a massive heart attack. I thought he'd fallen asleep in that old recliner of his." She glanced to her right. Off the small kitchen was a narrow hall that went left toward a bathroom and her bedroom. The entry to the small living room was to the right and the chair was still there. Kitzie couldn't see it from the stove but Carson knew her mother was "seeing" it anyway.

"What did you do?"

"I couldn't believe it. I mean, at first, you think someone's just dozing in front of the tube and maybe they're really out and not waking up." Kitzie left the stove and pulled a chair out from the table. She sat down slowly, carefully placing her healing knee in its best position, and looked at the placemat and silverware. She straightened the mat and lined up a fork evenly next to it.

"I was struck dumb, I guess. I mean, there I was, cleaning up the dishes and talking away and he couldn't hear me. I thought he was just really hooked on something on the tube." She smiled at the memory. "I went in there and said something like, 'Haven't you heard a word I've said?'" Her eyes lowered and the tone in her voice held a shadow of regret. "I suppose I sounded...I was...a little cranky. You know, annoyed. And I stood in front of him and repeated whatever it was I had said. But he looked like he was asleep. You know, he snored as he got older."

Carson felt embarrassed. "No, I didn't."

"Well, his mouth was slack and open and I shook his arm. He would get this awful dry mouth when he did that…anyway, it's just an awful realization that creeps over you, you know?"

Carson nodded numbly.

"When you go through something like that, there's all this activity. And you go through it. When he died and I was alone, it seemed I was drowning in a great ocean. Alone and sinking." Kitzie straightened herself in the chair and folded her hands neatly in front of her, wrists resting on the table. "Then it seemed I felt the shore just below my feet and when the ocean was calm, my feet felt the sand. Waves of grief still threatened to drown me but I knew that I could get through." She looked up at her daughter and smiled. Tears were silently making their way down her face. "Since you have been back, it's more like I'm up to my knees—or my one good one—in the ocean. And though the waves come, the trough after they pass is certain."

Carson wiped her face. "Are you facing the shore or the ocean?"

Kitzie smiled and didn't answer the question. She got up and went to her daughter, her only child, and hugged her. Carson started to say she was sorry but her mother shushed her. Carson choked back her tears.

Kitzie changed the subject and said, "Tomorrow night we'll need another chair. We'll use the one in the mudroom."

Chapter 21

Will Wyker pulled into the Turnbull truck stop in the south-central part of Oregon, close to the northeastern edge of Nevada. It was a combination gas station, convenience store, and market—a longtime family operation that was as ubiquitous as the highway itself. He took it all in as he slid the gear shift into park and noticed big changes to what had once been a one-horse stagecoach stop. The few houses in the vicinity, once spread far apart, had grown into a denser, modest community.

Wyker had the truck filled with diesel and tipped the attendant, who had diligently scrubbed the bug detritus from the windshield, washed it again, and squeegeed it without streaks. He even gave the tires a look-see as he walked his long-handled wand back to its frothy bucket. Will then pulled away from the pumps, parked off to the side, and walked toward the building, hoping Roxy Turnbull was behind one of the counters.

The wind came up, sudden and chaotic. Dust devils swirled across the parking lot. He shielded his eyes and out of habit, scanned the horizon. The weather was so odd and with the drought in its fifth year, all the ranchers were keeping a keen eye out. The chain of consequences had already begun up north but it was far enough away that no one seemed to be concerned.

Roxy was down-to-earth, loving, opinionated, usually on

point with her facts, and a true original. Wyker could not pass within a hundred miles without diverting to stop in to say hello or she would know, down to the day. He could never quite figure out how she did that. Somehow, she would sense he was in the area and had the uncanny knack of not looking surprised when his boots crossed the threshold of the store.

Wyker held the door open for an elderly gentleman, who made his way unsteadily to a sedan at the gas pumps. Wiper blades had carved broad, pie-shaped clarity into the windshield that struggled to stay clean. Wyker held the door after the man exited, looked after him, and saw that he was OK, then went inside. As he had hoped, Roxy was there and he knew he would be delayed for a few hours catching up, which was all right by him. Her lively, gray-blue eyes smiled as they connected with his, and her tiny frame was white-capped by a beguiling new hairstyle. He pointed to his own head, then toward her, nodded, and gave a big thumbs up. Roxy touched behind her ear and mocked a glimmer of a fashion pose, dropped it, and helped the next person in line.

Wyker looked around the well-stocked convenience store. To his right were two refrigerated units full of dairy products. He had always liked that brand of chocolate milk with the posing cow on it. He was glad Roxy still carried it, though his urgent hunger demanded something more substantial. A hallway led to the restrooms and the refrigerators continued along the wall to the left of that, where several men were looking at an impressive array of beers. Wyker was impressed and wondered for whom it had been stocked so well. The next section carried the heavily caffeinated beverages. This section at a truck stop made sense. In country where distances were measured in hours, not miles, keeping a driver alert at the wheel was critical.

And way out here, if you didn't have good neighbors, you didn't have anything.

There was an eclectic variety of sandwiches made fresh daily, or so the sign said. Wyker was inclined to believe it. As he looked at the choices, waiting to be inspired by a description, from behind the counter, Roxy's assistant rang up a purchase and a customer's voice caught Wyker's attention—murmuring followed by a phony, unfortunate braying laugh that choked out the music coming from the small speaker in the ceiling.

He froze and cocked his head to one side. He recognized it. It was familiar in a most unpleasant way and sent his memory back to the moment he'd saved Rio from the kill buyers at the Colorado BLM facility. He realized he'd never told CJ he'd saved his horse from the laugh erupting near the cash register at Turnbull's in Lakeview.

He checked himself and stepped back to let a man, who had chosen beer over caffeine, grab a sandwich. Wyker suspended his hunger and moved closer to the register. From the back, she might have been any petite woman with frizzy red hair but that laugh sealed it. It struck him how a single encounter could leave an impression that lasted forever. He was the type more inclined to give people the benefit of the doubt, but the alarm bells of his intuition knew that was undeserved in this case.

She was one-half of that couple from Colorado. She laughed again and it rang as harsh and phony as when he had heard it before. He stepped toward the window and looked outside for her partner. He guessed he was her husband. Then he spotted the short man at the diesel pump. They had a different rig this time—a longer, reddish-brown triple-axel livestock trailer with slatted sides. The crew-cab dually flatbed truck was filthy under a new layer of dust. There was a faded sticker on the back of the trailer that seemed to support finding homes for wild mustangs. Wyker found that ironic, given his previous encounter with them. They were not interested in doing anything of the kind.

He moved back to the sandwich section, though his appetite had temporarily waned. Seeing them this far west made him wonder. He knew the BLM had been eyeing the Kiger mustangs in the south Steens range, and he was concerned about the Big Summit wild horse herd in the Ochoco National Forest but he had barely kept up with the news. Why were they here? Were they just passing through? Then he heard her talking and moved to within earshot and shamelessly eavesdropped.

The cashier went on, "Things are crazy with the baby now. You knew I had a little boy? Well, it's just really tiring. Mum's helping out and we're doing OK."

The redhead gave her the side-eye, then feigned enough interest until she could launch into a story about her equestrian accomplishments. She was enormously proud of a belt buckle that consumed the center of her tiny frame. She redirected any further details about the cashier's domesticity and kept up an animated conversation about herself as she completed the purchase.

The cashier laughed at something the redhead said, which only encouraged her to continue prattling on about herself and her horses. Wyker tuned it out as he scanned the parking lot again, peering over a row of potato chips. Then heard the cashier say, "It's good to see you, Dixie. You and Cullen back for a while?"

Wyker made note of the names this time. Dixie and Cullen.

Thankfully, there had been no introductions when they had come to the wild horse holding facility where Wyker had worked, so she wouldn't recognize him. This pair had shown up periodically with a story about a program where they trained the horses they got from the BLM. But Wyker's third eye, his instinct for reading people, had called it correctly when he suspected that they just grabbed the horses on the cheap and moved them to be sold for their meat, probably to a Mexican slaughterhouse just over the border.

Dixie hedged her answer, which was lost on the girl behind the counter. She was a simple, kind person and Dixie easily manipulated the conversation and swung it back to herself without detailing any plans.

The cashier finally got back to her job as another customer crowded close. Dixie shot Wyker a look that revealed the true nature behind her act. She looked around him to check on Cullen, who was still out by the pumps near the trailer, looking toward the building. With his arm on the door, his head craned, the look on Cullen's face spoke "fetch" and Dixie picked up her things without a bag. She interrupted the cashier in mid-description of something she didn't care about anyway and said, "See ya!" and left the store.

The stacked heels on Dixie's cowboy boots, meant to create more height than was physically possible, added an element of misalignment that chopped her stride into awkward bits. It was an unfortunate gait that, at speed, became quite displeasing to the eye. The wind now blew in earnest. It whipped her short, frizzy red hair into a blizzard of mass confusion. Then a gust hit her with hurricane strength and sent her sideways. She almost tripped, ducked against it, which fanned her hair vertically up the back of her head like a demented halo, and she made a swift beeline for the shelter of the pumps.

Wyker casually followed, glad he'd left his hat and Tammy in the truck. He pushed open the glass door, walked to one of the concrete islands, and grabbed a handful of blue paper towels. He took his time moving toward his truck. His tall frame and solid build begged the gusts to try to alter his path. Out of the corner of his eye, he saw a monstrous dust devil start and bear down.

Washing his windshield again was a waste of time but it gave him the vantage point and excuse to take full measure of those two. He glanced into the cab of his truck and smiled at Tammy. But she wasn't looking at him—she was watching them through the window. Wyker sensed that she recognized the man. Her gaze was serious and focused. Wyker half-willed her to break off the stare-down and change the intensity of her energy. As if she knew his thoughts, she turned her head and looked at him. Her ears dropped and her eyes softened. He knew her tail wagged gently on the seat. He said, "Good girl," and she disappeared behind the dash.

Wyker hoped for a look at the plates on the rig, to see what state they were registered in. Both were filthy and covered with dirt, though he thought he could make out Colorado colors on the back plate. As he walked past the truck and trailer to throw away his paper towels, he put what he could discern of the numbers and letters to memory. He noted that the trailer was empty. He felt Cullen's eyes on his back and he moved on without a glance.

If pressed, Wyker couldn't easily explain his curiosity. He recalled Tammy staring past him down the breezeway that day when they'd come for the horses, and the way her eyes changed when she spotted the surly Cullen as he watched Wyker lead

Rio away from danger. Tammy was a damn sight better judge of character than most people he knew. She had picked up on this man's energy and did not like it.

"About time," Cullen said to Dixie as he checked the gas cap and locked it.

Dixie placated him, "Just being nice. Let's get going."

It was clear by Cullen's body language that he didn't care. Dixie walked around the front of the truck to the passenger's side as he started the engine and put the truck in gear. As she pulled the door open, she glanced briefly at a truck coming in for gas at the island next to them. The driver, a middle-aged woman, hopped out and waved enthusiastically at Dixie. Dixie chose to ignore her. The woman left her door open and hurried around the pump, waved, and said hello louder. Dixie proceeded to get into the truck and stared straight ahead as Cullen accelerated and the rig moved on.

The woman seemed puzzled, then crestfallen. A sensitive soul, she walked back to her truck and looked down at her keys. She found the right one and handed the key to the attendant, who opened the gas cap. He placed the gas cap on the edge of the truck bed and she handed him a card to slide into the machine. Wyker saw a pained expression on her face as she got back into her truck and watched the retreating Dixie and Cullen, as if what she thought she knew about someone was a mistake.

Wyker watched them go too and noticed a thick, oozy liquid dribbling slowly out the back of the trailer as they pulled away. It added a wet layer over the caked-on brown of the dried dirt on the license plate. He could have sworn it looked like blood.

Wyker turned back toward the store. He looked over at the

woman, her cheeks flushed, smarting from rejection, and he briefly wondered what awkward social dynamic was in play there.

Roxy watched as Wyker came back through the glass doors. He joined her by the window in the corner. Behind a small curtain was her cramped office. He put an arm around her shoulders and squeezed her. She reciprocated and quietly asked him what was up. Her tone told him that the question had multiple meanings and he did not dodge her, as he knew that she had been watching. "Those two, you know them?" he asked.

Roxy hesitated and shot a look over her shoulder at her gal behind the counter. She was straightening the shelves, dropped several bags of chips in the process, and the phone rang. She was torn between grabbing the handset and picking up the fallen items. She tried to do both, answered the phone, propped it between her shoulder and the side of her head, and gathered the chips in her arms.

Wyker's stomach reminded him he was hungry, and it growled loud enough for Roxy to hear.

"Jesus, Will, when did you last eat? Grab a cup of coffee and step into my office. We have some catching up to do."

He wanted more than coffee but figured Roxy had that covered. She led him toward the curtain. Her old brown Lab, Burma, took up a major portion of the floor and he lifted his head and thumped his tail when they came in.

"To your bed, Burma," Roxy said, and he ungracefully lifted himself off the floor and walked to a dog bed against the wall under the shelving.

"How old is he now?" Wyker asked.

"Hell, I really don't know," she replied as she put something in a microwave that was shoehorned onto a shelf, and turned it on. "I've forgotten how old I am." Convinced they wouldn't be overheard, Roxy picked up where they left off. "Little Miss Sunshine?

"Little Miss who?" Wyker smiled. "Cute. Sarcastic, but cute."

Her pursed-lips smiled. "Yeah, I can't say more than they're occasional customers. That one's quite enchanted with herself. My Sally out there thinks she's genuine, a real sweetheart. Her husband, Cullen, was probably with her. He's the one in charge, I think. I don't trust either of 'em, never have. Not that I was ever asked, mind you."

Wyker exhaled a short laugh of recognition. Roxy had grown older and walked with a slight limp, but those eyes still held a sharpness that missed nothing.

"Roxy, you're still a gossip, aren't you?" he teased.

"I can't help hearing things if people keep telling me things." And she laughed that cute, wicked little laugh of hers. "Or just doing stupid shit where I can see them," she added. She faced him with narrowed eyes and continued, "No, I'm not sure what they do. They were in and out of the area for a while. I think Sally said Idaho or something. Maybe Colorado."

"That's where I ran into them," Wyker said.

"Oh? And how was that?" Roxy asked.

"It was at the mustang thing I did with the inmates. Remember?"

She nodded.

"And those two showed up to buy." He shook his head in

exasperation. "It was bullshit though. Somehow they had finagled access and I'm certain they were acting a part."

"Meaning?" She raised an eyebrow.

Wyker shrugged. "Can't say for certain. I just didn't buy their crap story. I had the feeling that the horses they were getting didn't get trained and didn't exactly find…" He made quote signs with his fingers. "…homes."

"I see. Well, they're more gone than not, you know? I hear they've leased a place somewhere between here and the Steens. I know that's a lot of ground but until this moment, I really didn't care." She looked at her friend. "Should I?"

There was a paper plate on the corner of her workspace with potato chip crumbs on it. The microwave chimer dinged and Roxy pulled the item out and unwrapped one of her famous meatloaf sandwiches, thick-cut, and wickedly delicious. She handed it to Wyker and he didn't stand on ceremony, nor was intelligible beyond moans of culinary pleasure for a few minutes.

"Pretty good, huh?" she smiled. "Better'n one of those from the fridge out there."

Wyker nodded and continued to inhale the sandwich. A drop of sauce landed on his jeans, well-placed near his knee. He wiped it away with his hand, leaving an elongated stain. Roxy pointed to a paper napkin that peeked out from the edge of the plate. He gave her a juvenile wink, took the napkin, and wiped his hand. She laughed and he wiped the spot halfheartedly, not enough to affect the stain.

Roxy smiled. "You cowboys are all alike. Don't bother, it matches the other stains." Her eyes found the scuffed leather on his boots from a thousand rides.

Wyker facetiously hung his head, then leaned back in his

chair, feeling much better for the food. They spent the next forty-five minutes catching up. He told her about the Three Bit's rustled herd, how they had gotten them back, and the new arrangement with the Three Bit cattle and Harper's family on the McDermitt Reservation. He also told her a little about Rio and CJ.

Roxy could tell that he was especially proud of their progress together and she asked a few questions about him. "Sounds like it was a good thing," she mused.

Wyker agreed. "I think it's working out. Not the way I expected but then I'm not sure I expected much."

Roxy nodded. She was familiar with the type. Her late husband had worked in corrections in various penal institutions, retired after thirty years, and passed way too soon after.

Wyker drifted into talking about the plight of the West's wild horses and the conditions in the holding areas. She commented on how hard it must be to feed and care for so many horses—that, like prisoners, it must cost a lot to take care of them. Wyker agreed and somehow that led to the subject of feet—how the natural, free movement on the range kept wild horses' hooves worn naturally. But in captivity, that had to be physically managed. The horses were forced into a narrow squeeze chute, which compressed them to immobility. The machine tipped the animal to a horizontal position, with the horse's feet protruding out the bottom. The stress for a wild prey animal, held fast, was terrifying and there was no budget for sedation. Their hooves were clipped with large nippers, then roughly shaped with a metal file. The squeeze was then righted to a vertical position, opened, and the horse released. It was a production line with cowboys doing the trimming, not farriers, and there was little effort to balance the feet with the trim. Wyker wasn't fond of the process when he worked in Canon City, but he understood the necessity. He also knew that if the general public had seen the process, many would be upset.

His personal feeling was that the BLM was overreaching at the behest of an industry. He had seen the mass incarceration firsthand and he objected to it. It was an unnatural way to keep horses. He had done his part with the training program in Colorado but there were thousands of horses languishing in huge holding areas throughout the west.

Roxy was a great listener. It was her gift. Wyker hadn't realized it but he needed an ear and she lent one. The time flew and Wyker realized how late it was. It had been a good visit and he was glad for it. Roxy told him not to be a stranger and to come back soon. As an afterthought, she mentioned hearing about the fire that had started to the north of them.

"You might keep an eye out, it's not under control yet," she advised.

He walked slowly to his truck. It shouldn't have bothered him that much, seeing them again, but it did. Could this team be operating here? And how illegal was it? As he hit the road, he wondered where his old friend, Hy Royston, was.

Chapter 22

Bulldozer driver Jesse did not think of himself as an adrenaline junkie but some of the men he worked with might qualify. They did it for the thrill, for the challenge, for the money, and to make a difference and save lives. Dozers were an integral part of fighting large blazes. They were the invisible firefighters...until the operators died doing it. The deaths of two drivers in California while battling wildfires highlighted the dangers of using ten-foot blades to push aside the fuel—shrubs, grass, brush, and small trees—over uneven terrain so that fire met bare earth, stunting its progress.

The drivers faced serious hazards doing this job and they were acutely aware of it. Soft soil and hard, rocky ground caused them to slide precariously, and to tip and roll. Visibility was almost zero in the dirt they churned up and the thick smoke and ash. Fast-moving flames and shifting winds could easily burn them over. Sometimes they found themselves far away from backup, and had to rely on radio traffic and dodgy communications to tell them what the fire was doing.

Jesse had to admit that it could be a rush seeing the pandemonium of flames crowning 300 feet into the air, entire landscapes simmering red in all directions, and the sky black like midnight. An on-call heavy-equipment operator, he had gotten the call early as the fire incident had progressed at a rapid rate. Notice had gone out to those well past the ION region. The conditions had changed radically in a matter of hours. Continuous bolts of lightning found parched ground across entire states and the wind was doing the rest. The resulting firestorm that exploded to life shook the ground and roared as loud as a passing train.

Upon his arrival at base camp, Jesse parked his truck and flatbed trailer carrying his Komatsu 65 dozer and jumped out. The truck door was yanked from his hand in a wicked gust and it took effort to get control of it. He rushed to check in and was dispatched into some of the worst conditions he had ever seen. Uniformed men, faces etched with decades of experience at saving lives and protecting property, had a look that was different, and at first, Jesse felt it before he saw it. It was in their eyes. They were scared.

Embers floated through the air as the wind swirled and shifted. His manager looked exhausted. Dark bags under his eyes seemed to hold his N95 mask in place. The chaos of base camp was barely controlled as Jesse unloaded his dozer from his flatbed trailer and climbed into the cab. With limited resources, more support was not going to happen anytime soon. They would have to make do with the personnel and equipment they had.

Jesse found himself part of a crew that was stalling a swath of fire long enough for the local officials to evacuate houses in a small subdivision. At one point, the bulldozer glass was so hot to the touch that he opened the door on the other side to try to cool off. The fire laid down like a blowtorch with the wind on it. Jesse was several hundred feet away from the flames, but the radiant heat was so extreme, he thought his skin must be blistering. The dozer didn't like it much either and it coughed and sputtered in protest.

"Come on, baby…" Jesse spat through clenched teeth. He ducked as a gust hurled something that cracked hard against the windscreen. "You're a bad-ass and you can take this shit!" he encouraged his machine through his mask and protective gear. He yelled at the wind, at the fire, and swore as each blast came at him stronger and more determined than the last.

He didn't think it could get crazier from there but then the wind whipped with hurricane strength and threatened to knock him over. Behind his goggles, Jesse's eyes bulged as he felt the rig do battle with forces he had never dealt with before.

The fire they were working moved faster than anything Jesse had ever witnessed—at times, over a hundred yards a minute. With so much fire, they didn't try to put it out—they just tried to save people. People didn't believe the fires were coming until it was too late, then they wanted to stay and fight what was unfightable.

In another location, the blaze spotted around a fellow bulldozer driver in an open field while the driver attacked a line he believed would choke it of its fuel. Two other dozers worked alongside him, the field around them an ocean of rippling orange, the flames and embers in a dance as if alive. The driver was trapped, cut off, and he couldn't breathe. The dozer's engine coughed and began to overheat.

Cyclones of fire spun around and hit the dozer, gained strength, and turned into fire tornadoes. Wind-whipped debris pelted the windshield and broke it. Superheated air blew in and the driver's twenty-five-ton dozer pivoted counterclockwise. The driver didn't know what was happening and he willed himself to stay calm as white blisters bubbled on his fingers and hands. He tried to deploy his fire curtains but his hands were too burned. He was almost sucked out the side window and had to use a metal clipboard held in his blistering hands to protect his airway. When he finally deployed his fire shelter, he was certain he was dying.

The fire doubled back with tornadic unpredictability. Jesse's Komatsu had a speed of only three to four miles an hour. There was no quick escape. The area they had been directed to cut was one where the air warped and quivered from the heat. The wind seemed to follow the terrain as the firestorm spun uphill, then slowed and fell backward, attacking the same area again. Jesse had a few moments of abject terror as he and his colleagues crossed ground that was smooth and alien. It occurred to him that the fire was behaving in ways he'd never seen. It moved so quickly that he feared they might not know to evacuate until it was too late.

After working for the better part of thirty-two hours, Jesse fought back the fatigue with strong black coffee, long tepid in a large thermos, until it was gone. He was getting low on water too and he knew that dehydration was easy in these conditions. His buddy in the Cat behind him was a bit more rested than he was, but not by much. They were cutting a contingency line farther back to act as a backstop if the first line was breached. The sparks ran all over the place and Jesse wondered whether they were doing any good as he looked in the mirror to see the second dozer cutting one blade wider.

Jesse set the throttle in second gear using the controls in

his left hand. With his right hand, he controlled the blades and rippers and locked them in place. Using three-quarters full power, he listened as the machine lulled into a steady, mechanical rhythm. He tried to stretch his back out in the seat with limited success. His backside ached from sitting in one position for too long. He adjusted his pack behind his head and upper back for better support and rested his feet on the dash, then leaned back and closed his eyes for a moment.

Behind him, his buddy followed at the same speed. He was on his cell phone with his wife and the reception did not help the strained tenor of their conversation. The argument, really. He'd set his controls to match Jesse's and hoped to listen to his headset and nibble some chips, but no, she had called. The call getting cut off had not improved her mood and when he called her back, their argument resumed. He lost track of time and when she had hung up on him for the third—or was it the fourth?—time, he didn't call her back because his battery was dead.

Some thirty minutes later, Jesse was roused by his buddy's voice. Startled, Jesse bounded awake, his pack sliding down the back of the seat as he scrambled for the radio. "Uh, yeah. Copy," he mumbled.

"What the hell are you doing?"

Jesse looked at the radio in his hand with a perplexed expression. He rubbed his sweat-stained face and felt the sleep in his eyes as the realization of what had happened set in. Jesse unlocked the controls and brought the dozer to a full stop, opened the door, and climbed down. He looked around at the blackened wasteland, the ash so heavy in the air that he pulled his kerchief up over his nose and mouth. The need to move and walk might help him snap out of it.

Jesse walked the fifty feet or so back to the Cat. As he did, he saw a white, five-gallon plastic bucket, upended, its contents strewn along his path. Jesse squinted at the crumpled plastic. A section was warped and had cooled and hardened. Confused, Jesse turned and looked at his rig, then back at his feet. He saw the stunned expression on his partner's face, wide-eyed, and Jesse followed his gaze to a large gun sticking out of the freshly churned dirt. Next to it, something glittered. Jesse walked a few short steps to it, bent down, and stared. It was a necklace, tangled and dirty but obviously beautiful at one time. The diamonds didn't seem to be harmed…or maybe the heavy plastic bucket had taken the brunt of the damage in the fire-scorched earth where it must have been buried.

Jesse examined the bucket more closely and saw that it had been buried upright. The lid looked dirty and black in places, some of it looked melted, but he wasn't sure. He had no idea how deep it had been buried, maybe a foot or less. He dropped his mask to ask his partner if he had cell service when he saw the phone already in his hand. A waft of ash swirled in the godforsaken wind and sent Jesse into a coughing spasm. He bent over and wiped the tears from his eyes, then spied a path of jewelry leading to another busted five-gallon bucket, a third one, and a fourth, all protruding from the ground just ahead of the track of the other earth mover. Had Jesse not woken up, they would have missed it and the second Cat would have pummeled it all into the ground.

Jesse backed up a step and almost tripped over another piece of something black. He turned toward his shocked partner, then carefully bent down and pulled it from the ground. It was caked with dirt and he shook it, turning it to one side and holding his breath as he did so. He held it up toward the wide eyes of the other driver and turned it back to front, trying to figure out what it was.

It was a bulletproof vest.

Chapter 23

Wyker called Hy from the road and to his surprise, found they weren't that far apart. Hyland Royston was, among other things, an Oregon Ag agent with extensive law enforcement credentials and connections, and a longtime friend of Wyker's. Harper Lee knew Hyland as well, as Hy was his boss.

Wyker arranged to meet him at the Pine Tavern in Martin. As Wyker entered the establishment, he spotted Hy and his partner, Dave Clancy, at a booth by one of the big windows. Hy looked grim but then Wyker had never known him to be overtly cheerful. Dave was leaning on the table with his forehead in his left hand and he was laughing.

The men shook hands and Wyker started to sit beside Hy.

Dave warned him, "You'll want to sit here, by me. He's cranky."

Hy scowled at his partner. "I'm not cranky," he said, then proceeded to complain about Dave's driving and finished by muttering about how Dave drove like he still thought he was on the streets of San Francisco.

Wyker smiled, knowing this exchange was one to watch, not participate in.

Dave said, "He's been annoyed all day."

"Your driving caused it. Cause and effect," blurted Hy, pointing to himself as the effect part. He held up his menu, struggled, then it was flopped onto the table as he fished out his reading specs with a deep sigh.

Wyker thought he'd pile on. "What? You blind *and* angry, old man?"

"Who you calling an old man?" Hy raised an eyebrow and peered over his magnifiers at Wyker. "*Annoyed* was the word, and my eyesight has nothing to do with that."

There was a sparkle to his eye and Wyker, fond of his friend's dry wit, valiantly kept the smile from the edges of his mouth. Wyker laughed easily so this act was one of supreme self-control and Hy cracked what, for him, would be a broad grin.

Dave asked Wyker to let him out to use the can. As Dave slid out, Hy said, "You're a menace on the road. You're gonna kill someone."

Dave started away from them and over his shoulder replied, "No, I'm not. I'm an organ donor. It's right here on my license." And in midstride, he struck out his right butt cheek in an exaggerated way and patted the fat back pocket of his jeans, which his wallet occupied. Without missing a beat, he went through the doors to the bathroom.

While Dave was gone, Wyker and Hy did some brief catching up. Wyker admonished his friend about leaving out some salient details the last time they had spoken, shortly after they had rescued the Three Bit herd.

Hyland shrugged, held the menu up, turned it over thoughtfully to see whatever might be on the back, and found there was only one side. He looked at Wyker, then removed his glasses and put them carefully back in his pocket. "I wasn't interested in telling you everything. I was curious to see just how good Harper was and he proved himself, wouldn't you say?"

"More than," Wyker answered.

"His resume would surprise you, though I'm pleased you were impressed. How'd your con do?"

"Even better," Wyker smoothly answered.

Hy stared at Wyker, tipped his head to the left, and then decided he wasn't kidding.

"You're surprised?" Wyker asked.

"Yes." Hy pursed his lips. "Maybe."

"Just galls you that I might be a better judge of character than you thought?" Wyker smiled at his friend.

Dave returned and upon hearing the last comment, added, "And you're still friends with this guy?" He tipped his thumb at his partner and boss.

Wyker slid over in the booth. They ordered sandwiches and coffee and Wyker formulated his questions to Hy. He told the story of how he had saved Rio from the smarmy pair and made light of them, withholding his feeling that the guy part of the team was probably a more serious threat. Hyland listened and didn't ask questions. Wyker got the impression Hy was a step ahead of him.

"Anyway, just saw them again," Wyker finished.

Dave turned his head. "Where?"

Wyker told him.

Dave looked at his boss and whatever passed between them was silent and invisible.

Dave continued, "Why did they catch your attention?"

Wyker sat back against the worn plastic upholstery of the bench seat. "I don't know…" Air escaped his tightened lips. "Stuck in my craw the first time. It was like something caught in my throat I couldn't clear."

"What did?" Dave asked.

"Annoying mannerisms, phony crap you could cut with a knife, especially that woman's abrasive laugh." Wyker shrugged. "Just a feeling."

Dave looked at Hy. "Doesn't sound like much to go on."

Trina appeared and the plain-as-crackers food arrived. Hyland's iced tea and potato-salad sandwich were delivered by an older man that Wyker later realized was the chief cook and bottle washer. Thin-lipped and dour, Toby seemed to be cut from stone.

Wyker looked at Hy and asked what was going on with the buying of wild horses from the BLM. "These people sure the hell weren't trainers. Those were kill buyers. I'd bet on it."

Hy said, "There's been some chatter." He looked down at his sandwich as if he'd lost his appetite. "None I'd care to repeat to you." He shook his head. "What we've seen…it's just fucking ugly."

Dave nodded solemnly in agreement as the air went out of the room.

Wyker raised an eyebrow and Hy just shook his head at him.

"Won't elaborate, Will, cuz I know how much you care." He moved on and elaborated in another direction. "There're many issues overlapping this one. I've heard things got messy in Idaho, a big horse broker is finding the heat of federal scrutiny a bit too warm, yours and my tax dollars are lining some very fucked-up pockets…and now the money's moving. And the influence. It's like whack-a-mole."

Chapter 24

Never had Stiles felt like he did at that moment, or heartache so profound, than when he slid open the warehouse door and saw what he saw. It cut the center right out of him in an instant. His heart was the warehouse and he found it empty. He had nothing and didn't know what to do, and wandering around the empty building in a daze felt stupid and pointless. He searched her truck, which she had left behind, and it gave him a painful insight into her life. *This thing is a piece of shit,* he thought. It barely functioned. Even if he had a gas can and could fuel it, its overall condition was so poor that from motor to tires, he deemed it not roadworthy.

The sound of a tractor interrupted his dismay and he slammed the hood of Shiloh's truck closed. Stiles returned to the open door, peered out, then walked to the corner of the building. He had seen the old man, off in the distance in his field, several times when he came to the warehouse, went inside, and closed the doors. Stiles was the guy who rented the building and was never around. He didn't talk to anyone or even wave a glad hand in greeting. He just came and went. Each time, he deposited cash into his "bank"—the motorhome. It took most of a night to conceal his fortune and he had become very creative. He had done this more times than he could count. But when it mattered, when he thought his patient plan was about to come to fruition, it was gone. All of it.

    Stiles watched the old man on the tractor, and it was running very badly. In fact, to Stiles' ear, it was a miracle it was moving at all. And then, as if it heard him, it popped and died. He watched the old man struggle with the imbalance of time and infirmity as he climbed down off the machine. Once his feet were on the ground, he held himself steady with one hand on the tractor as he reached up for a wooden cane that lay on the floor of the rig. The tip of the cane was unstable in the loose dirt, and with what had to be pure stubborn will, the man wobbled as he stepped forward toward the engine compartment. Then the cane had nothing. It sank, his hand missed the save on the tractor, and he went down. He landed on his side, froze in a kind of winded recovery for a moment, then worked himself to all fours. The effort exhausted him and he remained in this position like a statue, his old eyes transfixed on the ground—his earth—now dry, barren, and empty.

    The old man was thinking that he had to get up, had to find the force within and will himself to go on. He groaned with the emotional effort that preceded the physical one, when a shadow enveloped him. A hand reached down, gently cupped his upper arm, lifted him, and said, "Here, let me help you." The old man squinted up into the blinding brightness. The backlit features were dark, but the hand was solid, so he went with it with grace.

    Stiles stayed there for several weeks and helped the old man. The tractor got repaired, as did the leaky roof on the house. Some plumbing in a bathroom was leaking too. Stiles fixed everything he could find and got a lot of satisfaction doing it. He slept comfortably in a spare bedroom whose décor was plucked straight from the fifties, chintz and all. The old man's wife was away caring for a sick cousin and her stay had been extended. He knew she was coming back but didn't want to hurry her. There was an abandoned truck behind the house and the old man said if Stiles could get it running, it was his. The registration was current.

"My wife pays it every time it comes. Probably shouldn't have, just never stopped," he told Stiles. "It used to run good."

Stiles looked at the Chevy 4x4 with its used cab-over camper shell. *Odd that*, he thought, *but what the hell.* He needed to ditch the truck he'd driven there for a while anyway, just in case someone was looking for them. He'd leave them in the warehouse with Shiloh's piece of shit. He'd left his horse in a pasture along the way, in a place where it looked like the horses were well cared for. The old camper truck was just what the doctor ordered.

Helping the old man provided an island of peace and a calmness Stiles didn't know he needed. In many ways, it felt good to help him and, without trying, the old man helped Stiles. Stiles left the day the wife was coming back, so he never saw her. The old man was grateful and gave Stiles some tools he didn't use anymore, a few bucks for gas, and thanked him. In the rearview mirror, Stiles watched him go back into the house and realized that he had been a godsend when he'd needed a sign.

He got to the highway and watched the weeds whipping along the road in the wind. It blew left to right and as he had no idea what was next, Stiles arbitrarily chose to go with the wind. Better to have it at his back at this point, he thought as he drove to the sound of the asphalt under tires.

Stiles stopped at a roadside convenience store and bought a few oranges. As he walked back to the old Chevy 4x4, he squinted at the faded quilt of stickers plastered on the windows showing places the rig had seen. Stiles had been to some of them when he was younger but most of the stickers were dated and worn, like he felt.

Road closures and detours around the fires that surrounded the ION region pushed him first this way, then that. He found some work digging fire breaks where manpower was stretched not only thin, but to not at all. There weren't enough emergency personnel and even the prisons couldn't funnel enough bodies to help out. Then there was clean-up work but he loathed the hazmat suit and the full head masks were awful.

Stiles seemed to go from one urgent situation to the next, and each time, he made enough money to put gas in the tank. He was fed with the rest, and he slept in the camper, so it felt like the work found him and he was occupied wherever he stopped.

The thing that bothered him most was the smoke and he coughed a lot until he was given a pack of N95 masks—a rare and needed find, but an uncomfortable one. The elastic was poorly placed, the design sucked, and it seemed like his face was constantly sweating under those things. His face broke out—an astonishing time warp back to prepubescence—and that bothered him as much now as it did then. He was buggered if he wore the protection and the same if he didn't.

Stiles was usually known as "that guy"—nondescript, not necessarily rude, just not friendly with anyone in the various places he worked. He kept to himself and did whatever the job required. He hadn't formed a plan, he just rolled with the flow. *Gawd, at my age,* he thought, *I'm saying shit from the sixties to define myself.*

He wrangled at a small outfit, bunked inside when it suited

him, and worked on his camper truck in his off-hours. Gradually, the days blended together and he fell into a rhythm. He liked ranch work, always had, and as he had no money, he was grateful for the wages and meals. And he knew the work, so his employers appreciated him. It made the cattle operations run smoothly with tested and tried buckaroos and not wannabes.

His gray hair grew long and he now had a mustache and a beard. Stiles was never much fond of beards, so he tried to keep it trimmed with scissors, but they were dull, and he soon gave up. In spite of the raggedy appearance, he adjusted and even began to like the way it looked. He saw a completely different man in the tiny, stained mirror in the camper, wondered why mirrors did that, and concluded it may have been what he needed to see. The "before Stiles" and all his grand planning had not yielded the expected results. This new face, with the same eyes staring back at him, might have a different history. Hopefully, a better one. Or so he told himself. Time was running out.

The fires so consumed the air that even the most vigorous phoenix could not rise from them. They burned like no fire before them, covering huge distances undaunted and mostly unseen for all the smoke. There was no measure of what was seething out of sight. The Three Corner country had erupted in the most destructive fire in history.

Eventually, Stiles moved on and for whatever reason, found himself heading toward the Jordan Valley. In some spots, fire-hazed skies glimpsed pockets of improvement. For days, he brushed layers of ash off the camper. He had to pick and choose his places to stay the night as he didn't want to wake up surrounded by an orange glow in the sky.

After driving into the night, Stiles parked off the road, down a deserted track, and set up camp well out of sight of passing cars. He knew the country, and as long as he had food, he could find whatever he needed. Except for money.

Stiles sat perched on a folding stepstool and watched the morning sky, tinged orange from the fire, become a hazy, smoke-scented day. For camping ambiance, he would have liked to have had a small campfire to take the chill off the morning, but the Great Basin fire had taken all the fuel. He cast his mind back to Shiloh for the millionth time and threw out locations she might have set her sights to. Geographically distant from there, for sure. He sipped the cup of instant coffee he'd made for breakfast and leaned back as a beam of sunlight fought its way through the haze and crested the shadow of a butte. He closed his eyes and relished the muted warmth of it. Every sunrise and sunset was cast in ghostly tones, and the days were not the right color. The high desert had a hue and a reddish-orange tint stubbornly clung to everything. He imagined the planet Mars had this odd coloring all the time. And with the ashen, lunar-type landscape, all the plants, shrubs, and trees incinerated, it well could be Mars.

He heard a bird. Something lived. Some creatures had made it through the hellfire and were singing. How extraordinary. He watched for as long as he could, curious to see what kind of birds had done the almost impossible.

Stiles fetched a day-old breakfast roll, set some crumbs on a nearby flat-topped boulder, and tried to mimic their sounds to call them in. It took a little while, but one, then two showed up and devoured the crumbs. He thought they might be thirsty and set a jar lid out on the rock with water in it along with a few more crumbs. That was the draw. He refilled the jar lid several times before he had to break camp and move on. He found a plastic food container, wiped it as clean as he could, and set it out full of water for his feathered fire survivors. He made a note to pick up some paper bowls when he had the money, to use something biodegradable to leave water for the survivors. He considered getting a bag of birdseed as well, if he happened to be particularly flush.

Stiles reached down and picked up a long, charred stick and poked it about in the mixture of ash, dirt, and fine pebbles. The fine ash puffed low and he could smell the fresh burn. It was interesting to him that the arrow of time continued, unabated, and the land would slowly heal, but the earth would bear the marks and wouldn't forget.

As Stiles drove away from his overnight spot, he thought about Shiloh again. He figured she was a survivor too and was adept at it. The whole point of his plan was to get to know her and without that crucial personal knowledge, even guessing about her plans was pointlessness cubed. To the hum of the V8 of his truck, he mused out loud to himself, "Where would she have gone?"

Chapter 25

Firefighter Cajun and his wife, Tish, an emergency medical technician, were, by all accounts, well-liked and well-matched. Both were farm-raised, big-boned, strong physically, and faith based. Their faith was a mutual priority in their lives. They'd met at church, tithed regularly, volunteered at ministry, and Cajun occasionally took to the pulpit and delivered moving sermons. They prayed many times a day—they prayed before they went to work on a fire and prayed when they were done. They organized religious services for the support personnel, dozer drivers, firefighters, and EMTs when out in the field battling blazes for weeks on end. They were the leaders and they understood their jobs, and everyone else's.

The massive Three Corner fire was beyond the scope of any wildfire veteran firefighters had ever seen. Chaotic scenes unfolded across the region as firefighters tried to evacuate homeowners and save houses, even as their escape routes were being cut off. People ran for their lives only to be stopped by walls of flames.

Cajun's team worked the lee side of a low mountain. The wind roared around them on the downwind side, sending flames stretching like water moving around a boulder in a stream. Cajun was on a line hand-fighting the flames. The rest of his crew, split between two trucks, moved to cut a break in another spot. As they made their way down a road, heat damaged the sides of their vehicles, most of their windows blew out, and they were battered by debris. One of the trucks was damaged on the driver's side and the other on the passenger's, even though both were only a couple hundred yards apart and going in the same direction. The firefighters pressed their bodies against the floorboards to save themselves from projectiles.

Fire vortices could maintain their rotational energy for long periods of time. No one knew exactly how long this one lasted, but it left a pattern of destruction over a mile wide and traveled a great distance. It was estimated to be more than two thousand feet wide at its base, and according to radar imagery, five miles high. Damage akin to that of a class-four tornado left trees uprooted and shattered, the bark scoured off by flying particles. Five one-hundred-foot-tall metal power line towers were blown off their bases. Another was severed from its base and landed over two thousand feet away, and yet another tower was torn apart and a steel pipe was found wrapped around a power pole.

Cajun felt the pressure change and looked around to find that he was alone. The noise of what was bearing down on him was terrifying. He knew he was in trouble but didn't know the full extent of how much. The fire tornado, generated by wind curling around the mountains and dragging along the ground, was headed straight for him. The rotating wind pushed the flames down to the surface and forced them into the vegetation, causing it to burn more fiercely.

Cajun didn't have time to think. He moved as fast as he ever had. He didn't even pray. He scrambled toward what looked like a rocky outcropping, then dropped his Pulaski ax and crawled on all fours like a cat to reach the rocks. Gravity caused the air to accelerate as it moved down the slopes toward the valley like water flowing downhill, and he could feel it helping and hurting him at the same time. He felt heat on his back and smelled singed material. Then a burst of high wind pushed him clear over the biggest boulder and blew him up into the air. As he cleared the top of the boulder, the gust briefly lost him and he rolled out of control down into a crevasse. His hand dug into a crack in the rocks and he gripped it as his legs were sucked out from beneath him. A *Wizard of Oz* moment flashed in his mind as he ducked his head against rocks and debris that hit him from all directions.

His helmet miraculously stayed on but he heard it crack, either from a blow or the heat, and instinctively tried to protect the front of his face with his hands and arms. His grip failed as he was knocked loose by something large and dark flying through the air. It felt like an animal and it growled and screamed as it hit him. He landed horizontally deep inside the crevasse among the boulders and passed out.

The inward wind generated near the ground streamed into the fire tornado, acting like a giant vacuum cleaner, sucking air and burning debris into its base, forcing it vertically up the core at extreme velocities, and spitting it out from high up, generating spot fires miles ahead.

As Cajun lay motionless among the relative protection of the rocks, a well-worn piece of paper half protruded from a small pocket that had broken open in his tumble. Cajun's singed hairs and torn bits of clothing pulled upward in unison as if a static charge hovered over him. The wind vortices pulled at its victim but could not dislodge him. The paper flapped and fought. It seemed to want to stay attached to him but in one last, ferocious pull, the vacuum won and the photograph of

Tish smiling at him when they got married flew up into the air. It bounced on the surfaces of the rocks, did a pirouette as if trying to fly out of danger, and then it was gone.

Chapter 26

Cullen had driven the rig all night, taking the back roads and keeping clear of the main thoroughfares. His nerves were still rattled. When he got back to Dixie, he poured out what had happened as soon as he had a beer in hand.

The truck and trailer were a dusted-out, dirty mess and she walked around the rust-red stock trailer, which was capable of carrying ten plus horses tightly packed. They'd worked the BLM's wild mustang round-up circuit for a while and their side gig was shipping horses illicitly to the meat processors in the south. Horse meat was a big market for shipment to Europe. The holding pens for the mustangs were overcrowded and it cost the government a fortune to care for them. It just made sense to cull—at least, Cullen thought so.

Dixie was a horse person. She had shown them her whole life but her convictions had shifted with her husband's. She made sure she got a finger on gossip, caught any tidbit of information she could, then spun it so it seemed that she knew more about things than anyone else. It was her mission in life to be all-knowing. Whatever it was, it was all about her, except with Cullen. She knew it was best to toe his line rather than face unpleasant consequences. And some unpleasant consequences had visited the job Cullen had been on the previous night.

Cullen held his glasses in his hand, nervous fingers

touching the thick, black plastic frames. "It was just the good ol' boys' shooting party. No problem, drink some beer and a few shots, and shoot some horses. Good fun and it was starting to feel like maybe a regular gig. I drove the load straight from the round-up and arrived at dusk. They had their spot all set and I backed the trailer up to the trap, opened the gate, and let them go." He waved a hand at her. "Get me another beer."

Dixie hustled inside the double-wide they rented by the month, grabbed a cold one for him, and trotted back. She handed him the beer and he twisted the cap off, tossed it on the ground, and swilled half before he took a breath. Dixie noticed the slight shake of his hand when he lifted the bottle to his thin lips. He noticed it too and his eyes went to hers. She quickly looked away. The scene played in his mind…

The stallion dashed back and forth and the parts of his herd that had made it with him tracked with him as best they could. A couple of yearlings were exhausted and some were injured. He paced. Dirt caked the dried sweat on his body and though his band was banged-up and half lame, he still held his head high. The alpha mare was beside him, scrappy, strong, and pregnant. Miraculously, she hadn't been injured in the melee when the helicopter had chased them into the trap. He'd lost part of his band and fought like hell to escape with the rest but couldn't. They were driven into a moving jail and released into half-darkness to another kind of hell.

There were other horses already there, to be funneled through panels to a swiftly constructed enclosure with a steep earthen wall that rose high above them—too steep to climb, though some tried. There was a ring of four-wheel-drive trucks, parked nose-to-tail, with a handful of lawn chairs set up in the beds, ice chests open and weapons all set to go. As Cullen drove away, the desert air was broken by automatic weapon fire and the earthen wall exploded with dozens of bursts of dirt. It was chaos under a few halogen spotlights trained on the trapped animals as the bullets mowed them down. The party had been drinking and it was a miracle they didn't shoot each other in the frenzy.

The stallion struggled to keep what was left of his band away from the other horses that had been delivered earlier. He ran them back and forth along the barrier, looking for a way out. The alpha mare was between him and the earthen wall that absorbed the shots that missed. The others fell away until it was just the two of them. He ran full speed at a rusted gate where there was the least amount of light. Someone tried to move one of the halogens to better light the area and lost it. It crashed to the ground and broke so part of the area went dark. That was perfectly timed for the stallion, who lunged at the right moment for freedom. A dinged and rusted end panel, half propped against the berm, was weak from repeated banging and had all but failed. The stallion went airborne, oblivious as hot lead wounded him fatally. His body crashed through and landed dead on the fence, destroying it. The pregnant mare had leaped in unison with her mate, their bodies mirrored as one. To the eye, it was one horse that crashed the gate. No one saw the shadow that flew past the fallen stallion and onward, not looking back as she ran through alone and disappeared into the dark of the high desert. Her bare hooves found smooth, even purchase and she ran to freedom under the stars of the high desert.

Behind her, justice was meted out when the shooting party was raided by darkened law enforcement vehicles, the sound of their approach masked by the gunfire. As the mare ran for her life, the shooting trailed off. Headlights blinded the shooters from the backside. The vehicles slid to hard stops, peppering the trucks that formed part of the kill pen with dirt and gravel. The shooters scrambled for their weapons. Those with just one weapon and faster feet scattered like rats fleeing a sinking ship. But not everyone got away. Those with bodies that betrayed them or who had brought more of their precious gun collections than they could carry or abandon were easily caught and subdued. The organizers of the mass murder of the wild BLM horses were harder to weed out and expose.

That Cullen was really rattled made Dixie feel better somehow and she didn't want him to see that. She folded her arms across her chest and stared at the ground, waiting for his story to come out. He set the beer down on the step next to him, then looked at his palms and rubbed them together as if they were wet, then dried them on the thighs of his jeans. When it seemed he'd gathered himself and the beer was starting to work, owl-eyed, he recounted what he knew of the events that had transpired.

"I hung with them for a little while and it got dark. I was in the truck, set to leave and they hit the lights and started in on their fun. The track outta there was so bad that I went down it at a crawl. Seemed to take forever to get off that gumbo road, and I was actually glad when I got to the turn and onto something better. It's still a tight deal with the trailer, so I had to swing it just right. There's a ditch there and I almost tipped it going in loaded. Missed by that much." He used his thumb and forefinger to emphasize how close he'd come to wrecking. "So, I'm making this tight left and that's when I was completely blinded. These lights came on suddenly and I hit the brakes and shielded my eyes."

"You didn't see them?" Dixie asked.

"No, dammit, my headlights hadn't tracked the full turn so I didn't see anything till they hit it. They had to have been there a while, lights out, waiting. They musta watched me coming for a good five minutes and I saw nothing but bad track and darkness." He hesitated, rethinking what had happened and whether he'd seen anything and just dismissed it as lights from a truck that was late to the party. "If it had been one set of lights, I mighta thought it was someone who was running late. Either way, they blinded me and I only had a second to crank it to the right to miss 'em. I took the whole rig off the road and punched it…I didn't think that son of a bitch would track but it did. It was a fucking miracle. It banged around pretty good. It's tight there, the road is barely wide enough for one truck to pass and I drove like hell." He pointed at the trailer and Dixie's eyes followed his finger.

She hadn't paid much attention to the rig except that it was covered in dust and was dirtier than she'd seen it in a while. But she followed his finger and saw it then—the back left section, near the bumper, was damaged. She walked alongside the trailer and touched the bar handle that latched the trailer's big back gate. It had a split-style door with a sliding section that allowed a quick way to prevent horses from slipping out as it was closed, or a full door that opened wide for hauling cattle. The latch was midway up and it was straight, but down below that lower left was the metal part that housed the taillight assembly. Whatever he'd hit, that was where the damage ended. The stock trailer had a dimpled dent that carved a hard scrape about a foot long to the end of the trailer's side and caved-in the bar that protected the assembly. The red plastic light cover had cracked and a piece of it was missing. Its jagged edge looked sharp, freshly broken, and it no longer concealed the reflective interior. She didn't have to bend down to see the bulb was whole and it looked like it still worked. Lucky him.

He stared at it in dismay. "I didn't even feel it, what with the rig banging all over as I drifted that turn. I didn't notice it till I stopped for gas."

"We could say we forgot we had the trailer on when we went into a parking lot and clipped somebody. Could pretend we're doing the whole insurance thing," Dixie offered.

He glared at her. "That's not the problem. The front plate wasn't covered. I didn't think about it. And I was caught full-on in those lights. I'm sure someone saw my face." He shook his head in frustration. "Shit, I was out in hell and nowhere, not a soul for miles."

Cullen almost leaped off the step, scooped up his beer as he went, and marched back and forth beside the rig. His hand gripped the neck of the bottle as he stopped and pointed a finger at her. "And I mean *nowhere*. Those boys have a big problem. Someone must've told them exactly where to go."

Dixie asked him a question softly. "What about the money?"

His head didn't come up all the way, his eyes rolled upward, and he snarled at her, "Of course, I got paid."

Dixie raised both hands, palms facing him. "So, what do we do?"

He threw the bottle. It hit something and shattered. "Make it fucking simple. We get rid of the whole rig, that's what we do."

Chapter 27

As the fire neared the area, a disaster preparedness meeting for locals—one of many in the past few days—was underway at Martin Ranch Supply. Lyle Martin had disaster kits available as the tinder-dry conditions persisted and anxiety levels rose. Information packets contained lists of suggested emergency materials and encouraged stockmen to determine the best place for animal confinement in case of a disaster. Wire cutters ran out quickly as the more experienced stockmen made sure each of their ranch hands had a pair.

Lyle was calm in the midst of the panic. There were conversations about nearby ranches that had not only lost animals, but forage for the ones they had managed to save. When the winds hit, the fire grew beyond anything anyone could contain. The animals' lungs were cooked in the heat as they struggled to breathe. Close to town, a dozen families had already lost their homes. Some only had time to grab a few pictures off their walls and were lucky to find the family dog or cat before they had to flee.

In areas with dense vegetation, the fire burned so hot that rocks split. In locations that had more trees, soil seared to gray ash and was sterilized down to mineral depths. The drought was the drought, but this fire spread, and the number of random fires had hemorrhaged into a perfect firestorm that left even seasoned firefighters lost for words to describe it. It was as if the country they had known all their lives had become an unrecognizable thing. It was soul-destroying and the speed of it caught people off-guard. They'd be as ready as they could be, but held tight, hoping the weird wind would spare their ranches and livestock. Then they were cut off from their planned routes of escape and squeezed from all sides.

During the meeting, it was suggested that everyone find alternate water sources in case power was lost and pumps were not working, or to have a hand pump available. Potential evacuation sites were discussed and identified, and an emergency neighborhood phone network was organized so folks could watch out for each other.

As the emergency preparation meeting wrapped up, muted, worried whispers filled the store as people dispersed. Kitzie poured coffee into a Styrofoam cup, reached for the creamer, and turned to see Buckets with a small box of new wire cutters. He set it on the floor, got a cup, and asked how Kitzie was doing.

Kitzie watched those enormous hands—she couldn't help it. They were so large and long that when his fingertips touched the black plastic lever on the urn, it looked like a miniature. And his fingers encircled the cup almost two-fold. Kitzie replied that they were nervous and worried about the fires reported to the east and north but so far, they felt they were not in danger. Then, under her breath, she added, "These winds…they're unnatural, like nothing I recall. You?"

Buckets turned and cast his eye out the windows at the front of the store and watched an aluminum can bouncing down the street. It spun and kicked up into the air, where the wind caught it and threw it out of sight. He took a sip of his hot beverage and as his hand came down, looked at Kitzie and shook his head gently. He touched the box of wire cutters with the toe of his cowboy boot. "I feel a little guilty buying out the last of Lyle's stock."

His weathered face was sheepish beneath his black hair, which was graying ever so slightly at the temples. The thing Kitzie always liked about Buckets was his eyes. There was a sparkle to them that she found appealing.

When the store cleared out and people made for the exit, Kitzie was silent as she and Jorge left to get the truck. The smoky air caught in their throats and they put on their masks. Kitzie had cut the elastic straps of the notoriously tight N95 mask, and retied them to fit around her ears as comfortably as possible. Carson had done the same. Jorge chose to leave his as it came and when he removed it, it left a red, mask-shaped welt etched deep into his face.

A thick layer of ash coated the truck. Kitzie turned the windshield wipers on so she could see, then looked at Jorge, who was settling into the back cab of the truck and greeting his two dogs, who had waited patiently for them to return. "That was a sobering experience."

Jorge forced a smile and asked what she thought it meant for them.

"This fire could set us all back to levels we haven't seen in a generation. And should the catastrophe not be as severe as they are predicting, forage and food will be scarce. Having that herd down on the McDermitt may be a really good thing after all," she mused. "Also, when we get back to the ranch, we need to get the trailers hooked up and pull them into the big arena. Once that's done, grab the horses from the barn. I think we'll just load them in the trailers. Can't hurt to contain them and be ready to run if we have to."

They picked up Carson, who had volunteered to stock shelves with donated items for the fire victims. Evacuees and families that had lost their homes picked up basic supplies at the donation center. Necessities such as food, water, toiletries, and clothes were coming in as the firefighters flooded in from all parts to help as well. It all needed to be organized and Carson was good at that.

Carson hopped in and they started for the Three Bit. They drove so close to the fires in some places that orange glowing streaks painted the inside of the cab and their faces took on a ghostly tone. The smoke invaded the cab and they drove in silence, masks on and the air vents closed. They were held at a checkpoint and watched helplessly as several free-running herds ran one way, and then, confused, ran back, terrified and doing their best to outrun the fast-moving fire. They moved on, then were stopped at a second checkpoint. A loose horse, closely followed by two large goats, trotted past them down the highway and disappeared. They had matching phone numbers spray-painted on their sides. Carson surmised that they were stable buddies and hoped they would make it to safety together.

Jorge's dogs were curled up next to him and he stroked their heads. He used a kerchief and wiped around their noses. He asked Kitzie if they had face masks for dogs. She shrugged and said someone should come up with that, then fell quiet and shook her head solemnly as they watched the chaos around them.

They sat there with the teams of firefighters, listening to the emergency radio in the cab and watching the fire dance in the air, huge, billowing clouds of smoke rising high into the atmosphere. The sun fought the smoky sky until it was hard to tell what time of day it was.

The three huge fires in the area had been collectively named the Great Basin Fire, though some called it the Three Corner Fire. They had melded into one event covering diverse ground, affecting three states, and setting records everywhere. Kitzie, Carson, and Jorge heard a report that the enormous fire could be seen from the space station as it circled the earth. Another report told of how the fire, its wicked winds whipping with an almost adversarial intelligence, had encircled a large group of tired firefighters. The swirling winds sucked one firefighter's safety helmet off his head. It spun up into the air and landed yards away. He chased after it, then all of them beat a hasty retreat to watch their previously defensible position disappear under an invading sea of hot embers, fire, and ash.

Garbage cans rolled in the wind down neighborhood roads, spewing rubbish and recyclables, some of which melted into the asphalt. The windstorm trashed the neighborhood before the flames reached it, then the fire finished it.

Closer to home, there were reports of ranchers and their neighbors cutting down fences. Though fences made their livelihoods possible, they needed to make sure the cattle didn't get trapped. Despite their efforts, depressing predictions of up to sixty percent livestock losses were to be expected.

When they were finally motioned through the checkpoint and resumed their drive toward the Three Bit, a devastated landscape reflected on unbelieving eyes. The scorched parts broke up the smoking areas, which fell into places still burning stubbornly. Then there were towering flames burning as if by themselves with no discernable fuel—the result of underground gas lines that hadn't been shut off. Whatever the embers grabbed, they consumed, then the wind turned them into multiple blazes. The fire took what it wanted, hollowed out communities, and destroyed lives. It feasted on brittle woodlands, brush, and grasslands as eighty-mile-an-hour winds scoured the sparks and rained them far ahead.

They passed a burned cattle hauler, its tires melted to the pavement. The undeniable smelled of cooked meat and hair assaulted their nostrils.

As Kitzie drove, her fingers clenched around the steering wheel, day became night and her headlights were nearly useless. Smoke-filtered sunlight backlit denuded trees, cloaking them in an almost ethereal amber light. In the foreground was complete annihilation, a tumble of burnt beams and timbers. Looking out the passenger's side, Carson could make out part of a chimney and the destroyed shell of a vehicle, all blackened and covered in ash. Rivers of melted aluminum from cars lay frozen on streets and driveways. More chimneys stood abandoned, like brick gravestones. Trees no longer looked like trees, now having morphed into something twisted and alien.

Kitzie, Carson, and Jorge passed a small enclave of burning houses and saw a few firefighters trying to save what structures they could defend, their images rippled and blurred from waves of heat. The skeleton of one house simmered stubbornly after being destroyed.

They crept through the dense smoke, their path impeded by escaping cars, abandoned vehicles, and emergency responders. Carson squinted to get a clearer look at what appeared to be lava, glowing orange, yellow, and red, simmering under a pile of burned wood. Through the cracks and crevices, it moved as if a volcanic force was at work beneath it.

They passed an old woman who sat on a high, uneven dirt berm by the road—a "country curb"—staring at the ground, seemingly unresponsive to the chaos around her. She cradled a brilliant red apple in her hand. Her eyeglasses, clothes, and hair were covered in ash, her face filthy. Her walker was parked sideways next to her. To the left of her, a man—maybe her husband—sat on some kind of crate, his dirty right hand resting on the handle of a metal cane, which was bent at an angle at the top. The ashy streaks that ran vertically on his upturned face reminded her of the tattoos on Harper's face. His uncut hair, a mixture of ash gray and black, was stuck to his forehead. His eyes were closed and in his left hand was a clean bottle of water.

Kitzie stepped on the gas pedal, and with a shudder, concentrated on getting them home. She didn't like how the winds had shifted toward the Three Bit. One look at Carson told her that her daughter was having similar thoughts.

Chapter 28

The little house with the peeling paint smelled of mold. Condensation dribbled from various locations and Mason had a runny nose to match. When he was outside and away from this place, his nose didn't run but in the house, he always felt slightly sick. He had always been a "sensitive," sickly child, lacking in the social graces and desperate for attention. He had been passed around to a series of homes after his mother had up and disappeared. His father had no use for a child and was in jail or prison more often than not, so Mason stayed with a smattering of well-meaning friends, distant relatives, aunts or uncles…some that treated him in strange ways. It was attention, of a sort.

Mason had locked himself in the only bathroom and could hear the news on the TV. His father was on the sofa, fully engrossed, and in a second would yell for him to get out of there. A lethargic fly with sepia wings crawled on the cloudy window, oblivious to the room's human occupant.

Mason's shoulders were hunched as he sat on the toilet. His stringy hair fell on either side of his face and he stared straight ahead at a worn plastic shower curtain. His body vibrated, his breath quickened, and he clamped his eyes shut. Then he lifted his head, leaned against the cool porcelain of the tank, and his facial muscles relaxed. His greasy blond hair fell away from his face, he felt the smiles of angels in Heaven looking down on him, and he was perfect.

Slowly, he opened his eyes and his dilated pupils beheld the peeling paint on the ceiling. A bare bulb, tinged yellow, feebly cast its glow, and Mason inhaled deeply and relaxed. A strange buzzing sound caught his attention. He turned his head and squinted at the lower corner of the window closest to the toilet. The fly had wandered into a small web there and his erratic buzzing was the last throes of his freedom being wrapped up and taken away. A little spider, the same size as the fly, had caught a prisoner and was mercilessly subduing him. Mason stared as the weakened fly's struggle against the inevitable waned to silence.

He reached behind him and flushed the toilet when he heard the TV go silent. The mute on, his father's heavy footfalls crossed the cramped excuse for a living room and Mason froze. He stared at the door and imagined his father's heavy, balled fist rising to hammer the hollow-cored barrier. Then he grinned because he was sure the hard edge of a hand was suspended in midair at the sound of rattling pipes swallowing clean water into the depths.

The voice penetrated anyway. "Get out here, we gotta go."

Mason hurriedly cleaned up and said through the door, "Go where?"

"Just get the fuck out here and grab your stuff," the irritated voice said as the sound of his boots retreated from the bathroom door.

Mason smoothed his thin blond hair, which reflected at him from the tiny medicine cabinet mirror. Curious, he opened the cabinet door and saw an outdated bottle of cough syrup, an old toothbrush, and an almost empty bottle of generic aspirin. He read the label on the cough syrup and saw that it had a measure of alcohol in the ingredients. Looking furtively over his shoulder at the closed and locked door, he cracked it open and took a swig from the bottle. The berry-flavored syrup coated his throat and descended downward with a slight burning sensation.

He turned the water on. It was cold. He rinsed his hands off. The towel was disgusting, as was his T-shirt. But his T-shirt was less so, and he chose it over the towel.

Mason exited the bathroom and saw that his father, Denny, wasn't on the sofa. He glanced to his left down the short hall, half expecting him to be lurking there to cuff him one. But he wasn't. Mason felt a wave of relief and a heightened sense of the pursued not knowing where the pursuer was, until he heard him in the tiny kitchen off to the right.

Mason crossed the space quickly and hoped he looked "normal." Whatever that was.

His father cast a side-eyed glance at him, his expression blank. He looked away. "I don't see your shit."

Mason disappeared and returned with a small secondhand duffel, his jacket looped through the handles. "We just gonna leave?" he asked.

"Yeah, don't you watch the news?" Denny said sarcastically.

"Uh, not really..."

"My money is out there and we gotta get it before it burns up." He pushed past him and opened the front door.

"We ain't gonna say good-bye to Marsha?" Mason asked, his voice a tad whiny. "She's been real nice."

Denny didn't answer. He had her car keys and he was unlocking the driver's side door to a worn-out seventies-era Chevy Malibu. Mason stood at the passenger's side door and looked pained. He knew Marsha slept hard during the day because she worked graveyards at the mini-mart gas station. She would need her car to get to work later. But Denny didn't care. He started the car and Mason dutifully got in.

Chapter 29

The walls and roof of the shop had been rattling and shuddering all day. Luis's noisy air compressor masked all but the loudest of the sounds of the building as it groaned against forces greater than it was. Then the wind shifted and a huge burst of superheated air blew into the shop. He was alone at the ranch, under a car at the time, when dirt and debris blew in his face. He turned his head and closed his eyes to wait for it to stop. But it didn't.

There was something unnatural about the air and Luis thought it odd. He finished tightening a few bolts, slid out from beneath the undercarriage, and walked to his workbench. He took a rag and wiped his hands, then stepped over and around all kinds of stuff to find the air compressor. He turned it off, cocked his head to the side, frowned, and slowly turned toward the open end of the building.

The air was thick with the smell of smoke. As a precaution, earlier, he had moved the horses from the barn to the arena, then forgot about them. They had been seeing ash and smoke for a couple of days, so he shrugged and turned back to the messy chaos of his shop, looking for a tool. Lately, the shop was even more cluttered, and it was harder to move about and find things. Even the shortest of tasks took twice the time.

His back was turned to the open sliding front doors of the shop, so he didn't see the hot embers running along the ground

Three Corner Fire

outside right away. The wind screamed as if a giant had exhaled right on top of him. A particularly hard gust distracted his concentration and Luis stood and looked about, slightly confused.

He didn't fully comprehend what he was seeing at first. It was as if hell had descended in an instant. Though he could not see them, he heard the nervous horses. He knew that if the red-hot embers landed in a mane or on fur, they'd sting and burn.

The horses clustered together and ran to the end of the arena near a wall of metal siding. Objects buffeted by the wind peppered it with a drumming sound and they ran in a group away from the barrage. But the superheated wind gusts swirled the hot embers there too and the horses bolted, trying to outrun their attackers.

Luis clambered over tires and wheels and around an open container of used motor oil. He lost his balance when his toe caught the edge of an aluminum-foil roasting pan and the oil splashed on his shoe and the leg of his pants. He skirted around a transmission and moved quickly to the outside. Once there, he ran through the skittering embers to where he had a better vantage point of the valley and the area around the Three Bit.

The smoke was much thicker and whipped in frenzied waves around him. It caught in his throat. He had a bandana around his neck and as he turned 360 degrees, he tied it over his nose and mouth. The fire was close and he realized he had to move. The others hadn't returned from the fire briefing, so he was on his own. He knew someone needed to free the cattle so they could run.

Luis leaped on the ATV and drove as fast as he could to quickly accessible places where he could open gates and cut the fences. He had a small ax as well as bolt cutters. There was no reason to be delicate about it. The wind was unholy, unnatural, and possessed a fierceness Luis had never seen or felt before. And it was coming…fast. He felt and smelled embers as they landed and took hold on his clothing.

The cattle would keep themselves ahead of the fast-moving fire and he could hear them even though he couldn't see them in the smoky haze, which grew worse by the minute. The air blew hot gusts and the kerchief over his nose and mouth didn't stay in place. He held it fast with his free hand as he drove. He stopped along the fence line and rushed to cut strands of wire at the stakes, and tried to flatten the posts with the ATV in a direction he hoped was away from the fire. He prayed the cattle wouldn't double back in a panic and gore themselves. Where there were wooden posts, he tried the ax, thinking it would be faster, but it was about the same so he used the bolt cutters. His arms grew tired from the exertion and his chest felt like he had smoked cigarettes his whole life.

The swirling wind intensified. Luis changed his tactics to opening up as much fencing as he could and pulling the wires away in a fan. Even pushed by fire, cattle would obey barbed wire until it was too late. It was an almost impossible task as most of the fence line was five-string fencing—the kind that took two fit men six full days to string a quarter-mile stretch.

It soon became too dangerous to stay out there and Luis decided he had done what he could, especially as more hot embers hit him and bounced across the ground in bizarre patterns. They had no set direction and caught everything around them on fire. The smoke was so thick, he almost lost his bearings getting back to the ranch.

As he came through the last open gate, a group of fifteen cows stopped him as they pushed through toward him, mouths open, gulping air and calves trying not to lose sight of their panicking mothers. He stopped to let them pass and the ATV stalled and died. He tried to restart it but it was too clogged with ash to get going again. He got off and ran to the fence near the big metal arena. The steel girders had a strange glow about them. Luis froze, then he saw a burst of flame and realized that the fire had reached the other side and structures were burning. *That damned wind,* he cursed in Spanish.

He dashed over to the water trough by the gate, wiped the ash from the water's surface, yanked his bandana off, and doused it in the water. He squeezed the water out of it, then put it back on to try to breathe better. He ran along the side of the arena and saw the small shed row barn that Wyker and CJ had worked on. There were no animals in it and there wasn't anything he could have done had it been on fire. There was an outbuilding used to store equipment and it was burning but it was too much for him to put out. The roof of his shop was burning. The entire back wall was engulfed, and the wind fanned the flames to a monstrous height. Then the wind shear blew part of it off in a flying wing of fire that jumped the metal, corrugated roof of a feed shed. As his eyes followed it, he saw it join with a fire that was burning the main house.

At first, he thought of his tools as he ran to the front of his shop and stumbled inside. The smoke billowed out and he couldn't see. The debris he'd jockeyed over just a little while ago hampered his every move. He tripped and bled from a dozen scrapes.

Luis turned to escape, then remembered the box. He covered his face, coughing and trying to use his forearm to create a way to breathe. He turned back around and looked at where he needed to go. The box was perhaps a foolish reason to run into a burning building, but the bottom part was not on fire yet and he felt he had to retrieve it. Luis looked up at the roiling flames and smoke that engulfed the tall, sloped roof. He edged between the cluttered workbench and staggered through the chaos.

Kitzie's repeated entreaties to clean up his space, to organize it, rang in his ears. He knew he should have listened and acted but he had just nodded, smiled, and did nothing. He still saved everything. He'd stashed open containers of oil and fluids underneath junk and out of sight. Beneath the slick black surface lay the used oil filters he'd pulled off and dropped into the used oil. Debris and precious junk crowded every conceivable inch of space and was stacked to the rafters. Now he felt a measure of regret. Quickly, he realized his predicament. He'd buried the special box under layers of his hoarding. There was no room to even turn around, it was packed so tight.

The metal box contained Jorge's birth certificate, proof of his citizenship, family records, and precious letters from his grandfather. Luis cursed himself for foolishly keeping them in the shop. He began to toss things aside about halfway in, and thought he remembered the metal cigar box being on one of the few counter-like surfaces at the base of the side wall under a shelf.

The roof began to crumble in at the back of the shop and a whoosh of hot air and rush of flames startled him. Luis felt his skin blister and it hurt like hell. Finally, he found the box and worked it free. He turned and struggled to navigate over his mess, straining to see through the smoke and flames, carrying the precious box in one hand and trying to grab whatever else he could carry to save. He loathed the fire for eating up his precious collections, so good…all of it.

He reached the door and pitched the metal box out of the

workshop as far as he could throw it to free up his hands to save more of his stuff, compelled to grab just one more thing. At that moment, all the improperly stored combustibles in the building ignited and blew the building apart with such force that car parts were strewn hundreds of feet away out the back—luckily, away from the arena.

The metal cigar box bounced from being tossed, then was pitched forward by the explosion, which sent it careening through the air to the edge of the arena, where it bounced off a pipe panel support and came to rest in the dirt.

Chapter 30

Rae Royston sat in her office and put the finishing touches on an email to a wild horse preservation group. She had decided to resign from the district attorney's office and find work that was more meaningful to her. She wanted to spend more time around horses and the people looking out for them. She had heard the phrase "the earth needs a good lawyer" many times, and she concluded that the wild horses of the American West probably needed one too.

Besides that, she intended to make some mischief and she couldn't do that where she was—not with Noah's political aspirations for higher office already shutting her down. His motivations were alien to her now anyway, and maybe that was as it should be. Theirs had been an odd working relationship in the best of times. Rae had always known that Noah was not the brightest bulb in the box and that he had simply been that guy in the right place with the right connections—that right place that she, as a woman, would never find herself in. She'd originally thought climbing this ladder was a good goal, and then the "good old boys" club repeatedly stole her thunder and eventually, her will to fight. When Noah's nuanced power moves stripped her team, it may have been they had mostly left her and their cause already, and she had simply missed it. They'd figured out how to get along…and that meant going along with things.

Rae wondered again about the guy she'd seen in Noah's office. She had enough information from the plates that she'd requested a check on them. There was something in Noah's demeanor that made her suspicious, but it was likely that she was making up conspiracies in her head and she told herself so.

And yet, her "friend" had called her on her cell and asked whether the inquiry was attached to a particular case. Rae wanted to hedge but was honest and said no. He pressed her, so she made up a little white lie on the spot. She said her team had been working for months on an influence case and had it pretty much sewn up, when the momentum changed and the air went out of the investigation (mostly true). Then she shared in a confidential, manipulative, gossipy way that her team was being picked off one by one and that the truck with the plates she'd inquired about had been following her (the lie). She wanted info about the vehicle's owner to see if there was a connection to her influence case.

What Rae couldn't have known at that time was there definitely *was* a connection. A dangerous one.

Rae rubbed her temples, then pressed her fingertips together, elbows on either side of her keyboard, the sides of her index fingers pressed against her mouth. She sat for a few minutes rearranging her plan, the momentum she felt earlier melting away. She logged on to her computer and saw a raft of messages and e-mails that needed her attention. One, in particular, caught her eye. It was from the anonymous sender in the BLM and they were upset.

The email informed her that with the "new" administration making sweeping changes to government, a lot of really nasty things were slipping past the watchers. The writer was upset and wanted Rae to know that of the sixty-something-thousand wild mustangs and horses in captivity, over forty thousand were to be slaughtered. The writer added specifics about the exact locations of the ones condemned to die and where they were going.

Rae sank back in her chair. She knew the horses were destined for an abattoir—likely the one in Mexico she knew about. The meat was no doubt destined for the prime markets, for human consumption, but that plant couldn't pass a mediocre health inspection on a good day. She swirled her office chair around, away from the screen, then kept the spin going by pushing off her desk at well-timed intervals. Rae liked the unmoored disorientation that edged its way into her brain when she did that—normal images oozing and blending into a kaleidoscope of broken pieces. The shards of her once-promising career trajectory rearranged themselves. She found the confusion strangely alluring. Perhaps her path would be one of discovering her path. She swirled back to face her computer, printed the email, then deleted it.

Rae put the printout into her bag. She went to her small closet and assembled the file boxes she'd been collecting for the past six months, then poked her head outside the office and told her assistant she was not to be disturbed. Rae locked her door and methodically cleared out her desk. She filled the boxes with files, then took the hard drive out of her computer and added it to the last box. Afterward, she used her cell phone to call down to the basement and asked for a favor.

By the end of the day, the file boxes—all ten of them—were discreetly removed from Rae's office and hidden in the depths below the building. Rae then called a friend who had a nondescript van, and made her way to the basement garage.

Her friend arrived in a delivery outfit and baseball cap, which disguised her gender effectively, and the file boxes vanished.

Rae knew she was done. She'd had enough. The very act of giving up was about to become a starting point. Satisfied, Rae headed back upstairs. There was one thing left to do.

Rae entered Noah's office, closed the door, and leaned against it. She didn't say anything. She just stared at him.

Noah didn't look up. "What's with the angry polite?" he muttered.

Noah sucked at personal confrontation. If there was a problem or issue to sort out, he always delegated.

Delegate this, asshole, Rae thought, and she stared at him until it forced him to look up and pay attention.

He tried the little smile and raised eyebrow thing, but he was so weak he couldn't hold her gaze, so he shuffled paper and mumbled something she didn't quite catch.

"What? Did you say something?" she demanded, any feigned politeness discarded.

"Um, I'm very busy… How can I help you, Rae?"

"You can start by telling me what the hell is going on. We had an agreement. You sabotaged my case. I demand to know why."

Noah looked down and rolled a pen back and forth on his desk.

Rae took a step closer. "You little shit," she whispered. "Answer me."

He looked up at her. "Don't talk to me like that." But he wasn't convincing in his retort. "Come on, you know how it is… It's just that other cases came up and I needed to prioritize. The budget cuts have really carved the heart out of the department. If anything, you should be thanking me. I saved your core staff from losing their jobs."

"That's bullshit and you know it."

He rocked back in his chair and there was something around his eyes that she recognized. She straightened up, folded her arms across her chest, and squinted at him. Rae could see that he was a little scared…but not of her. She didn't have his full attention…yet.

"Who's the cowboy?"

Noah looked startled. "What are you talking about?"

She pointed at the chair behind her. "The one who was sitting right there the other night." She leaned on his desk, palms flat on the expensive surface, her eyes hot coals.

Noah struggled with that one and tried to deflect. In a flash, his eyes darted to a file that was close to her hand, then back to her. Rae didn't let on. She played poker and she knew he'd never been at the table. To test him, she shifted her position and slid her right palm sideways to rest on the file.

A shine started developing on Noah's forehead, though it wasn't warm in his office and he was in shirtsleeves. "I don't know who you're talking about," he said nervously.

"The one who was in here a week ago, late." Rae rattled off the make and model of the truck from memory. "Ring any bells?"

He denied knowing who that was.

"You're a shit liar," Rae said, and then something her father used to say popped into her head. His voice reached out to her and she steadied herself. He'd said, "A snake does not bite because it has been stepped on, it bites because it *might* be." So she used it.

Noah had no idea who the snake was and it pushed him to make a mistake. His obvious discomfort coiled in the chair, sprang free, and he leaped up, sending the chair sideways to bang against the nearby wall. He walked to the dark window, his back to her. "Don't go there," he growled.

Rae didn't respond and waited.

He turned to face her, his eyes hard. "I mean it. This is not anything you want to mess with."

"Well, something has been messing with me, and I will make it my business to find out why."

When Noah was cornered, he paced, and when he was scared, he paced faster, which he now did behind his desk. He rubbed his forehead with his index and middle fingers, looking for a way through this. "Do you want a top spot somewhere? Name the office, I'll make it happen…"

Rae thought it best to let the air out a bit, to calm the tension, so she sat in the same chair the cowboy had sat in, and slid it to approximately the same position by the desk. Her elbows rested on the armrests and she mimicked the man's posture while Noah spoke. Her left hand raised to her chin and her finger crossed her lips, then she sat still to let the moment settle. Rae knew exactly what she wanted to happen now. She wanted that file Noah was so nervous about. She needed him to leave the room.

"…. with a generous signing bonus and a salary bump," Noah finished. He stopped pacing and looked at her with obvious relief on his face.

"Don't get happy yet, I want that in writing," Rae smirked.

"What do you mean?"

"*Your* handwriting," she said.

He worked his jaw and his eyes scanned his desk.

"And…" she continued.

He looked at her again.

"Go find the checkbook," Rae said dismissively.

He stared at her, the wheels turning.

Rae pulled out her cell phone. "I'll be right here, checking my email." She looked up at him over her phone while he gaped at her. "Oh, for Christ's sake, Noah, get going. I don't want to be here a minute longer than I have to be." She buried herself in her phone.

Rae didn't look up when he left, but she didn't hear him close the door either. "Noah!" she called, and he was back in the doorway in a flash. "Be sure it's a generous bonus, and a salary bump too…"

She heard him stomp heavy-footed down the hall. In an instant, Rae grabbed the file and opened it. It wasn't her email she had been checking on her phone, it was the camera feature, and she flipped through the pages quickly, silently shooting each page. There were three sections, each stapled together. It took maybe two minutes and when she thought she heard something down the hall, she finished and replaced the pages in order. She caught a glimpse of the cover page. The file was called "Cedar Wara" and there was a name—Dale something—and a short list of directors. Noah's name was on it, as was his wife's.

Interesting… Rae thought as she slid the file back to its original position on the desktop. Then she sat back and scanned through the pictures and was pleased. To be extra careful, she sent them to her home computer—insurance in case her phone had an accident.

Chapter 31

The day was blissfully ordinary, maybe a bit windy, but unremarkable. CJ liked the gray clouds rolling in on the horizon. When he'd been in his cell in prison, there was only a small window and all he could see was the clouds. It got so he watched that tiny square of sky like a TV. Weatherless days bored him.

His life on the Rez had taken to a consistency that he came to rely on. His world was compact and uncomplicated. Maybe not entirely trouble free, but any troubles were small things. The details were sensible and he had more than he ever thought he would have without being in jail for it.

He finished his chores and this day was his and Rio's. So, CJ tucked what he might need into a saddle pack, mounted up, and went out early, well before anyone could try to go with him. He checked on a small group of cows that were free-grazing near the Dugout, found them well inside the area near Uncle's, and left them alone.

CJ had the day to himself to disappear. He wanted to ride out to a small canyon he had seen from a distance but hadn't had the time to explore. When he had asked Uncle and Harper about it, Uncle had been vague, which CJ felt he did when he didn't want to share information. Harper tried to be more forthcoming because he thought CJ's curiosity was a good thing. It brought him out of himself and made for interesting conversation. When CJ opened up about subjects that he found compelling, there was a fire in him that seemed to transcend his dark past. They had all noticed the change in him when certain topics held the floor, such as their history, culture, and art. CJ had revealed that, as a boy in his native Australia, the Aboriginal culture—their stories and their mythology—had fascinated him. This was also reflected in his tattoos—another subject that Harper, Uncle, and CJ shared. Had CJ's life charted a different course, anthropology and cultural history might have been a career choice.

Harper had agreed with CJ that there probably was sign in the canyon. The old ones had left marks and information all over the region. Now CJ was on the hunt and he had his little book with him, thinking he would have time to sketch and be back before the weather went bad.

The cattle he encountered along the way were fine. He and Rio never got too close to them, just observed them in passing. CJ leaned forward in his saddle, elbow resting on the horn, rope reins slack and his mecate looped under his belt. He stroked Rio's neck as the horse nibbled on a patch of grass that still held some flavor in the fold of a small group of boulders. The grass was tinder-dry and it amazed him how the wild mustangs survived on it. CJ looked around and felt a grounded, grown-up sense of wonder, like when a sunrise surprised him.

At the wide mouth of the canyon, CJ let Rio pick his way into it on a well-worn deer trail. The clouds parted and sunlight fell freely through the rocks. Birds flew in and around the walls and their chirps echoed back and forth. Rio ignored it but CJ cocked his head and tried to beacon the direction of the layered sounds. He imagined how it sounded to the birds. What were they saying? Was it more difficult to hear in this chamber than up above, without the acoustics? They had a freedom he appreciated. They knew no bounds, yet they had invisible ones—strands of territory and family, and the air space they occupied and defended. They knew where the food and water were, and they taught it to the future. They knew the pattern of their days by the length of the light and the warmth of the air. They were free to go anywhere. CJ stroked Rio's neck and felt the same way.

Farther into the canyon, the walls rose on either side and it became deeper. CJ thought it would dead-end but instead, it surprised him by winding, first to the right, then left, then broadened and became shallow. He pretended that he was with a hunting band, that they were driving prey ahead of them into a trap. The layers of sediment visible in the walls led his mind to imagine the whole area underwater, and that he and Rio were submariners looking up into azure waters teeming with life.

As they made their way forward, the narrow path became indiscernible. Perhaps there was no water source deeper in and the deer had no reason to go farther. Perhaps they smelled water and just knew it was not going to yield a reward other than ungrazed ground or a predator's certain trap.

In the underhangs of the rock outcroppings, CJ thought he saw what he was looking for. He decided to explore those after he'd gone as far as he could go.

At a cramped, narrow point along the trail, CJ and Rio stumbled upon a mine of wall art. Unsure whether they had been discovered previously—certainly not by a white guy from halfway around the world—CJ was stunned by the complexity and symmetry of the drawings. Trapped in the amber of another time, he spoke to Rio as one would a trusted friend and companion.

"These things are incredibly beautiful..."

He pulled out his notebook—a diary of sorts—so he could document his finds. He recalled his disdain for the art therapy offered in prison, and didn't remember being especially interested in drawing as a kid. This was a new wrinkle and CJ found a certain kind of peace and introspection when he did it. He felt a kind of pride about it. He had a broader appreciation for it when he talked with Harper or Uncle, and sometimes the kids, about the meanings of the drawings. CJ had made notes from those conversations in the margins. His handwriting, once illegible, had developed into a readable form out of necessity and he annotated his drawings with the information he learned. CJ sometimes wrote about how he felt, or how Rio felt, on some of their explorations. He grew accustomed to the feel of the notebook's worn binding, its softened edges, and how it fit in his hand.

On previous rides, CJ had seen drawings that looked like directions and he'd been fascinated by the petroglyphs they'd passed while chasing after the rustlers. Uncle told him that the ancestors would leave the tale of a good hunt on a rock face as they dressed their kills and packed them for travel.

The wind whistled in the peaked rocks above them but CJ was engrossed in the geometrical designs in the rock. The deeply carved lines featured what Uncle called "tree-form designs"—a series of evenly spaced, vertical V shapes bisected by vertical lines.

CJ nudged Rio onward. They went deeper into the network of ridges and canyons than he meant to, but he kept finding sign and he felt like if he didn't look now, he might never. CJ found a smooth track that led up to a promontory and along that path, a storyteller had been busy. CJ almost wished Ely was with him, or Harper.

CJ shifted in the saddle and Rio stood quietly, a rear foot cocked, resting. "Maybe the symbols were meteorological. They look like clouds and lightning," he said to his horse.

At that moment, a bolt of lightning struck the cliffs above them. Rio jerked backward and CJ was blinded by the flash as thunder rumbled through the canyon.

CJ awoke and rolled over onto his belly. He heard a voice cry out, then realized it was his…only he could barely hear himself. He struggled to kneel but couldn't. On all fours, he rocked himself through the pain until he felt stronger. His ears rang and there was something wrong with his face. He touched his head with his right hand, then pulled his hand away and tried to focus on it. Through blurred vision, he could see it was red. CJ was too dizzy to stand. He looked to his right at the rocks, stretched out his hand to touch the wall, then drew back. The rock was hot. *How weird…* he thought.

There seemed to be rocks all around him that hadn't been there before…or had they? He tried to turn his head to see Rio but his brain exploded in pain the likes of which he'd never felt before. He rolled across the ground as if he could get away from it, and propped his back up against a smooth rock wall. This one wasn't hot and the relative coolness against his back calmed him back from the edge of panic.

CJ knew he had passed out—for how long, he wasn't sure, but his senses were returning. He began to think a shade more clearly and one thing that came to him was that he shouldn't sleep. He was thinking concussion. His head ached viciously. He tried to move his mouth to call for Rio but managed only a choked, strangled sound and he spit out blood and dirt. He had no voice. Or if he did, he couldn't hear it.

CJ rounded back to all fours and steadied himself. Time was unimportant. If it took ten years to move from that position, so be it. Then he smelled smoke. The thought of fire panicked him and he steeled himself, willed himself to move. He rocked back to take the weight off one of his arms, then used the sleeve of his torn jacket and wiped as much blood and debris from around his eyes as he could.

CJ straightened up so he was on his knees, found the rock wall within arm's reach, and braced a hand on it to struggle to his feet. The world spun around him and CJ focused on slow, steady breathing. His ears still did not cooperate and he felt as though he'd gone deaf. He started to feel panicked again, worried that he was so hurt he wouldn't be able to find Rio.

The smell of smoke grew stronger. At first, it was just the idea that something was burning nearby. Then it was constant. CJ leaned on the rock wall. He had to reorient his path. Was he coming or going? Should he go farther into the canyon or get out and try to get back to Uncle's? And where was Rio? Which way had he gone? CJ wondered how long he had been unconscious.

It was a toss-up where to turn so CJ staggered the way he leaned, which seemed the easiest thing at the time. As he grew more steady on his feet and more accustomed to the weird things his head and body were doing, he had the sensation that he was trying to run. Then another sensation—things falling from the sky and whipping around him on the ground, racing past him in a blur in the wind. The wind was hot and it hurt to breathe. He felt searing embers stick to him and smelled them burning his clothes. Some were extinguished by the layers of material, some made it to flesh and were put out by his blood.

A red-hot cyclone of fire crowned in the small trees around the canyon. The brush leaped with flames that looked like arms trying to grab him. CJ couldn't see Rio through the ripples of heat coming off the rocks and the embers that bounced along the canyon floor.

CJ lurched on unsteady feet through an unending vein of horror. He lost his hat. He had this weird feeling that he really liked that hat. He smelled burnt hair. There was so much smoke, he couldn't see. And he struggled to take a breath and felt faint. The air was as thick as milk and nothing looked familiar. CJ touched the back of his head and his hand came back freshly red. His body hurt. He called out for Rio, then for his dead brother. He heard screams but they were nothing he recognized. There was a sensation of tripping and then falling. The falling lasted forever…then he heard voices. CJ thought he was dreaming until strong hands gripped him. Instinctively, he swung and fought back.

A voice, faintly Southern and female, drifted to his ears. "…come on, buddy, I got you. I got you," she said as ash and debris pelted them.

The wind hurled rubble that became projectiles as his rescuers worked to keep CJ from further injury. CJ squinted to see the woman and saw a round face and thin lips. She wore bright-yellow firefighting gear and a helmet.

CJ thought he was hallucinating. He heard a male voice too and saw a shadow, not a face.

Overwhelmed by searing pain and struggling to breathe, CJ almost convinced himself they weren't real. But the voices were indeed real, as were the hands holding him. His mouth was open and his mind told him that his screaming for Rio was real. Then he tried to turn his head when someone asked him urgently, "Who is Rio? Was he with you?"…but something stopped him. He tried to grab at it. Something was there he didn't recognize. His fingers grappled with an oxygen mask. CJ ripped at it as he tried to get up but there was something on top of him. He grabbed at something alien and pulled it up to where he could see it. It was a shiny blanket. His hand felt it and he was confused as to how he had gotten it. He struggled to free himself, tore the oxygen mask off, and grabbed the woman's arm, a roiling mass of pain and panic, but the adrenaline that rushed through him gave him the strength, he thought, to get up.

His voice was raspy and unrecognizable to his own ears. "Rio!" CJ spit out the word but could barely hear himself say it. Then coughing exploded from his lungs and he couldn't catch his breath. His head hurt and he felt broken ribs chime in on his agony.

The woman took his hand and pried it from her arm. "You shouldn't talk. You have sustained burns to your airway and at the least, you're suffering from smoke inhalation."

He was strong but she was stronger, and he was surprised by how easily she handled him. Then he felt himself being lifted and placed onto something. There was chaos around him and it pierced his hazy reality. CJ was in pain but his heart was breaking, and he kept trying to tell the face in the helmet that he would not leave without Rio.

She reached for the strap under her chin, slid her helmet up, and removed it. CJ felt her face close to his and out of the corner of his eye, he saw an ash-smudged cheek. She aligned herself over him, her piercing blue eyes met his, and through her thick Southern accent, said, "My name is Tish and I'm going to help you. We have to get you to a hospital…"

CJ tried to calm himself and forced himself to breathe into the mask she replaced over his nose and mouth. He realized his head and neck were in some sort of soft, inflatable brace.

CJ rasped, "What the hell is this?"

Tish spoke in that even, calm tone that betrayed no drama in a situation fraught with it as the wind continued to sting them with ash, embers, and debris.

"I've placed something on your head wound and stabilized you. We're taking you to get help. We're loading you in the rig and we have to go. *Now.*"

Other voices urged everyone to get moving as the fire was cutting off their escape route.

CJ again fought to get up. His determination and will surprised her and she gently stopped him.

He grabbed her hand again. "No…you don't understand, I can't leave him!" Then he felt a prick on his other arm and tried to look at whoever did that. CJ looked back at Tish, felt her strong hands, and heard himself beg her to find Rio. No one else near him seemed to understand but then she leaned over and spoke into his ear over the din.

"I understand. You've lost your horse. I understand…"

CJ's eyes clenched shut as he felt whatever they'd injected him with start to smooth the sharp edges. "No…" he mouthed. "He can't be dead, he's too smart. He's out there…I have to get to him." He coughed again but it eased as she held the oxygen mask over his face and told him to breathe.

The voice was at his ear again but drifting farther away as she spoke. "My man, Cajun, is out there. If your Rio made it, he'll find him, I promise. You need help now. Let us help you."

Tish got into the firetruck and buckled in. She yelled to one of the others, "I think he's Australian."

Another voice said, "Man, what's he doing out here?"

"I think he's looking for his horse."

CJ kept saying Rio's name over and over as the roar of a diesel motor drowned out the sound of his voice.

Time washed around. CJ felt his arms being strapped to the frame of another stretcher and he felt Tish hand him off to someone who held the mask on his face. He felt a lifting and weightlessness.

CJ was sure he was dying. He lost consciousness with the image of Rio in his head, turning to look at him with those eyes, forelock blown aside, whinnying to him from across the pasture...

Chapter 32

The free-lance photojournalist was alone and savvy, and he moved with the different fire teams seamlessly. He never got in the way of the crews and was on a first-name basis with some of the firefighters and the police. He took stock footage as he photographed the cars and trucks that had been routed and rerouted around the fires, only to have the fires reroute them again.

He trained his camera on a beat-up, light-blue Chevy Malibu—or at least, that was his impression of it. As he trained his camera on the driver and waited for the right shot, the driver turned his head and looked at him. The photographer checked himself and lowered his camera. The look on the man's face wasn't just evil, it was worse. The photographer was glad he had his air filtration mask on as he didn't want those eyes to remember him or recall what he looked like. He had the impression that there was a passenger in the car but he couldn't be sure because the smoke and ash were so thick.

With the shot lost and traffic moving again, the Chevy was swallowed up in the chaos. Even brake lights and taillights vanished quickly as if in a thick fog. The photographer was relieved that the car was away from him and chose to go back the way he had come.

He heard the helicopter before he saw it. He couldn't believe it was in the air at all. The pilot struggled with the wind and visibility, emerged from the heavy smoke, and banked low over the roadway as the photographer snapped a series of shots with an emergency vehicle in the foreground. He smiled and looked at the results in his digital SLR. *Yeah,* he thought as he stopped on one in particular. *That's a good one for sure.*

Reporters, emergency personnel, and even a city fire engine deployed from Boise drove by. People scrambled around everywhere, frightened and confused. News crews with expensive gear made themselves more of a hindrance than a help.

Sherriff Spence's six-foot frame emerged from his cruiser and he lifted the mask that hung under his chin into place. He grabbed a set of clear safety goggles and put them on, then a sheriff's baseball cap with a large emblem on the front, and settled it squarely on his head. The wind tugged at it and he pulled it tight. With his Maglite in hand and on, he signaled the news van to pull back as the wind whipped embers along the pavement. The van complied and Spence got back into his cruiser.

His radio crackled that there'd been a disturbance, something about shots fired, and he got instructions to meet a road crew cutting fire breaks. He turned the cruiser around and hit the lights and siren. It was not yet night but in the bad parts, it was as dark as night. In some areas, Spence killed his headlights because the fires illuminated the darkness well enough, and sometimes the headlights made it harder to see in the smoke. The paint on the sides of the cruiser blackened from the heat and it was hot inside as well.

Spence navigated around flaming debris and passed by buildings engulfed by fire. And then it became instantly lighter and he picked up speed, silently hoping his tires were OK enough to get to the incident site.

Three hand crews, a hotshot crew, six engines, a water tender, a bulldozer, and a John Deere 210G excavator were among the equipment parked along the highway. One of the crew members flagged him in. They were digging a break and the operator of the excavator maneuvered a large boulder out of the path of a bulldozer using the mechanical thumb and bucket. Spence admired the operator's skill with it.

Spence drove past the work they were doing and guided the cruiser over the uneven ground toward a small group off in the distance. "This is not good," he said to himself and decided to find out what had happened.

Spence got out of the cruiser and reset his mask over his face. A wild gust of wind whipped a hard hat off one of the men and it skittered across the ground to Spence's feet. He picked it up, handed it back to its owner, and introductions were quickly made. The smoke was heavy in the air and Spence knew they couldn't stand around for long.

It's what was dug up that had caused some commotion. The guys led him to where the broken remains of multiple, white plastic five-gallon tubs were laid out on the ground. As they approached, Spence overheard one of the men telling another, "When the gun went off and chipped the window of the cab, we thought someone was shooting at us."

Spence looked at him. "What?"

Realizing that law enforcement was on the scene, the other man stepped aside. "Well, yeah, sometimes we run into these survival types and they feel all defensive against government 'intrusion,' even if it's to stop a wildfire."

Spence knelt and looked at what they'd discovered as the man, a heavy-equipment guy, stood over him, telling him the details. A team, led by an operator named Jesse, had been cutting a break and the man pointed down at the freshly turned ground. He gave a rough description of how far they'd been when they realized something was wrong and stopped.

"It's unnatural, what's been going on. This country just shouldn't burn like this..." The operator's eyes were red, and he was pale and tired.

"How long since you got some sleep?" Spence asked.

The guy just shook his head. He didn't know.

Spence nodded as he took in the myriad dirty items the broken bits of sealed five-gallon tubs had protected. "So, this is what you brought out?"

The guy nodded. "It kinda freaked me out when I got the call from Jesse."

Spence half hollered to be heard over all the noise and through his mask. "Where's this Jesse?"

"He's back at camp sleeping by now. He was up driving for over thirty-six hours and needed a break."

With his pen, Spence touched a well-wrapped bundle lying amid the broken plastic. He was about to unwrap it but stopped. The hand radio crackled that the fire had shifted and embers had caught, creating a situation where the heavy equipment was needed elsewhere. The team prepared to disperse, leaving Spence and a team leader in a county pickup truck to manage the site.

"You say someone shot at the crew?" Spence asked as he stood up.

"At first I thought one of these guys accidentally misfired one of the guns they'd found."

"*Guns*...plural?"

"Oh yeah, there're at least two handguns...and well, we thought maybe one didn't have the safety on, and *boom*." The guy looked around nervously. "Glad you showed up with sirens and lights."

Spence frowned. "You mean someone actually fired on you?"

"Well, I can't be sure but there was a car. Came up on us here slow like, coulda been an old four-door coupe, late seventies, light, maybe blue. I coulda swore there was an arm out pointing something at us and a flash out of the corner of my eye. I thought maybe it was another disoriented fire evacuee. This truck was here, look for yourself."

They stepped over to get a look at the back window. The truck had a bed rack for carrying loads. There was a shiny groove in one flat black piece of its metal frame and a fresh chip and small crack in the rear windshield glass.

"Looks like the frame deflected the shot," Spence observed. "Where were you parked?"

The guy showed him, and Spence lined up the road with that position.

"When the crew realized there had been a discharge, everyone stopped and one of the guys saw a weapon in one of the damaged plastic buckets."

Spence looked over the rest of the items and then saw the weapon, maybe a Glock with some serious damage, and a parcel. The parcel appeared to be heavy and large, compressed from being inside the tub and packed tightly against the other items. There was some kind of vest and maybe a glove, both caked with dirt.

"Bullet could be anywhere…" Spence muttered, more to himself than to his companion.

"Yeah, that's what I said." The guy looked relieved that everything was now in the hands of the authorities.

The man standing with Spence grew curious and he bent down to get a better look at the contents of the bucket at their feet. Spence's knee ached as he knelt, and he shifted his weight to one leg to ease his discomfort.

It was indeed a Glock and Spence carefully extracted and examined the damaged weapon. He knew from that and the bulletproof vest that this was serious business they had stumbled into. He'd make sure of his accurate documentation from this point on. He noted that the Glock was loaded and the safety was missing. It was also jammed and he couldn't unload the gun. He set it down carefully, aimed away from anyone, and considered how best to secure it for transport. Spence continued to open the bundle. He unfolded the edges carefully—it was layered and he didn't want anything, like drugs, to blow away.

"Officer, we have to move," the hard hat said in an urgent tone. "The rig that unearthed this is over there."

Spence nodded. He gently placed the Glock in his metal evidence case. He used a zip tie to fix the trigger and made sure to carry the case with care. The vest and the one glove he tucked next to the wrapped bundle and rolled it all up in a tarp, then tucked it tight to his arm. He followed the crewman over to the group that stood by the 210 crawler. They had picked up more debris from the crushed plastic buckets they'd unearthed, and handed the parts to Spence.

Spence used his cell phone to make a 360-degree video of the location and made sure he filmed where the tub with the gun had been buried. He got everyone's contact information, then they all moved quickly to leave. Spence and the crew leader were the last ones standing there and he looked around to mark any landmarks that the fire would not destroy.

As Spence turned to leave, something glittery caught his eye. He set down the case and evidence tarp and crouched to have a closer look. It was a piece of jewelry, filthy and dirt-caked, partially wrapped in another small bundle. Dirt or not, there was no mistaking the sparkle of a diamond.

Spence opened his kit and retrieved a pair of good tweezers and an evidence bag and picked up the piece. He dropped the diamond into the bag and looked at it through the plastic. It was damaged but it was of high quality. He thought of the well-wrapped bundle and got a queasy feeling in the pit of his stomach. The bundles had to contain something other than drugs and he knew he might have stumbled into a different situation altogether.

Spence rolled another flap of the bundle over and more jewelry was revealed—a lot of it—and there were more folds. The crewman whistled. This was an impressive haul and Spence was in a quandary. This needed to be carefully inventoried and the area searched more thoroughly and secured. But the fire was bearing down on them. Someone cursed the wind as ash and embers landed on him as he worked. Spence sat back on his heels and heard someone's phone chirp.

Spence and the guy walked to the rear of Spence's cruiser and he popped the trunk.

Looking around nervously, the guy asked. "You gonna call for backup?"

Spence didn't answer. He looked over the area as best he could. "Do you think you got all of it?" he asked.

The guy nodded but didn't look confident. "I guess so. We didn't dig for anything, they unearthed it and it was scattered close to the buckets. They said they grabbed what they could see if that's what you mean. Jesse and his partner were kinda freaked out finding jewelry and guns. And they were wicked tired."

"Are you good to give me a hand collecting this stuff? I need to look around and see if there's anything else." Spence opened his evidence case and removed a camera and some gloves and hurried to complete his examination of the area. The guy mumbled an answer and Spence thanked him for whatever he could do.

As he was finishing up and loading his trunk, Spence looked to his left at a few vehicles that had slipped in, heading in the opposite direction of where his patrol car was pointed. He noticed a couple of ranchers trying to get to livestock, and a street truck with a rusted scrape down the driver's side and no handle on the door.

The passenger of a light-blue car caught Spence's attention for some reason, staring like many do when a cop's lights are flashing—lookie-loos that slowed to look at an accident or some unlucky bastard getting a ticket. The car window was rolled up and the passenger appeared to be young, not stocky, and he had a bandana or some kind of cloth over his nose and mouth. The car hesitated, then someone directly behind it touched the horn and the driver moved along with the other vehicles. The traffic was confusing and it was hard to see what was happening ahead. Some roads were open, others closed, creating bottlenecks everywhere.

Spence had a brief line of sight on the passenger despite the smoke and debris raining down around them. He dismissed his uncomfortable feeling, though unconsciously made a note of him and the car's blue color and make. Then he closed the trunk, hopped into the patrol car, and sped past emergency vehicles that a manager was redirecting. With his lights flashing eerily in the smoke, Spence stepped on the gas as his radio crackled. He pulled out his cell phone and called Hy Royston. Hy didn't answer but Spence left a message to call him.

A few miles later, on clearer road, Spence checked his rearview mirror. He noted that emergency crews had gotten those few folks to turn around and they were behind him. He had dismissed the blue car and figured it wasn't back there.

As he refocused on the road, Spence got a call from a fire crew. They'd had a scuffle with two men—an older man and a younger one—who threatened a bulldozer driver.

"Another one?" Spence said with a sigh. "Did every crook on the planet bury their shit out here?" Shaking his head, he headed in that direction.

When Spence arrived at the fire line, it was chaotic and he had to walk in. He hoped to see the men detained. Spence looked around and saw two or three guys at the back of a pickup, its tailgate down and someone sitting on it. He walked up and found them helping someone. They cleared away when they saw the sheriff was there, and slipped back to their jobs.

The smoke was still heavy and particles of ash blew around them. The injured man on the tailgate reached behind himself and handed Spence a face mask. He pointed at Spence's face with a hand gesture that indicated to put it on. The man had a broad face with deep, heavy brows, and looked like he had some Scandinavian heritage. And he was big. It didn't take much to guess what position he'd played on the football team in school. He had a face that had seen more than a few hard blocks. It sported scrapes, swelling, and the looks of a good shiner developing fast. He'd been stemming the bleeding from a busted lip and stopped to speak. The wind howled and the noise of trucks, voices, and heavy equipment filled the air.

Spence had to lean in to hear him.

He told Spence he would recognize the guy and tried to smile, which cracked open the lip to fresh color. "Argh," he said through gritted teeth and dabbed at his lip again.

Spence asked the usual questions and the man produced a wallet. Spence opened it up, thinking that the man wanted him to fill in the blanks from the ID. But when Spence looked at the photo, he saw that it wasn't the Scandinavian's. It was a guy that looked like a million other guys. He raised his eyebrows.

The man shrugged. "Bastard wasn't gonna be reasonable. I knew that look. And the kid was a weasel, half gone outta reach. I couldn't take him down without knowing if they were armed. I'm not getting stabbed by a couple of guys for nothing. He was a dirty fighter."

Spence leaned back and looked him in the eye, frowning. "He was? You think he did time?"

The man nodded. "Near as I can tell," he said. "I made for him but wanted that." He nodded at the wallet. "I hoped they were more into runnin' than getting caught fighting with me. That's how it felt, anyway." Then he paused. "You got any Advil in your rig? My head's killing me."

Spence patted him on the shoulder and turned to see a shadow walking out of the smoke carrying a medical box. The mask over the figure's face and the helmet made it hard to tell it was a woman, even as she got close.

She pulled her mask down to introduce herself as Tish and looked at her patient. Spence introduced himself as well, then stood back. She asked the man a few questions, gently pulled the cloth away from a wound on his scalp, and replaced it quickly.

"You should get stitches in that one," she said.

Through gritted teeth, the guy said, "Got staples in your truck?"

"Not that many," she replied.

"Shit."

"Gonna transport you and we'll get you back on the line as quickly as we can, OK?" Tish told him.

She closed the lid of the box, then took his elbow to help him stand. She was a solid woman, all muscle, and strong. Spence took her cue and took the man's other elbow.

The injured man turned and reminded him to keep his mask on. "You too," he said to Tish.

"Bossy thing, aren't ya?" she said good-naturedly as she complied.

They got him to her rig and her companion loaded him into the back. She turned to Spence and said, "My husband, Cajun, is out there, and he's become separated from his team. Keep an eye out and call if you hear anything, will ya?" Then she handed him her card and was gone.

Spence had rough descriptions of the two assailants and a wallet. When time permitted, he'd begin the process of identification. He headed back to his car through the choking smoke and secured the evidence.

Chapter 33

Noah Bainbridge had no idea what was going on back at the office. His cell phone had been taken from him when Dale picked him up at the small local airfield to board the private jet.

During the flight, Noah settled into a plush leather seat and accepted a drink from an extremely attractive attendant once they were at altitude. Noah enjoyed the view—the one out the window and the long, crossed legs of the attendant in a seat next to the galley. He looked out at the broken cloud cover moving below them and thought about those shapely, tanned legs. The short skirt climbed dangerously high when she was seated, and the crossed legs brought it just shy of the smooth slope of her inner thigh. Noah was a legs-and-ass man, features his wife possessed in equal measure. The attendant possessed those fine qualities in perfect proportions and her moves in the small galley were almost choreographed just for him.

Which, in fact, they were. Dale liked insurance and the attendant was insurance. She was well versed in skills that Dale required on occasion, and was generously compensated for being extremely good at reading and manipulating people. Noah was treated to a certain show, a test, and Dale liked tests. He liked to measure his people's strengths. And even better, their weaknesses.

The design of the cabin allowed for privacy from the galley

with a heavy curtain. They placed Noah in a leather rotating recliner seat with a spectacular view. The height of the attendant was a consideration; Dale wanted the length of her skirt scant inches beneath her crotch and at Noah's eye level when he was seated.

Noah was halfway through his drink when she handed him a menu. He chose a croissant sandwich for breakfast, as Dale knew he would, and she sashayed to the galley to make it. She bent at the waist and retrieved something from a heated drawer and that skirt and fine ass did their job. Noah couldn't take his eyes off her. She moved like a dancer, nothing awkward about her. She did yoga and danced professionally, among other things, and she deserved what she was paid.

The croissant was already made and waiting but Dale had instructed her to go through the motions, to not make it too obvious. In fact, he said, "Make it look like you're not used to the role you're playing. Let his imagination work some."

The attendant returned to Noah to set up his tray. He acted like the view out the window had consumed him. The tray slid out, unfolded, and was secured by a small switch—a clever design accomplished with a little remote that she held in her hand. Noah raised his hands and enjoyed the technology. She noticed something the tray now conveniently covered, smiled, and returned to the galley. A muted pop sounded as she opened a bottle of expensive champagne.

With her back to Noah, the attendant finished preparing the tray with its real silverware and cloth napkin, a mimosa in a fine glass, and fresh fruit on the side. She put the prepared croissant sandwich on a warmed plate.

He turned away again and looked out the window so she wouldn't see he'd been staring. He looked up at her with a pleased and surprised look and she demurely asked if there was anything else he needed. He laughed nervously and said no thank you.

After the flight, they made their way to Tiny Belamy's estate in Dale's big truck. They passed through an enormous entry gate and Noah noticed a huge caretaker's home off to the right. He asked Dale how many square feet and Dale said thirty-two hundred. But there was a two-thousand-square-foot guest house as well, up by the main house.

The driveway meandered around the left side of the manicured hill and then up to a large parking area. The Tuscan-style estate was perfect. Enormous iron lanterns decorated either side of the biggest entry doors Noah had ever seen. It was interesting to see life at this altitude. He'd been a middle-class guy all his life. Nothing so rarified as this opulence had ever graced his imagination except on television and in magazines. It was perfectly manicured and diligently maintained. He had admired this kind of thing but could never quite appreciate the attainment of it.

What his pedestrian mind calculated was upkeep. What would it cost to do the roof, fix the plumbing, and maintain the insurance? And what about the taxes? His mind realized being truly happy in a place like this required a background, years of family training, and preparation for enormous wealth and responsibility. He pictured his wife and children adapting to this level of opulence and consumption, being raised and trained into an empire, not satisfied with upper-end suburban expectations. He succumbed to an intense desire to be the provider of that path for them.

Such was the lure of power. It was the management of this asset that Dale was calculating. He would position this dull public servant in the right place to be of use. He and Tiny knew how to groom a man congenitally lacking the acumen to understand how to accumulate real political power. They would be the architects of the power he would wield, then help him wield it.

A man opened the door, nicely dressed and wearing a tan jacket. Dale introduced him as Maxie, and as they entered the massive home, Dale spoke to Maxie as a familiar, an equal. Dale looked at Maxie as they made their way into a magnificently appointed foyer. He was an ominous, unreadable, brick of a man with unemotional eyes and a formal demeanor. There was something about him that made Noah wary—he had an edge that years of work in courtrooms had taught Noah to respect.

To the right was a large dining room with a vaulted ceiling, Tuscan-grape crown molding, and a long table that could easily seat sixteen. To the left was an octagonal office suite lined with dark-wood bookshelves and a huge desk in the center of the room. Framed by enormous, tall doors, the ornate crown-molded, vaulted ceiling finished the room exquisitely. Soft lighting provided a warm glow and Noah edged closer to fully appreciate it. In his heart of hearts that was his office in his mansion…someday.

He turned away and trotted to catch up to Dale, who had looked over his shoulder at Noah with a measured glance. Noah made a small, unseen gesture with his hands that conveyed he could not help it.

They turned right and flowed past the living room with its impressive wall of windows that looked out over an immaculate garden with a full-sized infinity pool beyond. The passageway led to a chef's kitchen, where Maxie and his beige jacket looked perfectly suited. Noah followed Dale to the left, where a huge, round table filled a large window seat area along with an octagonal bench seat and six chairs around the open end of the table. An expanse of stamped concrete went to the pool. Off to the right was a fifty-foot-long terrazzo with enormous urns at each pillar and a long grouping of the kind of chaise lounge furniture one sees at the high-end mega resorts of the rich and famous. Noah thought of his wife and how she would die to see this place. It was better than all her magazines, for sure.

Waiting for them was perhaps one of the largest men Noah had ever seen. Dale took a chair easily. Noah took the one next to him, seemingly a mile across that broad, inlaid table from the big man. He was then formally introduced to Mr. Tiny Bellamy by Maxie, who also took his place at the table.

Noah realized then just where he was and that this "fundraiser," as Dale had called it, was not about meeting a group of donors. It was about meeting one donor—and a rather nefarious one at that. Noah covered his unease and was startled when an espresso-bearing white coat appeared at his shoulder. Noah hadn't heard the machine and looked up to nod his appreciation.

Maxie, a statue of unreadability, moved his hand dismissively and the silent servant took a few steps back, bowed, and left. Noah turned back, tasted the espresso, which was authentic, and waited for this meeting to begin.

Maxie was deferential to the wheelchair-bound Tiny. Noah noted that it had to have been a custom chair to haul the man's girth about. While Tiny's disability was not explained to Noah, he guessed that whatever it was had rendered him unable to effectively communicate. Tiny had a pinched and shadowy look around his eyes and mouth and tiny beads of sweat gathered at his temples, yet he seemed to follow the conversation.

At particular points during the meeting, Noah noticed who Tiny looked at. Tiny was aware enough, trapped in his useless body, but it was evident that the reins of power had shifted to a blended combination of Maxie and Dale. Or Dale and Maxie. It was an even match. Noah couldn't decide who was more cunning, treacherous, and supremely manipulating. The way those two worked in concert together proved an impenetrable wall to Noah. Whatever he thought his role was on the way to the meeting, he felt realigned the second he got there, and completely in tow by the end.

Noah had wanted to be an insider when he boarded the jet. He acted the part, then he thought he *was* an insider. In the presence of these men, even the crippled one, he could feel just how far down the food chain he was and he would do anything to climb higher.

A phrase of his father's crept into his mind. "To dine with the devil, you need a long spoon." He hoped he had one.

Chapter 34

Disoriented and cut off from his team, Cajun crawled out from a wedge in the rocks. Upright but unsteady, he stood with his back to the sucking wind, ash, smoke, and embers that swirled mercilessly around him. He squinted to see where he was, looked for anyone else, and thought of Tish. He hoped she hadn't been caught like so many had, and prayed she was safe. He smelled burnt hair and skin, and thought it was his until he almost fell over the body of a dead animal. Other creatures fled past him, steaming from the heat. He heard them struggling to breathe as they ran in a panic, and smelled their singed hair mixed with the smell of the melted rubber soles of his thick boots.

Cajun tripped again and went onto a knee to catch himself. He had lost his Pulaski, a favorite tool of many a firefighter, and his helmet had been whipped away. He had trouble hearing and he wanted to pop his ears. The wind was deafening and it seemed that he couldn't get enough air into his lungs. He needed to shield his airway but he had nothing.

He put his hand up and felt the sting of embers as he tried to peer into the bad air. He blinked repeatedly through the maelstrom as a figure emerged from the wind-whipped, burning trees near a group of rocks. Cajun wasn't sure what he was seeing. It was similar in color to the stone. As it drew closer, its body was long and low, its beige fur unrecognizable and blackened with debris and burn marks. It stopped in midstride. It had the look of the hunted, not the hunter, and froze, looking at Cajun.

Cajun gulped as he knelt on the ground, level with the big cat, and felt his heart stop. In the howling firestorm that was bearing down on them, time stood still. Cajun loathed this slow-motion time whenever he was caught in it—it meant that something really bad was happening and he was in it. It was either happening to him, or he was watching events unfold, usually painful ones, and was powerless to stop it. He wished his Pulaski was close, and he knew from training and experience that if he looked away from those eyes to find a weapon and grab it, the big cat would close the short distance and be on him.

The cat crouched and postured, then a crash behind him caused him to launch past Cajun and run away from the fire.

Cajun sucked in some ash and could hear the fire making its run. He coughed and spun around, looking for a way out or through it. Then something on four legs trotted painfully toward him. The ground smoke settled as the wind turned, and as if the devil had decided he deserved a breath of fresh air, there was a clear moment. A tease, perhaps…some measure to give him hope that he would find his way out and back to Tish and their modest farm.

The smoke cleared briefly around the animal and it stopped and breathed deeply, then coughed. Cajun didn't move. It was a horse, filthy, singed, and scraped up. Blood from punctures and burns had swum together on his frame and mixed with ash. Much of his mane was gone.

The coughing subsided a little and the horse walked up to him. The animal didn't waste time. He used his singed nose to push Cajun.

Cajun fell over and his hand landed on the Pulaski behind him. Surprised that it had been there the whole time and he couldn't see it, he grabbed it and used it to stand. He got to his feet and leaned on the axe. The horse lifted his head and looked into Cajun's bloodshot eyes. The story, as Cajun would tell it for years to come, was that this horse spoke to him. He swore it. He said the horse told him they both had someone they loved and that it was time to go find them. Cajun swore he thought he would take the horse out of danger, but it was the horse that understood the way to go.

The horse turned painfully and started to move away. Cajun still leaned on his Pulaski, feet set into the ground as if rooted until a blast of superheated air and burning debris hit him so hard it blew him forward to follow the animal. Cajun knew it was the devil himself trying to get him but that the hand of God pushed him to follow the horse. A reddish horse. A devil horse.

The horse stopped and slightly turned his head for a split second. The effort stretched the purple-white blisters on his neck, which Cajun could see hurt like hell. The horse willed the man to get on with it and follow close as the fire surrounded them. Cajun would have never seen the narrow track and he grabbed what was left of the horse's tail. The burning he felt on his back and head was unbearable and the wind sucked his screams away.

"Not like this, God..." he prayed. Then he tried to get back to calm. "Don't make mistakes..." he admonished himself.

The track seemed to go down and became rockier as they went. It was a huge effort for them to navigate with the blowtorch beating on them. There was a huge boulder and steep chasm on the left. The horse deftly negotiated the passage even though it was more ideal for slenderer creatures. The overhang on a rock perched above scraped the top of Cajun's singed scalp.

Cajun had the sensation that the pressure of the wind was curling around them. The effect brought the superheated air to them from behind. The horse kept going until the track turned sharply between the rocks and into a crevice. The path was completely invisible to Cajun but the horse pushed on.

The roar of the firestorm seemed to be above them now. It reminded Cajun of his days in the Air Force when the jets would whoosh overhead just feet above them, and it was just as loud. The ash and embers still fought to get them but there was little to burn, so none caught. They simply stuck, withered, and became more ash. The ash swirled around them and piled in the cracks and crevices of the rocks like snow.

Painful steps on chipped, blackened hooves brought the red horse to a spot where it tucked itself against a part of the rock in an alcove that offered some protection. Then the horse did the darnedest thing. It took Cajun's charred shirtsleeve ever so gently in its mouth and pulled him closer to the rock wall.

Cajun couldn't believe it. He and Tish didn't have horses. He had no experience with them. Neither of them had ever ridden nor wanted to, both being a little afraid of them. Cajun was pulled into the safety zone the horse created and shut his eyes tightly. His eyes swam with tears as he imagined Tish and their dogs, all burned and dead. He had no wind left in his emotional sails. He was done. Maybe it was the damage to his lungs and the lack of oxygen, but he was done. In that moment, he stopped believing in God. He was crushed and felt death closer than ever before.

The fire had made its own weather and the last vortices of the firenado passed over them. Cajun's ears finally popped, and the horse tucked in even closer to the rocks as the atmosphere tried to stabilize. Cajun braced himself against the rock face by wedging the Pulaski into a crack and holding on to the shaft. He felt everything being tugged at and pulled, and turned his head and squinted to see the horse's tail being sucked out behind it, then drawn straight up for a second.

As fast as the weather event caught them, it was done. The air temperature dropped precipitously and they were enveloped by cooler air—a cause for celebration if he'd had the energy.

Cajun stepped out first. The gelding stayed, his exhaustion as complete as Cajun's. After the roaring abated, the red horse gingerly backed out of the alcove. He stood behind Cajun, head low, eyes half shut, and seemed to doze.

Cajun lowered himself to the ground and worked to find a way to rest on something. The parts that hurt the least were pressed against the dirt. The red horse slept for a short time, then stepped up to a tuft of something behind a rock. The sound of him trying to drink roused Cajun and he stood up painfully. The water was ashy and oozed from a crack somewhere above to refill the shallow divot that collected it, and the horse licked at it sparingly. As Cajun listened to his efforts, he touched his own face. It seemed puffy and felt fat. He chose to ignore it.

They shared this place for a time until it became night. Both needed the rest for what was still to come. The sounds of their labored breathing and wheezing concerned Cajun. The horse was in a bad way but so was he. He tried to take inventory of his injuries and knew that he needed hospitalization. As for the horse, that was out of his lane, but it was easy to guess that they both needed doctoring—and quickly.

The exhausted firefighter found a way to kneel on some softer dirt and he attempted to fold his stiff fingers in prayer. He relented and put the painful digits in a prayer position and felt as he had when he was a tiny boy saying his prayers before bed. He thanked the Lord for sparing his life and prayed for the strength to go on. He prayed that Tish was safe and when he prayed for his crew, he broke down in tears. It was as if the Lord had told him they were now safe with Him. He hoped the Lord had a greater plan for him because he didn't know why he was alive.

He didn't hear the horse come up behind him until the wheezing breath found his ears. The horse turned his head toward the entrance and made a painful, partial turn. Cajun tried to stand but couldn't. As a big man, he was used to feeling heavy, but this heaviness was alien to him. He had been a strong guy all his life and now he felt as weak as a kitten.

"I can't, boy. I'm sorry," he said to the horse.

The red horse returned to Cajun and took his sleeve with his teeth. The horse held his shirt and the weakened fibers threatened to tear right there, but the horse held it in a delicate balance. Then he let go and did a painful turn in the same direction. Cajun realized there was a purpose to his actions.

Through blistered lips, cracking and oozing with every syllable, Cajun croaked through a straight mouth, as if he was a ventriloquist's dummy, "I can't."

This horse had a reason and started away again, then turned once more. This time, the pain caused him to pin his ears and the turn back was a series of halted, small steps. He pulled on Cajun's arm until the Pulaski began to fall. Cajun felt it going and managed to catch it with his right hand, stepped around it, and moved toward the red horse. He swore there was a sigh of relief from the horse as he turned again and started to lead Cajun out of there.

The horse moved slowly, as did Cajun. Cajun became more aware of his injuries as they moved away from an area that was still smoldering to a rocky, boulder-strewn slope. Several times the horse stopped, waiting for Cajun. Cajun would come up behind him and touch his rump, and the horse would continue on. The lung damage had affected them both and it meant exertion that caused blinding dizziness that Cajun had read plenty about, but had never experienced firsthand.

The slope was gentle with turn-backs, and soon they were deep in the rocks. The superheated air had warmed them and they radiated heat on burnt skin. It was torture but the red horse continued to lead him. There was a crack in the rock, narrow but passable, and some greenery could be seen peeking out from under the ash that lay upon it like snowdrifts. The air felt a tiny bit better and a degree or two cooler. Just the promise of it pulled a thread of energy from within Cajun.

As the horse took him to some unknown destination, he realized that his eyelids were swelling shut. If he didn't get help soon, he'd be blind. He stopped when they were slits and he could barely see.

"Hey..." he barked as loud as his voice and lips would let him. He heard the horse stop. He put his hands out in front of him and tried to take a few steps, then waited.

To his surprise, he heard the horse approach. He felt him come around his left side and when he thought the rump was next to him, he found the singed strands of the animal's tail and grabbed it. The horse turned, seeming to know that the way needed to be less rocky for his human friend. For Cajun, the twists and turns were a mystery but he was able to shuffle his feet and navigate the barriers with the horse's guidance. He fell in a few places and went down, and the horse stopped. Cajun clambered to his feet and did his best because this animal was doing his. He remembered what Tish had told him once. She said nothing added more strength than dire necessity.

They came upon a bumpy patch in their way of going. Rocks were piled loosely and solid footing was impossible. Cajun went down and lost his grip on the horse's tail. The horse struggled to get himself over the rocks, let alone the blinded man. Cajun's sense of everything was going black. Even the excruciating pain seemed to ball into one big blur.

Cajun heard the horse scramble and slide, fall, and perhaps right itself, he wasn't sure. He heard dirt and debris roll until it stopped. With a leg, he felt the slope of the ground and tried to slide down it on his backside. But it hurt and he ended up rolling to the bottom of a four-foot berm onto a fire road, where he passed out.

Chapter 35

CJ awoke in a special care unit, unaware of how he had gotten there. He was on oxygen and felt terrible. He held his hands and arms up as best he could and saw he was on a drip for fluids. There were loose, pad-like bandages on unseen wounds and the skin beneath them was numb. CJ lowered his arms and assessed himself. He felt like he was wrapped up in a cocoon and he guessed he was heavily medicated for pain. Not good, he guessed. He heard voices and noises alien to the quiet of the high desert and the call of the cattle.

Rio...where's Rio... At the thought, he struggled to sit up and the effort swirled him into an abyss.

When he woke up again, it was dark, or the lights were turned way down. He wanted to talk to someone. Anyone. *Wyker...where's Wyker?* He tried to remember whether he had told someone to reach him. He didn't have any contact information, no numbers for anyone to find him, not even his parole officer. Would they think he violated? His mind swam and it made his head hurt. He tried to breathe in a way that calmed his heart and head.

A nurse came in and injected something into his IV. CJ felt a wave of calm and his pain lifted off of him like a breeze lifts a tablecloth from a picnic table on a sunny day. The cloth rose and the sun shone through it, and it parachuted up into the blue sky before it gently billowed back to earth, where CJ lay in a grassy field and watched its descent, drifting one way and then another, then above him and over him.

He wanted to know what was happening. He felt like he had an elephant on his chest. Even with the oxygen, he found breathing harder than he had ever experienced.

A presence in the room told him he was not alone and he waved the hand that was not attached to the IV. It felt heavier than his normal arm. Out of his peripheral vision, he could see movement to his right. He heard the rustle of plastic and a can, the flush of a toilet through an open door, water running in the sink, and something on wheels.

"Ah, you're awake," came a woman's melodic voice. She had a slight Hispanic accent. "I'll tell the physician. And I thought there was someone outside waiting to see you."

Her face was round and smooth with perfect skin, and when she got into a range he could focus on, CJ honestly believed it was the best face he had ever seen. The ceiling tiles beyond her visage had tiny perforations that expressed solidity that was wrong in every way. Her face blurred and those tiny holes became sharp and clear.

With his free hand, CJ pointed to the IV and the door.

The nurse laughed. "If that means you want to go, well, honey, that's not gonna happen for a few days at least."

His hand returned to the light, institutional blanket in a show of resignation and disappointment but it did not stay there long. He wanted someone to tell him what was happening and he tried to get the nurse's attention again.

He did his best to point to where he felt the door was, and he heard her rubber-soled steps stop. He pointed toward the door and made a come-hither sign with his hand, uncoordinated, jerky, and desperate.

"You want whoever's out there to come in?"

Slowly, with stiff fingers, he made the OK sign and his hand and forearm dropped again to the bed, exhausted from the effort.

"OK. Let me call the doc and see if he's still out there."

CJ lay there hearing the muted whispers and hospital sounds, and he wondered if he would drift off before anyone arrived.

In his dream, Wyker was coming. He wanted it to be Wyker. Wyker would find Rio. A tear ran down the side of CJ's face, coming unbidden from his heart. He reached up and wiped at it but it wouldn't move. It was like a glass tear stuck to his skin, or something in one of those weird paintings on fabric—big eyes and a giant, glistening tear. Where was Wyker? Where was Rio? He called to them but no sound came out. The effort of hoping and trying to communicate had brought forth a well of fatigue.

When he awoke, the doctor was there with a couple of other people, possibly in training. He thoroughly explained CJ's condition and treatment and it was more positive than CJ felt. He heard the whir of the hospital HVAC and the sounds of a functioning building—all the moving parts—and his mind wandered off into the halls, picturing the different people there in various stages of either getting what was wrong fixed or finding out that what was wrong couldn't be fixed. He wondered which of those he was. It frightened him for a second until he thought of Rio.

He felt like hours had passed and his frustration arced in waves of unreasonable hypotheses. He swirled in a drug-induced, oxygenated haze until he convinced himself that no one was coming and he'd better get up and go.

CJ's respiratory distress eased, though his throat was raw and he spoke little. He was motivated to get well as quickly as possible. The thermal injury to his upper airway would be denied by his will to find Rio. He even thought he heard Rio calling out to him. Then he shut his eyes against the memory of Rio's screams when he'd gone down. CJ sobbed and the coughing gripped him. He heard an alarm going off and footsteps, and then he heard nothing.

CJ's burns were not extensive—mostly first-degree, a small second-degree, and one on his arm that was almost a third-degree. Most of his external injuries were from escaping the canyon, and if he had been near lightning, it hadn't struck him directly. He had a persistent cough and shortness of breath associated with smoke inhalation. He was fortunate, and considering the many serious injuries the hospital was treating, his seemed minor to him. He began to wean away from the pain medications and he welcomed the lifting mental fog.

His whole life, CJ had stayed away from drugs, though he had associated with addicts in ventures he never should have. He always convinced himself that they had a handle on their shit. And if they got caught, well, they knew what they were doing. CJ found himself thinking more deeply and he was able to stand back from the events of his youth. He had been blinded by self-inflicted guilt, what he thought held a larger purpose. CJ could now see clearly in the moment, finding himself. He thought things through and set feelings aside. He had come to the truth about what mattered.

He endured his treatments stoically. The pattern of hospitalization made him concentrate on recovery until he could focus on Rio. There would be no getting used to it for him and he would not...*could not*...believe he had lost Rio.

Wyker phoned in and tried to be encouraging. He told CJ that people were out looking and that no one had given up yet. He believed CJ when he told him that Rio was alive.

"I can feel him. He's out there and he wants to be found. I *know* it. As soon as I'm free of this place, I'm going back out there to find him," CJ rasped into the phone during one of their conversations.

Wyker ended the call and was weary. The destruction was so widespread and yet there were weird pockets of unblemished land and spared structures. Many animals that had survived the conflagration exhibited symptoms of post-traumatic stress, though others seemed to have taken the devastation in stride. Some folks were trying to do the same. His friend, Roxy, had told him people were walking around with tears flowing down their faces, and that grief cloaked them like a veil.

As soon as Wyker found out what had happened to CJ, he moved as quickly as possible in the din and chaos that prevailed. The fires were still burning, people were displaced, and animals were injured or dead in droves. Within a couple of days, Wyker tracked down the team that had transported CJ. It took some doing, but he even managed to find and leave a voicemail message for an EMT firefighter named Tish. Her cell service was as spotty as his but he learned what he could.

When Wyker finally got to the hospital, he didn't find CJ in a room. With a few well-placed questions, he found CJ in a clinic waiting area. He had pushed himself and the doctor was pleased with his progress, and commented that he had a terrific recovery rate.

The list of injuries CJ had sustained was long and thankfully, it was a quantity versus quality ratio. He had suffered burns to his back, face, legs, and hands. He had multiple cuts and contusions, some cracked ribs, a concussion, and his doctors were deciding on more rehabilitation for the damage to his lungs.

CJ stood near the window, looking out at the clouds. Upper-level winds had made "mare's tails" in the sky, and these were particularly nice ones. They began at an imaginary base and the wind lifted the cloudy wisps, gracefully separated them like the fine hairs of a tail, and they flowed away. A whole herd of mare's tails decorated the brilliant turquoise sky.

Wyker joined him at the large window and broke the silence first. "Hey."

CJ looked over at him, and in a hoarse voice, replied, "Hey." And after a moment added, "Found me at last, eh, mate? Where the hell have you been." It was more a statement than a question.

Wyker tried a smile. "Been kinda busy. How are you feeling?"

CJ shook his head. "They say I'm doing well. But I hate it here."

Wyker slid a chair over and cocked it at an angle to the window so he could rest an elbow on the sill. CJ didn't look at him. The burns on his neck made it hard to turn his head for prolonged periods, and resulted in a mix of tightness and pain.

"They say you might've been hit by lightning," Wyker said. "What do you remember?"

"Not much. I don't think I was struck but I was awfully bloody close to it. I dunno, I remember rocks falling and things on fire."

Wyker knew him well enough to know that talking was not what he liked to do, yet he seemed more open than usual.

"Anything on Rio yet?" CJ asked.

"I have exchanged messages with a woman named Tish, who rescued you. Do you remember her?"

CJ shrugged. "I was really messed up, and whoever that was had a mask on and gear. Hard to say who." He thought for a moment. "*She?* She was strong, like…man strong. I think they strapped me to a board and I broke free, then I remember something about food." His eyes were on the clouds again, deep in thought.

"Food?" Wyker said with a quirky smile and raised eyebrows.

Someone behind them asked for CJ Burke. It was his turn.

"Yeah. Is Tish Southern? Like, I seem to think Louisiana, food… Weird. She injected me. Yeah, she gave me something and kept saying that this food would find Rio." He laughed. "Must've been good drugs, 'cause I don't remember anything after that for, like, days."

To Wyker's surprise, CJ motioned for him to join him in his appointment. "Might as well know what all's wrong and right with me."

Wyker sat in a corner chair as the clinician explained that the particulate matter CJ had inhaled was lodged in his lungs, and that he would be experiencing a process where the body eliminated the intruding micron-sized particles for months. They did not know whether he would develop asthma-like symptoms, they felt it was not certain, and for that, he was grateful. They cautioned that he would be especially susceptible to viral infections and bronchitis-type influenzas. The doctor suggested CJ get a pneumonia vaccination and an annual flu shot. These were alien things to CJ. He usually got whatever the prison infirmary gave out and their budget did not allow for fancy extras. On his own, unincarcerated, annual anything meant health insurance, and he did not have that. He toughed out injuries and illnesses. That was his way in the world.

As grateful as CJ was, the clinician explained that the effects of the trauma could last longer. There could be underlying sadness, a depression that was not to be ignored. He suggested counseling and maybe physical therapy for a few months.

CJ looked at the prescription he was handed. It was Ibuprofen, recommended Aquaphor applied regularly to the tight skin to promote healing, and rest. CJ had few questions and said little. All he wanted was a pass from someone that he was free to go. And he basically got it.

The nurse impressed upon Wyker that CJ needed to eat to heal. Maybe have food handy, fruit of some kind—anything so he would have something. She said the body used a lot of calories when it was healing.

"Upstairs," she nodded upward, "many are on feeding tubes. Their burns are much more involved and severe, but my point is, people do not realize that the body is burning calories when it's healing itself. He must eat. And," she added, "make him drink water. I mean it. He's a pain in the ass about it but the water is really important."

Wyker agreed and repeated it back to her.

As they returned to the waiting area, Wyker stopped midstride as an idea struck. "Food... Did you hear her say Cajun?"

CJ hesitated. "Yeah…Southern food. I was whacked out...told ya."

"No, you weren't. Her husband's name is Cajun. He and his team…well, there's been a problem." Wyker did not want to go down that route about the burn-over of Cajun's team.

"Anyway, we can talk about that later, but she says he's looking for Rio."

Wyker smiled and pointed ahead to a waiting room. CJ watched someone lean forward to look around the person in the chair next to him. Long black hair fell over his shoulders and the tattoos over both cheekbones crowned to a smile. Harper Lee stood and fell into step with them. CJ noticed new tattoos on Harper's chiseled face as Harper stretched his hand out. Stiffly, CJ took it and they shook.

CJ looked at him, tilting his head slightly left and then right. He pointed to the new additions. "Those are new."

"Surprised you noticed," Harper said as he handed CJ a small paper bag and CJ peered inside.

"Biscuits from Auntie, and the kids made you a card."

CJ thanked him and asked after the cows on the Rez. Harper told him they had gotten lucky. Everything made it through. The fire had threatened the reservation and their lands but skirted the Dugout. "Those warring winds changed up and shifted it away from us."

"No shit?" CJ said. "If only I'd just stayed closer to home, Rio and I would be fine."

Wyker noticed CJ had used the word "home."

"Come on. No room for woulda, coulda, shouldas," Harper chided as they made their way along the linoleum corridor. "You were more than half a day's ride out and you had no way of knowing." He pressed the elevator button. "Deer, coyotes, bobcats, mountain lions, and bear fled and countless died. Animals out of their territories are acting in ways my people say they have never seen. Heard of a story up north a ways about adult deer getting killed by black bear and that just does not

THREE CORNER FIRE

happen. That's how compressed the feeding areas are…what's left of them."

CJ and Wyker listened as Harper told of a tribal council on the Colville Indian Reservation that had voted to close tribal lands in the burned areas to subsistence hunting to help conserve a base population of animals. "They hope the populations will rebuild in time, maybe two or three years…"

Wyker commented that it reminded him of the restrictions on fishery populations and Harper nodded in agreement.

Harper told CJ to look in the bottom of the bag. CJ fished around and found a small deer-hide pouch with a symbol drawn on the outside, buried under the biscuits. He held it in his hand as the elevator doors slid open and the occupants crowded out. He turned it over in his hand and looked at Harper, who nodded to him to open it.

Wyker took the paper bag from his bandaged hands. CJ carefully loosened the tie string and opened the pouch to find a carving of a horse. It was somewhat crude and beautifully perfect at the same time. He turned it over and it was a little bigger than an elongated golf ball, but well made from some kind of wood. CJ looked over at Harper.

"Uncle said that is your totem. He said to tell you do not let your grief cloud your way forward. He says Rio is not dead, he's with you."

CJ did not speak. They got on the elevator and rode down to the main floor of the hospital. Harper got out with them and Wyker asked him where he was off to.

"I have something I need to check out for the boss and then we'll see, maybe the Dugout. Maybe I go see the Three Bit." Harper then added, "Keep me posted?"

"OK. Send my regards to Hy," Wyker said.

"I will." Harper turned to CJ, took his hand, and modified the pressure of shaking it.

CJ reacted with a touch of resistance, followed by relief when Harper was careful not to hurt him.

"We will see you soon, I hope," Harper said.

CJ nodded, unable to find the words. He looked at the totem and held it up. "Please thank Uncle for me."

After Harper was out the door, CJ said, "Take me with you."

Wyker turned and looked at him.

"Seriously," CJ added for emphasis.

"I'm heading to the Three Bit. That's where you're going if you walk outta here."

CJ looked down at the carved horse in his hand, then squinted at the brightness on the other side of the glass window.

"Fine," he said and the automatic doors to the hospital slid open.

Wyker stood, rooted. "Don't you need to get your stuff?"

"Don't have any." CJ kept walking and held up the carving. "I have everything I need."

CJ tired easily, though he would not admit it, and the effort to get out of the hospital taxed him. Wyker found a local place to eat and needed some time to get their bearings. It was a diner, nothing fancy, and CJ could barely sit still. He wanted to drive into the evacuation zone and find out about Rio. He was antsy that they were wasting time. He didn't have much of an appetite and he used Wyker's cell phone to call the number Tish had given him, got her voicemail, and left a message.

"Ah, yeah, Tish, this is CJ, the bloke you found and...um...helped. I'm out of the hospital and want to know if you've heard anything about my horse, Rio. This is Will Wyker's cell and he can reach me. Day or night. OK? Thank you."

Wyker ordered a burger and fries and rotated the fries part of his plate closer to CJ and took his time eating. Eventually, CJ ate a few fries and Wyker ordered a chocolate milkshake in a to-go cup and had the waitress put it in front of CJ with a straw. CJ scowled through the top of his eyes and the waitress retreated.

"Good thing you're weak as a kitten," Wyker said, holding up the burger and taking a bite.

CJ shook his head and stared out the window. Fatigue carved deep creases around his eyes. Wyker paid the tab, waited for change, and left a kind tip. In the reflection in the mirror behind the counter, he saw CJ put the shake back on the table and surmised he'd had a sip or two.

Better'n nothing, he thought.

He got a box for the leftover fries, then decided that was too disgusting—fried food did not get better with age. He spotted some fruit and bought that instead.

They walked across the parking lot and talked beside the truck. CJ voted to go look for Rio, to quit wasting time. He was ardent in his argument and Wyker let him run. He let Tammy out to do her business in a vacant area next to the restaurant, and when she trotted back to the truck, he gave her some water. CJ paced, tried Tish again, and stopped with his back to Wyker as he opened the truck door and Tammy leaped in. She took up a spot in the middle and watched Wyker approach CJ.

Wyker did not crowd him. He stood next to him and they looked at nothing in particular as CJ struggled to find his words. His breathing sounded like he had crinkled paper balled up in his lungs. Wyker sensed he needed to talk and that the confines of the truck cab were too restricting after his stay at the hospital.

"Thank you," CJ finally stated after a long pause. "Thank you for Rio."

Wyker put his thumbs in the pocket corners of his blue jeans. He imagined that his father had often felt what he was feeling then—a revealing moment of whether to offer advice or not.

CJ proceeded haltingly and he explained what he had learned about things while he was there. "There" being the hospital, Wyker thought, and his takeaway, his synthesis of what CJ said, was that the time he had spent with Rio had reshaped him. He had found peace—peace in his heart and with his horse. Rio had taken his failed, broken parts and rearranged them to be better.

"I made better choices around him," CJ said.

Wyker understood. In a strange and wonderful way, Rio was CJ's first experience with real love and CJ knew in his heart that he would never again be the man he was before...because of Rio.

"So, what I'm trying to make sure you know..." CJ fell silent for a moment. "...is that I am grateful for everything you have done for us."

Wyker touched him gently on the shoulder and turned toward the truck.

CJ opened the door and the weight of it took him a second to adjust to. Then he got himself in, managed to close it, and got the seat belt on.

Wyker put the key in the ignition but before he turned it over, CJ said, "I *have* to find him."

Wyker stared out the window for second, then said, "I know."

Chapter 36

Kitzie would never forget finally getting back to the Three Bit. The ranch sign was gone, a lone post all that remained of it, smoldering forlornly as she drove the three of them and the dogs back to what they had once called home.

They didn't notice the shop at first. All that riveted their disbelief was the house, what was left, and what was still on fire. No engines had made it there, no firefighters. Kitzie parked well away from anything that might still burn, and they got out of the truck. The ash and smoke stung their eyes and clawed at their throats. Carson pulled a bandana across her nose and mouth, and Kitzie and Jorge put on their masks.

"I think the dogs should stay in the truck," Kitzie said and Jorge nodded numbly.

Carson turned full circle, taking in the damage and the miracles. The wind swirled around them and Kitzie walked to her daughter, hand outstretched with a mask. Carson pulled the edge of the bandana from the tip of her nose, stretched the elastic over her head, and adjusted the mask to fit her face.

"Thanks," she said, then pointed at the big barn and looked at her mother's anguished eyes, her own eyes wide. "Can you believe it? The barn looks fine."

Kitzie looked at it, shrugged, and shook her head as she rotated toward the destroyed home she had known and loved for so many years. She looked at it with almost no emotion at first, as if all the things inside of it had gone silent. The memory of each precious thing was a blur in the almost blinding smoke and whirling debris. "The dogs…" she whispered, and headed in that direction, calling for Wyatt and Lulu.

Jorge instinctively went to the hose by the big barn, uncoiled it, and turned it on. It trickled. He recalled that there was a generator in the shop and he dropped the hose and jogged around the corner of the barn down the avenue that ran alongside the big, covered arena. Toward the end, well away from the barn and Kitzie's house, the first thing he saw was the destroyed shed row. Its five bays held the burned and crusted shapes of the ATVs, the tractor, and the backhoe. It was then that he realized what he *didn't* see. Partially hidden by the stubborn remains of the far wall was what was left of the shop. It too was destroyed.

A horse's call turned his head and he saw that all the animals had been turned loose in the big arena, protected by the aluminum roof, steel beams, and girders, but speckled with ash. They huddled together, terrified and shaking. Then they moved off to a far corner when smoke invaded their space, then uneasily looked for a safe place somewhere in the center.

Carson appeared next to Jorge.

Jorge looked panicked. "I don't see him anywhere… Papi!" he yelled into the din of unearthly sounds, the wind taking his words away before they had gone far. He yelled and yelled and began to run around the smoldering shop, then down to their damaged cottage, behind the shed row, and to the other side of the big arena.

Carson watched as his pace slowed to a walk and he began to cough. She stepped over some debris on the ground and realized that something was wrong. Bits of wood, metal parts in odd shapes, empty oil cans, and other junk was scattered everywhere. It was impossible to not step on some jagged, unrecognizable piece of something. She stopped, confused, and looked down at her boot. The toe had bumped into a small, metal box, scorched and dented, but still sealed with a hasp.

She rolled it with her foot and could feel items inside it. Carson bent down to touch it. It was still warm. She untied her bandana and used it to open the box. A gust threatened the contents and she closed the lid, then peered inside when the wind subsided. There were documents inside, official-looking at a glance.

Carson rose as a stiff wind peppered her with ash and coals and her gaze fixed on the fried remains of the shop. The crisped hulls of a couple of vehicles protruded grotesquely from beneath the scorched, collapsed roof. She looked at the walls and noticed they had been blown out, and part of one wall leaned, blackened, against the far wall of the shed row.

A dreadful thought occurred to Carson as she got closer to the shop and felt the heat radiating from its shell. She peered in around the smoking mess, tongues of flames still consuming everything Luis held dear. A waft of smoke, acrid and harsh with a chemical smell, reached her and she brushed it away as if it had wings. And then she smelled it.

At first, she froze and held her breath, then she sniffed through her mask. The uncomfortable sweating underneath it bothered her and she pulled it down and took another unencumbered, quick sniff. Then she spun and staggered the forty feet to the metal pipe panel of the big arena. Carson pulled the mask back up over her nose and mouth, grabbed the top rail with both hands to steady herself, and clamped her eyes shut. A strangled cry grew in her throat. Her back arched and before she knew it, her hand was back on the mask, ripping it off her face and breaking the flimsy elastic band. She dry heaved violently against the railing. It only lasted a few seconds but it hurt with its spasm and she coughed. She clutched the top rail with her other hand and pulled herself up straight as the wind hit her again.

She didn't hear Jorge return, and when her blurry eyes tried to focus around her, the fuzzy image of the huddled horses was the first thing she tried to concentrate on. The drifting smoke hung in the arena like a thick cloud. Carson found herself wondering how breathing all of this smoke and particles was affecting them. The sounds of their coughing made it apparent that they were struggling too. And they had no masks. She pulled her bandana back over her face.

Carson shook her head, turned, and saw Jorge's back as he stared into the burning shop. She heard him scream for his father, then saw him double over. He sobbed and coughed, and became so distraught that he fell to his knees, then dropped to all fours. She was afraid to approach him and looked for Kitzie. It was hard to read emotions behind mask-covered faces. The whole smoke-filled scene was strangely warped and unreal— faceless beings forced into unearthly situations they had no preparation for.

Carson twisted her upper body and neck, and in the maelstrom of blowing ash, dust, and embers, saw Kitzie approaching, her arms wide, with Wyatt trotting beside her. She held her daughter tightly. Carson broke their embrace and faced her mother, only their reddened eyes speaking, and it was in that awful moment that all three of them knew where Luis was.

The relentless wind still pummeled everything. Carson stood next to her mother and felt Kitzie squeeze her hand.

Kitzie leaned closer and asked Carson to make sure the horses had fresh water.

"Go check them more closely. See if they are banged-up. I saw ash in the other trough, a whole bunch of it. They may have to breathe it for a while. Let's be sure they don't have to drink it as well."

The noise of burning wood, wind, and other unidentifiable sounds tore at her words but Carson turned and went through the pipe panel and approached the skittish horses. With her daughter dispatched, Kitzie turned her attention to Jorge. His dogs were still safe in the truck and she moved toward him. As she got close, she bent down and found herself on her knees next to the boy. His face was in his hands, elbows resting on the ground, and his body shuddered with sobs.

Kitzie's hand hovered over his back. His spasms of grief raised it almost to her palm several times. She hesitated and waited for a break before placing her hand gently on his left shoulder. She soothed him with a soft stroke before she used her left hand to raise him up. He let her lift him to his feet and gently guide him back to the arena. They bowed their heads to avert the assault of ash and debris that blew and fought for air space in the alley between the burning structures and the arena. There was a broader space, a defensive perimeter around the big barn, and Kitzie wondered if that would be enough to completely save it. She watched embers and coals run everywhere and doubt crossed her mind.

She put Jorge in the truck with the dogs and heard something behind her. It was an engine—a big one. Through the smoke, it was hard to make out but whatever it was, it glowed red like everything else. Then she saw flashing lights.

The fire engine passed her and pulled up to the house, and

what looked like a fairly fresh crew leaped out and deployed. A smaller truck and an EMT were fast behind it and in a fourth vehicle, a familiar face rode shotgun with a battalion chief. It was Lyle Martin. He had the SUV door open before the driver had come to a complete stop and he rushed to Kitzie's side.

Kitzie was covered in soot, had ash in her hair, and her shoulders dropped as he approached. Lyle took her into his arms and looked over the top of her head at her destroyed house. He scanned left and saw that the barn looked mostly untouched. He was taken aback that one of the oldest original wooden structures on the Three Bit had not burned.

The crews had water and Jorge had gathered himself enough to get to the business of operating the generator and making the well water part of the battle. It would be hours before most of the fires were down to a smolder, and then the real toll would be evaluated. Jorge stayed away from his father's shop, his pyre, and the battalion chief notified the coroner of the fatality. It all became official quickly and a system took hold as control was carved out of chaos.

The battalion chief talked to Kitzie and kept her informed. "I'm afraid your house is a total loss. And there are some other structures I will have to red tag. Do you have a place to stay? Do you need the Red Cross?"

Kitzie had the big living quarters trailer in the arena. It had been effectively blocked from much of the fire damage because it was parked along the metal wall at the end of the enormous structure. Smoke and blowing ash were the only things that came near it. It had a gas-powered generator so if everything worked, it would be more than adequate. She told him there was a room in the barn as well, provided the barn stayed safe.

"I've got that," he told her.

Then she asked about the cottage on the far side of the row, and whether they had seen Lulu. "There's another small stable down there and a two-room cottage where Luis and his son stayed." Kitzie hadn't gotten down that far and wondered about their condition.

The chief told her that the cottage had sustained some singes along the outside of one wall, and they were conducting an assessment about livability there. A helmeted and suited member of his team approached and said the structure was sound. *At least Jorge will have a roof over his head,* thought Kitzie.

The whole thing was surreal. The chief and Lyle left forty minutes later to go to the next place that needed them. The big engine left about a half-hour after that, leaving Kitzie, Carson, and Jorge to stand amidst the drifting haze of the Three Bit.

Chapter 37

Shiloh maneuvered the motorhome into a long line of cars. Some were fleeing the fire and others were lined up in the opposite direction to get back into the evacuation areas, fire and clean-up crews interspersed around them, and it was controlled chaos. A heavy layer of smoke cloaked the top of a ravine off in the distance.

She'd had second thoughts about coming through this way and wondered why. Was she feeling a touch of remorse about her dad? Was she tempting fate that she would be recognized? She was taking good care of her new home, and it was hers...yet the tags would expire at some point, and then what?

Her paranoia chipped away at her confidence. There were times when Shiloh had nightmares—ones she forced herself to awaken from and got up so she could be anywhere else. This was like one of them. She was just passing through and would get out of the area quickly, but she hadn't planned on the fire or its aftermath. There were detours and delays and she crossed her fingers that she would be able to skirt around Martin.

Usually, news dried up when the drama of an emergency passed, but Shiloh found that there was still lots of stuff going on. She drove by people whose ashen expressions were as barren as the destroyed homes they stood in front of. Media trucks raced from one location to another, their satellite dishes ready to pop up like spring daisies. Star reporters, masks in place, huddled with news crews as they chose vantage points where the worst of the devastation made for compelling shots. Fire brought huge, life-altering changes to everyone affected by it. So did other things.

The traffic inched forward. Shiloh could feel it in the air—the heavy, smoky haze. Her mind wandered in the stop and go.

She thought of the circumstances she had just gone through and how it was all part of the past. She had put the pieces of her life together after finding the manila envelope, and had spent hours studying the materials it contained. Shiloh thought about her recent surgery and recovery. The hospital would have allowed her to park the rig in the parking lot for her treatment follow-ups but she chose not to do that. There was no reason someone should have her license plates on file anywhere. She didn't know if someone might be looking for her and didn't want to find out.

Shiloh had plenty of time to absorb certain realities. She had mixed emotions about Lawrence Michael Stiles. How had it all been worked out? Why had he done what he had done? After all the time that had passed, why was it important? Did he have some plan to help her? Get to know her? Make up for abandoning her? What would that change? And how should she feel about it all? She had no foundation on which to build even a rudimentary understanding. She was a creature of self-preservation, of survival.

Shiloh saw a woman sitting by the destroyed remains of a life, her face in her hands, sobbing. A tall man with graying hair stood, his back to the traffic, hands at his sides. The feeling she got was that he was in shock, unable to take it all in at once.

Seeing the man sent Shiloh's thoughts into a spiral. Time ebbed and merged and her mind drifted to the past. The *plop-*

plop of dripping water took on a cadence, like the ticking of a clock, as the drops splashed on her hands. She was wet from a shower and she was shaking. But she wasn't cold. Shiloh was trying to adjust to the fact that she had been brutally attacked. She sat on the edge of her bed, at her old place, wrapped in a towel, her wet hair draped over her shoulders. She couldn't remember how long she sat there. But something had changed and she wanted a name for it. She wanted an easily identifiable label for how it felt. What had happened to her was a violation and she had been afraid, but there was a layer beneath that, and she struggled to define it.

A car horn startled Shiloh out of her reverie and her thoughts came full circle back to the present. The image of that man—the silhouette of him standing there in a state of shock—brought an epiphany. He was alive. He had his life, yet he was missing things that he felt defined who he was. He'd once had a home with memories and treasured things in it, and now it was gone. Shiloh hadn't lost physical things, like the possessions the man grieved over, now in ashes and smoldering. But what was inside of her did the same thing in a way…

And then it came back to her. She sat a little straighter in her seat as she drove. It was spiritual theft. The thing inside her that made her who she felt herself to be had been damaged. Shiloh had lost something indefinable…and only just now did she realize that this was what was missing.

Had she come this way for a reason? Maybe she couldn't have sanity without familiarity. She needed to discover more than what she thought herself to be. She had to grow into this new self, inhabit her new spirit. Her body was recovering. Now she needed a goal for her inner self.

Shiloh shifted her thoughts to the money. She mulled over

her reaction to it. Finding the money, for someone not used to having a lot of it, was wonderful and terrifying. She wasn't prepared nor was she ever taught how to manage that kind of money should she ever have it. If she'd had an orthodox upbringing with stability, a home, and regular habits that education brought, she might have had a steady address, bank accounts, and maybe a stable life. That, however, was not the case and now Shiloh had a lot of cash that she hadn't earned. Just walking into a bank with it meant taxes, records, obligations, and she had no one to advise her. Thinking about the IRS gave her the shakes. She hadn't paid any taxes or filed in years, so she was sure she was in trouble there. It became a hamster wheel in her head. Shiloh knew she needed to stash money and exist under the radar.

She was in the mood for a good hamburger, and as traffic picked up, she looked for a place to get one that had space for her to park. What she came across was a small roadside diner—the kind most travelers avoided but where those in-the-know flocked regularly. They knew things that one wouldn't find in a travel guide—that this was a place that minded its own business, a place that believed in the Constitution, and one that was part of a network that supported freedom of rights.

Lonson and Bunny Rhodes knew it, and when Shiloh walked in, knew that she did not. It was the kind of place that had a weird feel to it. Shiloh felt she had made a mistake, and turned to leave. But then warm, motherly Bunny called out to her.

"Hi, honey, we're over here!" Bunny said in a slight Southern accent as she waved.

Shiloh turned to look behind her, to see who this woman was speaking to, but there was no one there. She then looked back and the woman indicated she was speaking to her. Her rosy-cheeked smile greeted Shiloh warmly and she rose from the booth and walked over to her. There was a genuineness about her that appealed to Shiloh. And she was hungry.

Lonson was ex-military police and had seen Shiloh pull in and park in such a way as to take in the road and the parking lot. He'd watched her sit and observe for a little while. She tracked people coming and going and only when she thought it safe did she exit the coach. Lonson was good at reading people and he read correctly that Shiloh was being more than careful.

A man walked by as Shiloh and Bunny headed back to the booth. The back of his T-shirt read: *No Trespassing*. Below that, *Violators will be shot*, and below that, *Survivors will be shot again*. The patrons ignored Shiloh and it was disconcerting.

The broad-shouldered man with coleslaw eyebrows and a mustache to match smiled a greeting as his wife encouraged her to have a seat. His cheeks were as rosy as his wife's and he wore a lumberjack cap and a Pendleton shirt. Bunny slid into the booth and Shiloh followed. Both sat facing the big man, their backs to the door.

Shiloh looked around with a question on her face—one that she did not put a voice to.

Bunny was softly helpful and said in a low voice, "Folks here value and preserve privacy. *All* privacy. Your business is private."

Shiloh looked at her, smiled, and nodded like she understood. But she wasn't sure she did. Lonson—or "Professor Rhodes," as Shiloh would end up calling him—did not miss that.

"I suppose I just violated that rule," Bunny said. She shot

a look at Lonson, who smiled at her indulgently. Bunny shrugged. "You looked like you needed a friend. If only for a little while. Like for lunch. Besides, you wouldn't know what kind of pie to order, and that would be a shame because they make great pie here."

There was a kindness to Bunny that was grandmotherly, yet there was another side that was extraordinarily strong and not to be crossed.

Over the course of lunch, Shiloh would understand many things she hadn't when she first walked in. And she felt that luck was still with her. Lonson was the perfect find for Shiloh because he absolutely adored Bunny and they were inseparable. For once, Shiloh's looks were not an issue and the relief she discovered from this was immense.

Bunny had some strong views, which she shared as she grew more comfortable with Shiloh. Shiloh let her run. She felt these two people had something she needed, like fortune had placed them in her path at the right time. And her hamburger was fantastic.

After lunch, they sat and talked quietly for the rest of the afternoon. Shiloh was surprised that no one asked them to leave. Lonson handed Shiloh some information on bitcoin and crypto currencies. Shiloh politely opened the literature and thumbed through its pages. Her eyes lifted and she looked at Lonson, at first with a touch of silent skepticism and then with growing interest. She may have thought that was the sum total of the lesson but it was only the beginning. And like a true scholar, Lonson could teach a master's class on how to disappear and take your money with you. Lonson was the first to admit that he didn't know it all, but what he had learned had served him well. Bunny nodded in earnest agreement as she took another bite of pie.

The first lesson was crypto currency. "Computers are used to make the complex calculations that verify a running ledger of all the transactions in virtual currencies around the world. It is surmised that countries under the thumb of sanctions, like North Korea and Venezuela, are using this as a way of propping up their sinking economies. As more bitcoin enters circulation, more powerful computers are needed to keep up with the calculations. And that means more energy."

Bunny patted Shiloh's hand gently and began to tell her where they'd just been, and that they were headed back home.

"When we were at that conference, we spent half a day with this currency guy. He called himself a 'miner' and he was involved in a company that mined bitcoin. In return, the miners claim a fraction of a coin not yet in circulation. In the case of bitcoin, a total of $21 million can be mined, leaving many millions left to create. We invested in the company, didn't we, Lonson?"

Lonson added, "Sure did, though I made sure we checked him out thoroughly. Lotta shysters at these things."

"How do you check someone out?" Shiloh asked.

Bunny answered, "We have ways. In the Redoubt, the off-grid community, we are part of a bigger collective and if someone doesn't get a clean bill of health, that group of people cuts him or her off." Bunny smiled and nodded. "The government took advantage of us and we are fighting back by not allowing anyone else to!"

Lonson patted Bunny on the back and settled her down. Then he looked earnestly at Shiloh, his hands flat on the table and his face serious. He could see she was just about full, her eyes had begun to glaze, and he assured her that after this part, they'd take a break.

"Keflavik, Iceland—a place where large virtual currency companies have established a base," Lonson was saying.

Shiloh struggled with concepts like the Redoubt, off-grid, second-amenders, and the ol' US-of-A being an enemy state. She had never read the Constitution and as a waitress, she pocketed most of her tips and hadn't cared about taxes much beyond whether the roads were drivable, did the lights come on, and that water came out of the tap. She paid no never mind to politics and did not conceive of the government caring much about her one way or the other. They pretty much ran the country and she lived in it. She didn't feel they had much of a say in her life.

With too much information being thrown at her, her bandwidth narrowed, and she interrupted, "Sorry…what's in Iceland?"

"You see, these companies need massive amounts of electricity. Iceland is blessed with abundant renewable energy. The cost of producing and collecting virtual currencies will soar and the place they will grow is there."

Lonson explained it at length, and it took a long time for Shiloh to even begin to understand it. But Lonson surprised her. For all his way-out-there ideas about the government and the end of the world as we know it, he was extraordinarily well-read and it juxtaposed oddly with his paranoia. Shiloh wondered more than once how diametrically opposing ideas could inhabit the florid thickness that was Lonson, but there it was.

He continued. "The geothermal and hydroelectric power plants…the population is so small that they produce way more energy than they'll ever use, and these computers get hot. They need ventilation and cooling. Hell, just opening the windows in a cold place like that will help."

He laughed and Bunny giggled too.

"Anyway," he said, "the guy expects Iceland to be the virtual currency mining center of the world and that currency mining will double and then triple its energy consumption to hundreds of megawatts per year. So we invested in the energy producers as well."

Shiloh asked how she could do that and still stay below the radar. Lonson winked at her and seemed pleased that she was on track with them, and said that they'd help her with that.

"The trick is to establish your identity offshore someplace." He winked again. "Where the taxes are hard to trace and the government isn't interested in small-time investors. See, if you were living in some suburb and paying all those damn taxes for every teensy thing the lying, cheating bureaucrats made for you, then they'd tax whatever you made right out of your hands!" His face reddened and a vein throbbed at his throat.

Shiloh leaned away, as it was a bit frightening to see it that close.

Bunny chimed in, "But we are out of those sons a bitches' reaches." And she rested that motherly hand on Shiloh's shoulder. "And we'll make sure they can't reach you either."

Shiloh accepted their invitation to park for a couple of days at their Redoubt in their sanctuary. Once there and set up, she slept too soundly for any dream.

Lonson Rhodes knew when to take breaks with filling Shiloh up with the survival skills he knew she needed. Shiloh extended her stay and expanded her education for a couple of weeks—enough time to do some investing. For the moment, it was a way of managing her financial life underground and she intended to learn more. She even considered settling at the Redoubt, at least part-time. On the road, she felt exposed. She was looking for safe places. She liked the idea of security and the isolationist ways and it reduced her anxiety.

One morning at breakfast, Bunny told her, "We got tired of living around folks that have no moral values and can't speak English. Not that we are racist or anything, it's just a fact that they erode American culture." The little jowl parts on the sides of her jaw wiggled when she nodded to punctuate her certainty. "Now, we pray to God it never happens, but if it did, we will be secure away from government overreach." She held her coffee cup to her lips and smiled at her husband.

Shiloh began to find their story interesting on a couple of levels. They had bought some land near a place called "the Steens" known as "the Second Coming" with several reliable sources of water, solar and other sources of energy, secure storage for at least two years' worth of supplies, and (this was very important) "a defensible location far from any main roads." They hunted for food and had even learned to melt lead to make their own bullets if they had to.

Bunny lowered her voice and leaned in toward Shiloh. "I can see you're on your own, and if you don't have protection, you should get some. We always carry. Got the AR tucked next to the driver's seat, my handgun between the seat, body armor, and plenty of ammo in the back." And she told Shiloh how and where to get whatever she needed, and gave her the card of a "friend" who would help her.

"Anybody with shit for brains can see the economy is failing 'cause of the national debt, no more manufacturing jobs, weak borders, and tons of welfare. And don't even start with me on crime," Bunny said as she cleaned her plate. Then she added, "Except our gun makers, why, they are doing good business in the US. You can get a custom gun where all that's original is the action and the serial number."

Lonson talked more about how they'd built their own bunker on their place and how they lived off the grid with their solar.

Bunny piped in, "Sure. It won't sleep six or eight people..." She looked at Lonson adoringly as she repeated verbatim what sounded like an advert for a bigger bunker. "But my man has built me an underground palace."

Chapter 38

Kitzie and Carson began to sift through the remains of the house the day after the fire. A few small things were plucked from the ashes and Carson watched her mother delight in their discovery. Some of the china had survived, though it was scarred by the heat. As Kitzie bent down in her mask and gloves, she brushed aside some heavier debris and unearthed a saucer, and then a teacup, in perfect condition.

"Now, how the hell does that happen?" her muffled, mask-cloaked words exclaimed.

Kitzie held them up for Carson to see, then set the cup on the saucer, lifted it with her pinkie extended, and faux sipped the contents to her masked mouth. The brilliant blue of the latex gloves was stark against the white, patterned china. Kitzie loved the English china set, its pattern ornate but uncolored. Carson remembered as a child her grandmother saying that colored china "argued" with the food. The dishes were her wedding gift to the couple and memories of special events and holiday meals flooded Carson's mind.

Carson's eyes filled up and her feelings couldn't be contained. Though the remains of the house were barely cold to the touch, sifting through charred memories was just too much. When Kitzie found Lulu's body, she broke down. How Wyatt had escaped was a mystery. Carson had never seen her mother cry like that. Carson carefully wrapped the body and buried her behind the barn. Kitzie mourned so many things—an animal she could not save, family heirlooms, and mementos that were destroyed.

Carson stood up with a bit of unrecognizable, melted metal in her gloved hand. She turned it over in her palm with a fingertip. The wind still blew with a vengeance and an ash dust devil swirled into the room. Carson shut her eyes and turned her upper body against it as it surrounded her, then moved off and fell apart. She wore a baseball cap and her auburn ponytail stuck through the hole in the back, so the wind's effort went unrewarded. But every part of her felt dirty. The wind took whatever was clean and ruined it. The ash was for extra measure.

Each tiny thing they found that had a connection to Tuff was especially poignant. Carson sifted through some ash and found a pair of earrings her father had given her mother eons ago. Kitzie had a habit of hooking her hoop-style earrings together, which was how these were found. They found his wedding ring, amazingly untarnished by the burn, shiny and like new.

Kitzie wore thick-soled, rubber barn boots that went up to her knees. She shuffled through the ashes and stopped by the only recognizable piece of furniture that was left in the rubble—the wire remains of Tuff's old recliner. Kitzie knelt and felt the cool ashes and scooped a handful into her palm. With a forefinger, she stirred them as if searching for feeling in them. Carson approached silently but stayed back. Her mother tilted her head and saw her out of the corner of her eye.

"You know," she started, "I used to feel him here, in this house. With all our memories around us, the familiar smells and sounds..." She sighed. "I was holding on to what was long gone. A cupful of time." She rose slowly and saw that the ash had stained her gloves a bluish-gray. She brushed them off on the thighs of her jeans.

Carson looked at the remains of the chair, then at the outline of the building, the skeleton of its foundation like a corpse at a crime scene. It dawned on her slowly at first...then, in a rush, she felt that her father was not really gone from the house. There was always some corner, some place, some fragrance or odor from beyond that brought comfort and longing.

Kitzie turned slowly, taking it all in again as if it wasn't real the first or the fiftieth time. But it *was* real.

"It's the first time...." Kitzie searched for the words. "The first time that I truly know he's gone."

The smoky sun cast long and orange, and Kitzie's shadow stretched to reach the outer edges of the foundation. In that moment, Carson saw that it was her mother who cast the shadow now, not her father. She saw that her mother was using her head and her heart to steer them all, to move past this crisis, to show them they would survive. She grieved for all the dead cows but held her head high, knowing that they could rebuild the herd. She saw Kitzie's resolve and strength.

Kitzie stepped out of the ashes, pulled the facemask down past her chin to her neck, and said, "I wonder when I won't smell like smoke." And she smiled at her daughter.

"How did you do it, Mom?" Carson asked.

Her mother took her daughter's hand and they fell into step together as they walked away from the ruins of the house.

"Had I never done any of this," Kitzie said as she waved her hand around, "I might've missed some difficult experiences. But I don't regret a moment. Now...let's check out the trailer."

The idea of using the old show trailer was an obvious one, and fortunately, the keys were in the barn office, so they were spared having to break into it. They explored its musty and long-ignored interior together. Carson sat at the little table and looked around. It still smelled the same to her. Her mother explored drawers and cupboards and a closet, and she returned with a pair of jeans and a pair of boots in her hand.

"I'll be damned, I didn't know these were in here," she said.

"How old are they?" Carson asked, elbows resting on the table. "I'll bet they still fit."

Her mother froze and stared at her quizzically with a lips-only smile.

"What?" Carson asked, leaning back into the bench.

"Oh, it's just the way you had your arms on the table, how you were sitting. You always sat that way, right there, when you were little." She shook her head and looked at the items in her hands, then set them down and opened another drawer. "Seems I left a whole kit in here. I have a couple of shirts, some toiletries...not a lot but something. I even have some underwear!" And she wiggled a bra through the opening—a graceful, disconnected appendage of floating underwear. She retracted her arm and added, "I'll spare you the panty-o-mime."

Carson laughed deep in her throat. "So kind."

"Well, this will do till I can afford to get supplies. Does toothpaste expire?" She flashed an exaggerated, toothy smile at her daughter. "I might even have shampoo in the shower..." Her voice trailed off as she looked.

Carson shook her head. "I think the air is thin in here. You're killing me. Help me hook up and let's see if we can move it."

Kitzie was behind her and asked, "Why?"

"Mom, it's as dark as a pocket here and if we get it over there—" She pointed to a location at the other end of the covered arena. "—it's closer to water and that big propane tank and the light will be much better."

"It's fine. The bearings are probably frozen anyway," Kitzie observed, her voice tinged with guilt for ignoring the trailer for so long. Tuff always bought the best available at the time and underneath layers of dust and neglect was a pearl.

They thoroughly cleaned it, vanquishing the musty staleness for fresh and wonderful. Jorge did the hook-ups to a bigger propane tank, power, and water, and ran a line out into the field for the gray water. The black tank was oversized, just as Tuff had ordered, but it was better that they used the barn bathroom and laundry facilities, and shared the shower in the upstairs apartment.

Jorge suggested that the surviving ATV, the "mule," be parked at the rig at night so Kitzie could drive to the barn if she needed to. Her knee was better but still bothered her at times, especially when she was on her feet too much. Carson suggested that they get a second one for the ranch if the insurance settlement allowed. Kitzie groaned at the mere mention of any more paperwork.

Kitzie quickly settled into a routine in the fifth-wheel. Jorge had found a couple of gravity chaise lounges in a compartment and a small matching table. He also found a large mat that went under the doorstep and set the step to stay out and not retract when the door closed.

On a day that began with smoke-diffused sunlight, Kitzie opened the trailer door, coffee cup in hand, and stepped barefoot onto the soft loam of the arena. She liked to sit at the little table in the morning and settled into a chaise. The morning sun cast rose-orange-tinged oblongs on the arena sand. There was silence but for the fluttering of tiny wings. Roosting birds had whitened parts of the metal framing and a flight of swallows mastered the sky. The chirping small birds filled the rafters. Their day had started earlier than hers, darting about like bullet streaks to capture early morning insects. There were fewer bugs, fewer everything, but nature bounced back and the tiny birds flew in and out with the certainty of success.

The firestorm and its aftermath had refined her down to her most essential self. If Kitzie thought too much about what was gone forever, she became paralyzed. When she stood in front of the carcass of her home, she felt almost catatonic. She wanted to walk, to take a long walk, but her knee was achy.

It was a beginning—the start of a process they needed to navigate. Within days, they had conquered a ton of details. Kitzie got lucky and an insurance adjuster was available to come out faster than expected. They had help with the initial clearing of debris from the Running Horse crew, which included Bodie Ransom. Buckets was relieved to find another "use" for him and their heavy equipment came in handy. To save time, they chose an area more or less out of eyesight for their dump—Jorge's idea and a good one. They could properly dispose of what they piled up there later.

The shop where Luis died had been completely destroyed and the explosion had blown pieces across a remarkably wide field. Jorge struggled with walking by it and did not want anyone to clear it except him. He was adamant and they gave him his space to work it out. He began by walking the arena because Kitzie had pointed out that the horses might step on some piece of something, and the last thing they needed to add to their pile was a hoof with a puncture or an abscess.

Jorge used a magnet and though he was doubtful he'd find anything, it was a good thing he did, and he was thorough about it. The explosion had sprayed farther than he imagined. He spotted some little things Luis had kept in the shop, blackened with soot. He treated each like a gift, collected them carefully, and cried.

That evening, Carson joined Kitzie inside the trailer. Kitzie picked up a piece of paper from a pile of insurance paperwork. "I know I've filled this out before." She looked up at her daughter. "At least twice." But she was stalling.

Carson stood in the doorway, her hands holding the trim. She sort of hung there as if the frame held her up. She had asked her mother, before the fire, to trawl back into time to a difficult period in her life—one so raw that it burned her to get close to it. Carson had asked about the circumstances of her father's death, but not how her mother had come out the other side of it. Somehow, with all the recent losses, she had to know.

"After it happened…after Dad died…after the shock of it all…how did you go on from the loss?" she asked.

Kitzie looked into her daughter's eyes and saw him. She saw Carson ride and saw him riding. The shape of her face, the cheekbones, the color of her skin and hair, the way she moved quickly when impatient. All the tells were there. She was her father's daughter. Her gaze drifted toward the back of the trailer. Carson looked over at the sofa and pictured her father, years ago, when she was small and they were on the road traveling with the horses. She turned back and saw that Kitzie's focus was on her again.

Carson stepped inside and moved to the corner edge of the bench seat next to her mother, cozy-like, and her mother scooted over. Kitzie folded her hands on the table and her right hand rolled her wedding ring on her ring finger. It was a habit she had when she was thinking. It was almost a meditational talisman, the smoothness of the white gold against her skin.

"It was so sudden and unexpected. One moment the world is as you've always known and come to expect, and then it's as if all the pieces shift irrevocably."

Carson was silent.

Kitzie didn't know what to tell her. The light above the table cast out the window to the corrugated metal wall of the arena. The shadows elongated as they disappeared into darkness. The rippled metal reminded her of sheets of rain and the regimentation of it soothed her.

Life had told her that she'd lost but a part of her was too stubborn to be defeated. Sure, there were moments where she howled at the storm, and when it didn't blow her away, she went on. Kitzie hoped her mouth translated those feelings somewhat coherently. She felt her daughter gently lean against her and rest her head on her shoulder. Kitzie reached up with her right hand and cradled the side of her face against hers. Her eyes were moist but no tears fell as she reached for a pen.

"The pain isn't what will defeat you," she started. "It's shit like this that will."

They laughed. Carson got up to retrieve a box from the floor and set it on the opposite bench seat. She removed the lid, looked at the pile that her mother had stacked at the far corner of the table, and offered to file. She noticed that her mother's shirt looked baggy and made a mental note that they should go into town and have a big breakfast in the morning.

Kitzie used a blade to open another thick envelope and added a last thought. "Be it personal loss or something like the fire, what matters is what you choose to do once the storm passes."

Kitzie was a realist and pragmatic. One of the first things she did after the fires was to rent a big propane tank and it was set on the outside wall of the big, covered arena. Some evenings would find Kitzie out on the chaise with her laptop, perusing ideas on Houzz and other sites. She discovered HGTV, watched reruns of older shows, and saw that there was a whole world of design that she had missed. She loved the way they found practical solutions to issues, yet was not convinced of that much change for herself as she considered rebuilding her home.

With all the fire recovery efforts, it was a confusing time, and there was uncertainty about how to proceed. Most of the high drama drifted away, the camera lights went dim, and the daily news reports dried up on national TV. Everything seemed distilled down to getting back to a new normal.

Kitzie waded through the morass involving insurance and made lists upon lists of things that were lost. Documents once taken for granted now held significant meaning. Finding records and replacing those that were lost depressed Kitzie almost daily. It wasn't the requests for copies of this or that; it was the repetition of the same requests when the head office or the voice in India or Bangladesh needed her to begin at the beginning…again.

One afternoon, Carson found some holiday icicle lights and hung them on the awning to cheer her mother up. They set up a little fencing around the area under the awning so when the horses in turnout came to call, they only got so far. And they found a propane-powered fire pit that they sat around in the evening.

There were so many details—the design and construction

plans, insurance, materials…it was never-ending. Kitzie would be warm for winter in the fifth-wheel if her house took longer to rebuild. And of course, they were realizing that it would.

The original house was old and not up to current building codes. There was now an opportunity to build something better. It was a lot of work and trying to understand it consumed Kitzie. The running of the ranch became Carson's job and that took her to a new level too. When her mother had to leave the ranch on research trips for things that would eventually go inside her new home, Carson was in charge.

Chapter 39

To break the pattern of clean-up and recovery, Carson rode out early, before anyone was up and about. The air was still, the sky full of chirping sparrows, and the saddle leather creaked with the motion of her horse. There was a brightness, a breathing, to the morning and she made her way to the hill where her father had taken that picture of her. She couldn't remember his dog's name, though the view was exactly as she remembered it...except now it was blackened by fire. It was a setting that grabbed her attention and inspired faith. Tiny white flowers peppered the stubble of the grass and as was fitting and right, the ranch was beginning to heal.

Circling back, she heard cow calls, from a single voice to a full-on polyphony, and she figured the cattle and ranch were stirring. Charred land stretched for miles to the rolling hills and beyond to the bluffs that threaded through to the open grasslands. Another spring would come and the green would spread. Patches of life struggled to say to the sky that they had survived and they would come back.

Carson stopped by her old truck, which was parked on the far side of the driveway, and rested her elbow on the horn of the saddle. From that side, the tires were flat and the paint on the bottom half of the truck was blistered. For the life of her, she didn't know why the gas tank hadn't gone up.

Leaving the reins looped over the horn, Carson used her

legs to guide the horse around to the other side of the truck. The damage seemed a little less there and her gaze rose to the gutted shell of the destroyed shop where Luis had perished. She looked behind her and tried to figure out whether that swirling devil of a firestorm had spun its way past her truck to kill him.

She dismounted and loosened the girth. She stroked the mare's face, glanced at the truck again, then led the horse back to the barn to put her up. As she turned the corner, she saw her mother sitting on the steps of the trailer, coffee mug in hand and a somewhat lonely Wyatt at her feet. He was still traumatized after his near-death escape from the house, and was lost without Lulu, so he stayed close.

Carson walked the horse over to her mother.

"I saw you up at the truck. How is it?" Kitzie asked.

Carson shook her head in amazement. "It shoulda burned but it didn't."

"What's your plan for it?" Kitzie stroked the top of Wyatt's head. He lifted it to meet her hand, eyes closed, and leaned in.

Carson bristled a little inside, partly because the question felt like when Kitzie would say "are you gonna clean your room?" when she was little. And mostly because her mess was much bigger now and she didn't want to clean that up either.

Carson rolled the rope reins in her hand and hesitated until she felt her mother's eyes on her. "Do you need me for anything?" she asked Kitzie.

Later, after taking care of her horse and some breakfast, Carson walked back up to the truck and it felt like the gravity of the earth increased with each step. She looked all around the vehicle with no expression on her face. Charred ground surrounded it and the tires were ruined. It was as if the fire had singed it and passed swiftly on to the shop to kill Luis...as if it had a reason to spare the truck. A whirl of ash had settled in a pattern on the hood and windshield.

The firestorm was arbitrary at best—miraculous in some cases, confounding in others. It skipped some things and chose to destroy others so completely that it took a leap of the imagination to recall how they had once been. Whole herds died and yet a mother and calf were found, unscathed. Along with the big barn, Carson's old truck—the one she had fled her once-perfect life in—was one of those inexplicable miracles.

The elastic loops of her face mask hung on her wrist like a bracelet. Carson rubbed her forehead and wondered if she had come there on empty in more ways than one. Her mind trolled back and she knew she had only unloaded the bare necessities when she'd pulled in. Her arms folded across her chest defensively and the feeling threatened to send her back down to the barn to put this off for later.

It was an effort to recall what she had packed and stored in the truck. Carson had been on the raggedy edge of losing everything she had worked so hard for and was in a dark place at the time. She tried to be optimistic that maybe there were treasures waiting to be unearthed, little discoveries of things that she had forgotten.

Her emotions surprised her and Carson sighed heavily as she unlocked the truck door. It stuck and required that extra bit of effort to open as it always had. When she had driven away from her obligations, she recalled thinking she was leaving with only things she truly owned. This truck was one of them, sticky driver's-side door and all.

A layer of dust coated everything inside. Carson flicked a finger at the plastic steering wheel and affectionately traced the wear marks. She looked at the blackened country through the dirty windshield, past the barn, and saw the work being done on the house.

Carson opened the camper shell lid and looked at the still unpacked boxes in the truck bed. She reached inside and pulled out a worn dowel. There was a divot in the lid's metal frame and a matching dimple in the bed of the truck into which she set her stick so the back window wouldn't crack her on the head.

She leaned in and looked around. Some of the embers had stuck. *Hot little suckers,* she thought. Random dots of light speckled her belongings. Carson craned her neck and looked up to see pinholes burned through the camper shell in places, and made a mental note to find some caulk to plug them.

The smell of smoke was overwhelming. It hung in the air as if trapped, even though it had been weeks since the fire. Carson coughed and stepped back to let some of the lingering evil escape. She slid her mask into place and started to unpack.

She wondered how she had gotten so much into the truck and how she had completely put it out of her mind. A large, square, wrapped object sat on top of the boxes. It stunned her to realize that it had survived the fire. Had it been in the house, it would have been destroyed. It was the painting of her as a child, sitting bareback on her horse, in the exact spot she had ridden to earlier that morning. Carson felt joy that something that special had survived, unharmed.

Upon seeing it, she remembered that her father's black lab's name was Cody. Her mind could hear the buzzing of that summer's insects and knew every brushstroke of the painting.

Carson sat on the tailgate, her feet swinging back and forth in an agitated kind of way as she looked out over the charred landscape. There were signs, subtle signs of recovery. Of redemption. She pulled a box out onto the tailgate and unfolded the flaps. It contained photo albums and high school memorabilia. She thumbed through a scrapbook of her baby stuff that her mother had made for her—a loving work of art. She flipped a couple of pages and then set it aside. Carson lifted out sketchbooks of little art projects, some old textbooks, and a couple of news articles from their show days. It was a mishmash and she began to feel the urge to organize. Not what she wanted to do now—it was more of an old reflex back to when she used to keep her office orderly and neat.

Carson placed the books back into the box and set the scrapbook carefully on top. She was glad they hadn't burned. She slid the box back in and twisted to check out another one. This one was marked OFFICE on the side and as she lifted the lid, the memory of packing it flooded back. She recalled sitting at her desk, half-lit and crying, pulling files out and plopping them inside, one on top of the other. Carson slid off the tailgate and rested her hips against it, her back arched, and flipped through a few of the files. One of her first realizations was that she had records. *Her* records.

Just recently, she and her mom had had "that" conversation—about what would happen when they were no longer. Kitzie had said, "When my lights go out..." It always started that way. When her lights went out. And she wanted Carson to get to figuring out her financial status because the Three Bit would have to go to someone...but Carson wasn't receptive. Kitzie persisted and one of her topics was sorting out Carson's legal financial situation.

Carson looked at the files and remembered a time when she had felt utterly confident and the total perfectionist. She was good at keeping records and taking care of business. But that was then, and this was a different circumstance. Time to contact a bankruptcy attorney. She hadn't filed last year's taxes and there was other stuff she should do. Carson felt stronger now. She'd found a place for herself and brushed aside thoughts of regret about her dad and all that.

As she stacked the materials to slide them back in the box, something caught her eye. She pulled out a large manila envelope, pried open the clasp, and peered inside. Carson recognized the contents immediately—copies of personal e-mails she'd sworn she'd destroyed. HE asked her if she had deleted them. She lied.

"Oh, shit..."

She hadn't thought of that house, her beautiful things, her new Jag, her tight tribe of a neighborhood, or him. No, she hadn't thought about him in a while. *Odd*, she mused. *He used to be on my mind almost constantly.*

At the time, through her financial decline, he was one of the last few of their group that still held her in regard. It was a self-serving regard to be sure, but it was the kind of attention that she needed to feel valuable. The sharpness of the memory flooded back and Carson felt her cheeks flush. It was an embarrassment, what she had done. Pretty much all of it.

As the financial crisis and the recession deepened, the community she'd worked so hard to be a part of had peeled away and avoided her. Carson remembered how easy it had been for her to fit in, and how she thought things would go. Her whole plan, a perfect life. When she looked back, there it was, her dream, her life puzzle, so painstakingly put together, now smashed apart and scattered before her eyes. She rewound the last year and a half of her stint in Silicon Valley—those final, pain-filled days when the hourglass was empty and had shed all her once tightly held expectations of herself.

In a moment of mental sarcasm, she shrugged. *That which doesn't kill us makes us bitter...* When she had money, she had friends. As her foreclosure situation deepened, an acquaintance approached her lender and tried to buy the property out from underneath her. Sure, it was simply good business, yet it still stung when she found out. Failure was never an option and she believed she could still save her house. To hear that someone close to her was undermining her was devastating news. The invisible categories of friendship became clear—they apparently included only the "successful," not the "stressful." What Carson thought were unbreakable bonds of friendship snapped apart as the tribe abandoned her.

Carson laid the envelope down on the tailgate, her hands pressed hard on the papers. She closed her eyes and let out a huge sigh. What an awful time it had been for her emotionally. She had blamed everything on someone else. But finally, she saw it for what it really was and blamed herself. But then she peered at the envelope again and pulled out a few of those cryptic e-mails.

"Crap, Carson," she said out loud. "This is such crap, girl."

She took a stroll through their history. She saw the dates and times on the e-mails. They were so consistent, there in print a track record of what they'd done on certain days and at certain times. It had gone on for a year the first time. *God*, she thought, *I was such a shit person.*

For Carson, it was her first affair with a married man—and her last. The stress of it was not good for her. She couldn't lie with his ease. He was the best liar she'd ever met, and she knew from his own lips that this wasn't the first time he'd cheated on his wife.

She'd read in the paper somewhere something to do with his startup, an IPO for his company. Carson looked at the email address. He'd sent many e-mails from his office. There was something in *The Wall Street Journal* about a billion-dollar valuation.

As she put the e-mails back in the envelope, Carson guessed that he was probably a billionaire by now. "Good for—"

"Whatcha got there?"

A voice from behind her made her jump damn near out of her skin and instantly annoyed her.

"What the fuck are you doing?" she barked at Bodie as she spun to face him.

He reached out to her, dismayed by her reaction. "Hey, hey...really, I thought you heard me coming." He put on his best puppy dog face and tried to touch her arm.

She recoiled and lost her grip on the manila envelope. It slid from her fingers and flopped onto the ground. He was quick and scooped it up.

"Give me that," Carson ordered, then didn't like the defensive tone she thought had crept into her voice.

Bodie tried to play keep-away with it as she tried to grab it—his juvenile purpose to maybe get her in his arms. Carson was really pissed off now, and the steel in her eyes told him he had miscalculated, so he complied and handed it over. She turned her back on him and shoved the envelope back into the file box, and quickly replaced the cardboard lid.

"What is that?" he asked, trying to smooth it over. But something about her behavior had piqued his curiosity.

"None of your business," she said simply. She was annoyed

with herself that she'd made a big deal of it.

Bodie paid attention. Beneath that attractive façade was the perfect combination of stupidity and naked ambition. That envelope didn't just call to him, it was screaming.

Chapter 40

Stiles pulled into town and parked across the street from Martin Ranch Supply. He sat in the truck, staring at familiar ground. Detours and road closures had driven him perilously close to the one place he still called home, where he'd grown up. Avoiding it would have been as simple as turning around and going back in the direction he had come—he knew he was tempting fate—but something compelled him to at least drive through, so he had continued on.

He saw that the Pine Tavern was serving the early birds, and that the town had taken a beating but not a defeating. Workmen were already at the Tavern and setting to repairs at the back of the building. *Must've been flying embers that caught,* he thought. The burn patterns were not from a full-on conflagration but the kind of damage from wind-driven embers and small catches that were put out soon enough.

He stared and in a moment of memory, wondered if the burn mark was still on the edge of the pool table in the bar. He had smoked briefly, but it didn't suit him, and he used to forget where he'd set the lit ones, especially when playing pool with his buddies.

Lyle Martin was unlocking the door to his store, his back to the street, and in the reflection in the window he watched a man getting out of a beat-up camper truck. He didn't recognize the truck, which was how everybody knew one another in those parts.

There was something familiar about the way the stranger moved as he looked around. Maybe it was the way he turned, put his hands on his hips, then ran a hand through his long, graying hair. *I know him,* thought Lyle. He lingered longer than he needed to, fussed with the lock on the door as if it were stubborn, and watched the man straighten as if he'd driven a long way and was stiff. The man looked around, as if taking in a place he'd not seen in a long time. He turned and reached for a cowboy hat and that's when Lyle had it—it was the way he put his hat on. Lyle stopped futzing with the key and turned around.

"Larry? Holy shit! Is that you?"

Stiles froze, hands up in the motion of adjusting his hat, and looked across the street as the man calling to him stepped toward the edge of the curb. There was a hesitation in his response and then, as if a decision had been made, he shook his head in disbelief. It had been so long since someone had called him Larry and he'd almost failed to respond. He'd been away from Martin for well over a decade and had gotten used to calling himself by another name. He worked his face into a smile of sorts, awkward and tentative, and started across the street to greet his old school chum, Lyle Martin.

They shook hands and Lyle looked sincerely pleased to see him after all these years.

"Even with that mealy muzzle, I'd recognize you," Lyle joked and Stiles ran a hand over the scruffy beard he'd grown.

"Seems the easiest thing these days. 'Sides, I think it makes me look respectable."

Lyle laughed that genuine laugh he'd always had. It was the thing that you could count on with Lyle—he was genuine. He'd always be truthful, even if it stung. Lying to a friend just wasn't in his DNA. Many years ago, he had warned Stiles about "that woman," but Stiles had followed his dick instead of good advice.

Because they'd been in high school and grade school together, there was a history between them. Lyle asked what Stiles had been up to and Stiles mumbled an answer that wasn't. Lyle said he had to open the store but that he made good coffee if Stiles would like to come in and catch up. Lyle unlocked the door and the store was busy almost immediately.

Stiles wasn't sure what to expect so he made himself scarce wandering the store. The steady stream of customers made sense considering all the repairs folks were trying to do before the bad weather set in. For ranchers and range men, being up early was a given and they probably had already done a day's work by the time the smoky sky felt the actual sun.

Stiles hung back until there was a break, though there were people in the store. He approached Lyle at the counter and said maybe he was too busy and that he'd come back.

Lyle finished a transaction in the register and said, "If you have somewhere to be, by all means."

Stiles chose honesty. "Nope, looking for work."

Lyle looked around the store with an eye that missed little. And it came back clearly why Lyle Martin was a pillar of the community. He commented, "The fire didn't seem real but now they're really living it."

"How so?" Stiles asked.

"Some are dealing with insurance companies—*if* they had insurance. They're being required to list everything they had and most are doing it from memory. And that process can be especially tough if they're suffering emotional trauma. We lost a lot of livestock."

"I saw the damage coming in and it was everywhere, for miles and miles." Stiles tilted a *Western Horseman* magazine and looked at the cover. "I almost didn't recognize where I was."

Lyle turned to help someone and replied, "A lot of folks feel the same way."

Stiles wandered around some more, liked a pair of leather work gloves, and pictured the ones in his truck that were so badly worn his fingers came through the holes. He needed a pair but it would take most of the cash in his pocket to buy them. That there was no sales tax was tipping the purchase in his favor. He listened absentmindedly to Lyle asking after each customer's family and their pets. He knew them all by heart. Lyle felt drained at the end of long days but was buoyed by the fact that he had helped so many with a kind word and an ear.

Stiles overheard some of the questions about things like rebuilding and if there was a streamlined process for getting plans approved once they had settled with the insurance company.

There was a murmuring that escalated, and Stiles tilted his head around a display and saw the back of a very large man at the counter. He ambled to a better angle and saw the high colored cheekbones of Irish descent. The man was upset and said loudly, "I'm fed up with bureaucracy. I'm living in a camper and I lost everything I loved, including Tank!" He looked like he wanted to explode, which was an unnerving prospect. It brought to mind a bull in a china shop, and he had the air of a man who wanted to break something.

Lyle sensed he was a man broken already and Lyle was not flustered by that much hostility separated from him by a tiny counter. He leaned in, not away from the man, and said something low and heard only by the big guy. He looked him in the eye and his body language said, "I'm your friend, I want to help."

Perhaps it was Lyle's earnestness, his belief in the good in people, and that his face still looked much the same as when they were in high school. Stiles heard him say kind things about Tank, and how sorry he was that they wouldn't see his hefty frame wander the ranch like he owned it. He praised Tank's resolve to never back down in the face of overwhelming odds, even if it was a pack of big dogs.

Stiles cocked an eyebrow, confused a little about this "Tank." Who was this? His eyes scanned left and right, and he saw fear in the eyes of people who had chosen not to approach the counter…just yet.

The big man stood alone at the counter and Lyle made no move to check him out. They talked out some of his grief and they exchanged Tank stories. A few moments with a calm third party was better than an hour of therapy to many, and Stiles almost wished he could have a "counter therapy session."

Lyle didn't ring up the purchases. He bagged them and set the bag on the counter, then walked out to stand next to the man. Stiles was impressed with how Lyle took his hand in his, held it in a sincere handshake, looked him squarely man to man, and said, "Tom, you can be depressed. Lord knows you have reason to. Or you can choose to go on and look for the positive things. Call anytime, day or night, if you need to talk or if you need help with something. Don't sweat the small stuff and count your blessings."

The big rancher thanked him sincerely and said some Christian response. It was easy to see that Lyle really cared about each of these people, aside from being a merchant. He wanted to look out for those who needed the most help.

After Tom left, Stiles said, "Tank?"

Lyle explained that Tank was a huge feral cat that had convinced himself and many others that he was really a big dog. The rancher was not a "cat" person, but this cat was no ordinary cat, a fact several dogs could attest to. Stiles smiled.

While awaiting the arrival of his help, Lyle started in on the civic details. "A recovery team was formed to handle logistics and the consequences for the community. We've lost a portion of our tax base and the general fund wasn't prepared for a disaster of this magnitude. We are talking to the State and FEMA for help with the shortfall. We need the staff to approve plans and things like that." Lyle checked himself. He could easily get into the weeds on the subject of the lack of personnel and a crisis in leadership in the tiny town council.

Stiles hung back and eventually the help arrived. Lyle beckoned Stiles to his office. Lyle was right, he did make good coffee. And he had some day-old powder biscuits that he popped into a little toaster oven and slathered with butter and jam. Stiles was on the hungry side and devoured three of the four. Lyle, the gracious host, looked on with barely concealed pleasure.

The two old friends caught up and Stiles stretched the timelines in his tale to cover the parts he didn't want to talk about. He was a carpenter and had done quite a bit of construction during high school and a few years after. Lyle said he could get him on a project rebuilding a house that had burned to the ground at one of the ranches.

Stiles was getting more comfortable and joked that he'd buy those leather work gloves after all.

Lyle smiled. "You'll get a discount."

"Thank you," Stiles said. And he was grateful.

"I'll make a few calls. Can you hang for a bit?"

He said sure and when Lyle left the office, Stiles did a quick sniff—the "pits" test—to see how presentable he was. He went to the restroom, where he performed a bit of a spitz bath on himself. He took his jacket and shirt off and hung them on a hook on the back of the door. Using dampened paper towels, he washed a few days of road grime off himself, and wished he had his toothbrush and toothpaste. He dried off and redressed, then took extra time to tuck in his shirt and looked down the front for any obvious stains.

He saw himself more fully in the narrow mirror over the sink, with its blackened corners where that odd mirror mold resembled paper that had been burnt at the edges. Deeply carved furrows in gray scrub stared back at him. His cheekbones reflected hard living and weather. He ran a hand down the beard that did its best to hide how thin he was. He looked at that man from both sides and was pressed to recognize himself. Lawrence Michael Stiles was his given name and he'd come home.

He was still uneasy about how quickly Lyle had spotted him, but there it was, and he was in the path. Maybe his luck would change. Summoning his courage, he glanced at his reflection again as he exited the bathroom. Perhaps there was a glimmer of renewed energy.

He returned to the open door of Lyle's office and Lyle waved him in. He mentioned a ranch Stiles knew—he'd recalled it from years ago. Lyle said it had changed a lot since then.

"It's called the Three Bit now…"

Stiles jumped slightly upon hearing the name, and hoped

Lyle didn't notice.

"...Tuff and Kitzie Collins' place. Tuff passed but Kitzie has managed through some difficult times. There's work there. Some people actually keep backup files in the Cloud...anyway, she settled with the insurance company faster than most. They're looking for help. Your kind if you still have those skills."

Stiles nodded that he did.

"She'll be expecting you. There may be some hands from the Running Horse over to help too. I have no idea what's been done, it would be optimistic to think some of the framing may have been started, but Lord knows if and by who. Will you check that it was done well? I hold this family highly. You need anything, just ask. And I mean that."

He offered to drive out there with him and make the introductions. Stiles was surprised he could get away.

Lyle replied easily, "For this family, I make the time."

Stiles suppressed the uneasy feeling he had in his stomach about this new job. But the decision was an easy one when he looked at his gas gauge and his remaining funds. He felt better about the beard and decided to keep it for the time being. He straightened the scarf at his neck and set his hat on the passenger seat, brim up. He turned the truck over and followed Lyle as they headed to the Three Bit Ranch.

The shocks were shot on the old truck and the camper shell swayed violently at each dip and divot as he followed Lyle up the Three Bit road. He knew where he was and steeled himself to the fact that if just one person recognized him, it was game over.

As he watched Lyle swing his truck wide into the large parking area, Stiles followed suit and parked ahead of him, nose pointing the way they'd come, and he left the keys dangling in the ignition.

Kitzie appeared from somewhere near the barn and watched the 4x4, teal-green and silver Chevy park. A dozen stickers papered the window of the camper shell. It was an older Scottsdale model and the engine pre-ignited in protest after the key had been turned off. She watched Lyle get out of his truck, and noticed places along the side where the paint had bubbled, and the rubber strips on the bumper were toast.

"Jesus, you had some touch and go," she said.

He shrugged it off and opened his arms wide.

"Really good to see you," she said and welcomed a hug from her friend. He asked her how she was doing and noticed the shadow that crossed her eyes.

"I'm sure there are those that have it way worse than us," she marshalled. "I can't tell you how relieved I was to get your call." She looked around Lyle toward the Chevy as the driver rolled the window down and opened his door from the outside. "So, he's a good friend of yours?" she asked.

Stiles stepped out of his truck and planted his cowboy hat firmly on his head. As worn as the first impression looked, the hat was immaculate. He walked slowly toward Kitzie Collins. The first thing he noticed was her penetrating, hazel-green eyes that seemed to see right into the being of the person she was talking to. They were the kind it would be hard to look away from. She wore boot-cut jeans over well-worn, lace-up boots, and a dark-blue, long-sleeved shirt, untucked, with the sleeves rolled up. She extended her hand and he took it. Her grip was solid and firm, and Stiles reluctantly liked her immediately.

Stiles looked at what was left of the family house and made note of a wonderful, big barn; an enormous, covered arena back behind it; and some burned outbuildings. He guessed that the house had been a traditional-style building, built in the fifties maybe, and his imagination clicked away with possibilities. Ignoring the others, he walked toward it, and got an impression of the job. His mind rolled back in time and he found himself planning on how to proceed—where he'd start, what materials he would need—and he subconsciously started lists in his head.

Stiles had almost forgotten how much he once enjoyed building things. The act of construction was soothing to him. He looked at the place and overall, saw that it had a good feel. When a place had that, it was almost impossible not to give what a location asked for. He knew by the ground under his feet that whatever he did there, he would feel good about for the rest of his days. Despite where he was and who he was, it was as if a shaft of sunlight had found him.

Tiny shreds of guilt still danced at the edges of his mind. But he pushed back on that and all the other disappointments, kept his expression blank, and tamped down the excitement he felt. Here was something he knew how to do, and in a way, he could sort of make up for at least one transgression.

After showing him the barn, they proceeded down alongside it to get the full view of the massive steel-beamed indoor arena and the big rig hooked up to the trailer.

"I'd forgotten about that," Lyle said. "I remember it now. That truck still runs?"

Kitzie nodded but quantified that it probably would need a bit of work first. "And that would be just to get into town." She laughed but then her face darkened. "God, it would've been Luis who would've gotten it road ready…" Her voice trailed off but then she brightened, determined that the day would not be a dirge. "Anyway, it's been parked for a long time.

Three Corner Fire

It's in no shape to do the long hauling it once did."

The Collins Cutting Horse logo was on the side of the truck, as well as "Not For Hire" neatly printed beneath it.

"Had quite a run, didn't you? Pretty heady days if I recall correctly," Lyle said.

"We had some good luck for sure. And since the fire, I must admit, that has been home and it's pretty comfortable." Kitzie nodded at the trailer, her arm resting on the pipe panels.

"Gives her the luxury of time in rebuilding," Carson said as she rounded the corner and introduced herself to Stiles.

Stiles was respectful and polite. Carson approached Lyle with a big smile, but her body language was hesitant.

Lyle Martin wasn't having any of that. "Oh, come on, girl, we're well past being shy. I all but held your hair back—"

She grimaced and put her hand up to stop him. Lyle laughed and grabbed her in a bear hug.

Carson's hat tipped off her head and she caught it in her right hand. Lyle mussed her hair affectionately, like she was a child. She smiled and waved him off, ran a hand to smooth a couple of errant hairs she really didn't care about, then replaced the hat on her head. Carson noticed Stiles admiring the horses but said nothing.

They walked down to where the small cottage was that Jorge had shared with his father. It had sustained damage to one side and Jorge had been fixing it on his own. Stiles looked at the job he'd been doing with what materials he had and was impressed that he had done so well with so little.

Softly, Lyle asked Kitzie, "How's the boy doing?"

"He hasn't talked much. He is obviously upset. Seems Luis may have gone back into the shop to retrieve his papers. A tin was found halfway to the arena and it contained family documents. Of course, we can only guess what happened." She turned to Stiles to be inclusive. "Jorge is an American, born here, but his father wasn't." Her voice choked, and Carson finished the story.

"It's pretty clear the explosion killed him."

"Jesus," Lyle said. "There's been so much death and destruction, you almost become numb to one more story." He removed his hat as a show of respect, looked toward the pyre, then placed it back on his head. "Is he around? I'd like to offer my condolences. He's a nice young man."

Kitzie said she wasn't sure where he was.

They walked a bit ahead and Stiles looked around for the farthest place where he could park his camper and still have power. There was the small barn that Wyker and CJ had worked on, where they had stabled Rio when he first arrived. Another miracle—it had been barely scorched by the fire. He thought he'd ask about parking on the far side of that. Then he cast a gaze over the destroyed shop.

"Ma'am, I'm sorry for the loss of your friend," he said and turned toward them as he finished.

Kitzie stared at the destroyed building. The blackened beams lay crumpled and thoroughly burned. Engine blocks and hardened pools of molten metal were everywhere. It had burned hot. There were so many old tires outside the back that they were still smoldering.

"What did he have in here?" Lyle asked. It was obvious that the structure had been stuffed with all kinds of junk.

Kitzie looked at Lyle and just shook her head. "They tell me he apparently didn't recycle any of the oil he drained when he worked on the vehicles. I didn't know how bad a fire trap it was."

Carson sensed her mother's guilt—guilt that wasn't hers, or so Carson believed. She looked at Lyle and he nodded.

"Come on, Mom, he knew what he was doing." She touched Kitzie on the back.

Kitzie nodded. "But still…" And that was all she could say. As her mother moved off toward the remains of the house, Carson added, "Everyone is still kind of in disbelief."

Stiles was trying to make a good impression and he walked next to Lyle as the women walked ahead of them, arm in arm, toward the destroyed family homestead.

"The repairs that Jorge has done on the cottage are good. Would it be OK to ask him to work with me?" Stiles asked.

Lyle told him that Buckets at the Running Horse was sending help. Stiles chose to acquiesce for the moment. If this was to be his project to oversee, there would be a time and place to assert himself.

Now closer to the remains of the house, Kitzie asked if they knew how many head of cattle had survived and Lyle said they were still trying to assess the losses. Carson asked if they had found a source of feed for what had survived. Lyle wasn't sure. She told him the Three Bit's stolen herd of cattle were on the McDermitt and the cattle were doing fine. She mentioned CJ and Rio getting caught up in part of the firestorm and that CJ was injured and had lost his beloved horse.

Stiles followed the conversation in silence. He walked a step slower because he had intimate knowledge of certain events. It was uncomfortable with them being so candid in front of him and it had him on his heels.

Carson and her mother talked openly to Lyle. They detailed how Wyker and CJ had found the cattle and gotten them to the reservation. Stiles' discomfort increased exponentially even though his curiosity about some of the peripheral details was being satisfied. Until now, he had only wondered about how the herd had been found and had no idea what had happened after he ran. And there they were, talking, albeit indirectly, about him. And they didn't even know it. He fell farther back and kept his silence. His mind reeled about the odd circumstances that had brought him there to the very ranch whose cattle he'd stolen.

Stiles looked around surreptitiously for any sign of the big man or the Indian. It sounded like the CJ character wasn't there. *So, he was a con*, thought Stiles. No wonder he didn't see Ramos again. The con must have gotten the better of him. Odd, that. Ramos was very good with that big knife of his.

Kitzie struggled with decisions about the new house. In her married life, it had been Tuff whose hand was on the tiller. He was in charge and though they talked about things, his decisions and preferences were the ideas that most often took hold. Kitzie hadn't minded as she raised their daughter and ran their business. The house was old and dated when they moved in and very little had been altered. Make that nothing—it simply wasn't a priority. Then it was more difficult as their lives changed when Carson left and then Tuff passed away. He was twenty-five years her senior and her world radically changed overnight. She took refuge in the familiar, then and now. And now that the familiar was gone, wrenched away from her world like Tuff, she was left to create her own space. She didn't want the responsibility, yet it was hers and she had to make choices.

Carson understood. The home she'd lost in the Silicon

Valley had been her canvas, a reinvention of who she thought she was. She created it, nursed it, and she lost it. She knew what that kind of distressing change meant. Carson felt that supporting her mother through this stress was the best thing, and she devoted herself to that end.

Carson's place of peace was the barn. Its serenity hadn't changed since she was a child. It was a consistent comfort, as solid as the thick wooden beams and trusses in the roof's rafters. Home to many generations of owls, the current resident kept watch over them as they came and went.

Her father's broad desk was a favored work station as Carson set up a computer for Kitzie. Carson had wanted to buy a new one, but Kitzie said it wasn't necessary, and Carson had stared in disbelief when her mother resurrected a laptop from storage, still in its original box, bought years ago and rarely used. Carson warned that there may not be software updates and they'd have to buy a new one anyway. But it didn't need to perform complex tasks and Kitzie didn't need any fancy programs. She just needed a better system for filing and record-keeping.

When Carson was done, she turned off the light in the office, closed the door, and stretched her arms. She did a few bends to loosen her lower back, straightened, and found the dull ache in her whole being soothed. Silently thanking her yoga teacher, she inhaled a deep breath and stared up into the rafters. The large barn owl stared down at her and she smiled at him. He'd survived the fires in this barn, another miracle, and they held each other's gaze for a moment.

Kitzie appeared at the barn door with Wyatt and asked if Carson was done for the day. She was. Both the owl and Carson looked at Kitzie when she asked about an odd email regarding a modified list of electronic equipment lost when the house burned.

"We didn't have much besides that old TV and the land lines," Kitzie remarked as she followed Carson, who was going up the stairs. Wyatt bounded after her.

"Oh, yes you did," Carson said. "How you could forget about all the state-of-the-art electronics that were destroyed, I'll never know."

Her mother froze mid-step and looked up at the profile of her daughter's face in the long shadow of the stairwell.

"There's a new 60-inch, flat-panel TV coming next week. They didn't have the exact model you lost, so they upgraded it. Kind of them," Carson added with a wry smile.

"What else did I forget about?" Kitzie asked as she followed her daughter up the stairs. "Carson?"

Carson disappeared around the corner without replying, causing Kitzie to ask with changed inflection, *"Carson?"*

Chapter 41

A brilliant beam of sunlight slanted sharply through the window and found Jorge's unopened eye. He'd slept on the couch again, which was too short by that slimmest of margins, so he curled up and felt like the small boy he used to be. The tiny bedroom with the twin beds was intolerable for him. His father's things were still there, where he'd left them, and Jorge felt paralyzed by his inaction.

Brightness warmed an eyelid and made it glow golden. The other stayed darker, cool in shadow. Thoughts crowded his mind, his brow furrowed, and he willed them to back off. The tiny, sparkling starburst patterns changed when he squeezed his eyelids tighter. Jorge imagined that maybe he'd "see" something through his closed eyes. Maybe a sign, a vision, a message as to what he should do.

Jorge rolled onto his back, knees bent, stocking feet on his father's favorite cushion, and opened his eyes to reality. The smell of smoke would forever make him think of his dad, and as that smell was pervasive, he thought about Luis constantly.

He sat up and put his feet on the floor, rested elbows to knees, and stared at nothing. Jorge willed himself to not cry, then wondered if he should. He felt guilty that he and his dad had been at odds with each other over Jorge's crush on Trina. He felt guilty that they were barely speaking...and now they couldn't speak at all. He felt hollow, blown-through, unobstructed, like the air would encounter nothing of substance and go on.

He puttered around in a T-shirt and sweats, made a cup of instant coffee, and stood by the window sipping on it. Maybe this was grown-up. Was this what men did? He knew he should eat, he just didn't want to. His dogs sat on the floor next to him, one on each side, faces upturned, and silent in their love. He looked down at each and pet one, then the other. They were hungry even if he wasn't. And his love for them was the wind in his deflated sails. They were his family now and he needed them more than ever.

There were chores to see to and fire damage clean-up around the ranch and he managed to pull it together, though he couldn't bear a smile as he worked. He didn't bother to turn away from Kitzie to hide a tear. Dratted things fell unbidden and he lamely played them off to irritated eyes from the ash and smoke. She handed him a pair of goggles and he was covered from chin to hairline. He sometimes felt that served to hold the feelings trapped inside of him. The foam padding at the bottom of the goggles was damp by the end of each day. Fortunately, it dried quickly.

Kitzie had commented that he was looking too thin and chances were when he saw her, she would hand him a PB&J and a bottle of water. She'd done that a couple of times that week, saying, "Stay hydrated," as she walked away, although her efforts to engage him about his feelings had ebbed because she was struggling with her own. They all were.

Feelings were strange all around and everyone dealt with their grief differently. Jorge's grief came in waves and his dogs never strayed from his side. Wyatt attached himself to Kitzie like a barnacle. And Carson found solace on the back of a horse. The pinched gray of her eyes softened and recent events blurred from sharp focus when she rode. She had a calling to make every horse better because they were the current, the tide, the life energy that she was privileged to share. The flow of rhythm and consistency soothed her mind. Balancing two bodies to move seamlessly as one tuned her in. It was inexplicable, those fleeting moments of pure communication, a toned palette where everything was true.

Jorge struggled with his feelings. He tried calling Trina for a distraction but got her voicemail. Frustrated, it darkened his mood that afternoon, and his dogs reflected that. Heads and tails low, they were like furry mood rings, predictors of the young master they adored. He had hoped Trina had heard about Luis and would feel sorry enough for him that she'd make more of an effort to be nice. Trina was unreadable, and as he had no experience with women, Jorge was at a loss to figure it out. He casually asked Buckets if he had any advice to share and Buckets replied with, "About what?"

Jorge stammered around an answer and Buckets tortured him briefly, even though he was quick to understand. He fake-punched him on the arm and told him he was messing with him. Jorge shook his head and cracked a quick smile, but looked at him in earnest and tried again.

Buckets looked away, then confessed a simple truth. "My quest to improve myself for a mate ran into my bad habits and an uncooperative physique." He flexed his long, slender arms in a mock pose of a bodybuilder. He looked like a tree with appalling branches battling gravity as he hurried toward the Running Horse truck. As he opened the driver's side door, he hesitated. "All I know is that when it's right, the planets line up and nothing keeps true lovers apart." Then he wished Jorge luck and left.

By the end of the day, Jorge still hadn't reached Trina and decided to drive into town to try to see her. He spent longer than he meant to cleaning himself up and was thoroughly underwhelmed with the effort.

He drove out the Three Bit Ranch driveway, maybe a little too fast, his mind going over what to say if he found her—whether to act cool and confident or go with his feelings and honesty. He bounced the two approaches back and forth until he was thoroughly confused.

Jorge stopped at the end of the driveway, looked left for oncoming traffic, then began a turn to the right and accelerated. He stomped on the brakes and jerked to a stop when she walked into the beams of his headlights.

She was a horse with a dirty, tangled, brown-gray mane, standing in the middle of the road. Jorge stared at her as he slid the gearshift into park. He opened the truck door slowly and she didn't move. She stood rooted, as if waiting for something. He hesitated and then thought he heard an engine. In the distance, he could see headlights playing on the telephone lines that remained on unburnt poles and he realized he needed to move quickly. He rushed to look for a rope in the back of his truck, didn't have anything, cursed, and removed his belt.

Jorge approached her as fast as he dared. He didn't want to spook her. The roar of a fast-approaching V8 spurred him to move faster, and when he could see he didn't have another second to spare, he flipped the belt over her neck and the end swung perfectly to his waiting hand. He tugged at her neck and ran toward the side of the roadway, pulling her with him just in time.

The rig honked long at him and swerved, which sent the

startled mare veering into Jorge, knocking him sideways. It was dusk and difficult to see, and he wondered why her belly had almost toppled him over.

He regained his footing and stood, heart pounding, next to his truck with the horse he had just found. He coaxed the mare to move closer to the truck so he could reach inside and turn the engine off. He saw his hand shaking as he locked the door and pocketed the keys. Jorge glanced down the dark highway at the retreating taillights and knew how lucky they had just been. It would have been a god-awful mess. Then he looked the other way, toward town, and thought of his missed opportunity.

The belt was his father's and was too long for him, which proved convenient. Jorge was saving a life with it. Something about that made him feel good as he maneuvered the mare to walk back up the drive to the Three Bit—a walk of at least twenty-five minutes, in the dark. There were a couple of moments when the mare stalled and he had to coax her forward. Jorge stepped on uneven ground occasionally, and wobbled to catch himself. She led easily enough, for which he was immensely grateful and he felt he almost knew her at the end of their stroll. He took her to the big barn, got her into a stall, and went to find Kitzie and Carson, who were eating dinner in the trailer.

Carson was the first on her feet. "You found *what?*"

He repeated himself and added, "She was easy enough to catch. She was standing in the road at the end of the driveway. I couldn't leave her there. Somebody would hit her." Then shook his head and rubbed his side. "Someone almost did."

"What's that?" Carson asked Jorge.

He had the belt folded in his hand and realized he hadn't

put it back on. "Oh." He held it up to show her. "It's Papi's…it's Papi's belt."

"You led her from the highway with *that?*" Kitzie asked as she put another bite of salad in her mouth, used a napkin as she rose, and grabbed her jacket.

Jorge nodded. "I'm sure she's had some handling."

Kitzie raised her eyebrows in admiration. "Even so, well done. Wyker would be impressed."

Jorge beamed. He had watched Wyker work his horses, openly admired him, and this was high praise indeed.

Kitzie looked at the young man and noted his smile—the best smile she'd seen on him of late—as he put the belt back on, arranging the extra length of it with a catch loop.

"Oh, um…that's either a really fat mare or she's about to pop," Jorge said, and told them that when she had bumped into him, that middle had almost knocked him flat.

The trio hurried out to the barn.

Looking at the horse through the bars of the stall door, Carson mused, "Fat? Or in foal big time?"

Kitzie said, "The latter."

"You sound so sure," Carson replied.

Kitzie said, "I am."

"A late baby," Carson murmured.

"Yes, not unheard of and this one wouldn't do well out there alone." Kitzie touched her daughter's shoulder. "Lucky for her, she's here, for more reasons than I can count. Besides other dangers, after the fires, there's no food out there."

Carson asked Jorge to get a rope halter and they approached the mare, staying close to her side. Carson touched the side of the mare's face, then ran a cautious hand down her back. The mare didn't shy away and let Jorge halter her easily.

"Tip her head this way," Carson said to Jorge. "Keep her head tipped toward me. That's it," she instructed. She extended her left arm and gently palpated the mare's rump. It was soft and pliable. "I don't see a brand…" Carson took the lead rope. "I'll hold her. We need to move her. Please go down to the foaling stall and clean all the shavings out of there." She turned to Kitzie. "Mom, do we have any straw?"

Jorge started to complain. "That's a huge stall. It'll take me too long."

Kitzie told him, "Hustle and you may still make it to town…"

"OK," Jorge said and shot her a look. "But I don't think I'm going anywhere."

"Why?" Kitzie asked the retreating ranch hand.

Jorge slapped the sides of his legs. "I don't have a truck!"

Carson looked at her Mom and said, "Oh, shit…" then added, "I think this mare is about to foal, Mom."

"Could be…"

It was forty minutes later when they put the mare in the readied foaling stall. Carson left her alone long enough to go to the tack room and call the veterinarian. Her call went straight to voice mail and she left a message. If someone was missing a horse, he'd be one of the first to know.

Carson watched the mare for a while. The horse stood quietly and dozed, back leg cocked, head low. She didn't seem interested in food, likely due to stress or pre-labor…but Carson would watch her for signs of colic too. She guessed she was a mustang. She was big but not tall, with good bones and a kind eye. She was barefoot but had good feet, and was likely broke to handle but not ride. Maybe she'd been adopted as a project. Carson wished Wyker was there. With one glance, he could have told them whether she was a BLM horse.

For the moment, they had no idea where she had been during the fire. She'd made her way to the Three Bit so she was their project for the time being, and Carson knew she would feel better if the vet took a look.

The mare seemed relaxed and showed all the signs of being close to term except for the obvious signs of labor. Without knowing an exact due date, it was more an instinctual thing for Carson, and though they had no idea whose horse she was, by mid-morning the next day, it didn't matter.

A few hours later, the vet skillfully backed his truck into the barn. His assistant and her entire family had lost their homes, so he was working alone and he looked awful. Carson walked over to him and saw the fatigue on his face. He was unusually quiet. An experienced large animal vet, he had known them since before Tuff died.

Their greeting was abbreviated and Carson said, "You look tired. You feel OK, Doc?"

He opened the back of his rig and pulled out his stethoscope. "Not really," he said. He found his glasses and looked up at the bright barn lights. "It's nice to see light for a change. Power's out just about everywhere."

He walked to the stall door with Carson and observed the mare for a moment. He seemed broken and barely there from lack of sleep. It was as if touching the feelings he felt would crack him into pieces he wasn't sure he could put back. Recent events had shattered him inside and holding it together for his patients had put a huge strain on him.

Carson reassured him. "I just need you to do an exam, make sure we've got this. OK?"

He tried to smile and apologized. He explained that there

were busy backhoes all over the area, and Carson's gaze fell.

"So much suffering…" he said. "I have put more animals—animals of ALL kinds—down in the past couple of weeks than I've done in my entire career." And then he somberly added, "Animals I brought into this world…" His voice cracked and trailed off. "It's nothing like I've ever seen. It's taken its toll, that's for sure."

Carson saw the gray tinge around his eyes and she knew he cared deeply for animals and their people. She slid the stall door open for him and they went in. She'd found a leather halter and left it on the mare, and clicked the lead rope on and held her.

Jorge and Kitzie stood outside the stall.

"She's a mustang, maybe ground gentled. That's a plus," the vet said. "Still, everyone be careful."

He proceeded with the exam—checked her vitals, listened to her gut, felt her sides, chose not to do an internal palpation, and asked Carson if they had the supplies they'd need when it was time. He noted that the mare had wax on her teats. Her vitals were good, and he said that without knowing more about her, they should just hope it would be fine. If she was in labor, it was early.

The vet got a call, answered it briefly, and had to go. Carson followed him to his truck. He handed her some extra vet wrap for the mare's tail, and apologized for having to leave so suddenly.

Between the three of them, there were eyes on the mare on the hour. Foal watch. Carson rooted around in the office looking for the camera system they used to have but was out of luck. Her mom didn't know what happened to it. It had been too many years, and it probably didn't work anymore or they had gotten rid of it. Carson considered sleeping outside the stall but she'd known mares that waited until no one was looking to drop a foal.

Kitzie couldn't keep up the rotation. She had a doctor's appointment for her knee in Prineville and wasn't sure when she'd be back. She needed to rest her knee for the drive, so it was up to Jorge and Carson to keep watch.

Carson had done many a foal watch. She remembered her first time as a young child and the wonder of it—the baby falling into the hay in its sack, all slippery and white; the mare licking at it as its head bobbled about and the foal lying on its side in the straw. The sack stretching and tearing as a wet muzzle appeared, the foal's flattened ears free of the case that had nurtured it for eleven months, and the soft, feathery-bottomed feet pushing free. She recalled the wet mess being her job. Even as a little girl, she had heaved the saturated hay clear and carefully separated the amniotic sack into a bucket. With help, she stepped it outside between the boots and legs of everyone lined up watching the miracle that was one of the prized stud's latest offspring—a baby that would grow up to be a champion.

Their two foaling stalls were twice the size of a regular stall. The stalls had turnouts separated from the paddocks on either side. When the mare and baby made their first forays out into the sun, the mares could be overprotective. Her father had designed the foaling stalls to be at the end of the barn, which provided a separation on the barn side and an open vista on the other. On the far side was a roadside path and pasture. Mares and foals felt the comfort of their own space so they could get into their new routines. It was important to put them in before dusk so that predators wouldn't try for the young foals.

This had been Carson's job, and she recalled the one afternoon when she was eight years old and late to the job her father had assigned her. She'd put the mare and foal in and as she closed the stall door from the outside, latched it, and went to hop the fence, she hesitated at the sound of a low, throaty growl. She shone her flashlight through the five-rail-tall pipe panel. The panels had orange rubber mesh zip-tied to them from the inside, which prevented the baby from hurting itself in a moment of youthful exuberance, and it was difficult to see through.

Carson scanned the light back and forth across the dirt track and along the opposite fence. She missed it on the first pass but on the second, a pair of eyes reflected in the beam. She held the light on the animal, a cougar crouched low, and watched its mouth open and heard it hiss.

Carson stepped back from the fence, frozen in surprise. She hadn't thought to be afraid for herself—her only thought was that she'd almost forgotten to put the mare and foal in. She backed away toward the stall door. The cat wiggled its butt, like she'd seen kittens do when they were playing. Carson felt the edge of the door at her tiny shoulder. Without looking, she fumbled for the latch, unclipped it, slid the door open a crack and slipped inside. Before she closed the door, she stuck her head out and fixed the flashlight on the spot where the cat had been, across the road. The animal had quietly closed the gap and was now crouched just outside the paddock fence, peering through the orange mesh.

Carson closed the door quickly with a clang and latched it from the inside. Then she realized she had a whole other set of problems. The mare was very protective, known to be aggressively so, and Carson turned to find the horse's eyes fixed on her as menacing as the cat's. Carson spoke confidently and cautiously to the new mother.

"Easy, mare, easy. I'm not going to hurt your baby," she said softly as she edged her body along the wall of the foaling stall toward the stall door into the barn.

The mare sensed the cat and had her baby tucked behind her in one of the corners, her ears pinned flat to her head. Carson didn't want her to get riled lest the mare hurt the baby by mistake, so she lowered her eyes to avoid looking at her directly, and set to opening the stall door and getting out. She latched it and breathed a huge sigh until she glanced down the alleyway and realized that the main barn doors stood wide open.

Carson ran to the doors and struggled to close one side, then dashed to the other. Halfway closed, it stuck. Terrified that the big cat knew, Carson tugged and pushed frantically, and in her child's mind, imagined the big cat running stealthily along the outside of the barn, knowing she wasn't getting the job done and trading one small meal for another. At what she believed was the very last minute before she was consumed alive, the door freed up and she slammed it closed. She held it closed to be sure, her forehead resting against the comforting wood barrier.

When she felt certain, Carson stepped away from the barn doors and sank to sit Indian style on the floor, her shaky post-adrenaline legs no longer willing to support her. She burst into tears.

When Carson didn't show up for dinner, Tuff went looking for her. She heard him calling her but she was too afraid to open the barn doors. She wanted to warn him about the cat, and was debating what to do when Tuff opened one of the doors. Carson jumped to her feet and pulled him inside by the arm, then, in a panic, shut the door behind him.

He stared down into her tear-stained, terrified little face and saw that she had been through something. He knelt and gathered her small body in his big arms and she disappeared into them. She sobbed on her father's shoulder in huge, air-deprived shudders. He let her cry. Then he pushed her back to look level into her face and asked her what had happened. He was totally calm. He asked if the mare and foal were all right. She nodded.

In remembering all this as if it were yesterday, Carson recalled that he didn't get up to go look. He picked her up and cradled her in his arms and headed toward the barn door. As he turned out the barn lights, she squeezed him hard and buried her face in his neck. He opened the door and looked outside both ways. The big light at the peak of the barn had gone on at dark. Carson was grateful that he believed her about the cat and was looking. Satisfied they were safe, Tuff exited, slid the door closed, and uncharacteristically hasped it shut. He then carried Carson to the safety and warmth of the kitchen.

The concern melted from her mother's face and her eyes changed as Tuff got his rifle and a flashlight. Kitzie conveyed an unspoken "be careful" with a look as he grabbed his jacket and went back outside.

Carson looked at her plate and wasn't yet ready to eat. She wanted to share her tale, but she and her mother seemed to be suspended in time until they heard Tuff's footfalls on the steps. He unloaded the weapon and returned it to the rack, and touched Carson's shoulder as he fetched a beer from the refrigerator.

"There were some good-sized tracks near the barn," he

stated matter-of-factly, and Carson looked nervously over her shoulder toward the door.

Her father assured her that he thought she had startled the cat and it had moved on. "To be sure, I'll go out at first light and check everything."

Then they encouraged her to eat her supper and tell them the tale of her courage and bravery over and over.

All these years later, it was still a fresh memory of her father...clear, concise. Carson saw his face, remembered the smell of his laundered collar, the scent of his skin, and the feeling of his arms tight around her. She wondered how that had escaped her in the intervening years...

The mare's rump was soft, indicating the hips were relaxing to allow the foal to come through the birth canal. Carson and Jorge wrapped her tail. They figured it would happen at any time and they were as ready as they could be.

The sound of shuffling hooves in the straw woke Carson from a fitful sleep. She'd left the door open to her room so she would be alerted if the mare paced in the stall and had slept in her clothes. Carson pulled her boots on, bounded downstairs, and flipped the light on.

The mare's coat was shining with sweat as she swung her head to nip at her swollen belly. She lowered herself into the straw with a groan and kicked awkwardly with her legs to roll. Failing that, she got up and resumed pacing the stall.

Carson watched her pace for another twenty minutes and was relieved to see Jorge's tousled head peek through the barn doors. As he squeezed through, he smoothed his hair and perked up when he saw Carson's eyes.

"What is it?" he asked and looked through the stall bars at the mare.

"I'm not sure yet. She may be a maiden mare."
"And what happens now?" he asked.
"We watch and wait."
And they did with increasing anxiety.
"It's taking too long. She can't deliver on her own…" Carson worried, then looked around and ran to the office. She called out to Jorge to get some warm water in a bucket and a twitch. She flipped open the lid of a trunk and rummaged through the contents, scattering the discards on the floor, until she dug down and spied what she was looking for. She grabbed a set of foaling straps and hoped they wouldn't need them. Still, it was better to have them close.

When Carson got to the stall door, Jorge was jogging toward her with a bucket that steamed slightly from the top.

They stood at the door. The mare was folding at the knees and getting set to lie down. Carson told Jorge to get in there and lay on her neck once she was down. He nodded and moved smoothly into position. Carson stripped off her sweater down to her T-shirt. She pulled out a long, plastic glove from its packaging and slid it up her bare arm.

Jorge watched her. She shuddered and he opened his eyes wide, questioning.

Carson said nervously, "It's cold."

She squeezed lubricant all over her gloved arm and quickly positioned herself on her knees at the mare's back end, away from where hooves could strike. She held the mare's tail aside and eased her slender arm inside the horse. It was an odd angle of attack and her arm muscles protested immediately.

Carson felt one soft hoof. The baby was definitely coming. She slid her arm in further and touched a nose. "Christ! Where's the other leg?" Carson hissed, fighting down panic.

Must stay calm, her father's voice toned in her mind. She turned until her arm was in up to her armpit and she felt the top of a knee. "Think, Carson!" she encouraged herself. Once she had the top of the knee, her fingers wrapped around it and she gently pulled to unbend it.

The mare grunted and struggled and through clenched teeth, Carson told Jorge, "Hang on to her!"

It felt like forever before the leg was straight, and then Carson felt both feet. She decided to take both in her hand and gently pulled. A series of contractions happened about the same time and the foal slid easily.

The mare grunted again and held her breath to push. Carson withdrew her arm as the soft baby hooves peeked out.

"OK, can you undo that halter?" Carson said to Jorge. "Great…yeah, now let her up if she wants to…"

Carson rolled away from the mare's hindquarters and stood up; the long plastic sleeve covered in a mixture of fluids. Her arm and shoulder ached.

It seemed like it was taking forever and Carson's hope for the foal wavered. She wasn't sure if the mare would stand and deliver. Gravity would help, and the foal's soft parts were designed to fall safely. The white sac was evident, and soon a nose and ears began to appear. The mare got up and circled. The head presented, the shoulders began to squeeze through, and then, with a soft *whoosh*, the body in its white slippery shroud slid onto the thick bed of straw.

The mare turned her body around and began to lick the sac on the baby. The foal lifted and bobbed his head.

"He's alive!" Jorge said, barely containing his relief. Unembarrassed, tears rolled down his face.

Carson reached down and cleared the colt's nostrils and

mouth. "I'll be damned. You made it, little one. Welcome."

Flushed from the exertion, she beamed up at Jorge, who was dumbstruck by the whole experience. While the baby lay there, Carson held the umbilical stump with freshly gloved fingers. Jorge handed her a squirt bottle of Betadine and a small bowl—treatment to prevent bacteria from traveling up the stump and entering the foal's body. Over the next few hours, she'd dip the stump in the solution several times until it dried up.

The amnion followed as hoped. Carson asked Jorge to get another bucket to put the sac in so they could examine it. "We need to be sure all of it comes out," she told him.

The new mother tended to her wet bundle and continued to lick away the milky-white sac he'd arrived in. While she freed him from the "room" he'd lived in for the better part of eleven months, she made soft, murmuring nickers to him. The bonding had begun, and the mare instinctively knew her role. The new mother was exhausted and finally lay down for a little while. With the sac off, the foal's fur began to dry. The tiny eyelashes, the ears, the little feathery feet—not hooves for a while yet—and the sweet muzzle mouthing the air delighted Carson and Jorge.

Handling and touching the foal during this period imprinted Carson on the little guy and in a way, his training had begun, yet she was careful not to interfere with the mare/foal bonding. Then there was the Fleet enema to do to free the meconium to prevent impaction, and that went as planned.

Carson was surprised at how much knowledge she had retained after all this time. Everything flowed to her as if by instinct and she felt a warm sense of accomplishment. She used the office sink to splash the sweat off her face. The air drying her skin felt refreshing and as she cooled off, she retrieved her sweater and brushed off the straw.

They watched and waited for the foal to stand. Carson went to the office and made two mugs of coffee, doctored one the way she knew Jorge liked his, and returned to the stall. There she found Jorge glued to the door, watching the colt's first comical attempts at standing. The fluid-soaked straw was slippery against the rubber stall mats and it was tricky going. Jorge wanted to help him. Carson handed him a steaming mug and explained that the baby's unsteadiness was normal and that they should let him stand by himself.

The foal was a delightful little guy and Carson and Jorge watched, ready to help him find his way to nurse. Carson got the cart and the rake and slipped in to remove most of the wet straw. The stall was thickly bedded so she pulled the cleaner straw from the sides to absorb the rest.

They stayed until the colt was suckling well. His spindly legs strengthened fast. It was hard to tell what color he was, but there were some signs when he was dried off. His face seemed to be predominantly black with the hint of a white star on his forehead, a snip of white down his nose to a pale pink muzzle. His ears didn't seem to be black...but maybe. His neck and chest were black. Then there was a large swath of white, and then what looked like brown, white, and more black. His eyes were dark brown. He had the most unusual markings Carson had ever seen. There had been nothing like him in the barn in all the years she'd been there. His legs were white to just below the knees and hocks, and black to his dark little hooves, still soft from their time in utero.

The vet arrived in the morning and thoroughly examined the sac and the afterbirth. He checked the foal over and was pleased. He examined the mare to be sure there was no evidence of damage during the difficult birth. Carson explained that the foal had one leg back and that she had managed to straighten it. The vet nodded and said well done. He was impressed. Then his cell phone went off.

"Gotta go," he said. "No rest for the weary. I'll be back tomorrow to check on the colt."

"Have you heard of anyone looking for a lost mare?" Carson asked.

The vet was in the driver's seat, fastening his seatbelt as he spoke. "Not a word. I kinda think we won't. You OK if no one claims her?"

Carson nodded. "It's just more mouths to feed. I've loved all the babies and I'll love this one too," she said, beaming with confidence that this pair would thrive, as had countless others before them.

Chapter 42

Denny chain-smoked as he drove the stolen Malibu and Mason, sullen, rode shotgun. Denny didn't think of it as "stolen." He called it "borrowed." He "borrowed" it from his girlfriend, and she wouldn't be stupid enough to report it. Besides, he rationalized, if he got his stuff back, he'd return it. She knew better than to count him out. He had come back before. And she was afraid of him.

They followed the cop. It was easy to blend in amid the confusion of vehicles evacuating or trying to get into evacuated areas. Driving conditions varied from impossible to smoky and ash-swirled. Emergency vehicles and livestock trailers added to the gridlock in some areas. Somebody put out the call and folks with trailers of all sizes came from all over to help evacuate. They lined the sides of the highway, waiting to be called into action. Once, when he thought the cop might have identified them, Denny pulled over between a couple of them and waited a few minutes before pulling out again in time to keep him in sight.

Denny did a slow burn about the whole thing. The dumb luck of those guys to run over the exact spot of his stash! He was angry with himself for warning them. He should have just killed them, grabbed his shit, and gotten gone before the cop showed. But no, he tried it the dumb way and now he was pissed.

Visibility was obscured in one way or another and that damn cop went everywhere. Denny watched the gas gauge with growing concern. When the cop was out in the open, he moved fast, and Denny didn't know the roads like he did so he was at a disadvantage. He would hit it to catch up, then round a bend and there would be a snag. More than once he had to drive right by the guy. Mason, the little shit, stared at the cop as they went past, even after Denny told him not to. Once out of sight, Denny right-handed the side of his son's head and Mason sulked against the passenger's-side door for an hour.

Too bad I can't just open the door and throw him out, Denny thought more than once.

Mason finally whined that everyone stared at cops when they drove by, like at an "axident." Truth was, he was growing antsy. Mason was bored and when he was bored, which was often, there was only one way he liked to entertain himself. He was like a smoker. He had to have his fix.

Denny pulled over and blended in where they could observe the cop as he worked the edges of the emergency zone.

Spence was never far from other people or his patrol car. He had excellent peripheral vision and was aware of Denny but didn't let on. He had his ideas about who they might be and what their interest was in him—or, more specifically, the trunk of his patrol car—but he didn't let his suspicions interfere with his work, though his hand was never far from his sidearm. After all, they could just be fire chasers or arsonists watching their work. If they were the ones who shot at the dozer crew, their motivations might line up with the arson angle. He'd read that arsonists admired fires, even if they hadn't set them; that they got a buzz seeing them. Spence doubted the arson scenario, though he tried to keep an open mind. The trunk of his car all but radiated the "heat" of its contents, like a Geiger counter running past something radioactive.

Calmly, Spence dealt with each crisis as his shift stretched into a double. At some point, he didn't see the Malibu any longer.

Denny had Mason look up the address of the closest substation, which was on the outskirts of Martin, and took the chance that, at some point, the cop would take the most direct route there. Denny drove leisurely in that direction. He got honked at more than once for driving like an octogenarian. He flipped those assholes off out his window each time as they roared by.

Secure in knowing that the cop was behind them, Denny searched for the right spot—a place to lie in wait for the dark, when they could run him off the road. Mason was leery of that plan, especially because he wasn't sure which side of the car Denny intended to use to make impact. They argued back and forth and Denny short cuffed him again for doubting his ability as an experienced "wheel" man.

"Quit bitching, you little girl, you'll be fine," he chastised.

Finally, the radio quieted and people started to behave better in the emergency evacuation zones. The National Guard had finally shown up in force and there was a level of protection that gave Spence a window to breathe, albeit with a mask on.

Spence parked by the side of the road and put himself in their position. He did a basic grid search, sat in a couple of places long enough, and felt reliably certain that they had left. But where to? If they didn't know the area well, they had to reconnoiter for the best ambush spot. And he knew they were armed.

Spence opened the trunk and slid the contraband aside to free up a dark, oblong duffle bag. He dragged it forward and unzipped it. Inside were a few essentials. He pulled out his helmet and tactical multi-threat vest that was glowingly advertised as enhanced to provide bullet, strike, and slash protection— *"Taser protection, defense against 9mm armor-piercing ammunition, sporting rounds, as well as common handgun rounds including .357, 9mm, 45acp, up to .44 magnum."*

Did he believe all that? Not entirely. But it sounded good. Out in this country, there was a smattering of shotgun wielders and the vest provided additional protection against shotgun rounds, including 00 buckshot and 12 gauge. The vest was well-made, comfortable, and effective. It had been an expensive investment but Spence had gotten a small stipend from the department to offset it. He had examined the deflected shot damage on the dozer and from the description of what the shots sounded like, he guessed handgun. He decided to be ready for anything.

Spence checked the contents of his patrol car and secured any loose objects that might become flying projectiles if he rolled it. He was reminded of his fun times at the demolition derby track and how an unexpected hit could upend his ride and roll him either onto his side or all the way over. He had to admit that that momentary moment of suspension, then being miraculously plopped back onto the track to continue the battle, was exhilarating. But then…no one was shooting at him.

He got into his car, set the helmet on the seat, and did the seatbelt nice and snug. Spence pulled out his backup weapon and set it into a custom holster he'd built into the door. He could pull it and fire either through the door to wound, or angle upward to make sure. When he put a revolver in there, the safety was off. If his hand went there, it was a committed act. Like his father once said, "You don't draw a gun unless you're going to discharge it. Period."

Ready as he'd ever be, Spence wondered briefly whether someone would know to go to his place and feed his fish if this went wrong. It dawned on him then that he'd never shared with anyone that he had fish. They were like family and they depended on him. Spence turned the key in the ignition and the powerful V8 roared to life. He knew he could arrive at the station looking like he'd come from playing paintball or his car would be a bit shot up and he'd be in one piece. He preferred no alternate storyline. Feeling that he was ready, Spence pulled out onto the road.

Denny and Mason were on knife's edge. Neither had the veracity or threshold for waiting, and their combined impatience made for the possibility of poor timing. Spence barely saw the car as it appeared and tried to hit his patrol car. He spun the wheel and dodged it, fishtailing on the road. The right-side wheels of his car lost purchase on the edge of the asphalt and flirted with the softer dirt. He fought the drift at first, then rode the two halves of the car, waiting for the right moment to fix it.

Spence was well trained and didn't make the mistake of trying to overcorrect it and flip his vehicle. He rode the edge, for a second scraping the undercarriage, which illuminated the darkness with sparks. Spence felt the moment and picked a spot to get the wheels back onto the pavement. At that moment, he checked his rearview mirror and saw a flash. He ducked as the rear windshield exploded, spraying glass all over the inside of his car.

"Son of a bitch!" Spence spat through clenched teeth.

The cage prevented the bulk of the glass from hitting him and he accelerated hard, then squirreled it around a slight bend in the road as another flash appeared in his rear view but went wide and missed.

The advantage was Spence knew the road. The disadvantage was, he didn't know exactly how capable and determined they were. They had no headlights on, and he couldn't gauge how close they were. He whipped it into overdrive, letting the powerful V8 run full-out. Spence widened the gap, picked his spot in a trucking turnout where there was just enough room to spin around, and set his trap. He killed his lights and waited at a place where many a wreck had occurred. With luck, they'd add to that number without his participation. He could almost predict how this one would end.

Spence idled the engine. His window was rolled down, and in the distance, he thought he heard them coming. Spence touched the dashboard of his cruiser for luck and waited…

But nothing happened. Spence killed the engine and listened. There was no sound of an oncoming car or a retreating one.

The radio crackled. Spence hadn't realized he'd been holding his breath, and jumped. A breeze blew from behind, through the broken rear window, and raised the hairs on his neck. He put the cruiser into gear and headed back to the station at high speed. With an eye on the rearview mirror, Spence grabbed the radio handset and reported the incident.

Chapter 43

The chute was set up in such a way that the trailers lined up, unloaded their terrified cargo, and left. Cullen had arrived late and was not happy he would be one of the last to unload. He could smell that the party had started when a gun-toting drunk wearing a cowboy hat swaggered over and, through Cullen's open window, breathed instructions he already knew.

Cullen heard the skip loader start up, its bright lights splitting the night. He could see it would be turning his way in a minute and grabbed his sunglasses and put them on.

Upon seeing this, Cowboy Hat tagged him on the upper left arm and asked if he was some kind of "movieeeeeeeestar."

Cullen was polite and said no. He knew how to manage drunks and he was especially respectful of armed ones. The sound of the rowdy group of armed men as they whooped and hollered about their shooting prowess drifted over the other noises to Cullen's ears. He dropped his load and wanted to get out of there as quickly as possible. Prior experience around these people had made him very edgy and if it wasn't for the money, he would have never done the job again. This time, he'd been more observant as he drove out to this location. No repeat of the last time, thank you very much.

The first batch had been driven through a barrier alley into a prepared shooting gallery. There was a series of them, and the skip loader waited nearby to bury the evidence.

Out of sight, on an elevated outcropping nearby, a lone rider watched, unseen, and the night vision lens of the camera captured the evidence before it was covered up.

Wranglers lined up another batch and drove the panicked horses down the chute. The victims had been rounded up by helicopter for the BLM, different herds, all destined for massive holding pens in the high desert. Contractors were supposed to deliver them to designated holding areas and well-meaning organizations tried to gentle the ones they could and get them adopted. But the numbers swelled and the holding areas were overflowing. A few bad actors had taken it upon themselves to do something about it, to gorge at the public trough and have their fun, and no one kept track of it due to the manipulation of the loosely followed "rules." This cabal of second-amenders had figured out a bullet-quick answer to a gigantic problem. They felt immune, entitled. It was like a Friday night club.

The rider, hidden beyond the boulders, bore witness. As their night wore on and the carnage moved from pit to ugly pit, rifle barrels grew red hot, gun smoke drifted low in the air, and the sounds of terrified animals were drowned out by the skip loader burying them, some still alive.

Before long, ammunition and alcohol ran low. Their numbers thinned as many staggered to their vehicles and departed in dust balls of confusion. A few fender-benders on ranch trucks occurred—the dings and dents indiscernible from the day-to-day use of the same vehicles. Some fell asleep in the beds of their trucks. A couple of wranglers brought their own horses and they high-lined them for the night and gathered near open fires to congratulate themselves about the "good" they were doing. By around one in the morning, the din had subsided, and the morons had had their fill of just about everything.

And that's when the rider went to work. It wasn't the rogue's first nocturnal raid. The horse, well trained, stood silent as girths were severed, rope lines cut, tire strips laid, and license plates documented. The rogue knew how to silently wreak havoc. The real damage would come from the use of the information against the perpetrators—ultimately more costly than sabotage. But that was pushing paper, expertly using the system against them, and unleashing a torrent of bureaucratic hell on those that organized the slaughter.

The psycho militia hated that someone was fucking with them. It was their God-given right to mess with the BLM and the overreaching government. They felt completely justified that they had standing. Some unknown was using well executed tactics against them and they resented it.

The lone rider didn't care. It wasn't about their stupid, shortsighted little fight. It was about the true wilderness. The wild horses had every right to be there, maybe more so than their cattle.

It was darkest before the dawn, and the rogue rider struck, shooting to mess with their heads and to run off their horses. Gunfire stirred groggy shooting party members, who fought their hangovers to catch up to what was happening. The dust rose faster than they did, and they never saw who cut their tie lines and ran their personal horses off. The rider ran them, driving them away, and they went willingly.

One outrider got a grip on his animal and was stunned when his saddle spun off onto the ground. His horse's halter rope was uncut, and he swung himself up bareback to give chase. The dust obscured everything, and, in the melee, he guessed at a path of retreat and got lucky.

The rogue rider felt the pursuer. There was no need to look behind in the swirl of confusion and dust. He was there. The rogue led the bareback man on a steeplechase, jumping shallows and dips, boulders and sedges, and this pursuer clung like a tick to his scrambling horse over unknown ground.

The rogue rider had made familiar with the ground in daylight and led this handy fool a-merry. If he wanted to be sore later and have a tale to tell, so be it. He'd have one. Including the part where he crashed to the ground within a hoofbeat of his quarry.

Chapter 44

Many of the people Spence saw after the fire were depressed and defeated. Some showed remarkable resilience, and some acted as if nothing bad had happened to them and were basically the same. Many were on the fence about rebuilding. Much of it had to do with the sheer devastation of it all. Where to start was almost a universal opening to conversations. The culling of injured animals took a toll that hollowed out even the strongest of men and women. There were so many dead and dying animals and the sound of distant gunfire drifted consistently on the wind. One thing Lyle Martin ran out of in the first few days was ammunition. The smell of burnt flesh and hair was everywhere.

Recovery task force meetings were very emotional, contentious, and a sense of hopelessness and fatigue had settled on some. Lyle invested every waking minute to helping the community recover. The Federal Emergency Management Agency sent people to Martin to register households requesting help for housing assistance and other needs. They set up a trailer office in the parking lot behind the ranch supply building and a steady stream of people made their way there to begin navigating a maze that would hopefully lead to financial aid.

Spence was driving his truck since the patrol car was in the shop getting a new rear window. He'd dropped the cruiser off late the day before, and the shop guy had said he'd get to it first thing. Spence hoped he would get it back that afternoon. He felt a little too exposed in his truck.

A break-in at the repair shop was the first of two unusual calls that morning and Spence went there to take the report. The door was kicked in but nothing was missing. No tools were taken, not even a can of oil. The man who owned it was a stickler for managing inventory and when the alarm had triggered a notification on his cell, he swore he was there in half an hour and saw no one. The only thing out of the ordinary was that the keys to the patrol car had been taken from the hook in the office and were found in the lock of the patrol car's trunk. And that's when Mike called Spence.

Mike leaned against his desk, coffee cup in hand, and said, "Yeah, that's it, the only thing amiss."

Spence frowned. "Are the keys still there and have you touched anything?"

Mike took a sip. "I thought about fixing the door and then I thought I'd better not touch anything. So, the short answer is, I have left everything as I found it."

Wisely, Spence had taken his evidence kit out of the patrol car before he dropped it off. He'd secured the evidence at the station, then locked his equipment in the heavy-duty, diamond-steel toolbox on his truck.

As Spence walked to his truck to retrieve the kit, he was acutely aware of his surroundings. He took a mental inventory of vehicles parked in the vicinity and any that drove by. Behind the building, in an open field, there was a smattering of parked vehicles, unwashed, with layers of ash on them. More than one was thoroughly dusted so that one could not see inside. The door handles, visible to him, were as ash laden as the rest of the vehicles, but if someone had jimmied a door on the far side, he wouldn't see that from his vantage point. Spence wanted to get the information on each of the vehicles before he left, maybe drive over there and look around.

"Hey, Mike, what's the story on those vehicles out back?' Spence asked as he returned to the shop.

"There were burned and abandoned vehicles scattered about during the fires. We're storing them. I hadn't thought about what to do if no one comes to claim them. At some point, I'll decide what's to be done. Probably auction. There's some with bubbled paint, heat damage, some were abandoned on the side of the road after they'd run out of gas waiting to get through."

Mike followed Spence to the patrol car through the open garage doors. "We had a whole lot out there, rigs with heat damage and I let folks stay in their motorhomes while they were evacuated." He took a breath. "Hell, we were really busy there for a week or so, it was good we could help."

Spence put on gloves, then dusted his own patrol car for prints. It felt weird to do that and he couldn't help but feel like a probationer practicing on whatever was available years ago. He followed procedure and collected evidence from the broken office door and any possible surfaces between where the keys hung to the patrol car. He took photographs of everything and almost felt he was overdoing it, yet something deep in his head told him to be thorough. Cautiously, he opened the trunk a crack, and with a bright penlight, visually confirmed there were no booby-trap wires or anything untoward waiting for him inside. Aside from evidence that someone had rifled through the contents of the trunk, it was normal.

Mike had to pump some gas, as in Oregon, customers were not allowed. Spence retraced his steps to the jimmied door. He closed it and stood outside, and imagined how it was done. Was it kicked in or pried? Did the perp care about noise? He pushed it open, followed with his head to peer around it, and it hit the wall and bounced back. Instinctively, Spence put his left forearm up, but not before the edge of the door clocked him on the eyebrow. He swore and rubbed his forehead.

Mike returned. "Oh, sorry, that door has given me more than one black eye."

Spence shook his head, rubbing it in the hopes it didn't just give him one too. "And you've never fixed it?"

Mike looked guilty. "Well, look at it this way, whoever heavy-armed it has a heeluva a shiner cuz he really muscled it, and it will definitely fight back."

"Grand," Spence said sarcastically and then asked Mike how he had found the office door when he responded to the break-in.

Mike wasn't sure. He had been a bit out of sorts and on edge not knowing what or who he might find. He told Spence that he was more than a little scared in the dark.

Inside Mike's tiny, cramped office, Spence noted that there was barely enough room for a chair. There was just one, in front of his desk. Spence walked in and stood in front of the desk and Mike squeezed past him, slid around the desk, and sat down behind it. Spence turned and saw the rack where the customers' keys were hung. A clipboard hung to the left of that. The tags on the keys corresponded to paperwork in the clipboard.

"So, the keys are just keys unless you look at the paperwork, correct?" Spence asked. He noted smudged parts on the doorjamb where someone working might grab the sill, stick their head partially in, and take the obvious key—a GM key for a GM car or other obvious make. Because the shop was so small, someone wouldn't necessarily need to come all the way in to reach everything.

"How many cars were in yesterday?" Spence asked.

"Well...there were two we left outside waiting for parts. And there were two inside. We'd a never left yours outside."

Spence's keys were unmarked—something one of his mentors told him to be sure of. "Always carry and use an anonymous set of keys," the veteran had told him. There was an interesting story of a hostage situation where an undercover operation was blown because the officer's keys screamed "cop" at an unstable perp, and that officer had died. And it was enough of a lesson for his mentor to make it one of Spence's rules too.

Spence ascertained that the perp would have had to look at the clipboard to see which keys went to the patrol car. He grabbed it and it immediately fell off the nail it hung on, and clattered to the floor. It startled Spence and he imagined it had done the same to the perp.

"Oh shit, I keep meaning to fix that, happens all the time," Mike said.

Spence was still wearing his blue, powderless gloves. Small sweat marks appeared through them as he picked up the clipboard and put it on the desk, then flipped through the orders to the third one, which was his. Large, red numbers corresponded to his keys and he looked over his shoulder to an empty hook.

"Where was this clipboard when you came in?" he asked Mike.

"Right about there, on my desk. I guess I did touch something."

"That's OK, easy enough to eliminate your prints and those of anyone who regularly works here." Spence dusted the large metal clip at the top of the clipboard and got a couple of clearly defined prints. He held the transfer up to the light and felt satisfied with it. His cell rang and he paused to answer it.

"Spence?" Dee's voice tremulously answered his hello.

"Dee?"

"Yeah, I...uh...I have a situation here. How far away are you?"

Spence did a quick calculation and answered her.

"Um, well...could you make it sooner, please?" And then she coughed and started to cry. "Much sooner."

Spence heard her tone and began putting things into his kit while she spoke. Dee had taken over Martin's small pharmacy—the only one for miles—after her father passed. It no longer had a pharmacist, but she managed to stock sundries and over-the-counter medicines. Occasionally, she made the trip to Redmond or Bend to visit a warehouse store like Costco to restock. To satisfy her own passion, she'd turned a small section in the back into a beauty parlor and nail salon—one chair and one nail station, and Dee ran both on alternating days so the nail polish fumes didn't overwhelm the hair customers. An old-fashioned barber pole adorned the front of the store, as Dee tended to the needs of both men and women. It had survived the fires undamaged. Spence got his hair cut there and Dee had Spence's direct cell number.

He hurried to his truck, clicked the door locks up, and placed his kit on the seat next to him. Spence put the key into the ignition and spun the tires in the gravel. He forgot to check the vehicles in the back.

Mason sat in one of the ash-covered vehicles in the field and had watched Spence's comings and goings. He should have rung his father, but he was engrossed in his cell phone, his imagination fully engaged with the images on the screen. He had his favorites saved in case he couldn't get a signal, which, where they had been lately, happened a lot. When they had stayed at that last motel on the way to collect their fortune, he'd been happy to take advantage of the free Wi-Fi and uploaded what he needed. His father had threatened to cut it off if he caught him at it again. That just drove Mason to be more creative with his habit. He closed his eyes and rested his head against the seat back as he ebbed like a flag in a dying breeze.

Denny had left him there to watch after he broke into the gas station to retrieve what was left of the damaged bucket and its contents. But it wasn't there, and the side of Mason's face smarted from the blow he'd received when he asked if his father had found it.

"Does it look like I found it?" Denny fumed.

He pulled up next to an abandoned truck, jimmied the door, and left Mason there to watch…watch until he got back.

"And don't fall asleep," he threatened.

And of course, Mason had slept straight away…even though the owner showed up less than a half-hour later because of the alarm. When he woke about three hours after that, he noticed lights on but he entertained himself instead of doing what he was told. His priorities were his dysfunction, something his father didn't understand and never would.

Three Corner Fire

—⁂—

Spence heard on the radio that the fire was still active in some areas, and the containment percentage sounded small as he headed to Dee's Boutique. When he arrived, Dee waved him over just shy of her shop and leaned on the sill of the truck window.

"Sh-sh-sheriff," she stuttered, and her voice caught as she straightened, turned her head away from him, and burst into tears. She folded her arms across her chest and paced by the truck until she regained control. She wiped her face with the back of one hand.

Spence noticed that her nails were perfectly done and he found the neutral color pleasing.

Then she leaned one hand on the door and said with a sob, "I know love today, sir. I truly do." She took a deep breath and continued, "You see that old car there? That old man, Tom... see him standing there?"

Spence nodded.

"His wife, Mary Elizabeth, has her nails done every week, same time, same day. Loves her nails. It's her only vice, she tells me, and she says how Tom felt she could do them herself, but no, this was her bit, her time, her special treat and he'd drive her to town every week, go off somewhere while she gets 'em done, then he picks her up. She bakes. Did I tell you that? She's a helluva baker and on her last birthday, ol' Tom, he surprises her with two of those special oven mitts she saw on the shopping channel and wanted really bad…anyway, Mary Elizabeth bakes up a whole bunch of her goodies for the folks that was evacuated and she tells Tom to get on in and deliver them.

They live a ways out and Tom did as she told him and then got cut off trying to get back to their ranch. Took him twenty-four hours best as I can get from him to get back there."

She was rambling. Spence started to interrupt but Dee wouldn't let him. She was almost breathless getting the story out.

"So, today's her regular appointment and so I see him pull up...and I come out to greet them and help him get her out and inside as she's a little unsteady. Well, she had the polio, used a cane or sometimes a walker thing. So, I come out and he's not right. I mean, he's really lost, talking and making no sense, and I think, oh hell, he's had a stroke or something. I sweet talk him to her side of the car. He's going on about how she has to have her nails nice. *'Specially now.* And I'm thinking he's confused or something....and..." Dee lost it again, dropped her head against her arm on the sill of Spence's car, and couldn't stop sobbing.

Spence gently opened the door and guided Dee over to the sidewalk, where she crumpled to a sitting position on the high curb. He had an inkling about what he would find in the old man's car. He reassured Dee, turned, straightened his belt and holster, and walked slowly to Tom's car.

The passenger's side door was open, and Spence approached it carefully. Cars were slowing, curious about what was going on. Spence closed the door partially and waved the gawkers on.

Tom leaned with his back against the car, staring blankly past Spence.

Spence asked him his name. "Tom? May I call you Tom?" he said politely.

The old man didn't look at him but nodded. He didn't make eye contact until Spence was next to him.

"Tom, I need to call this into the coroner. May I have your permission to cover your wife? I will be very respectful, sir."

Tom just closed his eyes and said nothing. In fact, he never uttered another word.

Spence asked Dee if he could use one of her customer smocks from the hair salon. Dee had recovered herself and was pleased to be of use. She fetched one and he took it around to the passenger's side. Mary Elizabeth sat propped up, head frozen in rigor mortis, her house dress charred black and falling apart, her skin blistered and burnt. There were few recognizable facial features. But on her hands were her favorite oven mitts that Tom had surprised her with.

Spence reached down and touched one of the mitts. He felt her intact hand inside and hesitated. He considered removing the mitt but realized that may not be wise. If it unstuck from the crisped skin, it might not be clean. He gently unfurled the rose-colored smock and covered her body.

Inside the mitts, protected from the fire that had destroyed their home of over half a century, Mary Elizabeth's hands were perfect, nails ready to be done.

Chapter 45

When the ranchers returned to their cattle pastures, it was a scene from a nightmare. Dead cattle carcasses lay scattered everywhere. The sudden loss of a livelihood, a home, or both could only be absorbed in waves of realization. Those who lost friends and family struggled to come to terms with it. Valued animals—from family pets to favorite horses to prized stock whose bloodlines went back generations—were lost. Health issues arose from the stress of losing everything and many hearts, irreparably broken, simply failed.

The harshest reality was the instant loss of income. One day people could pay the bills, and the next they could not. It was as if all the oxygen had been sucked away and left a hollowness, a shortness of breath. And it hurt to breathe. For some, it was too much to bear, the recovery an unimaginable string of steps with no clear map of how to begin. The damage to the dignity of normally hard-working people was almost total and the capricious nature of the disaster found ways to punish the lucky for their survival.

It was well past lunchtime, and the Running Horse truck was running late. Carson knew the sound of Buckets' beloved International Harvester and the Running Horse ranch truck. The Harvester reminded her of an old truck she'd seen somewhere as a child, but she couldn't recall exactly where.

She stood with the manure cart by the open barn doors

and waved to Green Eyes as he pulled in and stopped next to her, his window rolled down.

"What are you doing in Buckets' truck?" she asked him.

He put his finger to his lips, shushed her, and grinned. "I don't think he knows Ol' Belle here has gone on an errand. The other truck wasn't there so I borrowed her."

He looked around and didn't see Bodie ready to go, and muttered, "Where is that son of a bitch…" and then asked where Kitzie was.

Carson wasn't sure. "Try the trailer," she said and nodded that way. "Buckets is gonna kick your ass," she added.

"Not if I get back before he knows." He winked at her conspiratorially, then held up a manila envelope with Kitzie's name written on it in Bucket's neat print. "I'm on a mission. He left this on the seat. I'll deliver it. Be right back." He stepped on the gas and drove around the corner.

Carson plucked a manure rake from its hook on the wall. She pushed the cart to the closest barn door, slid it open, and went to the paddock door. The foal was stretched out flat, asleep in the sun, the mare standing beside him. Carson quietly slid the paddock door closed so as not to wake him, and left them in the paddock.

Carson was lost in thought as she picked manure and sodden bedding out of the stall and pitched it into the cart. She was procrastinating about declaring bankruptcy and hiring an attorney. She acknowledged that she needed to begin the journey to unravel and repair the damage she'd ignored for too long but still, she didn't want to know. She straightened and looked at the round, firm balls of manure that balanced on the tines of the rake and laughed. She was literally looking at shit. How prophetic. Then she muttered, "It's true. I don't want to know…"

"Know what?"

A voice from behind startled her. The rake wavered in her hands, dipped, and lost its contents. Carson looked down in dismay as the manure balls scattered, then she planted the tines of the rake into the hay and spun to confront a grinning Bodie.

"What the fuck!" Carson was furious. "What part of don't do that to me don't you understand?"

Bodie laughed. "Aww, come on, don' be like that."

He slid the stall door open wider with his right hand—just wide enough to lean on the smooth jamb. His tool belt was slung over his shoulder and his shirt was unbuttoned, revealing tanned skin behind a green plaid, short-sleeved shirt. A blush of sawdust had dried on his upper chest and traveled down to the top button of his faded jeans. He wore no belt and the band of his underwear teased from the top. Carson noticed the animal leanness of him, the natural way he propped himself against the door, so determined to steal the anger from her voice. The over self-confidence of an attractive man, even one covered in a day's hard work, was not completely unforgivable. Carson couldn't help but shake her head as she turned to retrieve her lost cargo with the rake.

"So…what don't you want to do?" he asked as he watched her.

"Oh, it's nothing," Carson said without looking, feeling exposed and slightly embarrassed.

"Seemed important…important enough to talk to yourself about," Bodie said.

She remained silent, found all the lost bits, and pitched them into the cart. The mare had returned to the edge of the paddock entry and stared at them through the bars, her ears pricked forward. The natural curiosity was one of the things Carson loved about horses. In spite of their place in the food chain, they continued to be curious about the hunter. And she felt a bit hunted at that moment.

Bodie changed the subject and asked if that old truck parked a ways off was hers. She nodded but guessed he already knew that.

"Do you want to sell it?" he said, making small talk.

Sell my truck? she thought. "I don't think so. Besides, the tires are shot."

Carson kept her focus on the task at hand and didn't look up at him but Bodie was determined to draw her out. She heard him lay his toolbelt down and enter the stall. He closed the door some but not completely. She felt him near and stopped scooping. Out of the corner of her eye, Carson saw his smooth belly and a perfect innie. He put his hand near hers and gently pulled the rake handle from her fingers. It was a decent attempt at a pass, and it had been an awfully long time since someone had tried. Her mind reeled for a second. It was a tempting thought…but not with this one. Carson leaned back away from him. She started to move to his left, to get out of the way, and his right hand came up to her elbow and gently blocked her. She looked up into that face and he leaned toward her.

"Easy, lightning," she said.

It was a phrase she used when an animal was skittish and moving too fast. She was uncomfortable and tried to lighten the awkward moment.

Bodie tried to lean closer, invading her space, and she backed away. Yes, he was good looking, but there was something dishonest about him.

The sound of footfalls startled him. Carson snatched the rake back, pivoted with it, and said loudly, "Thank you, but I don't need help, I've got this."

She stepped smoothly around the cart so that it was an effective barrier between them and went after a damp spot in the corner by the automatic waterer. Carson made a show of checking to see if it was leaking (it wasn't) and scooped up some urine-soaked shavings and plopped them into the cart.

Green Eyes appeared and started to smile at her through the stall bars until he saw Bodie. Bodie's false sparkle faded and with slumped shoulders, he slithered through the door past Green Eyes and scooped up his tool belt. He didn't look up.

Carson didn't hide her relief at the intervention, though the awkward tension in the air hadn't completely dissipated. They both heard the toolbelt land hard as Bodie pitched it into the back of the truck loud enough that she and Green Eyes both flinched.

"That sounded like it'll leave a mark," she tried to joke and ran her sleeve on her cheek as if to wipe away the vestiges of the unwelcome encounter. It left a dusty streak on the side of her face instead.

"Another mark among many," Green Eyes replied. "Man ought to take better care of his tools."

"Not sure that will happen anytime soon," Carson added, wiping at her face again.

Those piercing green eyes stared into hers. "He wasn't bothering you, was he?"

"Not much." She shrugged, rotated the cart, and dragged it behind her toward the door, then stopped in front of him.

Green Eyes meant to back off and open the door wider but on an impulse, he reached up to wipe the dust off that perfect skin. He tilted his head and half smiled. "You're a mess." He laughed and his index finger lightly brushed the smudge clear, then traced the line of her lower jaw and lifted it to fully meet his eyes.

That simple gesture sent an electric current down her spine and around into the pit of her stomach. Her breath caught for a moment and Carson became instantly aware of long-neglected parts.

Green Eyes stepped back. "There…all better," he said softly, and opened the stall door wider and backed up.

Carson didn't move and could think of nothing clever or witty to say.

Looking a little embarrassed, Green Eyes waved. "OK, see ya later." He turned and headed to the truck.

Carson heard it start and drive away, her heart doing a steady thud inside her chest. *Christ*, she thought, *was that two passes?*

A noise at the other door reminded her that the mare was watching. Carson pushed the manure cart out of the stall and closed the stall door. She opened the paddock door and the foal was the first through it. He did a little boinky move, excited at seeing her, and she paid attention to those little black hooves. They had firmed up quickly and were starting to look harder—enough that it was wise to avoid taking an exuberant kick from one. He dashed around his mom, lost traction in the hay and fell, leaped to his feet, and found a nipple to nurse, all in the span of seconds.

Carson exited the stall to leave them to it. After she closed the stall door, she rested her cheeks on the coolness of the bars and watched them. She closed her eyes and saw the fresh memory of those emerald-green eyes.

Carson found her mother by the remnants of the shed looking at the rubble and destruction. Kitzie's arms were folded across her chest as she looked at her daughter. "What's up?"

Carson laughed and joked that in the past twenty minutes she thought two men had made passes at her.

"Really?" Kitzie smiled.

Carson shrugged, hands out, palms up. "Yeah...I think that's what just happened."

"And?" Kitzie's eyebrows arched with curiosity.

"And...nothing. I think I'm losing my touch."

"Oh, well...I hear it's like riding a bike...you never forget."

They stood silently together. The smell of smoke and burnt materials still clung to the air, though it had been some weeks since the disaster. When it was the worst, one couldn't see because the smoke was so thick. Shades of reality matched the air quality and taking in the full measure of the damage was too much to interpret in one sitting. It was as if the fires were rocks tossed into a pool of water. The ripples extended inexorably outward, lapping against some things and washing over others. The rings begat rings and it took time for the full extent of what had happened to judge how it affected people.

Kitzie wrinkled her nose as she took a breath and soberly commented, "This kind of loss lives inside you for the rest of your life."

Carson nodded and bumped her shoulder against her mother's. "We'll get through this."

Jorge had the difficult task of deciding what to do with his father's remains. It was an expense he had never considered before, and he didn't have the money for it. There had been awkward conversations about it and weeks had passed, yet it had to be dealt with. He wasn't sure how to mourn his father without a proper funeral and he was too upset to consider planning one, even if he could afford it. But a resolution was necessary, and he finally asked for help.

Kitzie sprang into action. Her bad knee was stiff. She had overdone it and limped around the indoor arena until she found a cell phone signal, then negotiated a discounted price with the mortuary. After looking around furtively before being so blatant, and ensuring that Jorge was out of earshot, she argued that the fire had already done most of the mortuary's job. Kitzie hoped that her guilt over her inability to enforce the limits on Luis that would have changed the course of events, and broken the chains of causation, would be assuaged. But it wasn't to be. She knew hindsight was clearer and she struggled with it still.

When Jorge first realized why he couldn't find his father, he'd stood, stunned, before the crumbled building as tongues of flame leaped unsatisfied and the tires in the back refused to be extinguished. Kitzie had seen the light go out of his eyes and she wanted to reach out to him, to hold him like the mother he didn't have, to comfort him through the desperate loss. But cultural barriers held her at bay. The machismo of the Hispanic male made its first appearance in the body of the boy, now a man.

Kitzie sat in the trailer with her laptop. Tuff had taught her to do full back-ups of everything, monthly, and to put the discs in the fireproof safe. The safe had survived the fire, as advertised, and once again, it seemed that Tuff had reached out from beyond to guide her through tough times. The safe contained insurance policies, important records, jewelry, and the papers to all their horses.

Jorge knocked on the trailer door and asked if Kitzie could talk. She waved him in. He was concerned that even though he had his proof of citizenship, he had few ties to Mexico, and given the current political climate, he felt he wouldn't be able to come back to the US if, for some reason, he had to leave.

A few minutes later, Carson stuck her head in. Kitzie offered Jorge a beer, and opened one for herself while Carson uncapped a bottle of water.

"I wish your father had told me about the papers," Kitzie said to Jorge. "I'd have put them somewhere safe for you."

Jorge was spent, emotionally and physically. "Yeah, I knew that shop was bad but he would not let me clean anything up. Even the house was cluttered to the point that it bothered me." He tried to laugh but mustered only a dry cough.

"Jorge, whatever you decide, know that the cottage is yours. I haven't decided about rebuilding the shop or the other barn. I may just clear the ground where the shop was and leave it."

Jorge nodded his silent approval of that plan.

"Most of my energy will be directed at rebuilding the house. I have to see how far the insurance money goes." Kitzie looked at him and asked, "Would you please stay and help us?"

Jorge agreed to do that, and it made his mood a little brighter knowing he still had a future at the Three Bit if he wanted it. "It's a good thing you still had this," Jorge said as he looked around the interior of the trailer.

"It's plenty of room for me and Wyatt," Kitzie said and looked down at the little white dog. His head popped up at the sound of his name.

Jorge's two cattle dogs were lying outside, dutifully waiting for him. Jorge said he was sad about Lulu. Kitzie nodded.

Jorge got up. "Well...I have work to do," he said, and left the trailer, his beer unfinished on the table.

Kitzie got up and poured it out. "That boy will never be much of a drinker."

During a brief call with Wyker, Kitzie learned that the hospital was backed-up with fire-related injuries, a lot of smoke inhalation cases complicated by pre-existing conditions, and worse. They'd heard that CJ was improving and had left the hospital with Wyker. The stoic CJ had refused visitors initially, but Uncle had urged Harper to ignore that. He felt they needed to get CJ back to the Rez to heal, so Harper had gone to see them at the hospital. Wyker told her about Tish, who had found CJ. Said most of what he knew about the situation came from her, when he was finally able to reach her. Kitzie inquired after the herd and it seemed the cattle were thriving.

After the call, Kitzie filled Carson in.

"This Tish was part of a rescue team working in the fire area. She's an EMT, sounded like the one in charge. She told Will that CJ was quite the fighter."

Carson smiled at that observation.

"She said they thought another person was out there with CJ when he kept insisting he wasn't leaving without someone named Rio."

"Oh, God..." Carson looked pained. "He's really lost Rio then?"

Kitzie sighed. The angst of the loss was familiar. The last time she'd felt it was when it was time to put their prized stallion down. Every time she touched a horse, she felt the piece of her heart buried with him. When she stroked Wyatt's upturned face, and he closed his eyes, she could feel Lulu there with them. Kitzie was touching all the beloved ones that had come before. They had been there to make her ready, ready to love and be loved unconditionally. And to be prepared to let them go.

Kitzie tamped down her emotions and continued, "Wyker and Tish feel that due to the widespread destruction, Rio probably didn't make it. But she promised to try to get a message to her firefighter husband, to watch for him and..."

Kitzie stared at something on her screen and seemed distracted.

"And?" Carson prodded.

Kitzie looked up. "I saw something about a missing team on the news. I texted Wyker and he confirmed it is the same guy...look, even if Rio survived, chances of finding him are very slim." Sighing deeply, she continued, "Tish's husband's hotshot team is missing, and she hasn't heard from him. Crews are looking." She looked out the window. "You know, I needed convincing, then when I first met CJ, I wasn't sure about him, but watching him with that horse...it seemed he brought out the best in that man." She paused. "I hope this loss is not the kind that's always hungry. If it is, I am afraid it will eat away at him."

Kitzie looked back at her computer.

"Here's an email from the sheriff's office. They're sending Spence out to do a follow-up report on Luis's death." Kitzie sat back and looked sad.

"It's not anyone's fault, Mom, he didn't have to be in there when it was burning. That was just stupid."

Carson instantly regretted using the word "stupid." Her mother shot her a look.

"Sorry, OK...*foolish*. I don't know, maybe he was hurt and couldn't get out."

Kitzie indicated with her eyes that she forgave the bluntness of the remark. "I know, it's just Jorge I was thinking of. Has he shared anything with you?"

Carson shook her head. "He hasn't offered anything...and I haven't taken the time to ask, really..."

Carson had worked around him and avoided anything more than sincere words of condolence. As the days passed and the fire was no longer the first topic of conversation, a new normal had set in. There was livestock to doctor and feed, issues arising from the loss of forage to resolve, and the subject never came up easily. Carson thought it best to move on.

Carson asked, "When is Spence coming?"

Kitzie said it didn't say, it was just a formal notice. "Spence is probably pretty busy so it may be a while."

"Do you think it will matter that Luis was undocumented?" Carson asked quietly.

Kitzie looked at her daughter. "I don't know. I'd like to think not. A life was lost. That's all that should matter."

Carson dealt with the evening feeding for the horses that were still in the arena. Feet stomped and the smell of ash mixed with arena sand drifted into the air. The horses jostled for position and whinnied in anticipation of dinner. Carson had filled the hay bags in the barn and hand-carried them to the horses, and they trotted next to her on the other side of the pipe panels in anticipation. The trick to a peaceful, injury-free feeding was being familiar with the personalities, knowing the order and position of each horse, and getting everyone their food in a timely manner. There were four horses left in the arena plus they'd taken in a couple of ranch horses from neighbors who had lost everything, and Carson sorted out where to put each for the least drama. The Three Bit was well stocked for now but unspoken doubts about feed long term were not far from her mind.

Carson watched the horses eat. They quieted and muzzles vanished into the hay bags. Lips as sensitive as fingers explored the depths for their favorite pieces. The horses were separated enough that they could eat unmolested. This was a good group, and when the lead horse would move down the line to the next position, everyone shifted according to the established pecking order.

Carson called to one who had shifted but hadn't chosen well. "Hey, hey, get back to your spot." She started toward the offender, who wisely stepped back to his net and delved in.

Carson observed the hay that fell onto the sand. The horses would eat the sand too, when they cleaned up the last morsels of hay. She had located some psyllium on an online website, cheaper in generic bulk than through an equestrian supply, stocked up, and planned to feed some to each horse once a month. The last thing she wanted to deal with was sand colic or an impacted colon.

Carson looked up into the steel beams that supported the weight of the huge arena. It seemed like dozens of beady eyes watched her and she marveled at the tenacity of the sparrows. Their innate adaptability helped them thrive. The wind and flames had raged all around them for days and the suffocating smoke hung in the arched eves of the steel arena. The metal of the roof was marked by thousands of black dots where flying embers had descended, stuck, and died. Yet, above her, unfazed, were flocks of sparrows in their nests and flying around the arches of steel protection.

A few days later, Carson and Kitzie rode out to get an overview of where they stood on the ranch. It was a rare trail ride—something they used to do when Carson was a child. They had to consider the bred cows that had survived the firestorms. Some were struggling. They kept them pastured close by and Jorge was treating the injured. All over the county, ranchers who had stock survive were considering their options. Some families were completely wiped out and not all of them were going to stay. The Three Bit would have to take some stock to market because there was too little grass upon which to free graze. Everyone was looking at hard choices. *Market* choices.

Thirty minutes in, mother and daughter traversed a steep, narrow wash and rode up to a low hill on the other side, where a full vista of the Three Bit and the mountains beyond greeted them. The shadows were starting to stretch into the valley. Kitzie and Carson stopped and sat on their horses to take in the view. From several vantage points, they got a better visual of the damage to the land. They talked about which pastures were viable, which needed time to recover, and how much time. There were so many uncertainties. How many cattle could the land support? Which cows should they send to market, and which should they keep? How many more cows could the land near Uncle support? What would it cost to transport them?

Kitzie felt they should consult Buckets.

Carson agreed. "Let's show him our numbers and have him do an overview from his perspective. He has his finger on the pulse of the markets, an expert you could say. He watches the markets daily, like a trader should. Looks for trends before others know they're there."

It always seemed easier to talk in the saddle than from anywhere else. A good, well-worn boot in a stirrup and jeans pressed against leather always made a better setting than anywhere else in which to converse.

Carson felt stronger talking honestly about what had happened when she'd up and left her house in Silicon Valley, and now seemed as good a time as any to fill Kitzie in on some of the details.

"I walked away from huge debts, Mom. Shit-effing big ones, and just let the bank take everything. I left clothes in the closet and my Jag in the garage," she confessed.

It wasn't the first time Kitzie had heard bits of it but she had chosen to wait for the details rather than interrogate them out of her daughter. She knew Carson was in a bad way when she showed up and she needed time.

"Did you leave the keys?" Kitzie asked facetiously as she brushed a piece of hair from her eyes and leaned on the horn of her saddle. Her mare was relaxed, eyes half shut, and her back foot was cocked in the soft earth.

Carson let out a short laugh. "Yep. Keys to everything."

"All your nice stuff, clothes, just left 'em in the closet?" Kitzie inserted a little more levity.

"All…what was left…" Carson sighed. "Pretty much, though I did go back for one nice dress," she admitted.

"That was a good idea. Always nice to have that one good dress."

"I thought so." Then Carson inhaled deeply. "As it started to turn on me, I began to censor the impressions I gave. I tried to play this certain image and it kinda made me feel worse. I covered up not having any money, maxed out credit cards to conceal how much debt I was in. I felt that there was something wrong with me. I was in this socially constructed house of cards and my whole being depended on false impressions." Carson could feel the self-defeating chasm open up in her head and she fought it. That was then. She had left it and escaped. *Don't let that past reach out and grab you*, she willed.

Her mother didn't press, she listened.

"I fell apart, I became hypersensitive to every look, every gesture, and the simplest of greetings. I wasn't sure what was actual, imagined, or anticipated."

The insights were startling. *The voice saying this must belong to some other being,* Carson thought. There was a time in the not-so-distant past that this blunt retrospection paralyzed her to tears, it was that painful.

"Were you able to share this with anyone? Did you have a friend you trusted?" Kitzie asked gently as she gathered her reins and moved her horse to walk down the slope.

Carson smiled ruefully and owned it. "I was messing with something that wasn't mine. I kept a lot of secrets. I pretended things were OK and the wine helped me believe it."

"And yet the sabotaging behavior...what's your place with that now? And I'm good if that's a step too far...or too close, for that matter," Kitzie asked.

Carson looked at her mother's back as she followed her down the slope, and a flash of fear mixed with shame crossed her eyes. "Ah, fuck...I really cared about that group of people." Her throat betrayed her. She still did. "I didn't just want their approval; I *needed, craved,* their approval. I placed too much value on their opinions. I couldn't bear the thought of my clique judging me as less than."

She pressed her lips together to form a hard, thin line. But the face and eyes that met hers held only love and acceptance, not judgment. It was the wisdom of time and experience—something a woman of Carson's years might not have been ready for, but that Kitzie offered nonetheless. It was a clean question—her mother's attempt at pushing the barriers aside and encouraging Carson to get past it all.

Kitzie continued, "I get that it's hard to talk about." She shifted in her saddle and smoothed the end bits of her horse's mane at the withers. She laid it flat with her fingers, separated errant hairs, casually ordered them, and ultimately made it perfect against the mare's neck. "It's a risk to be open and reveal those secrets you worked so hard to keep. A risk of re-experiencing the pain. Avoiding shame is natural. We all do it." She nodded to the left as a sign that they were heading back.

Mother and daughter rode side by side in silence for a while. The footfalls of the horses blended, synched, and then sounded apart. In places, the ground was still blackened with burnt material and an ash smell rose when it was disturbed. The longer afternoon light laid gold on the black and created a strange beauty of its own. Tufts of color sprouted here and there. Carson pointed at something green pressing skyward, life renewed, and her mother nodded and smiled.

"Man, that fire ate everything out here," Carson observed, "and yet it will all come back." The tightness in her voice retreated. "Mom, I need to clean up the mess I left behind and I'm very reluctant to even look at it."

"We can look into it, talk to some people. I'm sure you have some records with you…right?"

"In the truck. I have file boxes in the back. Paperwork I've forgotten about." Carson hesitated, then forged ahead. "There's things in boxes I may not have unpacked since I left. Special sentimental stuff from childhood. I'll be my own archaeologist."

Her mother reminisced. "After I lost your father, I was confused about how to be without him. Every little thing had special significance and meaning. Some of it was silly, like a stale box of his favorite cookies." She smiled. "Did you know he hid cookies? I found them all over the place for months."

Carson laughed. "Yeah, I knew. He'd tease me that I couldn't find them. He was very good at that game."

"It took me a long time to have a sturdier sense of myself," Kitzie said. "It will heal. Everything will heal."

Carson wasn't sure if she meant the land or the people. Or both.

They rode single file down through a dry wash and loped up the other side. The ground was loose and soft, and the hind leg of Carson's horse slipped a little. She legged her up under herself and passed her mother on the right, then crested the edge at a lope with the momentum necessary.

Carson reached back to pat her horse's rump and scratched the base of her tail. "I had forgotten that *this* was the best time of my life…the horses and this country. I don't know why I ran away from it like I did. Ran as far from it as I could. And I hurt you and Dad in the process."

The sun was setting and cast a glow on the near end of the big arena, creating long lines that grew wider down the length of it, leaving a huge, fan-shaped shadow on the ground. Kitzie knew this was as close to an apology as Carson had come, and maybe would come, and she didn't push. It was good enough. She said nothing and moved ahead to open the first gate.

Chapter 46

There was a shared dismay when it was obvious that Bodie had noticed Carson. Around women, he had a knack for turning on the charm and being funny. Buckets wasn't blind, and when they were at the Three Bit, he distracted Bodie to tend to some detail or another as plans to rebuild Kitzie's house got underway. Green Eyes just wanted to punch him.

Carson didn't reciprocate the attention. This wasn't her first rodeo when it came to avoiding trouble. It wasn't their job to protect her and the thought of it irritated all of them.

One morning, after dropping Bodie off to Stiles at the Three Bit, Buckets and Green Eyes talked about it on the way back to the Running Horse.

Green Eyes had his fist hard to his mouth, elbow on the door ledge, and he stared out at nothing. Buckets asked him what was up.

"That guy's a shit."

Buckets grunted his agreement. "Ain't none of our business. Unless there's something more…"

Green Eyes shook his head. "No, it isn't like that. I have no call to be sticking my nose into the Collins family business. And if I had cause to, I'd be a helluva lot more respectable going about it."

Buckets smiled. "She is a fine thing, handy and smart."

Green Eyes removed his hat, rubbed his eyes, and

smoothed his hair before putting the hat back on. "Yeah, I know…it's just…" He grimaced as if it pained him. "Not *that* guy. Ya know?"

Buckets nodded in agreement as he turned the truck onto the highway and accelerated.

Bodie worked half days at the Three Bit, helping with the clean-up and preparations for construction on the main house. When he could maneuver it, Bodie liked to watch Carson work horses. She wasn't starting any, these were ranch-ready horses. Sometimes she'd work them on the ground and seemed to have a solid idea about what each one needed. She had the gift and made what the horses did look effortless. She knew how to rebalance them and smooth out any tightness that inactivity exacerbated. Working horses needed a job. Carson could feel where the imbalance occurred, work with their bodies to correct it, and they'd relax into that effort. She knew how to "dance" with them.

When Bodie had first started at the Running Horse, he'd heard some about Carson but had never met her. Now that he had, he tried to conjure up reasons to talk to her. He would make it look casual. To him, it was a given that women adored him and he was irresistible. Resistance and obstacles were surmountable. And in the world according to Bodie, when Carson knew he was interested, she would do all the work and come to him. He imagined she was already aware of him and would come around right away. But she didn't act like he expected her to and that was more than his fragile ego could bear.

His frustration was a distraction, though Stiles wasn't particularly bothered as he got more done alone anyway. But it gnashed at him that the idiot was drawing pay to be there.

Stiles liked an orderly work environment and assigned

Bodie clean-up duties. Bodie loaded a couple of days' worth of debris in the small trailer behind the ATV and maneuvered the load the long way down past the arena. He figured that she might be working in the big, outdoor round pen and he was right.

The round pen was old-style, constructed of roughhewn cedar logs lined up vertically and tall. It was big—much bigger than the standard sixty—and it was one of the first things her parents had restored when they got the Three Bit. There were several stories about the pen but no one was sure who had built it. It was surmised that it was originally meant for working cows because there were pens with chutes on one side.

In order for Bodie to talk to Carson, he had to be at the five-pipe panel gate. He purposefully stalled the ATV, then feigned dismay and gave her one of his "aw, shucks" best smiles, somewhere between "I'm embarrassed" and "hey baby…"

She stopped her session and asked what was wrong.

"I think I flooded it," he said sheepishly.

"Why'd you come around this way?" she asked.

"Oh…there were some trucks blocking the other way. I think they're delivering some lumber or something. And there's an insurance guy nosing around acting all helpful with your mom."

Bodie spoke like he was her confidante. He made some other small talk but Carson wasn't listening. She stood up in her stirrups and looked toward the far end of the covered arena but had no angle to confirm his story. As she turned back, he quickly dropped his head to fiddle with the ATV. He made sure it wouldn't start and she looked incredulous.

"Good luck with that," Carson intoned and turned her

horse away from him to get back to what she was doing.

He started to say something to call her back, when, out of nowhere, like an apparition, Stiles appeared.

"What are you doing?" he asked the startled Bodie.

"Jesus! Where did you come fro…" Bodie started to say before his words shriveled up.

Carson stopped again and looked over her shoulder. The edges of a knowing smile barely revealed her white teeth and she rested her hand on the rump of her ride.

Bodie, pretty much caught, tried to play it off. He thought for a second that Stiles would be understanding and give him a break. He mumbled something in his own defense, but Carson didn't hear it. Then, with a weak look on his face, he said, "Sorry, boss, I messed up."

Stiles said a couple of words she didn't hear either, but she didn't have to. It reminded her of her father. He chastised quietly and praised loudly. Whatever Stiles said, it was enough that the ATV started up immediately.

Carson imagined the muscles of Stiles' face frozen hard. She once had a mare that would get that face when another horse got too close to her food. He had made it clear he would not put up with this shit. Bodie pulled away with a skid and Stiles watched him go, then vanished behind the cedar poles of the round pen and retraced his steps.

Carson could see shadowy movement between the gaps in the wood. She loped over alongside and slowed to a walk. "You ride?" she asked the unseen figure beyond.

He hesitated for a heartbeat before he said, "All my life."

Carson stood in her stirrups but couldn't see more than the top of his hat's crown bobbing in and out of sight as he walked. "Really?" she asked.

Stiles covered the ground with long strides and avoided more conversation. He was like an onion—lots of layers and it wasn't easy to talk through them.

Through the wall of cedar, she persisted. "Wanna ride sometime?"

"Don't have the time," he answered without stopping.

Carson didn't take it personally. She shrugged it off and completed the rest of her ride.

Chapter 47

Kitzie walked with Wyatt around the ranch, a to-go cup of coffee in her hand. It was something she had started to do to keep her knee flexible and happy. The pattern she had fallen into was to walk as much of the Three Bit entrance road as she and her knee could manage without grabbing the Advil every day.

Layers of ash seemed to be waiting for the rain to wash them clean. A stubborn haze clung to the area, and in the patches where it dissipated, a strange light illuminated a march of small, fluffy seeds. The loners came first in single tufts, then clumps of fluff. A few stuck together, tumbling over the hard-packed gravel of the driveway. The wind danced them around, sending a whole army of them hurrying to unknown destinations. A swirl caught them in the eddy of Wyatt's legs, and he tried to catch one. Stragglers darted erratically to keep up with the ever-scattering main bunch. Kitzie watched, their delicate forms withstanding bumps, thumps, and stronger breezes that would separate them forever.

Kitzie and Wyatt continued their early morning walk up the driveway toward the house. A spider's night of work stretched across a charred wooden post, its ladder of webbing connecting it to the rusted barbed wire. An arc of light made the dew sparkle like diamonds.

Kitzie hesitated at the front of the new house and realized

she had begun to struggle with the memory of what had been and the reality that changed daily. Stiles had been there dark-early with a plan for what he wanted to accomplish so he'd be well along by the time Buckets dropped his "boy" off.

He tended toward a Zen-like focus, a tunnel vision of sorts, fully enveloped in his thoughts, and was startled when he saw Kitzie. Wyatt trotted up the newly built porch steps to greet him, his stub of a tail wagging.

Their ideas about the rebuilding had run into a wall on more than one occasion and their "discussions" often became vigorous. She had a vision of the past in her mind, not what could and maybe should be. But there were many code changes and the whole thing had to be built to them.

Instinctively, Stiles knew Kitzie needed time to consider the alternative approach he proposed so he kept a respectful distance until she sought him out. He did his best to hold back and listen to her before he spoke.

Kitzie had seen some drawings and reluctantly started to like the open concept Stiles presented to her. Carson was thrilled and Stiles greatly appreciated her enthusiasm. Kitzie had walked the new track that the foundation followed for a single-story home. They had been lucky to have one interior wall remain, so they called it a renovation or some such thing for reasons Kitzie neither understood nor cared to. It was out of her lane and she was relieved that Carson had taken an active interest in Stiles' designs and ideas. When Kitzie and Stiles talked about it, they seemed more adversarial and it stirred her up.

Loathe to admit it, Kitzie knew she would grow old in what Stiles designed and his ideas weren't half bad once she'd digested the reasoning behind them. Costs were slightly lower for a single-level structure and he had ideas not only for an open concept for the kitchen/dining/great room, but he was going to give the ceilings a bump up to add height and make the home lighter and airier. He had asked about a couple of skylights and an expanded mudroom with better organization.

Kitzie also noticed a window seat element in the drawings that he had avoided mentioning. He felt it would beautifully frame a view of the hills and taller bluffs beyond—a cozy place to curl up with a good book and watch the snowflakes fall.

Yes, they were good ideas. But the thing that was the most painful to Kitzie, especially right after the disaster, was the loss of the mementos from her life with Tuff.

Tuff's favorite old recliner had been destroyed and though she hated its ragged appearance, Kitzie had treasured it when he was gone. It was like a tangible piece of him she related to. Its springs and bits of its frame were the first things she had seen in the rubble and the most recognizable. All her photographs—or at least those that were in the house, her favorites—were gone. Carson discovered an entire file-cabinet drawer in the barn office full of years of pictures and Kitzie was grateful that they all hadn't been concentrated in the house. So that was something.

He noticed her grief and loss. Stiles kept his words to a minimum, never said too much, though there were moments when he opened up and when he did, it was usually in an easy, measured tone. "Those memories are the first we make and the last to go. But as real as the ring on your finger."

Kitzie looked at her left ring finger thoughtfully and set the ring to center with her thumb—a habitual thing she did many times a day.

They talked about the appliances and he encouraged her to

maybe get some magazines or go online and see what others had done. He suggested that Carson might help, and she had. They had looked online at "Pin-something" which had a ton of ideas—so many features and doodads that she'd never heard of. Everything in her old house had been over forty years old and each had its own little quirk to keep it running.

Kitzie turned at the sound of Buckets' arrival. He stopped the truck near her and a stocky Hispanic man and Bodie hopped out, both carrying toolbelts. They went to the back of the truck and unloaded a few things the Running Horse had sent over.

Kitzie rested her hand on the truck door and they did the pleasantries and briefly talked about what was on her plate. Buckets lowered his voice, touched her hand on the truck's sill, and asked, "How are you doing?"

"So far so good, I guess. This hole in the ranch will get filled. It still takes getting used to. Like, I'm surprised by it every day. I come around that corner and it's not right, you know?" Kitzie shrugged.

He nodded and watched the Hispanic man walk away from the truck, his head down as he adjusted the buckle on his toolbelt. "That's Mario. He's relatively new but is one heck of a worker. Stiles will like him."

Kitzie gave Buckets a thankful look. "Please tell Boss how grateful we are for the help. You'll let me know what I owe you, please?"

He said he would and that he'd be back after lunchtime.

One thing that impressed Buckets about Stiles was that he took charge and missed nothing. He prioritized the last part of debris removal and laid the groundwork for an efficient work site. He was an enigmatic person, hard to scratch much beneath the surface, so no one had a good bead on him. His manner was polite enough. He didn't seem to drink or want to share a beer with anyone after work. There was a haunting quality about him, like a huge part of the man was missing. He didn't seek the companionship of others to build himself up or validate his work. In fact, his work spoke more loudly about him than he did.

At the end of the workday, Stiles melted away. Buckets noticed that he either worked well past when others had quit or caught a glimpse of the man's back as he walked around the corner and disappeared. Kitzie had mentioned that she had seen him working into the night with a long, orange extension cord stretched from the barn to the house. He was compressing time, he told her when she asked.

Buckets inched the truck past the house, parked, and admired it. He walked through the house in its various stages of development, and despite Bodie being the weakest link in the chain, observed how well it was going. He said as much when he found Stiles working in the kitchen, and complimented his work. It was all in the details, Stiles said.

The wiring was top-notch, precision-labeled for ease of understanding years down the road, and Buckets noticed design changes that Stiles had employed. Stiles loved what he was doing and was talkative about the house. Buckets listened and asked thoughtful questions. Stiles articulated a vision for the bones of the house that would accommodate a re-imagined and updated home for Kitzie.

Buckets asked what had motivated him to keep the new structure one level and noted the practicality of it from an aging perspective, personally speaking.

Stiles paused. "No, it's her knee."

Buckets had almost forgotten about that. Kitzie didn't dwell on it and used her brace sparingly, so it was easy to forget she was injured.

"I doubt she would admit it but a great part of the strength in that knee is gone forever," Stiles explained. "Not that she has said anything. I've gleaned bits of what happened from Carson and I can see her favor it at times."

Buckets was impressed by the thoughtfulness of his answer and he pivoted to ask about the great room. It was open-concept for the kitchen and family room and because the footprint of the house was not large, Stiles had changed the downstairs bedroom configuration from three tiny bedrooms to a larger master suite and guestroom. He bumped out a wall for a small but well-thought-out walk-in closet, and in doing so, somehow created a master bath. He had nudged the ceiling up and added a skylight in the bathroom to allow more natural light, and he planned windows and other skylights throughout the home so it would be a light and airy place in which to live.

By expanding the footprint a little and modifying his plans, Stiles also created an office nook and tucked a cleverly designed shower into what would have been just a guest half bath. The window seat was one of Buckets' favorite elements. He admired the craftsmanship and found the view out the windows spectacular.

Stiles told him about something Carson had asked for. "Carson said you see softly rounded edges to the corners in some higher-end homes and wondered if I could do that.

Kitzie argued she didn't need fancy, but I'm gonna do it anyway." Stiles grinned under his thick mustache. "Not sure when we will be doing interior finishes and no one has said anything about colors yet. Carson is a big influence there."

His eyes went back to his "canvas" and he envisioned possibilities in the way the light would play upon his masterpiece. He then asked Buckets about Mario. "Hope you don't need that guy back," he said.

"I can give you more time. How long do you need him?"

"Oh, I'll take as much of his time as you'll let me," Stiles replied hopefully.

"When was the last time you built anything?" Buckets asked.

Stiles didn't answer immediately as they both went down the porch steps. His mood shifted, he became more cautious, and wasn't sure whether the curiosity was admiration or an inquisition.

Buckets sensed Stiles' reticence, so Buckets added, "I'm meaning that what you've done here, what you're doing here, is really great and I want to recommend you."

When Stiles heard that he felt a sense of pride. It took him a breath to compose his response as he reached the bottom step. He turned to Buckets' extended hand.

"That is, if you are going to be doing this kind of work in Martin for a while..." Buckets continued. "The town could sure use a craftsman like you, especially now."

Stiles, with a closed-lipped smile, gripped Buckets' hand. "Thank you. We'll see. Maybe."

As he left, Buckets thought, *That man has managed people, was a foreman somewhere. He certainly got Bodie to do what he was told.* He thought about it all the way back to the ranch. The job represented something more than construction to Stiles. Maybe a second chance at making a broken man whole again, or so he hoped.

As Buckets drove, he thought of men his age who had deeply cared about something earlier in their lives, then got swept up in events and life—like being caught in the current of the ocean, turning to see how close the land was, then not seeing any land at all. It made Buckets examine the course of his own life, and what eddies and currents had swept him to the Running Horse. He really didn't envision much more for himself than that and he was satisfied. He hoped the same for Stiles.

Under Stiles' guidance, every day was productive. They had accomplished way more than he expected, and he told the men so. Stiles knew that Bodie was easily distracted if he didn't stay on him. An exhausted Bodie was a good Bodie.

Usually, when the ranch truck arrived to pick them up, Bodie vanished for a bit, then reappeared slightly winded. Usually, he lingered as if looking around for something...or *someone*. Usually. But on this particular afternoon, when the Running Horse truck headed out with its personnel, he'd been the first one in. Buckets noticed, and Stiles did too.

Carson was out of sight, deep in the shadows just inside the barn door. She saw Bodie turn in the back seat and look out the window as they drove away. It would be the last time she saw him.

Stiles watched the truck go as he removed his toolbelt and set it in the box on the porch. The original porch configuration had been extended and now it wrapped around the edge of the house, forming a frame to the picture. Stiles imagined a cozy seating area and Kitzie sitting in a chair, a cool glass of something in her hand, relaxing. He set the area to rights as dusk closed in. The shadows were long, and he stood outside the house, hands loose at his sides, and drank it in. The new house was beginning to cast a more solid shadow and the lone figure cast his.

Cowboy hat in hand, Stiles started toward his camper. As he went, he heard someone drive up behind him. It was Kitzie, and she slowed the truck as she went by the house. He kept walking but could feel her taking a long look and hoped she liked what she saw. She'd been away from the Three Bit for the day. The truck idled forward and closed in on him, and he knew that he'd have to speak to her.

Almost anyone else would have approached the truck, leaned a glad hand on the cab, made friendly end-of-the-day banter, and accepted the offer of a beer. But not Mr. Stiles.

Clandestinely, Carson watched through an open paddock door for a few moments. She saw Kitzie lean her head out the window to say something to Stiles. He kept his distance, neither retreating nor approaching. His body language was all business. No frivolous chitchat from that one. He accepted compliments humbly and when he wanted to press a point, like a design change with her mother, she noted how carefully he went about it. Like he was handling a braced-up filly. He was a puzzle, thought Carson.

A short time later, Stiles lay on his bunk in the camper. He tried to sleep. He wished he had a beer, or something to dull the edges of his mind. He drifted off but awoke after the dream visited him again. His hand opening the sliding door of the storage building...the expectation of finally reuniting with his daughter...hugs, tears, a future together as a family. Righting wrongs and embarking on a fresh start. And then, complete darkness on an empty road with dollar bills fluttering in the wind.

Stiles squeezed the image from his eyelids and found himself staring into the quiet darkness of his camper. He heard coyotes calling and an owl overhead somewhere. He could feel it coming before he saw it through the window. Dawn was breaking and he was up before it.

Chapter 48

The two-man team was on a fire road, scared half to death that the fire would trap them. They had lost their bearings and no one answered the radio. They'd been driving for a while and began to stress about fuel. Were they heading toward or away from a better signal? Toward or away from a capricious change of wind and a rain of embers? They couldn't say and they rode in silence, each lost to his own thoughts. Both thought it was odd that on either side of them, the track was unburnt, like this road was immune somehow. Blessed by the gods. The fires had jumped this stretch and there was no reason why.

The driver slowed and cautiously rounded a bend that led to a long, straight stretch. Off to the right, the landscape was rocky; to the left was once scrub and trees. Way up ahead they saw movement. They both craned their necks forward and squinted as if that would help. The driver's foot came off the accelerator and they crept up on whatever had worked its way from the high side, down a dirt, sloped berm, and painfully onto the road. It was a horse, injured and spent, as if its last bit of strength had gotten it there. Another figure stood weakly behind it, holding the few strands of what was left of a tail. He lost his grip and tumbled forward and collapsed. Neither moved. Both were suspended in time.

The truck coasted to a stop. Painfully, the horse tilted its head enough for its left eye to catch motion in its peripheral vision and to cock a hairless ear to the sound of tires on the ground. He turned his neck straight and his nose drooped slowly closer to the ground.

The two men exited the vehicle, approached the figure lying in the dirt, and gently rolled him onto his back. What they saw took their breath away. His eyes were swollen shut, the skin on his face was scalded and singed in places, blackened in others. To their astonishment, the cracked lips moved and murmured something. He was semi-conscious. One of the men reassured him that they were there to help.

They'd been embarrassed to call in because they had no idea where they were, but now that they really needed help, they tried their radio again and miraculously, got a signal. Their eyes met in shock.

While one of the men transmitted their situation and asked about a Medivac, the other man looked up at the butt of the horse next to him and wondered if he should be concerned. A strong hand gripped his arm, it startled him, and he looked down and tried to reassure the injured man. The fractured lips moved and he murmured more words.

"What's he saying?" his partner asked.

"I don't know. Here, give me the radio. You try to make sense of it. He's definitely trying to say something."

They traded and the man put his ear right next to the damaged mouth, which moved and whispered some information. The firefighter pulled away and felt the hand grip his arm and try to shake it for emphasis.

He shook his head in disbelief and said, "I heard you. You need a hospital right away." Then he sighed. "Yes, don't talk, I heard you."

The prone figure couldn't talk but he nodded his head and then his whole body relaxed as he rested from the effort.

The fireman stood, frowning, and asked for the radio. He said, "I need to…I need a couple of things. You read? Over."

The answer was positive, and he asked for four things.

"Be sure you get this right. Yes, we need transport for a severely injured firefighter named Cajun. Two, we need to reach his wife, a firefighter/EMT, Tish. No, no last name, but it can't be that hard. Now this part, he's insisting on. You ready? We need a horse trailer." There was a crackle of a question. "Yes, a horse trailer NOW."

His partner leaned over and said that the good news was they'd been going in the right direction, so help wasn't that far away.

"What? What did you say? Repeat." the fireman said when he missed something squawking from the handheld. He listened and then acknowledged. "Roger, and can you find a vet to meet us there?"

"Roger," came the reply.

He handed the radio to his partner, went to the truck, and grabbed a fresh bottle of water from the cab. Then he saw the big plastic urn of drinking water that was mounted toward the back of the truck and looked around to see if they had a bucket. They did, and he directed his partner to get it. It was small but it might do. He took the bottle of water and went back to Cajun.

"Cajun?" he asked, careful not to jostle him. "Cajun!"

Cajun moaned and tried to turn his head toward the man.

"No, don't move, please stay still. There's a horse trailer on the way and they are close. That is what you wanted, yes?"

A strangled cry rose from Cajun's lips and a tear squeezed

from one of the red lids. A sob followed.

"Easy, easy, I get it. They thought I was nuts, but I get you. I understand. I saw. I will try to get him help."

Cajun cried. The tears pressed against his swollen lids, but he couldn't help it. The other man approached with the bucket.

"I don't know anything about horses, man," he whispered.

"OK, stay with Cajun, see if he wants some of this. But carefully." He handed his partner the unopened water and took the bucket. He went wide around the back of the horse and spoke to him the whole time so as not to startle him. "Easy there, easy." And he looked for a place with hair that wasn't singed or gone to touch him, then thought better of it.

He approached the head. The horse had his nose low, almost to the ground. The man bent at the waist and held the bucket out to him. *Him?* He looked under the horse's belly. Yeah, him. The left eyelid and eye flicked at him, as did the left ear, and the horse lifted his head slowly. The ears returned to a lax position of distress or pain…or both.

He held the bucket near the horse's mouth and nose and then tilted it so that the water slid up the side, closer to the top edge of the container. The horse sniffed it and worked his lips. The phrase "you can lead a horse to water but you can't make him drink" came to mind, only in this case, he'd brought the water to the horse. The horse's tongue came out and touched the water. It went back in and repeated that, then he put his muzzle to it and the man heard a sucking sound.

"Atta boy. Take what you can," the firefighter whispered to him. "Go easy though, can't have you drink too much at once." His eyes began a slow assessment of the animal's left side. What was left of his mane was on the other side of his neck, so he had a clear measure of his injuries on this side. He shook his head. These two had been through something awful.

He heard an engine. Something was coming. A snip of a girl driving a truck and trailer appeared out of the haze, her tousled hair just visible over the steering wheel. She couldn't have been more than twenty. Her eyes were red from wind and smoke, and there was a black soot mark on her forehead that she probably didn't know was there. She leaned out the window as she approached.

"I'm gonna turn around and we'll load him," she said without coming to a full stop.

It was a stock, two-horse trailer and he wasn't sure how she did it, but she must have known her stuff because she did it pretty fast and was back in moments. She pulled ahead of him, tipped closer to the edge of the fire road, and backed up. In no time, she was out of the cab, fixed the mess under a dirty baseball cap, opened the back of the trailer, and approached the horse easy.

"Oh, you poor thing," she spoke to the horse. "I'm sorry, it's not a slant load. We're gonna help you." She looked at the horse's face and sighed. "A halter is gonna suck for him."

"I agree. Do you think he'll go in without?" the man asked and he set the water bucket down. "You take one side of him and I'll take the other?"

"Let's try."

And they began to gently coax Rio into the trailer.

Rio took small, slow steps and when he got to the edge of getting in, he stopped and bent his head enough to catch a glimpse of Cajun on the ground. The horse stared at his human companion for a moment.

The girl and the man looked at each other. The man choked and looked away from her, saying he was sorry. He cleared his throat roughly, wiped his eyes with a dirty sleeve, and turned back to Rio. He leaned in close and spoke to him.

"Were gonna take care of him, boy. I promise. I won't leave him just like he asked me not to leave you." And tears rolled down his cheeks and one fell to the dirt.

The young girl watched silently, then she talked Rio into the back of the trailer. A front foot, the other front foot, a couple steps in farther and then the hard part. He had to bump himself into a little hop to get his back end in and he grunted in pain doing it. There was no point securing him inside. Letting him freely balance himself during the trip was the only way.

The girl quickly secured the clip on the latch of the trailer gate, then jogged to the truck door, yanked it open, and launched herself inside.

The man turned to go to Cajun, then stopped and said to her back, "Will there be a veterinarian, or someone who knows something about horses, waiting for you?"

She called back, "I'm his tech. He'll be there, and if he's not, I got this. Help him," she finished and jerked her thumb toward Cajun. She started the truck and headed down the fire road gently.

When the back of the trailer was almost out of sight, the two firemen saw the brake lights go on and the trailer squeeze to the right as it let an emergency vehicle, followed by an ambulance, hurry by.

—⚜—

Tish began praying when she got word that Cajun had been found. Though he was in a bad way, he was fighting to stay conscious until he could hear her voice. She talked to some people she knew at the command center where they were bringing him. She asked if he knew his team was gone but they didn't know. She asked why he wasn't being transported to a hospital and they said that would be optimal, but that nothing was flying. They had a field hospital of sorts set up and their plan was to assess him when he arrived, stabilize him if they could, and treat him if they had to. The command center promised to keep in close touch and Tish went about doing her job and figured out how to quickly get to her husband.

A technician was the first to see Cajun in the ambulance. Cajun was animatedly trying to tell him something. The tech did his job and noted that, through a slit of one eye, he tracked fairly well, which was encouraging. Word went ahead of the ambulance and a small crowd of firefighters had gathered to be there when it arrived. A couple of photographers hovered and got pictures of them surrounding the vehicle and hampering the crew that brought Cajun in. They crowded close as he was off-loaded by stretcher. One of them leaned in and with tears running down his face, expressed his condolences at the loss of Cajun's team. The picture went viral and almost won a Pulitzer.

The throng was cleared back and held outside the tent. As Cajun felt himself carried and heard new sounds and voices, the voice he most needed to hear wasn't there. And now, with the realization that he would never again hear the voices of his team, he was overcome with grief. Now he knew for certain they were gone.

An agonized cry welled up from somewhere deep inside him, so alien, he didn't recognize himself. His heart rate went crazy and someone worked on him as they moved him into the infirmary where there were beds set up for the seriously injured. Before they sedated him, he managed to get two words out—the first sounded like "Tish…" and the second, "horse." They texted Tish what he said.

Tish looked at her phone and frowned. "Horse? What horse?"

Chapter 49

Noah realized the meeting was over when Maxie and Dale left the table. He attempted a measure of participation and said to Tiny, "Good, we'll leave it at that then, shall we?" It was awkward and ignored. Mostly because Tiny had drifted into a semi-conscious state and Noah hadn't noticed.

Maxie called for someone on an intercom. His voice was deep and accustomed to command.

Noah had hoped to feel included, maybe invited to stay in some luxuriously appointed guest room—an offer he might refuse, but that would help him to feel more welcome in a different way. Maxie handed Dale a cold beer but chose nothing for himself nor did he offer anything to Noah. Noah knew he had been dismissed; he just wasn't sure who was doing the dismissing. Neither looked at him but his assessment of who was in charge changed. The big, florid man in the wheelchair had said little the entire time and looked like a meditating Buddha halfway through the meeting.

A substantial Polynesian man appeared. He smiled at Noah as he collected Tiny in his wheelchair, and disappeared.

After the time it took to drink a beer, Dale walked Noah out through the impressive front doors. Their panes of glass gleamed crisply with a view of the hills and mountains beyond. The broad, bricked path had rectangular ponds on either side, graciously framed by perfect landscaping. Noah looked for those big fancy goldfish but saw only the surface ripples of mosquito fish. Low hedges were clipped in symmetrical perfection and the huge parking area was bordered by plants that cascaded down the sides of short walls. The beige-colored driveway crunched beneath Noah's shoes as they approached the town car. It hadn't occurred to him that Dale was not returning with him.

He turned and shook Dale's outstretched hand and asked how big a place the villa was. Dale said he did not know but big enough. It was all very polite and formal.

As his handshake with Dale concluded, Noah thanked him for his support and guidance.

Dale pumped him up with, "You will do great things, I'm sure."

From the back seat of the car, Noah looked at the house again and caught sight of someone moving past the dining room windows. He took in a last look at the whole expanse of the place and wished he had been invited for a complete tour.

As the car whisked Noah away, Dale saw his nose all but pressed to the window as the car moved on. In a matter of seconds, it was around the first downward bend of the winding driveway and out of sight.

Noah felt a mixture of deprivation and ambition. That estate was the embodiment of his dream—not just the house but the wealth it took to feel comfortable and secure there. A hungry part of him gnawed at the edges of his own limitations.

The pilot waited for Noah at the retractable stairway of the jet as he exited the car. He touched his cap deferentially and reported to Noah their estimated flight time and weather conditions. Noah wanted this kind of respect. Always. He responded as if it were his plane and his staff. The same attractive attendant welcomed him aboard and it was just the two of them in the cabin. She guided him to the comfortable, overstuffed lounge seat that faced forward in the cabin.

The pilot had specific instructions, as did she. The jet cleared the runway with a powerful thrust, easily defying gravity. Hidden cameras bore witness to a part of Noah doing the same.

Maxie joined Dale on the driveway and the two men strolled the grounds. Despite Noah's flaws, neither threw away valuable tools because they didn't like their design. They both recognized Noah's usefulness and they would groom and use him. They discussed positioning the right mentor to improve his statecraft and to immediately recruit a competent speechwriting team. That there were other fine-tuning details to address was a given.

They settled into the seating area in the statuary garden near the guest house. The late afternoon light danced among the branches of the olive trees and played off the four-foot-tall statues on pedestals in the intimate garden. A small lizard darted out onto the warm slate stones. His head tipped this way and that, eyes swiveled, and his little arms did perfect push-ups as the colors of his belly gleamed iridescently in the reflected heat. The men conversed as equals and were served refreshments as they discussed carefully laid plans.

Tiny's health issues had precipitated some minor alterations, and his needs were tended to as business went on uninterrupted.

The Cedar Wara project was of growing import and Dale

was eager for that to be locked down as quickly as possible. Dale was the point man, pivotal in its success, and Maxie's direct partner. Securing the mineral rights out from under those more entitled to them had to be accomplished before the political climate changed. Elections had a pesky way of doing that.

Dale and Maxie concluded their business and walked between the guest house and main house, past enormous terracotta pots that lined the area between the arbor and the infinity pool. They stopped to take in the vista of the huge valley and uninhabited rolling hills, then walked toward the outdoor kitchen complete with a pizza oven imported from Italy. The men turned right, past another rectangular pond with tall, slender reeds protruding from the shallow water, and a massive concrete sphere on a tapered base that decorated a raised garden bed. Maxie and Dale retired to the wine cellar to choose a wine to pair with the enticing aroma of something rich and savory emanating from the kitchen.

The guest house was like a second home for Dale. He lounged by the pool, was waited on, and enjoyed a few days of downtime—from everything. He unplugged. After a few days off, he reluctantly packed his overnight bag and set it on the neatly made bed. His cell phone was perched on the edge of the bedside table, half on and half off the polished mahogany wood. Dale left his bag and went to the main house for breakfast.

The butler/handyman was having a good morning and he had his earbuds in, listening to music, as he arrived at the guest house and collected Dale's bag. His footstep to the side of the bed was vibration enough to cause the cell phone to slip off the bedside table and land between it and the richly colored bedspread. Its descent to the carpet below went unnoticed.

Chapter 50

Carson had fed and cleaned and saw her mother sitting on the broad, roughed-in porch steps of the house. She joined her and brushed off her jeans as she sat down, laughing.

"That horse," she started.

"Which one?" Kitzie asked, shaking off her preoccupied look.

"Oh, that Biscuit, what a character. He pretty much thinks all the mares are his bitches." She made air quotes with her fingers. "And at his age! What is he, thirty?"

"Or older. We were never precisely sure how old he was when we got him." Kitzie smiled. "And you're back in the country, girl, *thems* is a herd."

Carson shook her head at her mother's attempt at the vernacular. "Well, however old he is, he ain't old enough to forget he's a gelding. He gets them riled up in a heat and he has a kickstand!"

They giggled.

"I swear, his name shoulda been Randy," Carson added, laughing harder. "I'm in there with the apple picker, made a neat pile to scoop and he puts himself between me and the cart. He's wanting his belly scratched, which kinda means he wants his other part scratched too." Carson made a frustrated gesture with her hands. "So, I threw him a little hay to distract him before I started. But does that work? Noooooo. He wallers over and stands on the pile to be sure you have to give him a scratch. I used the plastic tines on the picker to oblige and the faces that boy makes..." Carson imitated the animated grimaces of the old horse, his neck elongated and down, lips twitching, head curved to one side, and eyes shut in ecstasy. "It's hilarious!" She stopped her pantomime and went on. "Seriously, there should be a tip jar outside his paddock."

Stiles was working nearby and saw them sitting together, shoulder to shoulder, and watched them laughing. Then Kitzie lowered her head and their voices took on a more serious tone. Stiles immediately turned back to work out of earshot.

Kitzie sighed. "I don't know what's wrong with me. I don't think of myself as a difficult person. Yet I keep struggling with him." Kitzie motioned behind her. "I can't seem to just go along and smoothly agree with all these design changes. I must wring out every last ounce of myself each time there's a decision to make. There are so many details and...crap, I'm addled. Too many plugs in too many sockets. I think I've blown a fuse." She put her face to her hands and groaned.

"Come on, Mom, you're doing fine. This is a lot and it's coming along beautifully," Carson reassured her. She glanced up and behind them at the new house. "I love what he's doing." Her tone dropped and it oozed affection.

"It's just that I had this picture in my mind of our old house, and this is so different..."

"Yes..." Carson paused, trying not to obscure her mother's genuine emotion. Then she leaned in and gently nudged her. "It's better. You don't need a two-story house. Everything on one floor makes more sense."

"Because I'm getting old?" Kitzie queried, lifting her head and looking at her beautiful daughter.

"Naaaaah, aging gracefully!" Carson teased, and quickly added, "And I don't think that and neither do you...but it's inevitable. Besides, the new appliances are so cool and more energy efficient. The whole layout has so much more natural light. The higher ceilings make it feel airy and open. I think it's fabulous," Carson enthused. "Our old house was so dark and cramped." Her forehead creased at the memory.

"I know. But it was what I was used to. Maybe I liked dark and cramped," Kitzie opined. "Maybe I'm dark and cramped inside."

"Well, not anymore...you were used to what was here because you kinda had to be. I remember Dad being all wrapped up in the ranch improvements but never the house."

"That's true. Then we bought the stud and the trailer, and we were on the road for months every year." Kitzie smiled warmly at the memories. She had loved the show-circuit days. They knew every show and every time was an opportunity to be with extended friends that were like family.

"This is an opportunity to make something better," Carson smiled. "This is the updated you. And I can't wait to sit at that kitchen island watching you putter about the kitchen, and eating your delicious meals."

Kitzie straightened her back. "I suppose...it may be that I've been stuck in the past too long. It's just that every day I seem to think of something, and I realize it's gone forever. It's sometimes too much to lose it all like that."

Carson wrapped her arms around Kitzie and held her tight. She kissed her cheek and rested her head against her mother's. The two of them stared at the big barn across the parking area in front of the house.

"You know...I kinda see something in the center of that

space. May I do something out there?" Carson pointed. "It needs a focal point, an island, maybe with a small gazebo for two and a little garden boundary around the outside."

Kitzie stiffened. "Gawd, more change?"

"It's a huge open space. Instead of a gazebo, what about a tree in the center? And some seating underneath? Maybe a couple of chairs to enjoy a picnic or an iced tea in the summer? It would create a circular driveway, but it would still be big enough for longer rigs to come in and go around. What do you think?"

Kitzie looked out at the expanse and could see what Carson wanted to do. She shrugged and thought, *Why not?* Carson was gesticulating her vision. Kitzie smiled at her enthusiasm and she put her arm around her daughter's shoulders and squeezed her. "Sure. I like it. You go ahead."

Carson asked her if she preferred one idea over the other.

Kitzie said, "Gazebo," and looked around at the covered porch. "Something that goes along well with this, maybe?" She smiled, getting into it with her daughter's obvious enthusiasm. "It will be a piece of you I'll always see when I walk out the door."

Carson loved the sound of that and said, "Oh, Mom..." and hugged Kitzie again. As she did, she looked over her shoulder and made eye contact with Stiles. He winked at her conspiratorially and she made a silent thumbs-up back.

When Kitzie and Stiles discussed design changes and plans, each vigorously defended or abandoned strongly held ideas, and somehow managed to work things out. Each time they were at loggerheads over something, a great compromise would come out of it and it kept surprising Kitzie. She struggled to understand his motivations because clearly, Stiles was invigorated to employ every good idea he had ever had on this project. As the days progressed, each encounter with Stiles accumulated on Kitzie's mind.

He talked to it—to the house. She heard him, early one morning, when she had just stepped onto the porch. She sneaked closer and ducked a bit to see him through a window cutout. His hand rested on the frame of an inside door, and his voice had a faraway tinge, almost nostalgic. "You will have everything a woman needs to make her feel strong and appreciated," he said, and he gave the frame an affectionate pat. Stiles then saw something move out of the corner of his eye and half turned toward her.

Kitzie thought he was supernatural, as she was sure she had eavesdropped perfectly. She straightened as if she belonged there and had nothing to feel guilty about.

He tilted his head and those piercing eyes grasped and held her from under the brim of his hat. Her lips parted to say something, but no words came, and she froze. In that light, he had a vintage Sam Elliot look about him. Kitzie couldn't take her eyes off him as he removed his hat, ran a hand over his long white hair, put the hat back on, and returned to work as if she wasn't there. Transfixed, she watched him turn away. It was as if the words he had spoken hovered overhead and she almost looked up to see where they were.

As she drove into town, those words echoed and sifted. It was like fish food floating on the water, then gently breaking the surface tension and floating to the bottom. What had just happened? What was she feeling...and why?

Kitzie put the shifter in the park position, killed the engine, and looked around Martin. It had been a close call for the small town. Had it gone up, it would have been devastating for those recovering. She watched the faces of the people passing each other on the street, most etched with fatigue and stress—a look, a smile in passing as if a door to the outside had opened, then shut as the weight of life pressed in close again. Unfair, carry on...that is what she saw in the faces of her community.

Kitzie glanced in the rearview mirror and tilted it to check on herself. *How am I looking to the world?* she wondered. There were new lines and the sparkle in her eyes that Tuff treasured had faded some. The image of her house sprang into her mind again and she thought, *It's priceless what we imagine home to be.* Her mind and her heart refused to let the images of her favorite things go. She knew that holding on to things just made it hurt more. But knowing it and convincing herself to let it go were two different things.

Suddenly, the exhaustion was overwhelming. Kitzie picked up her list, held the crisp paper between her fingers, and felt the urge to start the engine, back out, and go back the way she had come—to run back to the Three Bit. Her emotions almost won. That look that Stiles had given her, those eyes, and how she felt in that moment completely surprised her.

Kitzie watched the world outside through the windshield of the truck and her attention shifted to the broader picture and the moving parts in it. Her eyes found her hands resting on the steering wheel. Her platinum wedding ring had rolled to the left side of her finger again. She wondered why she bothered to straighten it a thousand times a day. She mused that she probably did it in her sleep too. Feelings crowded close. *I can't be this confused,* she said to herself. *I'm a married woman.* But a little voice deep inside said otherwise. She re-balanced the ring and pressed her fingers together firmly to hold it centered and in place. She spaced her fingers apart slowly and watched the ring's immediate slide to the left, away from her, and she dropped her hands to her lap.

The door to the tavern swung open and a couple of ranchers walked out, cowboy hats on. They spoke a few more words, shook hands, and went their separate ways. Vehicles cruised by. Much of the parking was taken in front of Martin Ranch Supply. There was movement behind the glass windows. Kitzie summoned the will to open the truck door and join the world. All she had to do was hold her head up and smile at everyone she would soon see.

The electronic ding of the door into the ranch supply announced her arrival. A couple headed toward her and she held the door open for them with a greeting. She had met them somewhere before but didn't recognize them enough to use names. It may have been an effort, but everyone seemed to muster a smile, their spirits undiminished. Kitzie watched their backs as they made their way toward a ubiquitous ranch truck. *We all have one just like it,* she thought.

They held her attention as she observed them through the reflections in the glass. Her mind wanted to see their faces as they each pivoted, opened the vehicle's doors, and got in—predictable, downcast eyes, no words exchanged, and that last ounce of strength to fasten a safety belt. The wife accomplished this before the husband, then her head dropped back against the headrest and her eyes closed.

Recovery had begun, maybe not as soon as the smoke cleared, but as soon as it could. Martin Ranch Supply was buzzing like a hive that had been stepped on. The indomitable spirit of the independent-minded cut a strong course through the Great Basin, yet many of the people Kitzie had seen seemed like shadows of who they were before their dreams had turned to ash.

Kitzie didn't show it but she was afraid much of the time. At night, she slept fitfully, often pacing back and forth in the trailer, hearing the suspension creak and waver, writing things down on pads of paper to try to clear her head. The refrigerator door was tiled with sticky notes. The constant worry was draining her, and she felt tired and fearful all day. There were so many details. It was all so overwhelming.

She pushed her cart down the aisles and checked each item on her list. Lyle kept the store sensible, and she easily found what she needed. The cash register line was three deep and the idea of small talk repelled her. Kitzie felt too fragile to perform. It depressed her that civil and kind was a chore. It felt alien to her being. *She* felt alien to her being. She liked people, never had a problem talking with anyone, and yet, she resisted. It was as though what energy she had she coveted and would only expend on with the people she really wanted to. She looked around her and thought maybe she wasn't alone.

When Lyle was free, he beckoned her to the other register. With her back to the entrance, Kitzie placed her items on the counter. Lyle was kind and solicitous, gracious and caring, as always, and maybe that was what broke her reserves. His eyes told her it was safe, it was OK. Everything would be OK. But it wasn't and now these new, confusing feelings muddled things even more. It was all too much. It was as if a dam suddenly used its spillway and the tears began to flow silently down her face.

"Here," Lyle said as he handed her a tissue. He recognized that her emotional fracture would not be contained and he came around from the counter.

Kitzie put her hands up as if fending him off because, if it was a hug, she couldn't manage to hold on to control. The whole store would hear a wounded animal losing it in the middle of Martin Ranch Supply. He held his hands in a way that supplicated and gently took her elbow and guided her toward the office area. It was off to the side, down a short hallway, near where the restrooms were located. Her eyes swam and blurred. Fuzzy shapes and linoleum tiles were the best she could do.

Lyle spun the chair in front of his desk around and gently made her sit. He slid the Kleenex box closer and placed a reassuring hand on her shoulder. Kitzie caught a sob in her throat, but it had friends right behind it.

"Kitzie, it's OK. Take all the time you need," he said gently.

The tips of his cowboy boots, dark leather against the industrial flooring, pivoted out of sight and Kitzie heard the door softly close.

She bent over and cried into her hands, and once it began, it seemed unstoppable. Kitzie thought if she could just find the bottom of these feelings, she could find a way through. It was as if pieces of her had come apart and wouldn't fit back together. A pile of used tissues accumulated at her feet. The waves of emotion calmed and attempts to clear her nostrils had little effect. Her stomach growled, she was hungry, and her eyes felt like an army had slogged through them.

Through an overhead vent, Kitzie felt air return to the room and the pounding in her head mimicked the beat of the ventilation. She pushed herself out of the chair and walked to the ladies' room. And though the cry had done some good, the reflection in the mirror begged to differ. She splashed cool water on her face. *Please*, she thought, *tell me I have my sunglasses in here*... She fished through her bag. Relief at seeing the case at the bottom was like a ray of sun piercing the clouds. The glasses restored a tiny bit of dignity. Kitzie squared her shoulders and returned to the cash register.

"Sorry about that," she said to Lyle as she paid for her purchases. He had bagged everything and held it behind the counter for her.

"Aw, it's OK. Here, I'll carry these out."

"You don't have to."

"Come on, let me carry them for you," he smiled.

She capitulated and they went out the door. "I feel a little embarrassed…can't say when that's ever happened before."

"It's been happening more often than you think," Lyle explained. "I've had grown men in that chair. And," he added, "you're much better looking."

She laughed. "So, you've perfected your 'chair-side' manner?"

"And ordered more Kleenex."

He set the bag on the floor of the passenger's side, then stood by the open door while Kitzie got in on the opposite side and fastened her seat belt. "How's Stiles working out?"

"I think it's going well, he's amazing." Both hands on the wheel, she confessed, "He frustrates me and then his ideas work, and I'm amazed."

Lyle listened and nodded knowingly. "What's the frustration?"

"It's all so different, the whole concept. I thought…in my mind, we were building the same house back. Like it was. You know?"

There was a pause so long he thought she might not go on.

"I think it's losing the house; it was my last anchor to the past, to who I was. Now I don't know…I don't have a clue who I'm supposed to be." Kitzie tried a wan smile.

Lyle looked at her with genuine affection. "Everyone fails at who they're supposed to be."

"Oh, that's reassuring." She made a face at him.

He winked. "It's supposed to be." And he closed the door and waved goodbye.

Chapter 51

Although the perpetrators of the mustang shooting parties thought their clandestine activities were untraceable, rumors had gotten out. Several sets of eyes hadn't missed it and they endeavored to prove the rumors true. But to succeed in that would be to risk their own safety.

One set of those eyes belonged to the rogue rider who seemed to appear and disappear out of nowhere. Horses rounded up and held were not there hours later. No one heard or saw where they went due to dark nights mixed with alcohol and lax attention. Swaths of fencing were laid down quiet as you please, and horses walked through the openings like they had pillows on their feet. In daylight, the tracks of the herds revealed where they had gone, and a separate set of tracks could be seen where someone had come in unseen and unheard.

The methods of access and egress varied. If the disruptors rode out from freeing the animals, their horses blended with the mustangs or they were riding trained mustangs who felt a kindred comfort with the animals they rescued. There were several theories on how this was accomplished…perhaps somebody was training horses for this specific work.

A graphic, disturbing video appeared on social media and was given to all news organizations. Under the Twitter handle "Wild horses need a good lawyer too," a mass shooting of a small band of wild mustangs was displayed to the world. High-beamed headlights and racks of spotlights mounted on bars over the cabs of trucks illuminated a stallion as he ran back and forth in front of his small band, which included yearling youngsters and at least one young foal. The mares struggled to keep their babies by their sides and the magnificent stallion pawed the ground and blew into the air to challenge the bright lights that blinded him. The dust billowed like fog around them. When the first shot erupted, it set off a cacophony of gunfire. Horses spun from the blows of the bullets and blood sprayed. The foal was one of the first to go down and was quickly trampled in the chaos. The stallion was hit several times and though limping from a shattered leg, he hobbled in front of his shrinking band, trying to fight what could not be fought. At last, he fell. A cease-fire horn rang through the air and two of the shooters went forward and finished off those that still breathed. From the disruptor's vantage point, the footage was clear and excellent. Though the shooters and their vehicles remained hidden by the bright lights, the carnage of their bullets was not. And all of it—the cruelty, the terror, and the suffering—was caught on camera.

The rogue rider, dressed in black, walked to a calmly waiting black horse and stroked its face. A gloved hand reached up and removed cotton wads from its ears and pocketed them. The high-end video camera went back into a custom pack and was zipped securely inside, the record of events and that night's location intended for distribution to several agencies, and especially to an agent named Hy Royston.

Three Corner Fire

The rider spoke softly to the horse. "Next time, we get their faces, their license plates, and we take them down."

The rider led the horse back along the deer trail they had come in on. Above the rim of the canyon, the stars created a blanket of infinity. With no streetlights for miles, the stars guided them out on the range. A long shooting star, then another, caught the rogue's eye.

The track merged with a broader road, maybe one traversed by the occasional vehicle or cattle, and the rider mounted up, then picked up a smooth, long trot and vanished into the black of night.

At the edge of a draw, there was one more task, and it was as expected—a small band in a holding pen and no one there. The approach was an exposed position but the intention to go down there and free the horses made it worth the risk. The rogue rider counted on the men being too far away to stop it.

The black horse was calm but coiled. He knew his job.

Out of the darkness, the rogue was joined by another horse and rider. The rider came alongside so silently that it startled her. She jerked her horse to a stop and reached for her pistol, on guard as she stared at the rider. His face was hidden by long black hair and he sat atop a scrawny black horse.

"Who are you…what do you want?" she hissed. She pulled her bandana higher over her nose to hide her face.

"So, this is what you've been up to," the man said casually. "That was a trap." He pointed at the horses.

She released her grip on her pistol. "*Was* a trap?"

"The barrier to the right is already down and clear."

It was hard to make it out in the dark, but then she saw that the horses were trotting out after the lead mare. The herd fled full force and the bravest of the horses led the way. The herd was fast, and like ghosts in the dark, they saw the landscape and ran it strong. There were a few trips in the tight throng of bodies, and one yearling fell and was almost run over by the rest, but they parted like a school of fish and he recovered and kept up. The whole mass ran well into an open valley floor before their pace slowed.

Their horses swiftly navigated the slope, which brought them level with the herd. Dust choked the air like a smoke cover. The two riders moved with the herd for a short distance, then broke off.

The sound of an animal one might hear in the dark quiet of the high desert made her stop her horse and listen. Was it a warning cry from a small animal to its brethren as an owl soared about silently? Her hand was over her pistol the instant she heard them coming from over her right shoulder. She turned to look back at the other rider, but he had vanished as silently as he had come.

She heard gunfire behind her and the *phiffft, phifft* of bullets in the dirt nearby. *Crap,* she thought and tugged her horse's reins. She made for the rocks and looked for a defensible position.

She and her horse tucked into a ravine of natural rock and scree. She walked her horse to let him catch his wind. It was hard to hear whether they were being followed or not.

Convinced she was alone, and had lost both her companion and pursuer, she made her way along a ragged rampart to further conceal herself behind it. The adrenaline of the moment flooded her extremities. That had been too close on a couple of levels.

A deer trail skirted along the lee side of the butte. The beginnings of dawn's twilight began and the shape of the land around her started to reveal itself. She walked and trotted some of the way, loped where the going was smooth and easy. She stayed in the shadows and got to First Spring an hour later.

First Spring was an ancient place where the spring ran creek-like through the rocks. The undiscovered rock paintings were faded where weather and water had all but erased them. The morning air was filled with the sounds of birds and a gentle breeze played through the tufts of grass that found hospitality near the water. She was tired. Being up all night crept at the edges of her being and she knew she needed to keep moving before the full heat of the day.

She dismounted and maneuvered her horse through a tight turn and led him up the path and out. The myriad bird sounds and rustlings ceased suddenly, and she didn't think much of it, assuming that it noted her passage. Her horse's ears flattened repeatedly and the skin on his shoulder twitched as if bitten by unseen bugs. She prepared to mount up.

"Thought you were fucking clever, did you?"

With one foot still on the ground, she released her other foot from the stirrup but didn't turn around. She froze at the sound of the stranger at her back, about twenty feet off.

"Where's the weapon?" demanded the voice with a rough edge to it.

She could barely breathe. She raised her gloved hands into the air, shoulder high, the reins in one. She worked to calm herself, to not panic. So far, no one had seen her face. She was facing the dawn and the brim of her hat shaded her eyes. Her kerchief lay at her neck, her hat held firmly by the storm tie under her chin. She felt it sharply, as if that were the only sensation in the world. She stayed frozen and held her breath, then shifted her weight and her horse felt her, ready to go with her.

Then came another voice from behind them.

"I don't think so," the voice said.

With a cry of shock and surprise, the man started to turn around. Harper disarmed him so quickly that the blow was unexpected, and the man dropped his gun on the soft dirt. As he fell, he gurgled something between a cry of intense pain and unconsciousness. The sound of him hitting the ground followed that and Rae spun to her left, her gelding dancing in a tight, agitated circle as the tension of the past few minutes was finally broken.

"You again! Holy shit," were the first words out of Rae's mouth. She walked the short span of steps and looked down at the man on the ground.

Harper had the assailant's gun in his hand, the barrel pointed down at him. Rae pulled a glove and touched the man's neck. He didn't move. It was a long few seconds before she found a pulse, and she stood up and looked down at the body.

"You didn't kill him," she said as her eyes rose to look at Harper. "I guess I owe you thanks...whoever you are..."

The edge of the morning sun illuminated the tattoos across his high cheekbones. The line of his jaw to the lower edge of his lip seemed carved from extraordinarily strong stuff. Dark eyes squinted at her in the brightness and frozen in the moment, the place, she didn't know what to say.

"That'll leave a mark," Harper said and he shrugged. "Oops."

A bit puzzled, Rae watched Harper return to his skinny black horse, who stood by quietly, untied. An excuse for reins hung straight from the headstall to the ground. The horse didn't move beyond lifting his head to look at them as they approached. Harper laughed as he took the reins.

Rae got on her horse. From the saddle, she asked, "What are you laughing at?"

He mounted and was still laughing when he repeated, "*That'll leave a mark*. I've always wanted to say that." He turned in his saddle. "Never thought the opportunity would arise."

Rae had more questions than answers and agreed with him that they should get some distance between what had just happened and what had happened earlier. There would be plenty of time to compare notes later.

"Gotta go before someone else looks for you," Harper said.

"That depends on who is looking," Rae replied.

"You mean besides your father?" Harper added as he started to ride off down the trail.

"What?" Rae was stunned. "*Who* are you?" she asked as she jogged down the narrow trail after him.

They were close to coming out onto the flat. With the increasing light, it was easier going.

On the ride back to where she had left her truck and trailer, Rae discovered who had sent her the information about the wild horses, and who had been sent to see what she had done with herself after she'd taken her leave of absence.

She asked Harper Lee if he would be in trouble for showing up and doing what he did. He said three words, "Leave of absence," then added, "Isn't that what you're doing? Oh, I'd say being a lawyer doesn't give you any cover either."

Rae nodded.

"I think your father wanted you to apply yourself to the problem a bit differently. Don't throw your entire career down the toilet."

Rae said that this wouldn't happen again. She would retire

the rogue.

"I'm glad. I don't think I could take it if you didn't. And I know your father certainly couldn't."

Chapter 52

The day was dry and still, with a thick buttermilk sky that cut the rays of the sun and let it hang low. Dale had been on the road for several blissfully quiet hours. His truck had an extra gas tank so there was little thought of stopping. A steady stream of his favorite country music pumped through a master stereo system and gave him nothing but joy.

He'd had to navigate around fire-related detours and found himself in unfamiliar territory. The first section of the detour was clearly marked, but he'd driven well past a sign that the wind had blown flat, rendering it invisible to an unsuspecting driver. At some point, Dale turned around and made a couple of tries down backcountry roads to get to where he thought he should be, certain his innate sense of direction was infallible. He remained convinced of that until he found himself on a gravel road in the middle of *no* and *where*.

Dale got out of the truck and looked up and down the desolate road with exasperation. He went around to the passenger's side and opened his speckled briefcase, still assured that this was a momentary lapse and that he would no doubt be on his way swiftly.

Dale was nonchalant as he reached into the briefcase for his cell phone, his manner confident and assured. With over a thousand dollars of new phone in his hand, he would soon be back on track. He mildly regretted not getting it out sooner for the GPS but he disdained technical assistance unless the need was dire. It was approaching, and he wondered if he would get a signal way out wherever the hell he was.

His hand casually reached into the briefcase, searched the interior, then searched more urgently. His brow furrowed and he pulled everything out of the case onto the seat. Papers slid to the floor next to a small ice chest that contained all he needed for the trip. Some of the Cedar Wara pages split off and fell between the seats but he didn't retrieve them.

His mouth open in disbelief, Dale realized that the phone wasn't there. He grabbed his overnight bag and pitched its contents in the same manner as the briefcase's. He stepped back from the truck, then looked up and down the long road and saw no signs of life or a semblance of direction. Dale walked to the back of his truck, removed his Stetson, ran a hand through his hair, and tapped the brim of his hat on his thigh.

His plan to get to the reservation evaporated. This was not the reality he had envisioned. *For Christ's sake*, he thought, *I slept at a twenty-five-million-dollar estate last night.* The irony of where he had been the night before and his current location was not lost on him. This just was not happening. Not to him.

He got back behind the wheel and chose going forward over going back. He could always turn around if need be. Dale saw himself as the architect of what was going to be, and in his mind, there was no doubt whatsoever that his plans would not be thwarted. He simply could not conceive the start of something that he would not see the end of.

The track bent and turned into something narrower. Dale kept going with the idea to turn around as soon as he found a good place. He didn't want to carve up the paint and he was confident there would be an opening. He spied a hidden turn, sharp to the left at the bottom of a hill. It was blind until he was on top of it, and he cranked the truck hard left to catch it. The instant he did, he thought he should have gone past it and backed up into it to turn around, but in his haste, he hooked the turn and regretted it immediately. The right edge of the track dropped off sharply into a soft shoulder. The right wheel fell away and Dale heard a sickening thud as the undercarriage got caught on the dirt. The whole cab tilted and the engine died. He swore, restarted it, and tried to put it in four-wheel-drive low to back himself out of trouble. It didn't work. The engine died again. He couldn't go forward and he couldn't go back.

Dale rolled down the window and looked outside. The ground on his side was a good three feet below the custom running board. He eyed the drop and wondered if, when he slid out of the cab, the truck would move without his counterweight. He thought the truck was too stuck and from what he could see of the slope, he hadn't managed to get hung up on a cliff. He shook his head and sat a little taller in the seat to see over the passenger's door sill at what lay below. None of it looked good and he wondered what towing company would come out there to pull him free—and what they would charge.

Furious with himself, and feeling the day slipping away, Dale pushed the driver's door open slowly. There was no shifting as he scrooched his butt uphill to the edge of the seat, which was no easy feat while holding the weight of the door. He had to strategize and coordinate his movements so as not to jar the vehicle. He swung his cowboy boot heels firmly onto the outside edge of the running board. He held the door open with his right hand and leveraged himself with his left on the frame. His plan was to slide the distance between the running board and the ground. It would be awkward but he felt he could do it.

It was farther than he thought and as his boots left the running board and gravity took over, Dale's feet swung under and his effort to control his descent became an exercise in flailing with a face-plant finish. He scramble-crawled on all fours away from the truck, half worried it would slide farther down the slope. It shuddered at the sudden shift of weight and settled, still firm in its wedged position.

Dale sat in the dirt, hands on his bent knees, and saw that the left rear tire was off the ground. He tilted his head to the side and spied the broken drive shaft underneath. After a maniacal kick, the cowboy-boot-imprinted sidewall spun, then gently rotated to a stop.

Chapter 53

Carson was "angry raking" manure in the paddocks—what her father called it when she was upset and raked horse manure. The ground around the piles held the welts of her rage. The apple picker didn't just scoop the poop into the cart, bits of dirt and pebbles pummeled the side. Some of it even bounced out from the force, and the longer she went on about it, the angrier the raking became.

The results were, of course, spectacular. Once upon a time, her father had teased that she should always be mad when she cleaned the paddocks. But that morning, Kitzie, who had first heard the tempo of the tines, and then watched Carson clandestinely for a little while, saw it for what it was. Someone was upset.

Kitzie stood next to the fence and waited. A few dirt clods had enough momentum to hit her boots and she was just about to speak when Carson stopped suddenly and threw the rake at the cart. It missed and its wire tines clattered on the ground.

"What's going on?" Kitzie asked.

Carson turned and Kitzie saw the anguished rage on her daughter's face. "It's gone."

"What's gone?"

"You know, I wondered why Bodie just up and disappeared. Buckets said it was for the better and he didn't complain about his absence at all. But now I know why he left."

Carson dropped her head and choked back tears. She couldn't believe she had been so stupid. He had seen the envelope when he watched her by the truck. She thought she had been smooth, that sliding it out of sight wasn't noticed. But it was.

"Goddammit!" she shouted at the sky.

Kitzie didn't try to assuage the rant. She knew she was getting to the why of the matter.

Carson stopped and looked at her mother. "He took it."

Kitzie did the "what?" look with the appropriate shrug and Carson approached her and leaned on the fence.

Carson explained that she had gone through her truck again, and had found more files and papers, and a couple of suitcases she'd forgotten about, which meant that she did have some clothes. Not everything had been lost in the fire. She brushed back a strand of hair and reset her baseball hat on her head. Then she said she found everything she needed except the one thing she wanted most to find—the manila envelope. Her mood darkened from there.

"Oh, Mom, I was an idiot. I lied to him."

"Lied to who? Bodie?"

Carson shook her head, frustrated at her inability to articulate and begin where it should have ended. "When I told him I destroyed all our correspondences, all the messages…I didn't. I lied. I copied all of it and saved them…and there may have been some letters where I poured my dreams and fantasies out onto paper and never sent. Precious memories and reassurances at the time. Mutually assured destruction if the wrong someone ever saw them. I foolishly saved it all. It was a comfort when I was lonely and there was no way he and I could get together." She buried her face in her hands. "Be together…"

"The married him?" Kitzie asked softly.

Carson nodded.

"And you think Bodie took the letters?"

"I'm certain of it," Carson replied miserably.

Carson was still upset and went to hide for a while in the barn office. She didn't like to be snarky around her mother—not when so much weighed on her mind. She felt childish, being upset and angry. She read somewhere that for therapy you could go into a room and take a baseball bat and be destructive…like a bull in a china shop. And then she looked at a picture on the wall of her father and it was like he was looking at her—or through her—and she snapped.

"Don't look at me like that. It wasn't my fucking fault! And no, I don't know whose fault it was. Shit just happened," she snarled to no one.

A shade of her old paranoia rose from buried depths into sharp relief, as if heavy smoke had cleared and revealed the truth. She loathed the feelings of inadequacy that bubbled up and roiled around all her best intentions.

Carson had come home, maybe for good, and things on the ranch had been interrupted by circumstances and new challenges. Now she felt guilty—guilty that her demons were fighting with her when, after the fire, she needed to be clear and strong. But she didn't feel clear or strong. She felt lost and strange. And there was the missing file and Carson felt vulnerable and deeply embarrassed. There were very personal things on those pages—things she'd rather have burned than have anyone see.

She swatted a brown plastic cup off the desk and it bounced against the wall. Carson wanted it to break into a million pieces but no, no satisfaction there. She paced until her internal rant wore out, then slumped down, ignoring her father's favorite chair, and felt the cool of the concrete on her butt.

"Goddamn it!" she cried. She accidentally banged the back of her head against the stucco wall and it hurt. "Fuck! Really?" she said to herself as she rubbed it.

The stinging pain caused her to pause. Still rubbing the throbbing at the back of her head, she rested her elbows on her knees and her head hung forward in the space her legs created. "Why are you so high and mighty? You arrogant bitch, you really think no one feels like you do?" she said to the empty room.

She looked up and saw the row of ribbons that hung across the top of the walls. Some were faded from age but remained years after being lovingly put there by her mother when they were flush with success. Carson liked winning and her eyes shifted to one of the saddles on a nearby rack. Under its saddle cover, she knew what it said on the fender: *Champion*. Yeah, she liked winning. She liked the hard work it took to create success. And she thought she'd done it. She thought she had it, and then it all went away. The sharp contrast between the comfort of lots of money and the spiral down to zero was an acute ache in Carson's being. It left a huge void she didn't know if she could ever fill.

Then, what about relationships? She had failed there too. She didn't have someone she loved and had committed to in the way her parents had done. She had "borrowed" someone else's—a matter of convenience she'd mistakenly justified at the time. Now, in hindsight, she knew it was all a lie. Maybe having all those things she had so desperately wanted was also a lie. If so, where was the truth? Tears filled her eyes, held fast, then rolled down her reddened cheeks. She was angrier with herself; more frustrated by her lack of understanding than tearful.

Carson lifted her gaze, looked up at the chair, and recalled a moment when she was little and had had a bad ride. And blamed the horse. Her father had been sitting there, his back to her doing something at his desk, and she thought he should have turned and bolstered her confidence, held her, and agreed with her.

"Nothing wrong with the horse," he'd said matter-of-factly.

It rang in her ears as if just spoken. Her father's voice echoed through the years. They were pretty crushing to a nine-year-old at the time and now, Carson's mouth hung slack, open in awe of the moment and the memory. A nine-year-old knew how to swear. Little Carson had heard the words all the time around the barn and she let fly. "Fuck you."

Her father was off that chair and kneeling in front of her as fast as any spooked colt, facing her at eye level, his eyes inches from hers and his cheeks flushed with fury. But there was something else in his eyes. As angry as he was, inside those pupils was a soul that understood her frustration. He understood the misunderstanding of who and what was there. The *why* didn't matter.

"Don't say things you don't understand," he whispered. "And never say anything that you will have to take back."

His face had evaporated with the years in between but the

shadow of it held fast.

The silence of the tack room office enveloped Carson. The soft sounds of the barn, some known and some only guessed at, found their way to her ears and her heart. She picked herself up, brushed off the back of her jeans, and grabbed the plastic cup she'd tried to break. It had a small crack. A small crack was the full testimony to her outburst, her rage. That was the sum total of it. She looked at it and wiped away her tears.

Carson set the cup on her father's desk, near his picture. She stared at the photograph for what seemed like hours. She extended a forefinger and touched her lips, then pressed it against the dusty glass and left a mark.

When Carson drove her mother to Redmond, Kitzie napped most of the way. Carson's mind and imagination were firing away. She hoped she was ready to shed herself, her vision of who she thought she was. She told herself she was ready to look at where she was, not where she thought she should be. And she knew. She knew that as nice as Green Eyes was, he wasn't what she wanted. He was like an arrow that fell just short of the target.

"Nothing wrong with the arrow," she murmured to herself. "Just not the right target."

The clarity of the statement made her smile and she felt strangely lighter owning it. In the imaginary moment, on her way to a fiscal guillotine, she felt that she knew who held the bow. She felt that if CJ pointed his arrow in her direction, it would find its mark. The CJ in her imagination had no furrowed creases between those brows. The eyes sparkled in a sweet gentleness and expressed joy at the little things, like just riding in the truck with her…anywhere. That kind of guy. Which he wasn't. Carson smiled at the foolishness of her imagination.

And then she was calm. The drive wasn't painful. Those past friends and lovers meant little to her now. They were behind, not ahead. And even though she knew it was farcical imaginings, a distraction, it felt oddly perfect and right. It was time she just went with it. It was time she stopped waiting for perfection and followed her flaws.

Carson found the attorney's office in Redmond and parked. Kitzie was going to take the truck into Bend to look at materials and ideas for the house and she was reticent about it. Carson got out of the truck and grabbed a file box, then waved at her mother and headed toward the small, nondescript office building. Kitzie slid over into the driver's seat. She started to head out, but then the brake lights went on and she turned off the engine. Carson turned back and Kitzie rolled the window down. They discussed something, and Carson shook her head and laughed, nodding, before turning back toward the building. Kitzie grabbed a design brochure Stiles had given her, and sat back to wait for her daughter.

The town had grown and people went about their business all around her. It was as if time had moved on and all that went before didn't matter. Carson was shown into a basic office and formal greetings were exchanged. The attorney was kind-eyed and explained everything thoroughly. He took her file box, gave her a packet of information for her to digest, and said he'd be in touch after he and his team had gone over the material. There were a few forms she would need to read and complete and he asked to meet again in thirty days. He was swamped with work and apologized for the time it would take to get to her case.

Across the street, a figure leaned against a building. He was looking down, the brim of his cowboy hat covering his face. The head lifted and Green Eyes observed Carson enter the attorney's office. It was a coincidence that he was in Redmond on an errand for the Running Horse. When he first spotted her, as she drove into the parking lot and parked, he wanted to say hi, and then he saw that Kitzie was with her. His hand rested on the wheel and his elbow on the open window. He opened his mouth to call out to her but something stopped him. He stood on the sidewalk and watched her. He turned and saw that he was in front of a small bakery. Along the window was a counter and a couple of women were sitting there having a bite to eat. They both watched him. He tipped his hat and smiled at them, and they looked quite pleased to be noticed. One quickly wiped her mouth to be sure no errant crumb spoiled her appearance.

Green Eyes looked down at the pavement, contemplating how to kill a little time. The ladies didn't look like they would mind him going in and parking himself nearby. So that's what he did. It was a nice place and the breakfast sandwich and black coffee he ordered were more than satisfying. The ladies chatted him up and they asked questions about what he did and was he a "real" cowboy?

Redmond had grown up, he thought. Yes, it was still a town that had its share of ranchers and wranglers but its proximity to the exploding Bend had caused some overflow. Housing prices had gone up and folks who couldn't afford or find a place to live in Bend came east to Redmond. Some commuted from as far away as Prineville. He was surprised at how much Prineville had changed when he'd driven through there earlier. A lot of survivalist types had retreated from the outside world to Prineville and he figured, correctly, that they were none too happy about the coming gentrification. Industry had found the town and the lower cost of living was appealing. The remote country attracted people who were tired of the crowding and expense of city living.

Green Eyes turned their question to him into listening to their answers to the few questions he put. His guess about the influence of growth in Bend was correct. One of the ladies was in real estate and she ran away with the conversation. It allowed him to eat in relative peace as he nodded and ate. Out of the corner of his eye, he watched the door Carson had disappeared into. She was there for a good forty-five minutes, and Green Eyes began to look at the clock, concerned that his true mission for being there was becoming impinged by his curiosity. He could hear Buckets grilling him when he got back to the ranch.

Buckets surmised that Green Eyes had a pretty easy time with the ladies—as evidenced by the real estate gal slipping him her card and pointing out that she had written her private number on the back. He was all charm with his pleasant, "Nice meeting you," and tip of his hat. He had the gift of directly looking at someone and it translated to a feeling that buoyed their spirits for the rest of the day. His whole demeanor was one of politeness and Old World manners, and these ladies obviously recognized a missing quality in the local menfolk.

Green Eyes watched the ladies leave and admired the way they'd put themselves together. Being treated with admiration and respect caused a person to carry themselves a bit taller, and they were quick and sincere to wish other passersby on the sidewalk a good day.

Their departure coincided perfectly with Carson's egress from the building. She hurried to where Kitzie waited, and climbed back into the truck. Through the window, he could see that both seemed happy as they drove out of the parking lot.

When they were out of sight, Green Eyes left the bakery, looked both ways, and crossed the street. He stopped in front of a door that had an attorney's name on it, and went into the office Carson had just left moments earlier. When he emerged, he held the attorney's card in his hand. He stood rooted to the sidewalk as he considered the information he'd gathered from the cute receptionist inside. He tapped the card on his open palm, then slid it into his shirt pocket. He crossed the street and decided he'd get the truck washed while he was there.

―◦⁂◦―

Carson looked at her hands and noticed how dry and scruffy they looked. She actually couldn't recall the last time she'd had a manicure. A manicure had been part of her weekly ritual in her Silicon Valley life. She laughed at herself and the memory of her previous existence.

Kitzie tried not to pry but did anyway. "How'd it go?" she asked softly.

"Oh, that went fine, I was just noticing that my hands are pretty trashed. It seems like my 'then life' and my 'now life' met in there when I saw the lovely nails the receptionist had." Carson held up her hands to show her mother.

Kitzie smiled.

Carson looked out the window. "They were very nice. We have started the bankruptcy process. The attorney has given me a list of materials I need to fish out of my files in the back of the truck. I can fax or mail them or we can make another trip."

Carson continued to stare out the window as Kitzie made the right onto 97 and headed toward Bend. Carson's eyes filled but the tears retreated and didn't spill. There was a bit of leftover anger—anger with herself—though it wasn't as overwhelming as it had been when she'd first returned home empty, broke, and feeling like a failure. The tears dried and the tightness in her throat melted away. The feelings of wanting to run away were easing as well. Carson liked being with her mom and after the fires, it seemed they were closer than they had ever been. She wondered if she would have come home after the fires had she remained in her old life.

Carson decided she wasn't that person anymore. The glitter of the things she once had now seemed contrived and false. She thought that treading water was the same as drowning, and she had been drowning back in California for a lot longer than she had realized. Her thoughts drifted to the personal e-mails and she realized they'd lost their significance. They were embarrassing but not treasured. With all that had happened, she'd completely forgotten about them and the reason they were once important to her.

The space between Redmond and Bend was dotted with

small ranches and open high desert. There were burnt areas along 97 and it reminded Carson of how far and wide the fires had been. A couple of the horse ranches had burned, and the empty paddocks made her wonder where the people had taken their animals.

She glanced over at her mother. Her profile was still lovely, the shape of her lips soft and her chin strong. She had a scarf tied loosely at her throat and Carson decided that she was aging very gracefully.

Carson continued. "I guess I didn't want to really look at it. I wanted it all to just go away on its own. But you were right to push me to clean up the mess I made."

"Do you remember what your father said to you after that show where you'd lost the cow and things fell apart?" Kitzie asked.

Carson wasn't getting it and held her response while her mother filled in the memory for her.

"You were so upset. Devastated. And he let you cry for a while and then he came and found you and he said…" She paused, knowing that her daughter would remember.

Carson looked ahead as the times rolled back in her mind. "Carson," she repeated from memory, "it isn't how you handle victory that matters, it's how you handle defeat."

Kitzie nodded. "You remember. I always admired your father's resolve to make a way that worked, whether it was for a person or a horse. He had the patience to see the best in both and to remind them of it."

"Mom…it's been so long. You still miss him, don't you?"

"Every day," Kitzie answered.

Carson looked out the window at the scenery as they rode in silence.

Chapter 54

Motion and an airborne noise caught Kitzie's attention. She looked over her shoulder and saw two birds comingled in flight. She straightened and pivoted to watch. She thought it was two doves in amorous pursuit. Their in-flight tumble shot underneath the belly of the horse at the tie rail, split apart, and they landed together nearby. The horse either didn't notice the jet that shot underneath it or didn't find it worthy enough to react to.

Kitzie came around the hindquarters, running her hand on the horse's side and rump, and looked at the two birds. It was then she realized it wasn't love. It was the dark eye of the sharpie hawk, having pounced upon its prey, that changed her perception of what she was witnessing. He stared at her from atop the broken dove.

Kitzie approached and the hawk took flight, releasing the dove. The dove was an unusually light color, not the soft gray she'd always seen. It was whiter and some of its feathers were on the ground. Kitzie approached it to try to help it, but its panic was fresh and it skittered under the nearby ATV. Kitzie got down on her knees to peek under it and try again. But the dove wasn't having any so she got back up to continue grooming the horse. Kitzie watched it for a time, and didn't see the tiny hawk, so she hoped the dove would recover.

The hawk reappeared and continued its hunt and the dove,

which could no longer fly properly and staggered to imminent death. Kitzie tried to save it again by taking off her baseball cap and capturing it, but it was in blind survival mode and found another tight place in which to hide, though the bird wasn't bright enough to stay there, she feared. Again, she backed off and hoped for the best.

Stiles watched the way Kitzie moved to still the bird's fear and to try to save it. Kitzie hadn't noticed his hammer was silent. He climbed down the ladder and reached for his water bottle and took a long, cooling drag off it. He set the hammer on the rung of the ladder and stood in the shade of the house. He felt better than he had in a long while and marveled at how a twist of fate had landed him back to doing a trade he loved. He'd forgotten how much he once loved building things, designing things, sorting out the various challenges, and creating something with his own hands.

He stared at his hands. He spread his fingers wide and turned them palm up. He made loose fists with them, releasing them, and turned them palm down. Working hands, he thought. His father's hands. When did his hands turn into his father's, he wondered? The skin was showing age—brown spots and imperfections from labor and weather. Like the erosion along the buttes nearby, sinew, veins, and bone were well defined. The bits inside of him hadn't noticed how time had changed the outside, and he felt like he was noticing it for the first time. He rubbed one hand with the other and looked up at the eaves, then to his right, and saw that Kitzie was watching him. A small smile touched the corner of his mouth and he tipped his head in greeting to her.

Kitzie chose that moment to drop the body brush into the tote. She went to the tack room fridge, grabbed two beers, and walked to the house, its framework still visible.

Stiles felt her approach and characteristically had no words. He had tried to stay aloof, apart, and be like a stone skipping across the surface of this particular pond. But he found himself feeling invested there and given his past transgressions, it created conflict within him.

Kitzie didn't say anything. She just handed the cold bottle to him, then walked along the edge of the building, looking at the details. She noticed little things; nuances he hadn't realized himself. It caused him some self-reflection, as if he questioned the effort. Was it guilt…or something else?

Kitzie noticed that he'd shaved the gnarly, stubbly beard off and trimmed his mustache. More of his face was revealed and she could feel him standing there, leaning his left elbow on something, his right hand at his waist, thumb in the front pocket, the neck of the bottle held fast, and his vest buttoned tight, like him. He stared, expressionless, a handsome face, and one that hadn't smiled since arriving.

Kitzie stopped and took a sip of her beer. She loved a cold beer on a hot day and this didn't disappoint. She tilted her head and looked at Stiles, matching expressionless for expressionless.

"You're pretty good at all this, aren't you?" she said more than asked.

He stayed rooted and just tipped his head in the affirmative.

"I thought I'd seen good work before but what you're doing here is different. It looks like more—maybe more than I can afford. I mean, the insurance is only covering what I'd call a minimum, and this is..."

Stiles set down his beer and walked over to her. He stood close but respectfully so. Both thumbs found pockets and he looked it all over. It was better than a basic hack would do. He'd be hard-pressed to admit otherwise. He was finding materials on the ranch, repurposing pieces of things that were pieces of things. He'd find something and see it in a whole new light. He'd done one whole side of the building in repurposed, corrugated metal. The rusted hues and varying shades caught the late-afternoon sun and dazzled. He mumbled something about not having to paint it ever, and he'd made good use of alternative material insulation—something he'd read about somewhere and tried.

Kitzie looked at him and he dared not look back at her, for in that feel of a look, he thought she could see right through him. He'd never felt so vulnerable around someone.

He moved off and went back to work with the over-the-shoulder statement, "Light's a-wastin'. Got a bit more till the day is through."

Carson enjoyed her mornings in the small, upstairs bedroom in the barn—the "miracle barn" as they'd heard it called in town. After the devastation that had surrounded it, the wood barn stood alone, completely unscathed by the fire. It was a bubble of peace and serenity for Carson, and a kind of spirituality from the whole area had fled the devil and found its sanctuary in this place.

Many peaceful childhood hours had been spent in the barn,

and when she was small, and too little to be of much use around the legs of the adults, she'd play for hours there. She sat on the edge of the bed and felt completely safe and it was a good feeling. She bounced her calves against the comfy bed and her thoughts drifted back to her childhood...

Carson would sit on a bale of straw, lean against the wall of a stall, and bounce the heels of her cowboy boots against the bale. She'd watch the dust in the light fall slowly toward the dirt floor of the barn. To Carson's imagination, fairies secretly danced in the beams, always when she looked away. They were clever and she would pretend not to look, or she'd give the beams the side-eye to catch a glimpse of one. She'd look away and spin back quickly, convinced they floated when you watched and flew when you didn't.

One time, Carson brought a small mirror and stood in the open door of a stall that was getting cleaned, hoping she could look into the mirror to see behind her back. She'd figured out that fairies knew when backs were turned. She'd draw pictures of them and make up stories about them—what they did, what they ate, and where they slept. She had a notebook that she'd drawn and written in but it had burned in the fire at the house.

Carson sighed as she looked at the light filtering into the little bedroom. She had no idea that they'd kept so many memories in the house.

On the small dresser, Carson spied a package of filter masks and saw there was one left in the box. She hated the masks. They made the lower half of her face sweaty, carved red trenches in her cheeks, and caused her skin to break out. She tried to wear just bandanas for the first few days and felt like a bandit. But the poor air quality and floating particles gave her a headache and a raspy cough. She thought after years of inhaling dirt and dust out riding and working cows, not to mention the copious dust of the hay and the barn, that it wouldn't be any big deal. But this was different, her mother told her. The fires had vaporized structures and cars near and far, sending toxins into the atmosphere to rain down indiscriminately on everyone. Even the buckaroos took to the masks right away. The smell of smoke had lingered in the air for weeks, making everyone edgy and depressed.

Carson dressed and ran a brush through her hair, then grabbed the mask and went down the stairs. The big barn's doors were closed but that hadn't kept the smell of the smoke out. In some of the confined spaces, the smell was stronger and that caused more than a few panicked moments.

Carson turned the lights on and fed the horses in the barn. When she was finished, she turned the lights off again and headed for the door to the left of the big sliding doors—no need to let in a bunch of bad air, she thought, though she missed them being open. The owls in the rafters knew when they were open and went in and out through them. Carson stopped and looked up into the darkness and knew they were there somewhere but couldn't see them.

As she stepped outside and started to stretch the rubber band of the mask over her head, Carson sniffed the air, then took a deep breath. The distinct smell of fresh morning air struggled to compete with the odor of the smoke. She held the mask in her left hand and walked straight out into the drive and rotated 360 degrees, looking for the haze, the smoke, the silence, and there was none. A bird chirped happily nearby, and the sky was clear. A healthier sun rose in the east, not yet clear of the nearby low butte of the canyon. Carson closed her eyes and sucked in the fresh, wonderful air. She would have dropped the mask right then but knew to be wary. The winds had changed mercurially before. But this morning felt different. It felt like…hope.

She stood rooted in that spot for many minutes and surveyed the damaged structures all around the open drive. For the umpteenth time, she wondered how the house had burned to the ground so close to the old barn, yet the barn had survived. She could see the edge of what was left of the shed row and workshop where Luis died. And the ramshackle, twisted, charred remains of the other buildings. The tractor, parked next to one, looked almost new. Why didn't it burn? Another mystery. Someone had washed it recently, though a layer of ash had quickly stuck to the effort. Carson smiled, then walked toward the tractor on her way down to the big arena to have coffee with her mother, which she knew was already brewed.

Chapter 55

It took forever to get off the uneven, dusty track and onto good, even highway and the young vet tech resisted the urge to pull over and check on the horse. She feared he was already down or dead. She tried the number in her cell. Her speakerphone on the visor chirped and went to voicemail. She didn't leave another message and headed straight to the clinic.

Though just out of high school, Janine had experience beyond her years. She wasn't a certified vet tech but she was the vet's daughter. Motherless from an early age and raised by a single parent, Janine's father had worked hard to set up a large animal practice pretty much in the middle of nowhere. And he was in the middle of the biggest disaster any large animal vet had to contend with. She was worried about him as she hadn't seen him for almost a week. His voicemail greeting over the speaker was almost unrecognizable and she wondered how to even ask him to come back to the office for the injured animal she had in the trailer.

By the time she reached home and the clinic, she knew her own animals waited to be fed, but she had to move quickly to treat her patient. She backed the trailer as close as she could to the clinic doors, clambered up onto one of the aluminum wheel fenders, and looked inside. An ear twitched and a slightly swollen right eye looked at her. He was alive. And he had traveled facing backward, so he had turned himself around in the trailer during the trip.

Janine hurried to unlock the office, slid open the door to the clinic, and found something soft to loop over his neck to lead him inside.

The horse was remarkably cooperative, though he was stiff and almost tripped and fell when she unloaded him. To evaluate him, she guided him to a set of stocks in the center of the treatment space, then clipped the chains behind his butt and in front of his chest. She called her father got his voicemail again. She knew there was no time to waste. She had listened to him talking on the phone to clients with injured animals from the fires and she surprised herself by how much practical knowledge she had absorbed.

Janine felt a flash of panic that her lack of comprehensive experience would be an issue but she didn't really think about it as she went to work. Her patient stood calmly as she hooked up an immediate IV to combat fluid loss and shock. She knew that she shouldn't use a lot of fluids because she'd remembered something her father had said about overhydration. *Watch that*, she said to herself.

She grabbed a chart to enter the name of the horse. What to call him? She hadn't gotten a name. They didn't know it... She chose the name of the man he had been found with, Cajun. She took his vitals—respiration and heart rate—and what she didn't think of she found on the form and it acted like a checklist. She started to assess the obvious injuries she could identify without cleaning him off yet. When she checked the capillary response on his gums, she looked at the singeing and partial burns around his muzzle and on his face. The forelock was curled and singed to just below his ears, his muzzle hairs and eyelashes were gone, and the lid tissues were reddened and puffy.

Janine did an inventory and categorized the burned areas by severity, along with areas that were lacerated or punctured. There were several shallow cuts, maybe two that would need suturing, and the eyes. There was an instrument she needed to look at his eyes...where was that kept? As she opened and closed drawers, her cell phone rang and she quickly plugged her earpiece in and answered it. She was relieved to hear her father's voice. She explained what she was doing and he was silent to the point that she thought she had lost the call, until he said that he wished she had waited for him.

"When can you get here?" she asked.

He didn't know.

"Well then, I'll tell you what I have and you start talking," she commanded. "I started his chart, already have the IV in, and I've got his stats."

"We use about 20 liters of fluid, no more. You said he's an adult horse?"

"Yes. A gelding and could be a red roan. He's a mess, hard to tell what color he really is."

"Did you find the Banamine?" he asked and instructed her how to administer it for pain and inflammation. He mentioned Pentoxifylline to help with circulation, depending on the grade of the burns, but told her to maybe wait on that.

"Keep checking his hydration status, lung sounds, and cardiovascular—"

The connection was lost.

Gently, Janine measured Rio's weight with a tape, entered it on the chart, and administered the correct dosages. She started to dab clean some of the injuries with a weak chlorhexidine solution. While there were several punctures, the ones that she felt needed immediate attention were a set of wounds horizontally positioned on his thorax.

The soft hum of surgical clippers echoed, and bits of hair drifted down in odd clumps. In the hours that followed, fluids and blood splashed onto the smooth floor, and gravity guided them into crevices etched into the concrete that led to a metal drain. At times, a steady stream of sterile saline washed clumps of hair and unviable tissues into the depths of the drainage system that ran under the clinic.

At midnight, the vet returned home. Their animals let him know they were hungry and he frowned. He was sleep-deprived, emotionally wrecked, hoarse to the point of no voice, and while he knew the crisis had placed a huge responsibility on a seventeen-year-old's shoulders, this would not do.

He looked for the mail first and thankfully, a package had arrived. He had euthanized so many animals that he had put in an overnight order for the drugs needed to humanely put them down. He fed everyone and looked for Janine.

"Where are you?" he wondered when he didn't find her in her bed.

He went outside and around to the far side of the clinic building and saw light coming from within. He slid the door open to the loud sound of someone snoring.

Janine was asleep, upright on a chair outside one of the stalls. Her head rested on the stall door, her mouth agape. She was still wearing one of the aprons and it was smattered with the efforts of her labors. Her hands, palms up, were still gloved and held an open book on her lap. He glanced around in dismay. It looked like a bomb had gone off in the treatment room and he shook his head.

He put his hand over his eyes. "Oh, crap..." he mouthed.

He could feel the fatigue in his bones and was sure that his skin was all that held him together at this point.

He turned at the sound of Janine's patient in the box stall. He looked through the bars at the horse, then down at the chart on the hook on the stall door. He tilted the chart to check it, realized he needed his stethoscope and his cheaters, found both, and picked up the chart.

"Well…Cajun…what's been happening with you?" he whispered, and his eyes bulged as he read.

Rio gingerly pivoted and started toward him. Over the cheaters on the bridge of his nose, they looked at each other with matching sets of red eyes.

A Penrose drain had been placed in a lateral wound on the thorax. There were two puncture wounds about a foot apart, her notes said. In a scrawl only a doctor could interpret, she described probing the puncture wound with a gloved finger and identifying an object directly beneath the skin, which turned out to be a shard of wood. She had enlarged the hole and removed it with forceps. She used a Chambers mare catheter to determine the extent of the pocket and finished with the drain. He was stunned when he found the offending piece of wood in a bag on the counter and surmised that it was probably part of a sharp branch.

He glanced down at the book and saw that his daughter had been reading up on burns. Janine had circled the paragraphs on first- and second-degree burns and had underlined that these wounds generally healed well without grafting. Under the heading "Equine Burn Injuries," another underlined passage read, "Most are first-degree burns similar to sunburn; only the top layers of skin are affected."

Hmm, he thought, and looked through the bars at the groggy horse.

The vet stepped into the stall and approached Rio carefully. To his relief, the animal gave no immediate cause for concern, so he checked his vitals and looked at his daughter's work. He was impressed. Rio seemed hungry, so he got a half a flake of alfalfa, softened it with a little water, offered it to him, and was relieved to see him eat. He made some notations in the chart.

The most severe and largest burn, second degree, was on Rio's left rear loin, flank, and haunch. The vet noted that the vesicles and blisters were intact. Wise, as they should be left that way for twenty-four to forty-eight hours after they formed. The blister fluid provided protection from infection, and the blister was less painful than exposed, raw skin if the blister was broken. After forty-eight hours, he would excise the blister and apply antimicrobial dressing to allow the eschar, something like a scab, to form. He shook his head. This animal had been through hell.

He prescribed further evaluation of the burns and noted, barring infection, that the prognosis should be good. He looked to see what Janine had administered for pain medication and noted that she hadn't tried to guess at antibiotics. *Smart girl,* he thought.

He went about double-checking and doing his own follow-up evaluation for medications. He noted everything he did in the chart and hung it back on the hook. He watched Rio eat a little bit of the hay and judged his overall physical condition as excellent. The horse was trained and well-mannered, even in pain, so he surmised he belonged to someone.

He cleaned up the treatment room and made enough noise that it roused Janine. With sleep in her eyes, and a bit confused about where she was and why, she mumbled that she'd get it. Her father turned her toward the door by her shoulders and told her to get to her bed.

Chapter 56

The bankruptcy attorney was efficient and the office communicated with Carson several times by phone. Carson faxed some things from Lyle's office at Martin Ranch Supply when Kitzie's machine developed a glitch. Kitzie felt the poor thing was exhausted from overuse from all the insurance crap.

"It burned out," she said, and then started laughing at her pun.

Carson cracked up too. It seemed she swung from crying to the opposite, they laughed so hard.

There would be a follow-up appointment with the attorney, and she dreaded it. No, she more than dreaded it…but it had to be done. She had to face the costs and figure out how to get back on some kind of track. The bankruptcy attorney would guide her, and she trusted him.

The following day, late in the afternoon, Carson took the initiative and saddled two horses. She ponied one to the house and waited by the porch until Stiles caught sight of her. Reluctantly, he came out, his face disciplined, his voice flat.

"I thought I was clear," he said.

Carson's face disappeared behind the rim of her hat and her neck scarf hung from her neck in neat folds. She looked back and thrust her chin out stubbornly. "The day is just about over and there's time for a short ride before dark. Come on," she said. Her hazel eyes pleaded, eyebrows high, and she flashed a funny, toothy grin, then scrunched her shoulders up in a comic attempt to break through his resolve.

His lips formed a firm line and he scratched his ear, looking away from her. "All right, but lose the saddle and meet me at my camper." He turned on his heels and closed the door.

Carson brightened and jogged the horses back to the barn and pulled the saddle off one. She trotted them down to Stiles' camper and found him waiting outside the small barn holding a saddle pad and a saddle. Without a word, he placed both on the horse that Carson had brought and put foot to stirrup.

They set the horses in motion with Carson leading the way. It was obvious that Stiles was not just a rider, he was a seasoned horseman. So, she upped the difficulty level and pitched down a steep draw and took the next slope at a gallop, then loped easy up a gentler rise to a vantage point high enough to get a good lay of the land and the ranch. There wasn't time for more than a quick tour and they made a half-circle around the other side, where Stiles got a bird's-eye view of the house. He reined up and sat looking at it for a moment.

The last of the sun would be gone soon. Carson looked at the house too and it was coming along well. From this view, Stiles' vision had a whole new meaning. Then he pointed at something off to their left and loped off in that direction. Carson followed.

They stopped at an old piece of farm equipment partially buried in dirt, like bones picked clean, the remains of spring grasses starting to grow through its bare tines. The last of the sun's rays struck it and Carson's eyes widened.

"You know, that's really kinda pretty," he said.

She agreed with him. He suggested it might be an interesting addition to that center garden instead of rotting away where it was.

It was darker when they jogged back toward the barn. The lights in the arena came on and Carson looked at him.

"Let's go..." she encouraged, hoping that he was not quite ready to be done.

He was reluctant and she goaded him into it. It may have been a short arena ride but Kitzie watched as each did their own thing for a little while. She liked to see horses in there again, and though her mixed feelings about Stiles were genuine, she appreciated the other dimensions to the man that she had been unaware of only a few months ago.

Stiles finished his ride quickly and excused himself. They watched him go and Carson said she would come to get the horse in a minute.

Kitzie asked Carson how that had come about.

Carson laughed. "Just me being pushy and stubborn." She grinned at her mother. "Wonder where I got that from..."

Kitzie shrugged innocently.

As Stiles disappeared around the corner, Carson added, "He's a horseman, for sure."

Her mother nodded in agreement, ran her hand through her hair, then went inside the fifth wheel to start dinner. With a half glance over her shoulder, she asked Carson to ride by the cottage and ask Jorge if he would like to join them.

Stiles had unsaddled and was walking the horse back to the barn when Carson met him next to Jorge's cottage. He handed her the mecate. His voice sounded strangely nostalgic and he thanked her for the ride.

"Hey, I'm grabbing Jorge to invite him to dinner, care to join us?"

Stiles politely declined and retreated to the privacy of his camper.

Chapter 57

Spence discovered that the ID in the wallet the fireman had given him was a fake. There was a smattering of business cards inside it that proved irrelevant. The picture on the license was very poor, but he guessed it might be the only real part of it. The fuzzy image might match mugs shots, so he focused on a different track of research.

Spence wasn't sure how many jewelry robberies there had been in Oregon, when they occurred, or where. The task of tracking down the source of the contraband wasn't easy. There had been a lot of robberies and he wasn't sure when this one had occurred. He got a map and marked the Three Corner country in large, concentric circles, then logged the cities and larger towns in each ring as it went out from the recovery site. He also called Hy and Dave for a few insights into the minds of these guys.

Dave had a better handle on what Spence was asking due to his extensive police background, though he jibed at the inference. "What, you think because I arrested perps like these I have a clue how they think?" And he tried to sound insulted.

They were on speakerphone in Hy's car and Hy piped up that Dave drove like a criminal, so it wasn't that big of a stretch. They started a running diatribe and Spence finally stopped laughing long enough to interrupt them.

"You guys ought to do stand-up together...you're a riot."

Dave told him he would get back to him, that he had an old, retired detective friend who might be able to narrow down the search. "OK if I give him your number?" Dave asked Spence, and Spence gave him his cell.

"I'm hardly in the office lately. It's nuts out there."

Hy, now serious, added, "I'll bet. You OK otherwise?"

"I'll have stories for you next time I see you, that's for sure," Spence added wearily.

Hyland's friend was quick and the list was short. Spence looked at his map of circles and the names of places that had been robbed, what was used in the robbery, and what was stolen and that thinned it down fast. He found the number to one of the jewelry stores and dialed it. He left a message and hoped the call would be returned soon.

The next morning, Spence received an excited call back. It came in as he started to file his many reports. The owner of Gem Jewelers was breathy in his haste to learn everything. The return of the stolen jewelry had been part of the plea bargain, that was true, but the jewelry was never found. The hapless owner recounted his conversation with the DA, which left Spence speechless. The handling of the whole affair was just shy of incompetent. On a scratch pad, he doodled and then made a note of the DA's name—Noah Bainbridge.

The store owner had a bit of an odd follow-up rumor he had heard. Seemed an older, eccentric female customer who came in only sporadically had appeared a few months before the perpetrators were scheduled for release. She'd heard a tale from a young man with long, unkempt hair who was bragging about being rich when "his old man got out," that they'd go dig up a fortune buried way out someplace she'd never heard of, but east of Redmond a ways. Spence considered the face he had seen in the car, the younger man, probably this guy's son, and the description of the hair fit.

Spence wasn't at liberty to tell the jewelry store owner why he was asking exactly, and he chose his words carefully. He said he'd keep him posted on what he found and hung up. His next calls were to the probation officer to get that violation paperwork rolling. Then to contact someone in the district attorney's office where the case had been adjudicated.

During several conversations, Spence discovered that the worthless DA who had prosecuted the case had gone on to greater things and that his replacement seemed more than aware of his many shortcomings. It wasn't hard to read between the lines that he'd been the unhappy recipient of several flawed cases, unhappy victims, and legal complaints.

The new DA said in a frustrated tone, "God help us all."

Spence discussed the particulars of what had happened and they both easily guessed that the bounty from the robbery had been buried there and the fire had prompted them to move fast to find it…too many feet marching, too much fire-altered terrain, and they couldn't wait any longer. The partner had already violated his probation and was back in. They discussed how to proceed.

"Do you think the dozer destroyed the jewelry?"

Spence said, "No one on-site saw anything but dirt and smoke. It's bad out there, we're still not anywhere close to containment and they are working hard and fast staying out of harm's way. One operator was very lucky after being in a rollover accident."

The DA said he would re-examine the case.

Spence stood up and stretched his tall frame. He was weary, almost missing the boring days of Martin. He walked to the window of his office, cracked open a bottle of water, and took a sip. Mentally, he reminded himself to drink more water and looked out the window at the parking area. All the vehicles were coated with ash. Wiper-blade marks streaked windshields not touched by rain in months. The air was heavy with that smoke overcast. The fires were not yet done, and Spence knew that this might be a brief lull, like the devil needed to inhale before using his fearsome breath to drive more devastation.

Chapter 58

Very near where her journey began, Shiloh was glad that her tank wouldn't necessitate stopping for gas. But damn, she did have to pee. So she pulled off at an empty turnout. She chose it just for that reason. Her paranoia still made her jumpy—after all, it was a small world. What if Stiles was in the area and just happened to cruise by the coach? Oh, God...she didn't care to hazard a guess as to how that awkward encounter would go.

Shiloh shook her head. Enough with the what-ifs.

When she was ready, she checked the mirror and pulled back onto the highway. A short distance away, she saw a figure walking alongside the road, arm extended and a thumb indicating intent. Her foot eased on the accelerator as she looked at the back of him. Nice looking maybe, and from the back, nice ass in those blue jeans. He must have heard the slight change in the sound of the big motor because he turned around to walk backward, thumb still out. He carried a rucksack of some kind and a jeans jacket over his left shoulder. One more step backward and their eyes met, and he smiled.

Shiloh had a moment of weakness and pulled over. She cursed herself as she looked into the side mirror and saw him jogging to the coach. She considered hitting the gas and getting gone, that she had made a mistake, but he went to the driver's side window, which was pretty high up off the ground, and looked up at her. A look of recognition flashed across his face. Shiloh kept her Ray-Bans in place and pressed the electric window button to roll the glass halfway down—just enough to be sure nothing funny happened and too high up for him to reach inside.

He had to raise his voice to be heard over the idling engine. He pushed his sunglasses up onto his head and his slightly longish hair played perfectly around his face. He stood respectfully apart from the coach and his eyes scanned its length admiringly.

"Wow," he said, then asked for a ride and added, "I know you."

"Where are you going?"

It seemed the only question Shiloh could think to ask. She remembered him from the Tavern. He had come on at the Running Horse just before everything happened. He was quite charming and very easy on the eyes. But she wasn't interested in any company. She had too much to lose stashed in the coach, and a curious guest could spell disaster.

Regret at stopping edged her face and he was perceptive enough to say, "Anywhere but here," and he turned up the wattage and the charm. He held his hands apart in a cute, supplicating gesture. "Come on…Shiloh, isn't it? Take pity on me."

Shiloh turned away and looked straight ahead, down the road. She again considered just stepping on the gas and letting him eat her dust. She'd never see this guy again. What would it matter? Nothing to gain by being generous.

She shook her head and the word "sorry" formed on her lips. He changed the open hands to prayer hands and made an even cuter face.

Shiloh couldn't help it. She smiled, dropped her forehead to her hand, and rubbed her left eyebrow. "Get in," was all she said, and she unlocked the passenger's side door.

He ran around the front of the motorhome and gratefully climbed in. He set his pack on the floor between his feet, found the seatbelt, and clicked it into place.

"Don't know if you remember, I'm Bodie," he introduced himself.

Shiloh didn't reciprocate. She didn't confirm his guess at her identity and he didn't press. He just smiled at her and said, "Thank you. I really appreciate this."

Over the next few days, Bodie made himself at home as they traveled. It was as if he'd been cruising around the country in the motorhome all his life. Shiloh felt that was a bit much but she had no choice but to tolerate it and indulge him. She hadn't realized how alone she'd felt and there was a kind of entertaining value in his company. She kept her room locked and was guarded about everything. That he knew who she was needed careful managing, she decided. Best to keep close track of him for now.

Bodie was a talker and as Shiloh listened to his stories, she asked a couple of questions that addressed his immediate past. Lucky for her, he was his own favorite subject. He talked about the Running Horse and his boss, Buckets, and that "he-thought-he-was-better'n-me" Green Eyes guy. "Scum fucker," he muttered.

Shiloh smiled inwardly. She knew each person he mentioned right down to how they liked their eggs and coffee. She didn't give herself away until he started talking about working on rebuilding a house on the Three Bit.

"I'll bet that bastard Stiles is wondering where I lit off to without a word," he said.

"Stiles?" Shiloh asked, curious for the first time.

"Yeah, some grizzled old guy, friend of that owner of the supply place." Bodie fished a piece of gum out of a side pocket in his backpack.

Shiloh kept her eyes on the road and her hands on the wheel. She didn't want to seem too interested...but she was. *Whoa...it has to be him. Christ*, she thought, her brain doing cartwheels. *How in the hell did he end up at the Three Bit? How awkward and dangerous for him... Why would he go back to Martin at all? Why risk it? Me? Was he looking for me? Did he think I'd come back here? Crap, I am really close.*

Shiloh pushed her paranoia aside. She glanced at Bodie and considered that no one would look twice at her traveling with someone. Maybe she was safe for now. While her thoughts about Stiles floated close to the surface, she knew men well enough to know that Bodie had an agenda, and for the moment, it was not her.

She made certain he was never alone in her home to rummage around—and she knew he would if given the chance. And he was never far from his backpack, so there was something there he felt he needed to protect.

Road closures and detours became more stop and stuck, and parking anywhere for an extended stay was not going to happen. Bodie spotted a Staples and cried out that they should pull in and see if it was open. Shiloh parked, and noticed that Bodie seemed to think that she wouldn't drive away and leave him because the only thing he carried in there was a manila envelope. She hadn't seen it before and wondered what it contained. It was the only time he'd left the backpack unattended, and she knew that was what he was protecting. But why? He was inside long enough that she started the generator and chose a movie.

A confident Bodie returned with a certain smugness and satisfaction he hadn't possessed before, and when he sat in the chair in the salon, he didn't talk, but he was smiling. He put the manila envelope back in his backpack. His previously secretive posture with it was replaced with nonchalance, almost as if he didn't care that Shiloh saw it. Then he put his hands behind his head and watched the movie that played on the big screen.

Shiloh muted the TV and he turned and looked at her with a look that said, *What the heck?*

"What are you playing at?" Shiloh said it with a seriousness that she'd begun to develop lately.

"What do you mean?" he said, his boyish charm in full play—so impressive that even she believed him, except that she was just as good at bullshit.

She pointed to the backpack and raised her palm as if to silently say, *I know all about it.* She wondered if he had ever played poker and guessed correctly that he had not.

He was silent and stared out the window for a long moment. He pursed his lips as if considering how to lie. Then he leaned forward, elbows on his knees, and his eyes sparkled. "What the heck. I have this great opportunity and it just fell into my lap. I couldn't walk away from a potential fortune."

Shiloh didn't miss the word *potential,* and she kept her face emotionless and waited. Her silence drew him out and he confessed to most of the story.

He'd tried to have a go at the daughter at the Three Bit but the girl was distracted, she wasn't interested. "Shit, maybe it was her mom's house burning down. If it hadn't been for those fucking fires…" He frowned as if someone ignoring him was completely offensive. "Stuck up... I couldn't get anywhere with her. And believe me, I tried. That Stiles asshole was on my shit and between him and Buckets..."

Shiloh inwardly winced at the mention of her father but gave no outward sign. She knew who Buckets was but she kept that to herself. She liked that she was working Bodie rather than the other way around. This guy was a one-note song and Shiloh knew exactly how to play him.

He was talking now and running on, quite stuck on himself. He was selling her and she knew it. She also knew he'd made his play and that was why he'd spent the afternoon in Staples. He was talking about the file and the very personal e-mails he'd stolen.

She felt her body language lean in a little, her curiosity piqued. "What kind of 'personal' are we talking about?"

"The kind this man wouldn't want his wife to read personal." He laughed and it was a sticky, smarmy laugh. "Nor would that Carson. You see, he won't know who sent it to him." And then he looked at her like she should appreciate how smart he'd been.

"What did you do, exactly?" Shiloh pressed.

He leaned back a bit and she thought she might have overplayed it, so she mirrored his body language. That smoothed his ego enough to keep going.

"I copied everything. All of it, on a zip drive, and I put a note in that I cut and pasted together with gloves on." And he held up his hands, fingers wide, and wiggled them at her. "And I mailed it. Found his fancy company address online." He shook his head and smiled at the good fortune about to befall him. "I mean, maybe she knows he's done well with that start-up of his, maybe she doesn't. I don't know and I don't care. I mean, the ranch got damaged and maybe he'll think she's the one who needs the money…except…" And he paused for effect. "…I directed him to put the money in an account that only I control."

"What kind of account?"

He was almost flushed with giddiness and he had to move, so he stood and paced the length of the salon. "Crypto currency," he finally said. "Virtually untraceable."

Shiloh sat back. She knew this ground well. She'd bought higher than she'd wished but was still well in the black. Just not as black as the high. She had spread her risk some by investing in a "miners company" and she had been considering ways to invest in the power companies in Iceland, but she needed to get back to the Redoubt, to Bunny and Lonson, and she wasn't about to bring this creature there. Of the many questions rolling around in her head was one of surviving, longevity, and when to lose this guy.

Circling back to the excited Bodie, she found him getting too close physically and she pointed at the table opposite her, motioning for him to sit. He was on a roll. Just talking about his grand scheme had pumped him up and she needed to deflate him some.

"So, you're into blackmail." She said it not as a question but as a statement of fact, in a tone laced with an edge of judgment, and it effectively checked him. "And you've used me to perpetrate this." Another statement.

"Well, you don't have to put it that way…exactly," he began. "You haven't done anything and staying here with you really helps me. I'm a moving target, so to speak. I'm good with that." And he opened his palms in that supplicating gesture of his that said he hoped she was larcenous enough to see the wisdom in it.

And there the rubber did indeed meet the road.

"What's in it for me?" Shiloh asked, staring at him unsympathetically. It was just business.

Bodie was silent for a moment and Shiloh waited for the answer she knew he didn't have. Then it came out and his deflation was complete.

"I don't know…"

She got up, opened the refrigerator, and pulled a bag of salad out. "Well, that's the first true thing you've said."

"You don't believe me?" he whined.

"Fuck no." Shiloh pulled one of those big cans of soup—a real one—from the cupboard and a small bowl to microwave it in. It would be enough for a cup for each of them and a small salad.

Bodie looked miserably at the sparse meal she was going to serve and instantly missed the chow line at the Running Horse. There were always platefuls of hot food and all of it was delicious.

Then, in a half-facetious tone, Shiloh said, "I'd like to, truly I would." She pulled a plastic bowl out for the salad ingredients. "But so far, you have a whole lot of nothing and I don't see you ponying up any money for gas or food, and this is just some fool's idea of a sure thing that might not be. Woo-woo…" Shiloh waved a hand in the air to accentuate her point.

His head jerked up and he glared at her back, then his look softened because it was such a nice back. Defeated, he stared at his folded hands on the smooth surface of the table and the precarious nature of his position trickled down. It was as if Shiloh had sprinkled truth on the surface and the facts held fast, neutrally buoyant, then they gently submerged their way down to the bottom of the pond that was Bodie Ransom.

Chapter 59

Carson again stood before the contents packed in the back of her truck. She still felt a bit ill about the missing e-mails but that was waning. She wasn't there to dwell on the past this time. She had a different agenda.

She ducked under the camper shell and gently slid the wrapped painting out of the truck bed. It was large and awkward to handle but she rested it on the top of the tailgate, then wrestled it to balance the frame on her right hip. She tilted her head and caught sight of the house and Stiles moving around inside.

During the night, she'd had an idea. It was as if all the dark feelings were pushed aside and a beam of sunlight had burst through the clouds. And now, the edges of her mouth turned up into a smile at the thought of her revelation.

Carson surveyed the area to make sure Kitzie wasn't around, then walked the painting down to the house. She waddle-marched herself up onto the porch and set it down. She called for Stiles and he cautiously looked around the corner of the front doorframe. Carson waved him over.

"What?" he asked.

"Are you working alone?"

He nodded.

Carson turned the bundle sideways and gripped it from the top. She shuffled her feet over the threshold and carried it into the room where Stiles had been doing finish work. Carson leaned it against the wall and undid the little strip of masking tape on the brown butcher paper. She peeked inside to check that the painting wasn't upside down, then carefully pulled the paper away.

Stiles gazed at it and didn't say a word. Carson grew impatient after a few minutes and struggled to keep her mouth shut, until she finally blurted, "Well?"

Stiles didn't take his eyes off of it and inhaled a deep breath. Then he said something opposite of what Carson expected.

"I wish I'd had the opportunity to love my daughter as much as your father loved you." He set the tool in his hand on the wood counter, turned away, and walked out to the porch.

Carson stood there, dumbfounded. She had expected a different conversation, something along the lines of where they could put the painting to surprise her mother.

She eventually followed him outside and didn't see him at first. He'd gone around the edge of the wraparound porch and was leaning on one of the supports. The railing pieces were not on yet so he stood where the railing soon would be. His back was to her and Carson stopped at the corner of the building, not sure what to do next.

He sniffled audibly and Carson watched him pull his kerchief out of his back pocket and wipe his face. Then he blew his nose, folded the kerchief up in a way she assumed contained his sorrow, and slid it into his back pocket.

"Guess that needs washing," Carson said.

Stiles tilted his head in her direction, removed his hat, and ran a gloved hand through his white hair. He needed a trim, he thought. It was getting to be too long. Then he put the hat back on and shook his head in a slow measure of resignation. Carson was sure it wasn't about the handkerchief.

She boldly made her move. She walked by him and sat down on the edge of the porch, feet dangling, and stared out at the view. There were, amazingly, tufts of green sprouting everywhere. It had been weeks since the fire had blown through. She squinted to be sure she wasn't deluding herself.

"No, that's real. It comes quickly, like a healing, and then it makes the high desert new again in time," Stiles said.

He surprised her by using the support to gracefully lower himself down off the porch to the ground a couple of feet from her, and they stared out into the expanse together.

Carson swung a boot back and forth, her palms planted on either side of her legs as she leaned forward, watching that boot. She realized it was something she had done as a little girl. Finally, she said, "What happened to your daughter?"

Stiles audibly sucked wind into his lungs and let out the longest exhale Carson had ever heard.

"What *didn't* happen is more like it," he said.

And then he began talking. It was thirty minutes before he was spent and Carson didn't say a word the whole time. She didn't ask any questions, not a one. She just listened. She realized later it might have been the first time she had truly just sat and listened to anyone.

There was a long silence after he stopped talking and Carson wondered if it was too long. She'd always jumped in to fill those.

"Mom has never seen that painting," she said.

Stiles turned and looked at her, his rugged, weathered features framed by his white-gray mustache and eyebrows. "Really?" he replied.

Carson turned and looked at him, her neckerchief

complementing the color of her eyes. They matched her mother's. "Really."

Stiles started to smile at her. "Then I have an idea."

Carson smiled back. "I was hoping you'd say that."

They both got up returned inside. They found a safe place to hide the painting from Kitzie, then went their separate ways as Kitzie emerged from the trailer and walked toward the house.

Chapter 60

The haze from the fires hung in the air and the sun was a coward as it struggled to pierce the overcast, orange-tinged sky. Wyker looked at the N95 masks on the dashboard of the truck. He hadn't really thought about them much but as the visibility decreased, he wondered whether they would have to wear them inside if it got worse. He thought about Tammy and the other animals. How could they be protected and what were the health effects on them?

CJ slept for a while with his head against the window, then he awoke to make a fresh argument to go find that Tish woman, or look for Rio themselves.

Wyker handed him a bottled water and said, "Drink." He reminded him that they were headed to the Three Bit.

CJ shot him a frown and reluctantly took some water.

Wyker continued, "If he managed to survive, he'll know how until things settle down and then I promise, we'll load up a couple horses, go get your posse on the Rez, and we'll find him."

CJ sighed. The effort of making his case had drained him, as Wyker figured it would, and he again dozed off with his head against the headrest. The tightness of his injuries made finding a comfortable position almost impossible. He was easily frustrated and his handsome features held a stone-like quality as he suffered in silence.

After a potty break and some kibble for Tammy, Wyker fastened his safety belt and he and Tammy watched CJ's back as CJ slowly walked around outside the truck. Wyker insisted that he get out and move some, try to stretch a little. Stiffness after so much inactivity made parts lock up.

"I should know," Wyker joked.

CJ said, "Try this shit if you want to feel old, mate," in his Australian drawl.

He moved better after a few moments, but didn't do full range-of-motion exercises completely. Stretching his neck was agony and his arms and shoulders weren't much better.

Wyker teased that there might be some liniment in the tack room at the Three Bit that would help. He joked about the healing benefits of frozen bull semen. But even laughter caused CJ discomfort.

A few minutes later, CJ rejoined Wyker and Tammy, and they left with Tammy curled up between them. CJ stared out the window mostly, and Wyker let it all be. He drove to the sound of the engine and the road beneath his tires. It soothed his mind and without the weight of the trailer behind him, the mileage was much improved. After a while, Wyker reached for the radio and turned it on to hear the latest about the fires.

"Stop! Stop!" CJ yelled suddenly, startling Wyker.

Wyker hit the brakes, quick-checked the rearview mirror for traffic (there was none), and skidded to an awkward stop near the right guard rail off the side of the highway. CJ craned his upper body and neck stiffly to look back over his right shoulder and ordered Wyker to back up. Wyker slid it into reverse and began rolling backward using his mirrors. When CJ pointed to something off in the distance, Wyker stopped and looked too.

"What's that?" CJ asked.

Wyker wasn't sure, so he turned the emergency flashers on, made Tammy stay in the truck, and they got out and stood staring into the high desert. Wyker grabbed his binoculars and looked, lowered them, and sighed. CJ had already climbed over the guardrail and was sliding down a short slope to the high desert scruff and brush. The line of sight was better from the road but they had the general direction and it wasn't far.

CJ tried to jog, then slowed, partly because running was too hard on his lungs and the bloody bits on his body had opened and oozed, causing bandages to shift. But he didn't care. He was completely focused on a body that lay in the chaparral.

Wyker caught up to him, then slowed and let CJ approach a second animal standing over the body. It was a foal, maybe a week or so old. Its partially dried umbilical stump dangled under its belly. The foal stared at CJ and CJ stared back. It was confused and distraught, working its mouth and nickering at the prone body of its mother. It looked sucked-up and dehydrated.

Wyker looked around and saw no sign of other animals. No herd lingered. "What did you do, girl?" he murmured. He approached the body from the crest of the back in case the mare was still alive, and flailed or kicked. The colt danced around some and Wyker cautioned CJ to remember where he was.

"Watch her feet," he said.

CJ acknowledged with a nod, his focus totally on the foal. The frightened baby stared at him and took tentative steps toward its mother's body.

Besides various scrapes and surface cuts on the mare,

Wyker could see a couple of wounds, likely from bullets, and the trails of blood that stained the mare's hide. Somehow, she had managed to get away, to get this far. Had she given birth, hurt like this, he wondered? Had she guided her foal this far and succumbed?

Wyker touched the mare's neck and it was still warm. He frowned. She hadn't been down long. He watched her side for breathing and there was none. He knelt by her mane, hoped her head didn't flip up and hit him, and touched his fingers farther down the base of her neck where he knew a large vein should be pumping its life-giving blood. There was no pulse. He slid both hands under her neck and it moved freely.

"I think she just died," he said.

He looked up and was surprised to see that CJ had his arms around the foal. The foal's lips worked open and closed and there was dried milk on them. He'd nursed recently. Wyker stood up to get a better view of the mare's underside and saw milk on the teat he could see.

CJ weaved and struggled to stand, his breathing loud and wheezy. In spite of his condition, the foal let him wrap his arms around his tiny body and hold him. Bent over, it took CJ a moment to gain leverage and gather him in his arms. Wyker watched CJ lift the foal and start back in the direction of the truck.

"Help me," CJ croaked through clenched teeth.

It took a little while to manage it and the back of Wyker's shirt was damp by the time they managed to get CJ and the foal settled into the back seat of Wyker's truck.

Wyker stood outside, not knowing what to say. He heard CJ speaking softly to the foal, reassuring him as best he could. Then he had an idea. He went to his toolbox in the back of his truck and rooted around until he found a large baggy containing various syringes and sterile needles. He didn't need the needles, but he grabbed a 60cc syringe and kept its container cap.

He pulled his knife out and looked for a spot on the guard rail post to cut the tip of the syringe off as cleanly as possible. He wanted a slight lip to remain for better suction. The idea was so weird and farfetched, and probably wouldn't work. He didn't tell CJ where he was going, just signaled that he'd be back and he retraced their steps to the inert body.

Wyker studied the mare's body. She looked to be in good condition, probably part of a wild band, so her stallion had cared for her. He had no other clue to read other than to surmise she'd been shot, fled, had her baby, and had cared for him as best she could while she was dying.

He risked postmortem muscle contractions and set about to try his idea. Fortunately, the mare had no leg contractions and he was spared injury as he knelt by her hip. A few minutes later, surprised he had gotten anything, Wyker looked at his handiwork in the syringe, acknowledged that it was paltry at best, and used the syringe's container cap as a makeshift seal. He spoke to the mare as though he knew her, then removed his hat and said some words to her under his breath. He saw a shadow and looked up to see buzzards wheeling in the smoky sky.

Wyker knew that in men of a certain kind, there were no reservoirs of affection for people but there were untapped ones for animals. CJ would not be talked out of what he was doing and Wyker knew better than to try. He knew the foal probably wouldn't make it and that this heartbreak piled on top of another wouldn't be good for CJ. But if CJ had heartbreak in his arms, so be it.

Wyker returned to the truck and opened the door. Tammy had stayed up front, though she turned around and watched. There wasn't anything to say and a few miles down the road, Wyker looked in the rearview mirror to see CJ and the foal fast asleep, CJ's arms around the orphan and the foal's head nestled against CJ's chest.

Chapter 61

Back at the Three Bit, it was close to feeding time and the afternoon shadow of the barn cloaked the ground as Carson passed through the sliding doors. No one had come forward to claim the missing mare. The new colt slept like a rock star and the mare took advantage of his downtime with some of her own. She was an excellent mother. If she was a maiden mare, she was naturally born to nurture another.

After a peek at the mare and foal and finding them content, Carson noticed a beam of sunlight that stretched across the floor and felt it point its long finger at her. She was drawn by an invisible hand as she walked toward the spot where the light touched the dirt floor. As she approached it, she saw the dust particles, mixed with ash filaments, dancing like magic wishes in the light. Carson stood just outside of it and closed her eyes. She reached her hand forward and felt the moment her fingers pierced the beam. The sun's warmth was strong and Carson felt the brightness through her closed eyelids.

She opened her eyes and looked at her hand in the beam, held out the other to join it, palm up, and remembered the easy times when she was little. Those memories didn't come without digging like a miner. Sometimes they seemed so far away. She remembered the deeply painful, the embarrassing, and the hurtful moments readily. They were crisp and fresh and she resented them. Later, in her frustration with her father and her life, she had begged the wishing dust for fame and fortune and to be gone from there. She had tried to catch wishes in a tiny glass jar, pour them out quickly, and trap them under her pillow so she would dream of a glamorous future like in the magazines.

Carson extended her fingers, felt the warmth, and closed her eyes again. She imagined she had a wish fairy in her palm and she gently cradled it. She closed her other hand over it and made a wish. Carson spoke to the fairy and asked her for a miracle. She wasn't specific, she wasn't petitioning for a certain thing, just a gift. "A gift of hope…" she whispered. "A gift of strength and renewal…" Then she opened her hands and let the wish and the fairy go free.

Carson opened her eyes and knew she wouldn't see her wish fly high up into the rafters but the thought was comforting. She had forgotten this magic until that moment. She stepped forward into the slender beam of sunlight and lifted her head, eyes closed, and extended her arms, turning slowly like the ballerina in her old childhood jewelry box. She felt calm and the old urges to run and hide and be angry melted away.

Carson stopped spinning and sank to the dirt, where she sat cross-legged in the beam of fairy dust. She wanted to feel whole, not part, and she was afraid she would never figure it out. This place and time, when she was with the horses, were when her self-loathing took a break. A hungry nicker broke the spell and she murmured that she was coming as she stood and dusted off her jeans.

Carson fed everyone, checked their water, picked some manure with the apple picker, and swept up the bits of hay that fell as she carried it. After making a bucket of warm mash for the new mare, she leaned against the stall door and listened to her eat. It was a simple sound, reassuring, like listening to the ocean waves or a creek. The baby lay undisturbed and wrapped in a cloak of warmth and security, his little sides inflating and deflating with each dreamless breath. It was all so familiar, having a new life in the barn. Carson recalled the planning and preparation it took to breed a champion—to raise and train it, learn each one's strengths, and build confidence in their weaker points.

The foal stretched as if he knew he was on her mind. A sleepy head lifted, then resettled in the bedding, and continued his bliss.

The sounds of the barn made Carson's vision swim as if a lens had been dialed to "blur." In a faraway place, she heard footsteps—those big boots and the gentle stride of her father. She struggled to remember him as clearly as the pictures on the tack room wall as her imagination conjured the clear sounds of his footfalls coming toward her.

She shut her eyes, willing the footfalls to stop behind her and to feel his big arms envelop her tiny frame. Carson imagined leaning her head back against her father's chest and him holding her without saying a word.

The footfalls faded. It was her mother's hand on her shoulder that brought Carson back to reality. Kitzie didn't say anything, just snuggled her shoulder next to her daughter's and together they watched the mare eat some from the bucket, wander outside for a moment, then return.

Stiles hadn't taken any liberties. He felt it was respectful to stay in his own lane even when invited to explore the ranch, but he couldn't resist visiting the rail every morning, to watch the foal from a distance, as he went back and forth between his camper and the house. They had put up the soft, orange plastic fencing to prevent injury and the baby moved around freely in the 15x30 foot enclosure.

The real entertainment was the colt's first turnout in the soft loam of the big arena. Carson and Jorge moved the arena horses to the outside round pen for an hour and Jorge helped Carson walk the mare and foal down to the arena gate to release them. He had fashioned a baby halter out of a soft lead rope and Carson led the colt. He was a handful, but both Carson and Jorge had been doing some light training with him in the stall and paddock, so it wasn't a completely alien concept for the little guy.

The mare enjoyed the bigger space and ignored the foal's antics as she indulged herself by rolling in different earth, free from the confines of her paddock. She wandered the perimeter, gazed out at the hills and alien surroundings, and breathed in the new smells while the colt expanded the bubble of his world. His long, gangly legs propelled him into a realm full of interesting sounds and smells, and the occasional bug or butterfly to greet. His returns to his mother improved after banging into her more than once. He crashed, tumbled, and recovered, shook off each maneuver, and bolted with limitless energy to the next new thing. During one of his energetic outbursts, Kitzie and Jorge had to run a block at the end of the arena, where Kitzie's trailer was located, and the foal surprised them with his moves as he dodged them. That had sparked a comment from Carson to her mother, "Looks like a true Collins!"

Later, Stiles found himself drawn to the barn. Hesitantly, he stepped through the sliding doors, and as his eyes adjusted to the dim light, he was taken aback. The well-crafted, beamed structure possessed a soaring cathedral space over a central, open area. Perhaps it was the angles, or a moment of something inexplicable, but he unconsciously removed his hat and held it over his heart. His pulse rang in his ears until he realized he had been holding his breath. He inhaled deeply and the warm air smelled of horses, hay, and leather. The deep creases in his forehead cleared above serious eyes and Stiles felt as if he had entered a church. The space was like nothing he had ever seen. It had depth and scope, and he was drawn to the center of it. He looked up and turned full circle to take it in. If ever there was a place where he could ask for forgiveness or redemption, this was it.

It was perfectly balanced, the way the stalls were lined up on the edges, and there was a passage off to one side, a door to what he guessed was a stairway to the room Carson stayed in. From the peak of the roof, a windowed cupola beamed streaks of sunlight that pierced the center and cast a pattern on the rough floor. It had a spiritual quality and he reveled in the peace of it. Stiles looked back to the outside and wondered why, in the time he had been at the Three Bit, he hadn't gone in there. It was like the heart of the ranch, sacred ground, and he almost retreated from the building. But curiosity got the better of him when humming drifted through an open door and he peeked around a corner to see Kitzie working at the desk on her laptop. He cleared his throat and she turned to look at him.

"Hey," she said.

He nodded a greeting and she invited him in. Stiles saw that she wasn't wearing her knee brace as he entered the long, narrow room. Kitzie noticed his glance, and without looking up from the screen, said her knee was feeling better.

Stiles looked around the room full of pictures and framed articles from various equestrian publications about the Collins Cutting Horse operation. He slowly made his way down the wall. He read some and looked more closely at the pictures.

Kitzie was aware of him as he became engrossed, and she realized he hadn't been there before. Maybe he didn't know the history. She saved what she had been doing and looked up from the computer. "It seems like yesterday..." she began.

Stiles listened, thought about a couple things he'd had rolling around in his head, and stifled the urge to speak. He moved down the room and half turned to take in the row of ribbons that ran along the ceiling. He looked at the racks of saddles, some of which were trophy saddles that hadn't seen a day's ride in a decade or more. Several must have been special, as they had custom covers with a fine layer of dust on them. He guessed which was her husband's favorite—it had the heaviest layer of dust. It was tucked into the far corner and on the wall near it was a photo of a stallion. He bent lower to get a good look.

"I buried the stud up on the hill. I've been trying to grow some wildflowers over the spot without success," Kitzie said, and a faraway look passed through her eyes—not one of regret or sadness but of treasured fact; a personal moment shared. "I've tried and tried to put something there... I guess I don't have a green thumb. Carson was always the better gardener," Kitzie mused over pressed fingertips. She looked back at her computer screen.

Stiles noted that she seemed perfectly relaxed, perhaps a rare encounter. At the moment, they weren't at odds with each other over a design element or idea. He started toward the door, careful not to wear out his welcome. He heard her clear her throat and thought he felt her eyes on his back. Stiles stalled, then turned his head when he was halfway out the door.

It was an impulse, one he immediately wished he had ignored when he said, "Ever thought of marrying again?"

Kitzie laughed and made light of her answer as she tapped her fingers on her keyboard. "Never considered it. Who'd want this much work for so little reward?"

A moment later, she looked up...but he was gone.

His silent steps slowed as he crossed the center of the barn. The light from the cupola reflected long angles and as Stiles lifted his chin and felt the warmth of the light on his face, his eyes closed and he mouthed silently, *I would*. Then he looked back toward the office, blushed hot, and straightened his hat.

Brushing the foolishness aside, Stiles walked with purpose to his camper, unlocked the door of the crew cab, and lifted the edge of a saddle blanket. He stared at his saddle and bridle. He ran a hand over the cantle leather and felt the back of the seat. The smell of that barn had kindled memories. Better times well before his bad deeds—simpler times he now wished he had never left.

He picked up the bridle and the split reins slid off the seat and draped onto the ground. He held the bridle up, then collected the reins and looped them over the top. Out of habit, Stiles slid the bridle over his arm, where it had rested a million times before when he had carried it from tack room to ride and back. He turned and leaned his back on the side of the truck and watched the sun disappear behind the shoulder of the land. Stiles closed his eyes tight and felt drowned by the shadows. Then he opened them, returned the bridle to the back seat, covered it, and closed the door.

The days had been full enough, but the nights were bad. Stiles was always restless; he couldn't see the future without being haunted by the past. Time crawled by as he lay in bed, staring into the darkness. Outside, the wind had dropped and the sounds of cattle drifted to his ears from far away as his mind wandered. An owl screeched to call to another and Stiles drifted off into a restless sleep…

Sunlight reflected off the water in the trough and sent light rippling across the wall of the barn. The slender fingers of a woman's hand ran along the surface of the weathered wood, adoring its many imperfections. Fascinated, Stiles watched her fingers interrupt the reflection, as if the barn's wall was water. Barbed wire, strung between posts, met the barn and her fingers caressed the rusted wire. Naughty strands of white hair refused to stay in place and blew across her face. His reserve melted away, replaced by a feeling he hadn't known before. He touched the hair and gently smoothed it back into place. His fingers continued and traced the curve of her cheek, the strong line of her jaw, and lingered under the tip of her chin. She looked up at him with eyes that shone like the morning sun through a bedroom window—the most beautiful eyes he had ever seen. His fingertip discovered every detail of those perfect lips and there was no resisting the urge to kiss her, but the face spun away from him as if a wind vortex had sucked the whole of her being into nothingness. The edges of her swirled and vanished and those eyes were the last thing to go.

Stiles sat up halfway, suddenly awake, and his heart pounded. He rolled over, hungry, hollow, and lost for words.

Chapter 62

The recovery on the ranch began to slowly make a kind of sense. Although everything was different, chores were still chores and had to be done around rebuilding. Despite that, the colt was impossible to ignore and he was the darling of the ranch. Carson spent as much time as she could with him, as did Jorge and Kitzie. It was much better than working. Carson set up a couple of stools near the paddock, and Kitzie took to having her morning coffee there. The foal boosted morale considerably as the horrors of the fire were set aside, and there was an increased level of procrastination with everyone. Both Kitzie and Carson noticed that Stiles took uncharacteristic breaks to watch the foal, his laser focus on construction briefly interrupted at least a couple times a day.

The colt would lose his foal fur between three and four months of age and soon the nights would get colder and the days shorter. Though he was only days old, they discussed looking for old baby blankets because he had been born so late in the season. There used to be some in the barn and Kitzie wondered aloud if they still had them. Her eyes misted as memories crowded close. Carson found that her ability to listen and not interrupt had improved, or so she hoped. In reflective moments, she felt she needed to be a patient friend instead of a needy daughter. Their relationship changed and grew almost daily and in unanticipated ways.

As they stood together at the stall door, the feelings shifted and it was back to business. Carson mentioned it had been a long time since they had needed a foal blanket, that caring for a late foal was more work, and they needed to be ready for the harsh weather. She pointed to the old heat lamps hanging in the stalls and wondered aloud if they still worked.

"I'd be hesitant to trust them," Kitzie observed.

"Can we afford to replace them?" Carson asked.

Kitzie didn't answer but had a dubious expression on her face.

Carson looked down at her boot tip and felt impotent. There was a time when money wasn't a concern for her. Now that she had none, she felt ineffectual and frustrated. They had other decisions to make before the weather got bad, and though they had a plan, culling the herd was one that was still too hard to make. Buying feed for a whole winter was not going to be possible, even if they could find it, and transportation, storage, and winter feeding were expensive. The colt was indeed a much-needed distraction from a fast-approaching reality.

Both redirected the conversation back to the colt and Kitzie observed that, with so many ranches and farms damaged or gone, it was likely that no one would inquire about the mare. They had no history on her so there was only speculation about any vaccinations or care she'd had before they found her. They discussed a titer test with the vet, to check for the presence of antibodies, bacteria, or disease, and he said when things slowed down some, he could do it. In the meantime, they would watch the foal closely for any signs of illness or failure to thrive. While he seemed fine now, they both knew that anything could happen without warning.

Three Corner Fire

A week later, Carson retired early. The days felt like they blended together, some intolerably long and filled with too many decisions. She felt physically exhausted, then found sleep elusive. She discovered a book in the office. Propped up with an extra pillow, she had forgotten how much she had enjoyed reading in bed. She looked around the tiny room and came to the conclusion that it had a similar feel to her old bedroom. The pang of knowing that space was gone forever had begun to dull at the edges.

Carson awoke with the light on and the book on the wrong page. She felt refreshed and positive. The barn was quiet below and she would feed, get coffee, then clean. She had a plan and decided it was going to be a good day. It was time, with the new life here, for things to really start anew.

She dressed and bounced down the stairs to the nickering of hungry horses. Carson slid open the big barn doors, flooding the interior with light. She went to the mare's stall door and peeked through the bars. She saw the mare nuzzling the foal, who slept in the hay, and started to walk away—but checked herself and remained to stare at the tiny body. She didn't see his side rise and fall and the mare wasn't acting right.

Carson opened the stall and entered. She crouched beside the foal. The minute she touched him, she knew, and her heart fell. He wasn't quite cool to the touch and the what-ifs started to roil in her head, then grew to relentless quickly.

The mare nosed her baby and tried to rouse him from a slumber he would not wake from. Carson touched her on her nose and stroked the side of her face but no amount of reassurance would do. She heard footfalls coming and turned to face Jorge. His expression was one of expectant joy but when he saw Carson's face, he stopped.

"What is it?"

Carson couldn't speak. She just shook her head as he came into the stall. He went to the baby's body and touched it, stroked it, and whispered prayers in Spanish to it. He begged him to come back. And then his voice choked when he said, "Come back, Papi," in Spanish.

Carson's eyes swam at the sound of his anguish and she left the stall and slowly slid the door closed. She went outside the big doors and leaned against the barn with her back to the aged wood. She felt the heartbeat of the building that had survived when others did not—the building that had contained new life and a new start, and now contained another ending. Carson willed herself not to cry. She knew Jorge had broken down in there and she left him to grieve.

Carson sensed movement to her left and saw her mother round the corner with two mugs of coffee in her hands, Wyatt trotting at her feet. Kitzie was watching the mugs, being careful not to spill as she walked. She stopped short when she saw Carson sitting owl-eyed outside the barn. One of the mugs sloshed and Kitzie winced as the hot liquid found skin. She set the cups down on the ground and shooed Wyatt away. He trotted into the barn, found his snuggy by the tack room, and curled up in it. His expressive eyes knew they were upset.

Carson felt like a little girl and wanted to cry in her mother's arms. She put her hand on her mother's arm and held herself back from releasing the floodgates.

Kitzie saw she was about to break. "What happened?"

"I don't know...he was fine last night." Carson closed her

eyes and struggled for control.

Kitzie touched Carson's shoulder and looked inside the barn. Carson meant to stop her but her mother went in. Carson almost followed, but she stayed rooted to the front of the barn, the palms of her hands flat against the wood siding. The day had taken on a leaden stillness as if the world had stopped and was mourning with them.

Carson heard the stall door slide open and voices, then a long period of silence. She stepped inside and tiptoed to the edge of the stall door. Jorge was being held by Kitzie and she just stood there quietly, letting him cry. Jorge let go of her, left the stall, and disappeared out the other side of the barn.

Carson went to her mother and the two of them stood silently outside the stall door.

"We didn't even name him," Carson whispered.

"I think Jorge did, just now," Kitzie said.

Carson looked at her.

"Papi," Kitzie said softly.

"Ah. That will do." Carson looked in the direction of where Jorge had disappeared. "Where did he go?"

"He's getting a shovel and picking a spot," Kitzie said. "I figure we'll let him..."

Carson nodded. It was almost too much. "I hadn't realized how much having a young one here again meant to me."

"Me either," Kitzie said.

Carson headed to the office.

"Where are you going?" Kitzie called after her.

"I'm gonna call the vet. Put it out there that we have a nurse mare. Maybe someone has an orphan that needs one. Though the chances of that are small...it's pretty late and...what am I saying? After the fires..." She stopped walking, took another step, then stopped again. "Oh, what the hell, I'll call him anyway."

They left the baby in the stall with the mare until Jorge had dug the hole. The mare continued to hover over the foal, occasionally nudging it and nickering to him. They let Jorge carry little Papi out of the stall while Carson and Kitzie saw to the grieving mother. It was hard to say what she would do but removing the body went well. For hours after he was gone, the mare ran up and down the paddock, calling for the baby, which broke everyone's heart to hear.

Kitzie retreated to the motorhome to make sandwiches that would go uneaten. Carson walked down to the other end of the ranch and found Jorge making a mound over the grave. She had picked some tiny, late-season wildflowers growing in a bright spot near the arena fence. Jorge stepped away and turned his back to her. He stared out at the denuded hills where the fire had approached the Three Bit while Carson removed her hat, put the flowers on the mound, and rested her hand there on the coolness of the freshly turned ground. When she stood, she was surprised to see Jorge walking out into the pasture, his dogs beside him. He wouldn't return for several hours.

Carson put her hat back on and walked slowly toward the barn and the frantic mare, whose cries still resonated across the Three Bit. She watched the dirt-mixed ash puff into the air with each footfall of her boots. When she was near the arena, her mother called her over. Carson climbed the fence and walked toward the motorhome. Kitzie had set a table outside and half a sandwich awaited Carson.

"Mom, I'm not really hungry."

"Try some. And have this," Kitzie said and handed Carson a fresh coffee.

Carson smiled. It was nice that her mom was trying in a way that wasn't pushy or intrusive. They didn't talk and she ate the sandwich and drank half the coffee. Then she got up and said she needed to check on the mare.

"Carson," Kitzie said, "I think we should talk about breeding horses again…"

Carson turned and looked at her. It felt right to at least consider it. Those were good times and having the colt, even for a little while, had brought that feeling back. She nodded and left.

Carson walked into the big barn and grabbed the apple picker and cart. She wheeled the cart to the stall door where the mare was running back and forth—into the stall, out of it and down the long paddock, over and over, her nostrils flared and her neck slick with sweat. Carson watched her and realized she needed to remove the mesh. It should roll up easily, she thought. And she considered sedating the mare.

Kitzie walked up to the house. Stiles told her he was sorry to hear about the colt and he looked as sad as they felt. He asked Kitzie if she wanted to be alone and said he could work outside. She shook her head and leaned against the wall by one of the windows—the one that would have the window seat. It pressed out onto the deck area and Stiles had shaped the deck to mirror it. At first, it was just going to be a window, but it spoke to him that someone should be curled up in it, with lots of pillows and a throw. If Kitzie sat with her head at one end, she would see the driveway and the paddock, and could maybe watch young horses run and grow up. If she sat with her head at the other end, she would see the mountains and rangeland. In the winter, she could watch it snow and gale, and in the summer, see acres of wildflowers and grasses feather in the wind.

Stiles busied himself in the kitchen area and the room was filled with one of those long silences that brimmed with the surrounding sounds and smells. There seemed to be a pall, a shadow over everyone, and Kitzie stared at nothing out the window. Her focus was far away when Stiles asked, "How's Jorge doing?"

She blinked out of her reverie. "He went off somewhere, haven't seen him in a while."

Stiles saw a rag on the kitchen island. He reached for it, wiped his hands, and tossed it into an open bag.

"Those need washing?" Kitzie asked.

He nodded.

"Carson can do them. Or I will. There's a washing machine in the barn…"

He nodded again and stood at the other side of the window seat. He stared out and said, "This is my favorite side. I like this view." He looked at the floor, then over her way. "I've noticed that when you come in here and walk around, this is where you end up."

"Really?" Kitzie said.

"Every time. I think it's your favorite view too."

"I see that you've framed the bench part but stopped…"

"I was going to ask if you would prefer drawer storage underneath or access from the top and open storage. I could make a hinged lid…" He stretched his hands out to mimic the parameters. "You would lift the lid here and put whatever you want under there." He pointed. "Of course, you would have to pull the cushions and pillows to get to it but if you stored something like…" He suddenly felt awkward and didn't want to say the wrong thing. The day had been difficult enough.

"Like Christmas decorations?" she smiled.

"Well, yeah, like that."

"Can I think about it?"

He nodded, then tilted his head to look around her and she turned too. Way off in the distance, he saw a cloud of dust. Someone was coming in on the Three Bit road—fast.

Chapter 63

Carson turned on the old radio that sat on the shelf by the door between the office and the stairs up to her room. She didn't care what it played and the signal wasn't the best but it worked. It was so covered with dust she probably couldn't have found a different station if she wanted to.

She locked the mare out of the stall, and the grieving mother did her calling outside while Carson worked inside. With the stall door open to the barn alleyway, she parked the cart where she could fill it and set to clearing the foaling stall of everything that smelled like the baby. Carson started with the most soiled straw and wheeled the cart out the back barn door, on the arena side, and made a pile. She would spread it later. On her way back, she felt the grief again and let it come. She dropped the rake, took her hat off, and cried. She pressed her forehead against the cool metal wall of the stall as her breaths came out in jagged gasps. She visualized the emotion that Jorge had shown and realized it was the first time she had ever seen him do that. She hadn't known him long, so that wasn't saying much—it was just *why* he had cried. The overwhelming loss of so much…it crashed in her head and spilled out.

The radio suddenly stopped. Carson wiped her face and looked up at the flat metal of the wall. Its dust and blankness were a comfort and to turn away from it meant thinking. It wasn't the songs she needed, just the background noise. She felt a flash of anger toward the old radio and stomped past the cart. Her thigh slammed into the handle and Carson cursed as she pushed it away. In her impatience, she launched out of the stall and careened into someone.

Carson bounced backward and stumbled as she tried to keep her footing. Her baseball hat fell off as she caught her balance. She saw boots and her eyes traveled up a body that was now bent over and groaning from the impact. It took Carson a moment to recognize the man who had turned away and was now swearing. Her mouth hung open in shock as she stared at him. He looked so different from the last time she had seen him.

When CJ could manage the pain, he straightened and looked at her. Neither spoke. In the awkward silence, a breeze tossed Carson's auburn hair across her tear-streaked face, and a strand caught at the edge of her mouth. Her face was a mess, her hair dancing wildly, and it stirred a memory in CJ. Unaware of his actions, he reached up and gently freed it, so lightly that Carson could barely understand it.

A commotion from behind CJ broke the spell. Tammy ran into the barn, went straight for the water bowl, and lapped at it, and a shadow appeared at the door. Eyes wide, Carson stood rooted there for a moment, confused. She knelt to scoop up her hat and moved around CJ to see who it was.

"Jesus, CJ, what are you doing?" came Wyker's voice from the shadows. His voice was barely recognizable and it looked like he was carrying a dog.

Carson flashed a look at Tammy. Her eyes adjusted to the light and refocused on Wyker as he came farther inside. The something struggled in his arms and she could hardly believe what she saw.

"If I take one in the jewels, I'll be singing in a higher key," Wyker added hoarsely.

Wyatt scrambled around the big sliders and went to Tammy for an excited reunion.

Kitzie, not far behind, came in and said, "Hey! I heard your truck come in and—"

And that was as far as she got. Kitzie stopped and craned her head back to look at Wyker's truck. There was no trailer behind it. She gave him an inquisitive look and held her hands up in front of her.

"Don't ask. It's a longer story than I can tell right now. I have some milk for this little guy but I need help feeding him."

CJ gaped at him. "How did you get milk?"

The foal wiggled and Wyker came close to losing his grip on him. The baby started whinnying.

"Jesus, come on! I can't hold him much longer," Wyker said through clenched teeth. "Milk...yeah, it wasn't easy..."

Carson guided Wyker toward the stall door and she asked someone to close the main barn doors in case the foal got loose. "You can set him down, I've got him," Carson instructed and leaned over to hold him with one arm around his chest and one around his butt.

The mare appeared at the stall grille, calling constantly, desperate to reach the baby.

Wyker straightened his back with a groan, then looked at the frantic mare. "Hope you have Advil," he joked.

All of CJ's attention was on the little guy. Wyker turned to Kitzie and hugged her. He apologized for coming in so fast, and said he would be more respectful next time. She made a face at him and smiled.

"You're forgiven." She nodded toward the little one. "This time." Then she added, "Advil is my best friend. I think we need a big bottle…"

Wyker shook his head. "Great," he said, rubbing his back. He nodded at CJ. "I told him he wouldn't make it but he refused to believe me."

"Where did you find him?" Kitzie asked.

Wyker took her arm and guided her over toward the barn doors. He told her about the dead mare.

Kitzie's face clouded, her eyes angry, and she shook her head in disgust. "This kind of thing doesn't happen. I mean…"

Wyker didn't let her find the words. He knew what she meant.

"You couldn't have known we had a milk mare here," Kitzie continued. "Was this just dumb luck?"

"Dumb, probably. Luck?" Wyker looked over at Carson and CJ. "We'll see." Then he raised his eyebrows. "Wait…you have a milk mare? This changes everything…"

Kitzie nodded toward the mare.

Carson held the baby in her arms, his spindly legs on the ground. He seemed tired and she said to no one in particular, "We kinda need to decide how to do this, he needs to nurse."

CJ was ready to help but he had no experience with this sort of thing. Out of fatigue and some pain, he leaned against the wall and watched. He looked pale and spoke little.

Carson called over to her mother. "Mom, I need you."

Rolling with this new set of circumstances, Kitzie took charge. Wyker secured the mare in the outside paddock. CJ managed to spread what was left of the straw around the stall more evenly. Kitzie went to the pile Carson had removed earlier and retrieved some of the soiled bedding—the dirtier the better. Anything with the baby's smell on it. They needed to make the orphan smell more like the mare's baby, or at least try.

After spreading the dirty hay around the stall, they proceeded to introduce the orphan to the mare. They cracked the stall door open a few inches and placed the foal's face where the mare could see him. The orphaned colt nickered and mouthed, and the mare strained to get as much of her muzzle through the crack as she could. She arched her neck and struck the door with her unshod hoof. Kitzie slid the door closed and the mare cried outside it. The mare ran down the length of the paddock, then returned and stayed by the stall door.

"She's too wound up," Carson observed.

"It's going to be OK," Kitzie said

The baby nickered and the mare continued her frenetic calling. Wyker watched her but was careful to keep clear.

Beyond the stall door, Kitzie heard the murmured greeting between a subdued CJ and an equally subdued Jorge.

"Well, another country heard from," Kitzie said, welcoming Jorge. "Seems we have all the players. Let's get to the program."

Jorge opened the paddock door and slid through. He managed to halter the mare. There was a moment of confusion about who would hold the colt and how best to do that. Carson decided that on the fly, and Jorge was either too spent or too preoccupied to argue. Wyker opened the outside door and the mare all but dragged Jorge through the opening. Tensions were fraught as everyone tried to position themselves safely and yet allow whatever was going to work out happen.

It was awkward and took a little bit of time but the mare accepted the orphan. Getting him to nurse took another chunk of time. The foal would eat a little and give up. They needed him to do better than that, so he had help for the first few hours.

When things settled down, Carson left CJ and Jorge in the stall and fetched a fresh bale of straw, opened it, and added a thicker layer of bedding.

Though his color was not good and he needed rest, CJ stayed in with the foal the longest. Kitzie disappeared for a little while and returned with a baking sheet she used as a dinner tray. On it was a cup of soup, some warmed bread, and a bottled water, along with a paper napkin folded around a spoon. She told Wyker to get CJ and went through to the tack room and set the tray on the desk.

CJ was easier to guide, as worn out as he was. He checked himself, shook his head, and let Kitzie take his arm to seat him. He didn't give her any guff. He obediently did as he was told, ate the meal, and looked the better for it. He thanked her and said it was delicious.

"What did they feed you in that place?" she asked.

He shrugged. "It was OK." He didn't add that he was grateful for gaps in his memory.

She offered him more but he declined.

"Maybe later." He nodded toward Wyker. "He's been bugging me to eat and drink water."

She pointed to the unopened bottle on the tray.

"Crickey, not you too..."

Kitzie folded her arms across her chest, cocked her head, and raised her eyebrows in her best "do it or you do not get up from the table" face. She asked if he needed to take anything for his pain, and he said just basic pain reliever, nothing special. His body was stiff and sore and CJ vaguely wandered through waves of pain. Watching the foal sleep with a full belly and an attentive mother next to him was soothing beyond anything that came in pill form.

From the house, Stiles had watched things unfold. He stiffened when he saw the man carry an animal into the barn. He had missed seeing the first man who had entered. He was distracted from his work and he felt that the world had just shrunk a little. With his guard up, he tidied the work area and retreated. As he made his way back to his camper, he ran into Jorge, who was heading to the barn. Jorge had asked him if that was Wyker's truck that had come in. Stiles answered honestly that he didn't know.

Stiles now glanced around and felt every paranoid nerve in his body tingle. Out of an abundance of caution, he checked his tires and made sure he was clear in case he had to make a swift departure.

Chapter 64

Some cowboy boots are great for riding, some for driving, and some are good to dance in. The ones that Dale wore that day were not good for walking for miles on a dirt road. He stepped on a rock wrong and half turned his ankle. Though it didn't hurt him, the way his luck had turned, that was the last straw. He got mad at the offending rock and kicked it out of his way. And of course, he was sure he had a blister forming on a bunion.

He saw a large boulder and sat down to rest his feet and consider his options. He was dirty, sweaty, angry, and tired. This was so not how he thought his day would go. He had pictured himself arriving close to the reservation, finding some shit motel, and devising a plan to check up on his parolee. Dale had no knowledge of what had happened and that CJ wasn't there.

As Dale got up off the boulder, he spotted a track, narrow and recently used. Curious, he followed it. It bent and twisted, and he rounded a bend and saw a gate. He approached it with care. Plastered everywhere were warnings against trespassing, and lots of references to weapons and the freedom to use them against—what else?—trespassers.

Dale looked around respectfully for surveillance cameras or motion detectors. He held his hands up in case he was on camera. The last thing he wanted to do out there was piss off some gun-wielding hick. He knew they'd shoot first and not ask questions. Dale knew the type. Hell, he *was* the type, and while he more than respected the right to bear arms, at the moment, his need was greater than theirs, and he felt he could talk his way out of any situation. Dale didn't see where he had a choice, so he broke in and started walking.

Bunny's eye cracked open when she heard something. She had fallen asleep in her chair by her vegetable garden with an open book in her lap. She read aloud to her veggies and swore that was why her harvests were so good. Their postern path ran alongside the garden. It was their escape route, just in case. The gate was heavily fortified and hard to see from the dirt road. And along the path was a collection of old farm implements, half-hidden in the overgrowth—sharp-tined tillers and hay cutters, some rusted and falling apart, others salvageable, or so Lonson insisted.

She heard it again. Someone was on the path and making a fair bit of noise through the overgrowth. She heard a man swear. Lonson was on the other side of the property and out of earshot and she regretted not having her shotgun. But Bunny had her bat. Her book slid to the ground as she reached for the trusty handle. Her eyes were narrow and sly when she rose, quiet as a cat, to position herself to surprise the enemy.

Lonson heard Bunny's voice stretched thin and high, screaming for him. He dropped what he was carrying and ran from one end of their stronghold to the other. She ran into him, and, out of breath, couldn't explain the emergency. He held her away from him and saw no injury or blood.

"For Pete's sake, Bunny, what are you yammering about?"

Her hand shook as she pointed in the direction of the garden, and the two scurried together back that way. It all appeared to be normal. Lonson gave Bunny an exasperated look and started back toward the house. But she grabbed at his arm and pointed to the path and said "he" had gone there.

"Who did?"

"The intruder!" she exclaimed.

"What did he look like?"

"Big! He had a hat on and when I swung my bat...." She stammered and bent over, struggling to catch her breath.

"Did you hit him?" Lonson asked.

She shook her head. "Oh...I think I'm gonna pass out..." She wobbled back to her chair and landed in it heavily. At that level, she was able to take in that her husband was armed. "Oh, good, you got your gun. Go get him. I think he went that way." She pointed to the path again. "He may have retreated the way he came."

"How many were there?" Lonson asked as he looked in the direction she pointed. "Where is your bat?"

"How do I know? It fell outta my hand and I ran."

"Well, get up and find it and then we'll go see where that fella went."

The bat was found where she had dropped it. Lonson picked it up and handed it to Bunny, then they followed the path single file. Before long, Lonson stopped and Bunny ran into the back of him.

"Jesus, Bunny," he hissed, a bit nervous, more so after he pointed down to something in the dirt. "Don't step in it," he cautioned.

But it was everywhere and it was hard not to. They rounded

a turn in the path and saw the red-stained leather soles of a large pair of cowboy boots attached to a very dead man.

"Holy shit, Bunny, what did you do?" Lonson asked, frozen in place. "Did you hit him on the head?"

Bunny leaned around Lonson with a horrified expression on her face. "I don't think so," she whined. "Truth is, I think I missed. He was quick for a big guy, ducked just in time."

Lonson handed Bunny the sidearm and told her to use it if the guy tried anything. "Be sure you don't hit me with that thing."

"I'm much better with a gun than my bat."

Lonson approached the body carefully and got to the hatless head. "Musta lost his hat somewhere." And he noted that there was no obvious blood around his head, so Bunny hadn't gotten him there. *Then what the hell happened?* Lonson wondered.

One arm was above the man's shoulder and the other beneath his frame as if he had crawled the last few feet. Lonson touched the man's wrist. It was still warm and he felt for a pulse. There was none. "Christ...he's dead."

"You sure?"

"Near as. Here, help me roll him over."

When they turned the body over, the first thing Lonson noticed was that the guy's eyes were still open. He looked the body up and down and saw that the man was bloody from the belt down, and his pants near his crotch might have been torn. There was a lot of blood. He was doused with it and it had barely begun to congeal.

Lonson rose and looked back down the path and saw disturbed brush. As he walked past Bunny, he took the bat from her, tracked the blood to where it started, and used the bat to hold the brush aside. Beneath it was part of a cutting attachment for an old tractor, with a row of long, sharp spikes. A particularly nasty one on the end was bent at an angle and stained red.

"Holy shit," Lonson muttered as he looked back to the body. "He bled out, all right." He pointed at the spike. "He must've tripped around here…" He looked down and retraced a few steps. "Yeah, looks like this branch is stripped, it kinda spun him and he…" Lonson slow-walked a possibility, then said, "Sure, that's as good as I can see it."

Bunny and Lonson stood next to each other and looked at the body for a few seconds, then Bunny said, "I'll get the backhoe, you get the tractor and a rope?"

Chapter 65

Shiloh maneuvered the motorhome through a series of detours and traffic jams uncomfortably close to Martin. She had taken to wearing a hat and her dark glasses and she considered changing her hair color. Her jeans accentuated the obvious, so her best disguise was baggy sweatshirts.

Bodie managed to get more tiresome by the hour, and though he never suspected it, she found him barely tolerable. Though Bodie was convinced his good looks and magnetic charm would win over this gorgeous woman, Shiloh was the master at stringing men along with little to no effort on her part. Many a man had tumbled in the wake that was Shiloh, convinced they would be the one to "get her," only to find they had spent a lot of time, energy, and money in a fruitless pursuit. She had no intention of keeping Bodie around any longer than she had to. The fact that he had recognized her presented a problem and she was confident she would find a way to jettison him soon.

Remarkably, his flurry of messages had yielded results, and quickly. This surprised her. He wasn't that bright. Whatever he had on his mark, he had played just enough of it to get a down payment. Unfortunately, that made him even more nauseating than before.

He had made his deal with whatever devil he was courting, and his little bitcoin gambit had apparently paid up. Shiloh surmised that all his dirty little secrets lived in his pack, which he still guarded. She didn't really care. She had her own secrets and she was successful at keeping them from Bodie.

The more he talked about the work he did on the Three Bit, the better picture of things she got.

"Yeah, that asshole Stiles ordered me around like I was an idiot or something," he complained. He tapped the backpack in his lap. "Well, this changes everything and that stuck-up bitch Carson, she didn't know what she was missing. I fixed her good...this is pure gold."

He alternated between calling Carson Collins a stuck-up bitch and obsessing over her. Maybe the little shit was bipolar or something. Shiloh felt like she had a hairball caught in her throat. She'd had her own memorable encounter with that Carson bitch, which had resulted in a black eye for Shiloh that makeup barely concealed. That Bodie tried to hit on her was just gross. He had never seen Carson like she had. Though, to be momentarily fair, the woman may have had her reasons. Still, that night at the Tavern, Shiloh was just trying to be nice and Carson didn't have to react to her kindness the way she had. Shiloh was told that Lyle Martin had marched Carson out of the bar, which Shiloh thought was fitting, and she was sorry she'd missed it.

Without tipping her hand, Shiloh put more details together. If she was right, her father was working on one of the ranches they had stolen cattle from. How the hell did he let that happen? And how disconcerting playing that part must be. She didn't feel an iota of guilt at taking his life savings. She felt that she'd earned it, that he owed it to her. That was how she resolved any internal conflicts she may have briefly entertained. Her needs took priority. She was done serving others.

Shiloh continued to wonder how that all had worked out. Asking Bodie directly would have been a mistake, so she fed him just enough rope to hang himself. He was never the wiser that she had more than a passing interest. Bodie was his own favorite subject, so it was easy, and Shiloh was more subtle than he could guess. She showed no emotion when he ranted on about all the people who had done him wrong. She knew how to encourage him to believe she was on his side. He mistakenly thought there was a "we" in the motorhome. There was not.

Vans with dishes on the roofs were peppered throughout the vast area that was either burning, had burned, or might burn. The height of the chaos around the fires created a media frenzy. Like pigeons after crumbs, they raced from here to there to get the story. And there were a lot of stories to tell.

As for the fire crew that had perished, each member of that team had a family and a background. The waves of scrutiny made the grief and loss unbearable for the loved ones. Reporters clambered to get the shot. Recovering the bodies proved to be the first intense and dramatic story, and because so many had died, the human-interest stories fanned out from there. There were hourly damage assessments, containment updates, and gruesome body counts. A water tanker crashed, an engine went off a road somewhere. Damage and cost estimates changed hourly. Updates abounded and no one had the time to check accuracy. How could they? It was old news moments after it was news. There was footage at six, ten, and eleven, miles of smoldering foundations, and amazing, uplifting stories of survival. There were stories of beloved pets and people reuniting. The flow of media was almost never-ending, and the more dramatic the better.

At first, the attention paid to shell-shocked fire victims drew a helpful kind of attention. Supplies, money, and acts of kindness overwhelmed. As quickly as the promises of aid poured in, the fire blazed fresh horror and drained the attention to another area. Many of the grand promises dried up like drops of water on parched ground. Generosity had its limits. Under the glare of the spotlights, donations and promises of financial aid were lauded. Grants morphed into low-interest loans after the lights went down and the crisis surged elsewhere.

The last to mine that field were the real storytellers—the writers who asked the right questions, presented the most moving encapsulations of real strength, accurate timelines, real heartache, and deeper explorations than the snapshots of what had been lost. Fact-based books began to appear about family, fathers, sons, lovers, and generally good people who had fought a good fight against an intractable foe and lost everything. The truth of the fires was laid bare in a kind of detail television and daily news didn't have the time slot for. Approaches varied. The science of how it had happened was destined for documentaries, lengthy reports, and autopsies of disaster on channels that relished back-to-back catastrophes. The personal stories of survival and love became big pieces in sections in Sunday papers, magazines, and special features.

The lone survivor of the fire crew was as sought after and hounded as much as the relatives were, and they tracked Cajun down to the hospital he had been taken to. Fortunately, they couldn't get at him. The hospital staff was efficient, hardnosed, and only Tish and select friends could run the gauntlet successfully.

But one intrepid reporter managed to slip inside. She convinced the staff that her husband was a patient, the victim of a car accident. She hung out on the floor near intensive care and watched for her chance. She was hungry to catch a break, to talk to someone to get an update—something more personal than the daily briefing bull her colleagues were getting from the media liaison.

It was easy to spot Tish and the reporter figured out a possible "in" when she managed to surreptitiously follow her as she left the ICU. Tish said something about the chapel to one of the nurses on her way to the elevator. The reporter timed it perfectly. She took the stairs and was in the chapel praying when Tish arrived. The reporter sensed this was not a woman to trifle with and she ended up respecting her privacy. She struggled with what to write and hoped that an angle would present itself that wasn't too awful. She held back and waited for her chance.

Tish was needed in the field but remained close to her husband. She was in constant contact with her crew as they carried on without her. She and Cajun were the spiritual glue for a lot of people and their absence was keenly felt.

Initially, Cajun was kept sedated. His body fought off infection and it was several days before he knew where he was. When he came out of the fog of the first few days, the face of his wife was there waiting for him. With tubes protruding from almost everywhere, they held hands and prayed. They prayed for the crew that had died in the fires and tears ran down Cajun's cheeks. Tish took a tissue from the bedside table, leaned in close, and wiped them for him. Their eyes locked and he smiled, and then he tried to ask, via a pen, about the horse.

Tish hadn't been able to sort out what had happened to him yet but she had spoken to the men who had found him. They had described the horse and she had no idea if it was still alive. She knew that Cajun had been adamant about saving him and one of the men thought the girl who picked up the horse said she was the vet's assistant. Tish was frustrated that no one had gotten the woman's information. She didn't even have a first name, let alone a last. How could they miss getting information from someone and just hand over an animal like that?

She told Cajun that she found out what kind of truck and trailer the horse had been transported in and she meant to contact every veterinarian in the area and track the horse down. But help had poured in from all over the west. The horse could be anywhere.

Cajun had been on a ventilator but it had been removed, much to their relief. Yet Cajun's voice was barely a whisper and if the infection got worse, he would be back on it. Right now there were bigger issues to be concerned about besides a horse. But this horse was on Cajun's mind despite his serious condition. It reminded Tish of the other man who had struggled with injuries and still fought her to try to get to his horse. *What is it about horses...* she thought. Or maybe the question was, what was it about *this* particular horse?

"Saved me," Cajun croaked, his voice stretched as thin as spun filament. It was as if the smoke was still caught in his lungs and made it impossible for him to take a full breath.

Cajun coughed uncontrollably and spit up dark-colored phlegm. Buzzers and alarms sounded and people filled the room.

Tish stood back and they worked to stabilize the coughing

fit that had dropped Cajun's oxygen level to a point where he almost lost consciousness. The two competent floor physicians worked the situation and there was a flurry of activity as they disconnected his bed and Cajun was wheeled to the operating room for the solution to his breathing difficulties.

Tish retreated to the downstairs waiting room, and an hour later was told that he had stabilized and was moved back up to the intensive care unit to be carefully monitored. She went up the elevator to that waiting area, where a familiar woman was seated in the corner of the room, reading a magazine. She lifted her head and smiled at Tish.

Hours later, Tish was in Cajun's private room. There was a discussion with updates from the attending, and for the moment, he was not intubated nor did they do a tracheotomy. He had stabilized, though he was plugged in with fresh tubes and sensors and looked like a very large bandaged pin cushion under a thin sheet.

When the staff cleared out, Cajun's eyes told her he would not let it go.

"I will do what I can but right now we need you to get well. Everyone is so worried about you." Tish gently rested her hand on his chest, over his heart where she was reasonably sure he didn't have a burn or a bruise. "You took quite a beating, my man, and I need you. The team needs you. We all need you back."

He drifted in and out of sleep and in between that he was calm. He looked awful and Tish was deeply worried. Sensing that he was drifting back to sleep again, Tish promised him once more that she would investigate, that she would get after it immediately. Though "immediately" would be later. Things were crazy with the fire and Cajun developed an infection in his lungs that scared everyone.

Tish spent a lot of her time in the ICU and in waiting areas. It was where she found time to make calls, and she searched out various veterinary practices. She got voicemail on one number repeatedly and she rubbed her forehead, imagining how busy all of them must be. One was a small animal place, and one did a mixture of both and didn't have any horses at their location. They were treating animals off-site.

She went to the chapel and sat on a chair. Tish did a prayerful meditation, then the hospital chaplain came in and they prayed together. As she was leaving the chapel, she spotted the woman she'd seen in there the day before. The woman approached her, introduced herself, and got as far as her first name when Tish's cell phone chirped.

Tish apologized that she needed to take the call and answered. The woman watched Tish's back as she started to slowly walk away, but not far enough that she couldn't overhear Tish's side of the call.

Tish stopped between the door to the stairs and the elevator. The woman positioned herself nearby, ready to take either. She pretended to press the elevator call button but didn't.

"Hi, yes, thank you for returning my call." Tish introduced herself and then went on, "I'm looking for a horse, my husband is a firefighter…yes, that one. Um, he's doing OK considering, thank you for asking. Anyway, he was found with this horse and I'm trying to find it…what?" She stopped, listened, then said, "No, we don't know what the horse's name is." She listened further, her eyes wide. "Wait a second, you have an injured horse there that you picked up?" Tish shook her head. "I'm sorry, what was your name?" She was quiet for a moment. "Oh, hello Janine, you're my first bit of luck on this."

Tish leaned against the wall, her cell phone pressed hard to her head, her eyes closed with relief that she would have good news for Cajun. From the corner of her eye, the reporter saw the white of Tish's fingers pressed hard on the plastic and could almost feel the strong grip of this woman. She could have dented the sides of the phone with her intensity.

Tish popped off the wall. "What did you say the horse's name is?" A big smile played across her face and she shot a sideways glance at the woman, who smiled awkwardly back.

To make her stance by the elevator appear legit, the reporter looked up at the lit floor indicators overhead, huffed an exasperated breath, and pressed the call button for real. She made "huh?" sign with her hands and Tish nodded that she got it, then turned toward the door to the stairwell.

"He will love that…that you called him Cajun," Tish continued.

Tish smiled as the woman decided to look like she didn't want to wait for the elevator and moved toward the stairs. She walked by Tish with a friendly wave. She pushed the door open, offered to hold it for Tish, guessed which way Tish might go, and went up.

Tish did go up and the woman listened as Tish mentioned the veterinarian's name. When Tish hung up, the woman picked a floor at random and exited the stairwell. In a flash, her notebook was out and she wrote down the vet's name, the name Janine, a horse, and Cajun. She snapped the notebook shut with a smile. She had found her story angle and got that tingle she sometimes got when a good story landed in her lap.

Bodie jumped in his seat. "Oh, I love those!" he yelled and pointed excitedly at a sandwich shop across the highway. He was childlike in his enthusiasm, almost impossibly so, and he pleaded with Shiloh to pull over. He pulled his billfold out of his pack, got the cash he needed, shoved the wallet back inside, and used his heel to wedge the pack under the seat, tucked tight. She pulled over to the side of the highway, off the shoulder.

"Why aren't you pulling into the lot?" he whined.

"It's packed and too small. I'm not getting stuck in there," she replied. Her hands and arms rested on the steering wheel as he looked over and said nothing.

"Oh, and take that bag of garbage with you and put it in their dumpster," she said.

"What?" Bodie looked incredulous. "What do I look like?"

"A guy about to carry a small plastic bag of garbage over to a dumpster."

He hesitated but thought this might be his last chance to get his favorite Philly cheesesteak sandwich that he was certain he could only get there. He hissed, grabbed the garbage bag, and went to the door. He disdained the garbage errand. He started to open the door and said, "I'll do it *this* time...but we have to talk."

Shiloh didn't watch him trot across the highway. She was doing a slow burn on his misogynistic comment about "having to talk."

"About what..." she muttered under her breath. *What an asshole,* she thought and looked out her window with a grimace.

It seemed to take him forever. Shiloh didn't actually see what happened, it was more that she heard it. The horns sounded, there was sudden braking and the sound of sliding tires on pavement, then an odd thud followed by a creepy silence, more honking, then excited voices. She caught a glimpse of a cheesesteak sandwich splattered on the pavement before a large van blocked her view.

Shiloh put the turn signal on and edged the motorhome back onto the highway and accelerated. In her rearview mirror, she saw the traffic behind her bunch up as rubberneckers slowed to see the body on the asphalt.

Chapter 66

It was time to face the music. Carson's heart fell when the bankruptcy attorney called and another appointment was set up. Kitzie reluctantly embarked on another shopping foray, and joined her daughter for the trip.

Kitzie pulled up to the curb to drop Carson off near the attorney's office. Carson looked at her mother and found it amusing that she wasn't excited to go shopping. She opined that most of the Silicon Valley husbands did nothing but pay the bills for shopping, and that they'd give their eye teeth for a wife like Kitzie.

Kitzie smirked and said that looking at stuff was tiresome. She suggested waiting so they could go together after Carson's appointment.

"You're not going into Bend. Here," Carson said and pointed to the paper on the seat near her briefcase. "Here are some addresses of some cute shops that I researched for you. It's not like a mall. There are people there who will really appreciate you shopping at a local, small business."

Kitzie picked up the paper and looked down the street. "Huh, looks like one place may be right down there."

"I'll call you when I'm almost done. Who knows? I might just walk down to where you are and clear my head." Carson opened her door and got out.

She turned to reach for her briefcase—the last remnant of

her once-aspiring Silicon Valley dreams. Its soft, expensive leather and design were timeless. Next to her jeans and boots, it was a classic juxtaposition and not entirely unflattering. A briefcase like that looked good everywhere. She straightened and pulled her well-worn, down jacket close across her sweater. The day had a distinct chill to its overcast gray.

Carson smiled at her mother. It was one of resignation and she said, "It either didn't take as much time to figure out or there's a bigger mess to make things right." She turned and looked at the building's façade. "I've got that heavy, bad feeling. That can't be good."

"Don't assume anything. We've been through worse. A historic fire didn't destroy us. Your bankruptcy won't either," her mother said with encouragement. "Though not being able to feed our herd…"

"We'll work it out, Mom." It was Carson's turn to see beyond the immediate challenges to the future.

They looked at each other without words and communicated as only two people who love each other can.

"We have options, and maybe we can send more cows to the Rez," Carson said. "Buckets gave us some other contacts. Some old chum from his game days, I think… That one in Butte Valley? We have some calls to make, for sure."

Kitzie mulled that over for a second. "We'll see what kind of deal we can make on the feed."

Carson liked the way Kitzie said "we." She shut the truck door and gave her mother a small wave as Kitzie pulled out and merged into the sparse traffic.

The attorney's office had the quiet morning hum of a reasonably busy practice. Since Carson's last visit, her attorney had made some changes, expanded, and apparently had taken on a new partner. There were new names on the door and more staff.

A couple in familiar ranchers' clothing sat next to each other in the waiting area. The wife looked stoic and the man's eyes were ringed red. They could just as easily have been in a funeral home as a legal office.

Carson sat across from them and she and the woman looked at each other. Carson smiled the smile of a fellow sufferer and she put her briefcase on its side on the chair next to her, pulled her jacket off, and laid it across her lap. Down jackets object to lying flat and Carson futilely tried to fold it into something resembling neat. The outer shell crinkled loudly and there was a kind of hiss that emanated from the inner workings as she smoothed its unruly surface with her open hand.

Carson gave up and studied her hands as they lay folded on the material of the coat. She pondered two things; she really needed a manicure and the skin on the back of her hands was dry and looked much older than she realized. She lifted a hand and studied her nails. There was visible dirt under most of them and she looked around to see if there was a restroom nearby where she could wash them. She looked up again and saw the woman watching her. Their eyes connected and the woman's look indicated that she'd noticed what Carson was probably thinking.

She smiled. "It's around that corner and on the right."

Carson smiled in return. "Thank you." She got up, her bulky jacket over her arm, and carried her briefcase down the hall to the restroom. She stood at the sink and used her longest fingernail to free the trapped dirt from under the others. The warm water felt good and she reached for a towel to dry her hands. Carson looked around the restroom and noted the new designer tile, the subtle wallpaper, and tasteful countertop. She ran her hand over it and thought something like that would look nice in her mom's new house. She fished out her cell phone and snapped a shot of it to share with Stiles.

The bathroom was an oasis. Even the fan in the ceiling had a pleasant, soft hum to it. Carson picked her coat up off the counter and for a moment longed for something at least a touch more dignified. Then she thought about the frost that was on the ground when they had walked to the truck in the dark that morning and decided that being warm had its advantages. She exited the restroom and walked back to the waiting area. The couple was gone and as she set her briefcase on the chair, she heard someone behind her.

This was a new face, and she was dressed business casual, quite appropriate for Redmond. The woman approached her and introduced herself. Her demeanor was dignified and respectful, but friendly, as if they were at some function that wasn't in a bankruptcy attorney's office.

Carson made small talk to cover her discomfort as they walked down the hallway. "Been some changes here since my last visit," she said politely, not really caring about the reason.

The woman walked next to Carson, not ahead of her. She explained that there was a new staff and they now had a separate trustee who used the office for collecting and distributing payments. They were also in talks with a professional credit counselor and they were forming a full-service business that would give borrowers more tools and options other than traditional solutions to their problems.

"We felt that if we had professionals with proactive connections to the banking industry, we could help people explore other options, such as mortgage modifications."

Carson nodded but said little as they approached the attorney's office door. The woman gently tapped the door, then opened it, entered, and held it wide for Carson. Again, her expression and demeanor made Carson feel respected... which was nice. Awkward, but nice. That wasn't a feeling she was prepared for. This whole process was one of degradation to her—of failure on such a scale that its taint would stick to her for the next five to seven years, depending on what chapter she would be forced to file under. Carson assumed the bad kind, the worst kind, as she had no income to make payments. Inside, she felt gray and tired.

The attorney rose from his desk, then came out and around it with an expression of pleasure at seeing Carson. He shook her hand warmly and thanked his associate for bringing her in. Before the door shut, the woman asked both if they'd like anything and Carson said some water would be nice. Her mouth suddenly felt parched, as if the walk down the hall had been through the Sahara.

The associate returned with a bottled water in hand. Carson thanked her and the woman left.

The attorney cleared his throat and began with a series of questions that he wanted more clarity and detail on. Carson listened to the information he was required to give her. It was a set of parameters that might influence her choice of how she'd care to proceed. She accepted some paperwork that she figured he was also required to supply her with. All Carson wanted to know was how bad it was—specifically, her back taxes.

The attorney sat back in his chair and seemed to be contemplating how to say something. Carson felt the gnaw of impatience and opened her mouth to hurry things along. She wanted to get to the point and then beyond it as quickly as possible.

"I've rarely been surprised by much in this business and going through your information was a revelation," the attorney began.

Carson closed her mouth, the harsh words stifled. She looked at him, completely confused by what he was driving at.

"May I be impertinent and ask a personal question, please?" he queried as delicately as she had seen any man ever try to be. It was as if he was uncomfortable even asking her permission.

Carson nodded.

"Um..." He looked down at his desk. "Who was your friend?"

"I'm sorry...my friend?" Carson was immediately uncomfortable, like a kid in school called on by the teacher to answer a question in front of the class.

He looked taken aback, then he looked again at something and mentioned a stock.

Carson's mind raced. Stock? She got up from her seat and her briefcase tilted against the underpinning of the desk. She needed to pace and her mind sifted through things she had been trying, and succeeding, to forget.

The attorney waited and looked concerned. He didn't want to upset her and started to say so. Carson raised a hand to stop him, then stopped in front of a rather nice landscape painting he had on his wall.

In the back of her mind, she seemed to recall that *he* had arranged for her to purchase some shares. "Suggestions," he had called them. Investments for her future. He gave her gifts for her birthday, Valentine's Day, and Christmas. "Pillow talks," he called them. And NSO (no special occasion) gifts. All the color drained from her face when she wondered whether her situation had gone beyond some back taxes and a foreclosed house. Was she in a real kind of trouble? Had she taken something without knowing it? Her fear was palpable and the attorney asked her to sit back down.

"Let me explain," he said with a slight smile.

"Am I in a serious kind of trouble? I truly don't know what you are talking about…" Carson started.

He leaned forward. "I don't mean to frighten you. I don't need to *know know*. It's just that whoever they were, they were *very* good friends."

"I'm sorry, I'm a little confused…" Carson mumbled, rubbing her forehead. She hoped a clarifying moment was coming, and soon, or her head would explode. She had been so anxious about facing reality and thought she was ready for the worst. She had geared up to be strong, and this weirdness wasn't at all what she had expected.

"So were we," the attorney continued. "And that was the part that required us to reassess our whole approach. You see, the real estate thing is all gone, that was a very good piece of property you bought, and the bank made money on it. They're satisfied." He opened Carson's legal file. "I can show you if you'd like."

"Maybe later. Is the really bad news my taxes? Back taxes and penalties?" She felt her palms grow sweaty as her fears began to consume her.

"Please, relax, it's not as bad as you think." He smiled. "It's not every day that I approach one thing that seems straightforward only to find out it's something completely different. It definitely challenged my assumptions."

He expanded with some market history that Carson was unaware of. She had tuned out and hadn't listened to the news, and they really didn't get any news out at the Three Bit anyway. "The back story that was really interesting was the IPO of a certain company, considered wildly overvalued at hundreds of millions in 2012. It is worth over one hundred billion today. And it now delivers tens of billions in revenue."

Carson was starting to think he was going off on a tangent. "And this is a stock you purchased at some point?"

"I did, in 2000, and I'm feeling rather good about it…as should you."

Carson shook her head and gave him a look like he was on something. "What are you talking about?" Why was he telling her about his personal stock purchases?

"At the time, I became convinced I'd made a mistake and was going to sell when this company made certain moves that solidified its dominance in modern communications. I wanted to sell it because I didn't see that they would lead the way into the future." He paused. "Fortunately, my wife didn't let me and now it's a large part of what will be our retirement."

Carson wondered where this was going and her raised eyebrows said so.

He smiled. "Life is full of these lyrical little moments and it's nice to be part of one." And he turned a sheet of paper around in his hand and slid it across the desk in front of Carson. She leaned forward on the edge of the seat and started to read. The reaction to the information he presented was stunned silence.

"Perhaps you were so wrapped up in failing that you failed to see where you had succeeded," he said softly.

Carson murmured, "That's so well put I might have to

write it down and use it to explain this to myself later."

The apprehension that had possessed her for months shifted. It felt like she had been skating on the thin edge of the ice, all the time, and now this turn of events was completely unpredicted.

He asked her if he could bring an associate in to talk with her. "One of the changes we have made is to be more full service. We added an investment counselor and I want to be very clear that we are separate entities under the same roof. Would you like to speak to her?"

Carson nodded, still numb and not sure how to feel at that moment.

While they waited for Maryann to join them, the attorney tried to move on to the tax liabilities that needed clearing up. He estimated that she owed several hundred thousand dollars when all was said and done, though he felt there could be some negotiation on that.

"And depending on the decisions you make with that…" He nodded to the paper still resting quietly on the desk. "…there are some moves you can make regarding financial planning." He rose at a tap on the door and a diminutive woman, dressed in a business suit and attractive, sensible jewelry, entered. He came around the desk and did the introductions.

Maryann had a wonderful handshake and wise eyes that connected directly with Carson's. The attorney excused himself, offering them his office, and left the room.

Maryann took the chair next to Carson, rotated it to face her, and handed Carson her card. Maryann Feldman, CFP, Financial Planner and Investment Advisor. She explained her qualifications and background in straightforward terms.

"It seems you've had a bit of a surprise," she said with an East Coast accent, New York most likely.

Carson replied, "You could say. I thought I was here to file for bankruptcy and now it seems I need something entirely different."

"It looks like you have made some very good choices and are capable of managing your affairs, and I'm here to offer my services to most effectively help meet your financial objectives, both personally and professionally." Maryann handed Carson a compact folder, which Carson opened to see the heading: *Wealth Management Planner*. Maryann continued by saying something along the lines that if Carson chose her to work on the objectives of her plan, she would be committed to fully assisting her and her advisors in all aspects of the process.

Carson got stuck at the word "professionally." She had been a professional and had crashed and burned at it. She was distracted and Maryann asked her the question again.

"Was there something you wanted to pursue? A career?" She was asking about what Carson wanted to do.

Carson didn't hesitate. "I'm a rancher." And then she shook Maryann's hand again and said, "Hello, I am Carson Collins of Collins Cutting Horses and the Three Bit cattle ranch. I think I'm ready, let's begin."

They spent the next hour discussing her current financial situation, investments, and general estate planning.

Kitzie texted what time she would be back to pick up Carson and Carson laughed.

Maryann looked at her.

Carson said, "I don't know what to say to her. I mean, I hadn't thought about the things…all this…and what I thought would be happening, well, it's all a great deal to take in."

Maryann was a great listener and she offered no opinion on what Carson "should" say to her mother other than, "What do you want to tell her?"

Carson shook her head, at a loss. "I don't think I want to say anything...for now, I mean. Is that OK?"

"You do what is best, there's no reason you need to tell anyone."

When they parted, Maryann reassured Carson again and finished by adding, "Money is like life. You have to decide how to spend it."

Chapter 67

The almost bald tire slid right and crunched over the gravel as the truck came to a hard stop. The cab-over camper shell swayed on weary shocks. The sun played shadows on the ground and illuminated the license plate frame, which was crooked. Stiles took the truck out of gear and put it into park, slowly set the brake, and killed the engine where the Three Bit road met the highway. His heart pounded as if he had been chased and his breathing seemed to synchronize with the *tick-tick-tick* of the engine settling to stillness. It was that kind of fear you hold on to, that you have inside, and for the first time in his life, it was tearing him apart.

He rested an arm on the open windowsill, looked both ways, then glanced at his side rearview mirror, where his gaze and his heart lingered. It was the moment he realized that he hadn't thought about his daughter recently and couldn't remember when that had faded from his purpose.

What if Wyker hadn't come back? Wyker and that CJ. They didn't recognize him with his long hair, mustache, and beard. He had been sent there by Lyle and there was no reason for them to question his references. He had the best. Their last encounter was a different time and he didn't know then what he knew now. He was in a different context and he felt different. He didn't want to be a threat. In his mind and in his heart, Stiles wanted to make it up to them…to her.

"We were all preoccupied with the colt," he said out loud. He smiled, thinking about watching the little guy. He'd hung on the pipe panel fence and saw how well the adopted orphan was doing. CJ was around but kept to the main barn and the colt. And it seemed he mourned. Stiles thought there was some undefined tension there—the way CJ was around Carson, all busted up from the fire, that he had lost that red horse. That was a big deal and he'd half expected Wyker and CJ to leave at any moment and go look for him, they talked about it so much.

When he arrived to work on the house early and saw that Wyker's truck was gone, he'd breathed a sigh of relief. One less person who might have a suspicion. Then he heard that CJ wanted to go look for Rio, and that made him feel hopeful. If they weren't a working part of the Three Bit, he could manage to stay clear and it might be that he could stay. Maybe not at the Three Bit but close, in Martin. Do more of this kind of work. He liked building things. He wanted to do that. Talk of more projects had already come his way and the light at the end of his dark tunnel seemed to be in sight. Stiles could be someone else...

But CJ and Wyker didn't go any further than Martin Ranch Supply. And there was another visitor...

Stiles felt like he could only be so lucky and his anxiety level made him quieter. He recalled the feeling he had, standing by the sawhorse workbench and putting his tools away. He had unplugged the long extension cord, coiled it neatly, and was careful to stay organized as he checked off the day's goals accomplished in his head, and the ones to accomplish tomorrow. The wood of the hammer fit his hand comfortably. Relaxed, he stood staring at his work and felt a connection to it that he knew he would always be proud of. He told himself that the crowd wouldn't stay there forever, and it was all going to be OK. He half believed it until he felt movement out of the corner of his eye. Hoping it was the evening visit from Kitzie, he turned to face her and the almost smile froze on his face.

He hadn't heard the Indian coming until he was really close. Quiet, he was.

He saw me, thought Stiles. *He stared and stared and said nothing...*

Stiles hadn't physically jumped from the fright but it felt like it—his eyes flinched and his heart sure did. He knew exactly who it was, kept his composure, and slowly faced him, his hammer in hand.

Harper Lee looked at him and Stiles felt the chicken skin on his arms. Harper's eye flicked to the hammer and Stiles put it down carefully on his makeshift sawhorse bench. Time seemed an eternity and Stiles felt a bead of sweat travel down between his shoulder blades. The cool of the late afternoon was well started, yet he was uncomfortably warm.

Harper's expression was inert, unreadable, and he didn't speak. His black eyes looked down over his aquiline nose and his lips pursed. The tribal marks across his cheekbones almost seemed to glisten, as if freshly cut on his skin. His long hair hung loose and framed a face that could have stood on any field of battle. The wind picked up his long hair and blew it into a halo that framed his head, as if he was a native Medusa and the ends of the tendrils possessed tongues. Stiles was truly alarmed. Then Harper released him from the stony gaze and stepped back a few paces, though his eyes never moved. Then Harper turned and silently walked away. Stiles knew that Harper had recognized him, so he waited.

His head swam and he slowly turned his back to the

retreating Harper. He brought his left hand up and covered his eyes, then slid the hand down over his mouth. He smelled the wood he'd been working on; it permeated his skin and filled his nostrils with what he knew to be real. He inhaled the odor deeply and looked at the house. Still so much left to do. Would there be time to do it? Suddenly, he felt that his time had run out. He rested his palms on the workbench and felt the queasy crawl of the adrenaline find his bowels, then his knees. He lifted his head quickly and looked around, wondering if anyone was watching. The old paranoia came back as swiftly and silently as the Indian.

When the two had met before, Stiles had held a rifle on him. He had only hoped the rifle would be a good enough deterrent to send him off. He didn't know and he might have shot him. But a shot from nearby—he suspected Wyker of it—had startled him and thankfully, the shot completely missed any mark. The rest of it was a blur, though Wyker coming after him he recalled clearly. And that horse of Wyker's knew that Stiles was aiming for him and pulled up short just in time. But he was too far off so he felt Wyker wouldn't recognize him. And besides, he had stayed well out of their way.

Stiles kept his head down and made sure no one noticed him much. When Wyker and CJ looked at the house rebuild, Stiles left to take a leak or went to his rig and disappeared inside for a break or something. He was a shadow, a specter as a carpenter, though his work showed a skill that was above ground.

That was where he'd been. He looked at the wheel and shook his head. It could be so simple. He bit his lip as he struggled with how he was feeling. He'd never been more conflicted about what to do. When he'd realized Shiloh was gone and that she'd taken everything, there was just shock. No choices. He had always been easy about leaving a place, and this place should have been no different. Was it the unfinished parts that gnawed at him…or was it something more?

Stiles wondered what had changed in him. Something had. He wanted to tell her everything. He had never been honest before, never told anyone everything, and yet leaving the ranch like this felt so wrong. This part was usually easy. He was good at this, yet he was hesitating. There was a definite difference this time and he really struggled with it.

He had met someone that he believed in, that he knew he would always believe in. Stiles had fallen for Kitzie in a way he had never thought possible, and certainly well past possible at this point in his life. And he knew it would never go away.

He started the truck and as it rumbled to life, he picked a direction at random and pushed it hard to speed, as if to convince momentum to make the choice for him. He hoped that distance and speed would dull the pain he felt at running away. But instead, it grew worse.

Chapter 68

Janine was in the house when she heard a car pull up. Her dogs barked and she walked to the door to see a woman she didn't recognize. Janine walked out and asked if she could help her.

"I'm looking for a horse," the woman said as she got out of her car.

Janine looked her over and frowned. "And who are you?"

The woman stalled and seemed to be considering her answer. Janine crossed her arms in front of her.

The woman looked down and rummaged through her purse. She pulled out her identification and walked toward Janine. "I'm a reporter."

Janine leaned over and looked at the proffered qualifications. She wasn't about to make it easy for this lady, so she kept her mouth shut and let the lady talk herself in if she could.

"Look, I'll be honest with you, I'm not sure I'm in the right place. Is there an injured horse here that has anything to do with a firefighter named Cajun?"

"What's it to you?" Janine asked as she sat down on the top step of the porch.

The gal shook her head and smiled. "You're not going to make this easy, are you?"

Janine smiled sweetly at her. "Nope."

"OK, well, I'll tell you what I think and what I'm hoping to do, then could we go from there?"

"You can try," Janine said.

The reporter shared what she thought she knew and thought there might be an interesting story about the firefighter and this horse.

Janine told her that she needed to talk to someone, then they would see about horses and stories. She pulled out her cell and called the other woman involved in this. Tish.

Things had moved along. Cajun was making steady improvements and he wanted to see the horse. Tish had wondered if there was a connection to the Aussie she had worked on and whether this animal might be his, the one he'd lost. It was a far-fetched idea and she didn't want to get the guy's hopes up only to find out that this horse wasn't the one. The hang-up was, who could she call to figure it out?

After talking to Janine, Tish felt the reporter might be the key and she agreed that the woman could interview all of them if the point of the story was to reunite the horse and its true owner.

The three-part series ran in all the national papers and even made it onto "PBS NewsHour," the BBC network, and the Chris Hayes show. Fox was only interested if there was a certain political spin on it, so they passed.

The TV was on in the Pine Tavern. Jorge was there keeping Trina company early in the evening when he saw the story. It was quiet in the bar and the volume was up enough and he recognized Rio right away. He almost fell over when he saw him. He immediately called Kitzie, who put Carson on the phone.

Chapter 69

Spence pulled up to his home and took a cell call from the coroner as he turned off the engine and undid his seatbelt. It was a brief conversation about the dead pedestrian from the highway incident, and he confirmed there was still no identification on the guy. In the fire's smoky confusion, there had been several unfortunate pedestrian/vehicle encounters, and more than a few animal versus car reports. When he had looked into the accident, Spence was surprised by how much traffic thronged around him and how many people asked questions he had no answers to.

It had been more than a long day—long *days*—and when he opened the door to his double-wide and stepped inside, Spence said, "Hi, honeys, I'm home," but without the humor he usually had for the fish in his fifty-gallon aquarium.

Spence had always had fish, mostly a long series of goldfish, but they seemed to be the most stalwart of companions, always oblivious to the vagaries of his job, his career path, and the occasional change of locale. The only parts of *their* locale that changed were the plants or the occasional new sea creature that blew bubbles up to the surface. Spence liked the treasure chest that filled with air, then the lid opened when the chest was full and burped forth a collection of bubbles.

His fish were always happy to see him, and he was fastidious about water temp, pH levels, and that they had optimal conditions in their forced captivity. He could sit and watch them like a person watched TV. In fact, they *were* his TV. Their lives were as interesting to him as any binge-watched HBO series.

But this night he decided that he would shower, change into jeans and a shirt, and have dinner at the Pine Tavern. Maybe play a game of pool. It had been the kind of time where he wanted to be with people. So, Spence cleaned up and felt better for it, then went down to the tavern. He walked in and was greeted warmly by half the room before he made his way to the bar. As he slid onto the seat, he slipped the bar menu from its metal holder and tilted it toward the light to choose something for dinner.

As he smiled at Toby, who was friendly this time, he noticed a figure down the bar, holding an untouched mug of beer and staring straight ahead. It was Dee and she was just shy of catatonic.

Spence looked at Toby and asked how long she had been there, and more importantly, how long she had been like that.

"For about forty-five minutes," Toby replied.

"Oh, that's no good."

"No, it isn't."

"Toby, I'll have two Club BLTs with fries, please."

Spence got up and moved down to the empty stool next to Dee. She turned and looked at him, unseeing for a second, before she folded her mouth into an impression of a smile and said hello.

"Hello," he replied simply and sat next to her. He didn't try to chat her up, draw her out, or boost her spirits. He just sat by her. When the food arrived, he ate as if it was the most normal of things to do and she stared at her plate, then looked at him, wondering what was expected. He just smiled, a silent companion, and after a time asked Toby what game was on. "After everything I've seen the past few days, some mindless sports is just what I need."

Toby got the remote and started the scroll search. "What do you want?" he asked.

"Anything," Spence replied. "I really don't care."

Dee took a fry and dipped it into Toby's special aioli. She looked at Spence, surprised. "Hey, that's pretty good."

"Haven't you eaten here before?" he asked.

"No. I'm usually home with my cat," she answered. And then she started laughing at how lame that sounded.

He leaned over and said, "I'm usually home with my fish."

They both started to giggle. Her laugh was that goofy, infectious kind that did an out-of-breath wheezing thing when it got going. And before a minute passed, they were in uncontrollable, tears-down-the-cheeks hysteria. Over nothing. It took many minutes and some Kleenex to clear their sinuses before they settled into the game and dinner.

It turned into one of the more pleasant evenings either of them had had in quite a while. After a couple of hours, they both felt it was time to go and Spence paid the tab. He helped Dee put on her sweater, held the door open for her, and walked her to her car.

Dee was still rattled and she fumbled for her keys. They fell with a clatter to the pavement and Spence bent down and gathered them. He found the proper key, inserted it in the lock, and opened her car door.

Dee stood staring at him for a long minute. "How do you do it?" she asked.

"I'll tell you something my good friend Hank told me

once."

Dee leaned in to get every word.

"There are two wolves inside of each of us. One is regret and doubt, and one is love and hope. Which one of the wolves wins?"

She smiled broadly. "I know this one!" And then she blushed. "The one that you feed."

He nodded and smiled. And then, totally out of character, he asked her if he might kiss her good night.

Her face filled with a kind of glow he'd only seen a few times in another person, and she replied, "Yes."

He touched her chin gently with the tip of his finger and kissed her softly on the lips. And she kissed him gently back. Then he guided her into her car and wished her sweet dreams. Dee started her car, put her safety belt on, looked up at Spence through the window with a smile, and mouthed, *Good night.*

Chapter 70

Harper's visit was slated to be brief, yet he hesitated to go. He meant to be up before dawn but was more tired than he thought and it was well past eight when he walked down to have a word with Mr. Stiles. He'd had a few hours to consider things and it was still a shock to find a cattle rustler on the very ranch he had rustled cattle from. That he found him at the Three Bit was disconcerting and that he hadn't told anyone that he recognized him was an issue as well. Harper had been struggling with it since facing Stiles the day before.

The dedication Stiles had shown to the Three Bit and Kitzie confounded him. The detail work in the house Stiles was building for her was extraordinary, and that was one element of his presence that needed adding up before Harper decided what to do. That meant a conversation.

The sun had crested the hills and was casting long shadows everywhere as Harper walked down the length of the covered arena. Much about the Three Bit was impressive and he could see elements that spoke of the man who had built it and why the Collins family had been so successful at one time. And why Will Wyker was Tuff Collins' friend.

Harper wished his mood matched the growing brilliance of the morning. He saw the sunrise glitter on the surface of the water in a big round trough. Tiny bugs bounced on the surface like spirits. Life was beginning all over again, like the colt, who grew stronger and surer of himself with each passing hour.

Wyker...what to tell him? He apparently didn't notice who Stiles was when they had arrived. Granted, there was still a lot going on. And Stiles' appearance was different—the longer hair, quite white, which was short and hidden under a hat before. There had been no mustache or beard, and what he had grown was effective.

It took some reflection to pinpoint what it was about him that had tipped Harper off, and Harper credited some weird sixth sense of his. He felt it on his skin like one feels the rain. He had only seen the rustlers on horseback, so it wasn't the man's walk or bearing. There were no observable mannerisms that flagged Harper's attention because he hadn't seen any. It wasn't a for-sure thing until the moment he had faced him alone. His play had been a complete bluff. It was a test, and one that Stiles had almost passed. Harper paused in midstep with the realization that it was the guilt—that was what gave him away.

The night before, Kitzie had improvised a darn good dinner at what she called "Chez Arena," which she thought sounded better than "dinner at the trailer." She and Carson had become adept with a Weber grill and they had made hamburgers and salad. Kitzie had invited Jorge, but he had gone into town, and Stiles declined, which was apparently not unusual for him. The little bits of information created a picture for Harper—one he hoped would clarify what should or should not be done.

Next to the trailer in the arena was a propane fire pit. After dinner, it was surrounded by lawn chairs. Harper let the conversation about the house start innocently, organically, to learn how Stiles had come to the Three Bit. It was of interest to learn that Stiles had grown up in the area. Harper spent much of the evening thinking things through and wondering whether he was obligated to push what he suspected higher up…or let it go.

Carson even nudged him once and discreetly asked why he was so quiet. She nodded toward CJ. "He has an excuse to be so but you…"

Harper shrugged it off to quite a few miles and some night work that he didn't elaborate on, and redirected the conversation to learn more about the Three Bit. To Kitzie's delight, everyone enjoyed taking turns telling stories about the place.

Carson explained the cutting horse business and, after the tragedy of the fire, what a big lift to everyone's spirits it was when there was a new foal there. And how upset she was when she found that he had died. Wyker did a decent retelling of CJ marching off into the brush and coming back with a colt in his arms. It was the one time during the evening that CJ's face lightened up. He had been affected by the little guy. Carson was most animated about the colt and his adorable antics of the day. The light of the fire lit the lines of her face which, it seemed, CJ had come to know as well as his own.

As CJ watched her talk about it, he smiled, though laughter and sitting were uncomfortable for him. He had hollows under his eyes and didn't mention Rio. No one did, but his absence and the lack of news about him was like an elephant in the room—or rather, the arena. It was impossible to miss.

It was easy to see it would be an early night for CJ. Carson had relinquished the room in the barn and moved into the trailer with Kitzie. CJ excused himself after dinner and Carson watched him go. She felt he was particularly down that evening. She looked at her mother and raised an eyebrow at her.

Carson was dying to tell him, but Kitzie shook her head and lowered her eyes like a period on a sentence.

With a sigh, Carson called his name with a question mark in her voice. He made it clear that he could manage the stairs up to his old room, and stiffly, he made his way there. A heavy weariness was setting in fast, though the beauty of the moon had a freshness to it as if he had never seen it before.

The stairs took effort, and after climbing them, CJ sat on the bed in the dark. Moonlight poured through the window and softly found the details of the room. It was familiar to him and it was reassuring to be back. The sounds of the horses shifting positions below, the gurgle of an automatic waterer topping up, and the owl's distinctive call found his ears.

CJ kicked off his boots, stretched out on top of the bed, and watched the moon's progress across the window glass. Not a breath stirred the air. *What a difference from the weeks of wind,* he thought. The double-paned, insulated glass made two moons when he closed one eye, and it reminded him of his childhood. But there he was, so much pain later. He imagined that the closest thing to rest his discomfort would allow him was perhaps a fitful doze, yet he fell asleep as soundly as a child.

"No, you sit, I'll do clean-up," Carson told her mother. "Besides, I'm your roommate and I have to pitch in." She smiled at Kitzie as she gathered the dishes and went inside the trailer. She enjoyed the sound of her mother relaxed and at ease.

Harper and Wyker would rough it in their respective trucks. Wyker had the less-comfortable arrangement as his truck wasn't set up for overnight sleeping. Harper's truck had an old fiberglass shell on it, and he had a bedroll and mattress in the back. He offered to share with Wyker but he passed.

"I've heard you snore," Wyker teased. "You woke your ancestors at Sanctuary."

"That wasn't me," Harper protested. He looked at Kitzie, palms up, and repeated, "It wasn't me, I swear." He spoke up to Carson as she returned from the trailer. "Come on, Carson, you were there. Was I snoring?"

"I'm not sure who it was," she laughed.

Kitzie felt a demonstration was needed and she looked at Wyker with raised eyebrows. Carson suspended clean-up and waited with a similar look. Harper begged him not to, which encouraged Wyker to do an imitation that left the four of them laughing. It was laughing at the others laughing that spun them all into coughing fits at the end.

The evening had worn down easily. Harper had enjoyed visiting and told them so. He also said he would be leaving early and kept his own counsel regarding his suspicions about Stiles.

Now, on this new morning, Harper Lee passed the remains of the shop where Jorge's father had been killed. The debris had been removed and all that remained was a scorched concrete pad etched with scars. He wondered how Jorge handled it. He saw that their cottage was quiet and noted his vehicle parked beside it. He must have gotten in late.

Down a little farther was the barn where Wyker and CJ had stabled their horses. It marked the place. Stiles' camper would be on the other side. Harper rounded the building and saw nothing. He continued the length of the paddocks out the back, looked all around, and it was missing. He looked around on the ground and confirmed that this had indeed been where Stiles had been parked.

Maybe it was the coward's way out or maybe it was honorable. Harper was about to pick the coward's way for himself. He didn't want to be the one to tell them Stiles was gone. Best they discover that for themselves, long after his own departure. He said his good-byes and left the Three Bit without giving anything away.

It wasn't long after that they realized Stiles' rig was gone and when he hadn't returned by midday, they started to wonder where he was.

Stiles tore open an ancient bag of potato chips and cracked open a water. He'd been driving around, thinking. He didn't have a direction and drove past a truck stop where a motorhome was getting gas.

All night he had struggled about leaving Kitzie. He felt he had to tell her why. He felt the loss of her intently and couldn't resolve it. He made the decision to go back, talked himself out of it, and drove on.

After some distance was behind him, the front end of a familiar motorhome nosed into traffic. Shiloh was determined to leave the area and was headed to Bunny and Lonson's Redoubt. She needed to mine their knowledge about the unexpected windfall she now had access to—Bodie's ill-gotten bitcoin gain. Bunny and Lonson said they would sell her a plot, get her set up, and watch her back, and she believed them. But were they far enough away from Martin?

Cars pulled onto and off the highway and the gap between

the camper and the motorhome grew smaller.

Larry Stiles could hear the highway breathing, or in his distracted state, he thought so, until steam coming out from under the hood intruded. He didn't need to look at the temperature gauge and immediately pulled over. He knew he had a problem—he knew he had several—and the truck was sending him the next part of the message: *You must stop. You have to look a bad thing in the eye and break the spell.* When he popped the hood, steam cascaded into the air and he stepped back until it dissipated.

Less than a mile away, the motorhome bore down on his location. A short line of cars was caught behind Shiloh and she knew they were anxious to pass. She would be more than happy to let them as soon as a decent pull-out presented itself. A sign said one was coming and she slowed to give them the road. But as she neared it, she saw that somebody was broken down smack in the middle of it. Some camper thing and it looked to be smoking. Or maybe that was steam? *What the fuck,* she thought, then realized she couldn't make it so she accelerated and kept going. In the rearview mirror, she saw a man bent over the engine but didn't think any more of it.

Chapter 71

Spence drove to the station early in the morning and parked his truck around the side. He strolled to his locker and changed into his uniform, opting to keep his black turtleneck shirt on underneath as it was quite cold out. As he hung up his jacket, he looked down at the five-gallon plastic bucket—the only one that had survived intact—that had held the jewelry, money, and guns. He had taken everything he'd collected—the bulletproof vests, as much jewelry as they could find, and all the weapons—and secured them in the evidence safe. He had a lot of paperwork ahead of him.

The square mirror in the office didn't accommodate his full frame and he ducked in and up to be sure he looked his best. Spence cared about the uniform in a way that bore him the kind of pride his father had instilled in him. His father believed in polished brass, shined shoes, and a clean, pressed uniform. It was a holdover from his military days and as a young man, Spence would sit and observe him as he prepared for his watch.

As his father left the house, he would tap the top of his cap on his son's head. Sort of bounce it off his noggin. As he got older, Spence mistook the repeated action differently and his mother had set him to rights.

"Your father needs luck like some men need air. He has a ritual that he adheres to because he believes it will bring him back to us safely every day at shift's end. That tap of the cap is the last part, the most important part, of his ritual. You are his good luck."

The memory made Spence smile and he bent low to see his reflection, smoothed his hair, and saw his father's eyes smiling back at him. He tipped his cap to the mirror and mumbled some words to his father that someday, he would have a small noggin to tap the cap on.

He didn't turn on all the lights in the front office, just his desk lamp in his small, windowless office near the locker room. The message light on his phone was blinking. He caught the messages on a pad. He liked pen and paper, and he always had a supply of sticky notes in his drawer.

A few minutes later, Spence was out the side door and around the corner to where his patrol car was parked. The windows were frosty but he felt good about the new rear window and admired the job the garage had done, though he needed to get in there with the vacuum because he saw bits of glass sparkling on the back seat.

He started the car to warm it up, then slipped back into the building through a cloud of exhaust. It was colder out than he thought, and it was like walking through a fog.

Mason was startled awake when his father smacked his arm.

With gun in hand, Denny ordered, "Let's go," and got out of the car.

His father was faster than he was, and carrying the heavy crowbar unbalanced Mason. He had never been athletic and ran like a girl. Denny had really worked out in prison, Mason thought as his father hissed at him to keep up.

They came at the idling patrol car from the passenger's side and as he ran, Denny crouched and scanned the empty parking lot. It was still dark out and the condensation on the windows hadn't cleared. But Denny didn't wait. He stopped, raised the gun, and pumped several shots into the car, aimed at the driver's side.

Denny barked at Mason to jimmy the trunk and see if their shit was there. He lowered the gun a little and kept his focus on the car, then glanced at the building with plans to get in there and find their stuff if it wasn't.

Jimmying the trunk with the crowbar was harder than Mason thought it would be. As he struggled, it crossed his mind that he hadn't asked why they were looking in the trunk at all—their stuff wasn't there when they had broken into it before. But his father thought that it made sense, and who was Mason to argue?

"Dammit, open it!" Denny yelled and started toward him as it sprang open and Mason was lost from view. There was a strange thud and Mason crumpled to the ground near the back bumper.

"What are you doing?" Denny asked and slid sideways to get a look. He saw Mason's feet and the corner of the car. A disgusted look crossed Denny's face. His first thought was that Mason had slipped and fallen. "For shit's sake, you moron, get up." And that was as far as he got.

A voice ordered him to drop the gun and Denny spun and fired blind. The bullet destroyed the side mirror on the passenger's side of the patrol car. The next shot caught Denny square in the chest. He flew backward and was dead when he hit the ground.

Spence's shoes crunched on the pebbled asphalt as he cautiously crouched and approached the body. He reached for the rifle first and picked it up. The muzzle of his gun never left its target and Spence called for the kid to come out from behind the cruiser.

Spence went wide around Denny's head, more convinced with each second that Denny was dead. He started to check around the back of the patrol car. Its trunk lid was still up. He stepped back and trained his gun on Denny, then at the back of the patrol car. When he got to where he could see, the billowing exhaust cloud lessened and wisped through the increasing light of dawn.

The crowbar lay there, abandoned, but the skinny kid was nowhere to be seen. There was quite a bit of blood on a spot on the ground. Spence trained his gun around in a circle but nothing came at him. He kicked the crowbar under the car with his toe, bent down, and touched wet blood. He scanned around him again and then called for help.

Hours later, when Spence read the file, he learned that they were from Redmond and the elder of the two had been out of prison less than a year. He discovered that almost five years earlier, they had robbed a jewelry store in Redmond. They had forced their way into the store while a customer was there, were armed, and wore bulletproof vests. The owner and customer were forced to the floor and they stole a hundred thousand dollars' worth of jewelry. They were caught and the naïve district attorney in charge of the case had pleaded the pair down to a sentence of four years in exchange for the return of the jewelry, plus a sentence reduction from armed robbery to a lesser charge that omitted the brandishing of weapons.

"What a sweet deal," Spence murmured, considering that

both had a track record for multiple offenses. Spence was astonished to learn that the jewelry was never returned or recovered, and that the DA's notes revealed he had told the store owner that the deal was a good one for him because he could pursue them for damages once they'd served their time.

    Spence read the reports twice and sat back in his worn chair, incredulous. "You've got to be kidding."

Chapter 72

CJ watched the colt's head nod sleepily in the straw. The mare stood next to him, hind leg cocked, head drooped, half asleep. CJ smiled. His heart melted each time he watched him. A smattering of raindrops fell on the roof of the barn and he looked up into the cupola. The owl watched him and the sounds of the barn were soothing and calm.

CJ walked to the barn doors as the rain increased. Without wind, it fell straight, and the coolness of the air felt wonderful on his skin. He closed his eyes and listened to the orchestral sounds of small, misty raindrops as they fell on the plants and surfaces nearby. Larger drops built momentum and the droplets sounded deeper as surfaces resonated to their beat. A few minutes into the symphony, accumulated roof rain trickled through downspouts, ting-tinged at the bottom, and added another layer of depth to the music. The crescendo of the musical performance ebbed as the squall moved through and was replaced with a brilliance that turned pupils to pinpricks while clinging droplets sparkled and danced.

CJ was at peace. There were no demons trying to chase him away. Despair had taken him in when he had nowhere to go but now all that had changed. He returned to the stall door and gazed at the colt, whose heavy-lidded eyes found him. They watched each other for a long moment until gravity won and the foal's head nestled back into the straw. His right front leg stretched out with a tiny shiver before tucking back in. CJ felt the love that Rio had given him being renewed.

His fatigue returned and he headed toward the stairs for a bit of rest. Another gentle wave of weather found the roof and CJ hesitated when he caught movement out of the corner of his eye. Carson, who was walking to the barn from the house, stopped and looked up as the drops found her face. He stood in the shadows, unnoticed, and watched her. Childlike, she opened her mouth to taste the rain. She lifted her arms and spun in circles, her boots stirring the damp dirt.

Tears from heaven bade the ash to become ground and raindrops willed what remained of the fires to become part of the land again and heal. The wind owned the fire and the two had possessed the country for weeks. The fires had burned away the parts of people that didn't matter and left those who had nothing to start over with even less. Yet they remained.

CJ found himself halfway to her. Rain dotted his shirt and found his face and hair. He reached out his arms in a dancer's pose and waited until Carson's rotation lined her up perfectly. She was startled when he caught her outstretched hand and smoothly led her into a two-step to music that no one could hear. It was something long forgotten, yet returned in an instant, and Carson followed effortlessly. The ease of it astonished her and she let CJ move her around in the dirt of the drive, the rain making quick work of connecting the damp dots on their clothes.

CJ's eyes left her face and he led her on the driveway dance floor to an older country tune he began to hum. He stepped expertly and gently turned her in a single spin to the beat of the rain, then guided her into a turn and changed directions.

CJ looked down at Carson as she looked up into his face.

He felt that his fall through time and space had stalled, that he had new ground beneath his feet, and he stood taller. He remembered another dance move and almost managed to lead it. It crumbled a bit and he looked at Carson, half expecting a critical look. But instead, she giggled and winged the bobble into an entirely acceptable mistake that they both finished well.

CJ let her go, stepped back, and looked at the ground. He brushed the top of his hair with a hand and wet droplets flew as he wiped the rain from his face. Carson stood, rooted, and watched him. Neither said a word. The moment hung in the rain that fell between them.

A huge drop, well aimed, plopped onto Carson's forehead and startled her. CJ smiled. A real smile on CJ was quite a wonder to see and it caught Carson by surprise. The drop held in place for a second, then started its gravitational path down her face. CJ stepped in closer and with a finger, gently stopped it at Carson's eyebrow, redirected it around her eye, and onto the back of his hand. Neither moved or spoke.

Carson saw the line of his mouth, his well-shaped nose, and the hazel eyes that stared into hers, just inches away. She felt awkward for a second and dropped her eyes to his chin. There was a small dimple there she hadn't noticed before and without thinking, she reached up and her index finger gently found it. He watched the wisp of a frown pass over her brow and his smile deepened at the feel of her touch, tinged with the amusing notion that she was discovering his face for the first time.

Carson looked up again and her lips—those remarkable lips—parted with a question and an answer inside. CJ grinned like a child and leaned down close and kissed her. He felt the sharp intake of breath, the millisecond of indecision, then the returned pressure of their first kiss. He opened his eyes and saw her lashes meeting the shadow of her cheekbones—those lashes that were naturally curled and unadorned, the skin that was perfect and wet from the rain—and he pulled back a few inches to take all of her into his forever memory.

Their eyes locked. When CJ smiled, his whole face was different, and his long brown hair waved from the center and cascaded around his face. Carson shook her head in amazement and planted her forehead on his chest, letting out a sigh of relief and release like she was breathing for the first time in a long while. CJ brought his hands up and cradled her head. Tilting it up to face his, he kissed her again more deeply. Their lips worked well together and both liked what they found, their rhythm and timing easy and well matched.

The rain slowed and they were soaked. Carson shuddered and CJ wrapped his arms around her. The horses called out to let them know it was close to feeding time, so they hurried back into the barn. CJ disappeared upstairs, then returned with two towels.

"Those are your only ones," Carson said with a smile.

"Yeah, I know."

He smiled back as he brought a towel around her shoulders and up onto her hair. His hands smoothed the terrycloth in an attempt to absorb the dampness, then he used the towel to draw her to him and kissed her again. The intensity increased and Carson pushed him gently against the door to the upstairs room—not to go up, just to kiss him properly back—and he responded. CJ leaned against the door and wrapped his arms tightly around her. He rested his chin on her head and glanced up into the rafters of the barn. The owl stared down at him with those all-knowing eyes. Then it winked at him, fluffed its feathers, closed both eyes, and went to sleep. CJ laughed. Carson pulled away and looked at him. "What?"

"See our friend up there?" He pointed to the rafters.

She nodded.

"He just winked at me, at us, and then closed his eyes. It was probably nothing but it was the way he did it...like he was saying 'about time.'"

Carson tipped her head at the sound of a nicker from a stall. "I suppose it's about that time. Reality calls," she said.

He touched her chin, lifted it once more, and kissed her gently. "Reality can call all it wants. It'll never be the same again."

They began feeding and when CJ wasn't looking, Carson surreptitiously glanced at her phone. They were almost done when the sound of an engine neither of them recognized intruded and they stepped in tandem to the big barn doors. They laughed at their sudden awkwardness and both found their self-consciousness amusing. Carson and CJ peered out the doors to see a rig they didn't know haul in and make the circle past the house. The driver was a girl and there was a woman passenger.

Carson tried not to give it away as she waved them over, and as they came even to her, the passenger rolled her window down and asked, "Are we at the Three Bit Ranch?"

Carson winked and asked if they were lost. The woman looked at the girl who was driving and they grinned at each other. It seemed that the long drive had made a friendship.

The woman grabbed a camera bag, looked up at the clearing sky, and held up a finger. "Give me a second. I have to get this out, hold on..."

She got her Nikon camera and took the lens cap off.

Carson looked at it and complimented her. "I used to have one of those. It was in the house..." and she crooked a thumb at the new structure.

"Oh, that is a shame. I love this camera. It puts up with everything." The reporter laughed. "It puts up with me!"

CJ held back just inside the barn doors, unsure if he was any party to this. The woman got out of the truck, introduced herself to Carson, and handed her a card. CJ missed the first part but caught a last name.

The reporter craned her head to look around Carson and caught a glimpse of CJ standing in the shadow of the barn door. A smile started at the edges of her mouth and she quickly lifted the camera and snapped his picture before he could object or realize what she was doing. His taciturn face on, he edged back into the shadows, out of the lens's range. She turned back to Carson and her eyebrows went up in admiration—the universal sign between women that he was hot.

"Sorry," she said, and stepped around Carson, who was still eyeing the card. Janine leaned over and motioned to Carson. Carson stuck her head half in the truck and they began speaking quietly.

The woman approached CJ, stood too close, and he backed away uncomfortably. "Please tell me you are CJ."

He raised his eyebrows, then squinted. He hesitated to say yes or no until he knew what the hell was going on.

Carson had turned away from the quiet conversation in the cab of the truck and now watched CJ closely. The driver's side door opened and closed, followed by the sound of the back of the trailer being opened. An animal shifted its position inside and stomped a foot.

The woman moved quickly away from CJ to the back of

the trailer and disappeared behind it. Without a word, Carson followed her, her head cocked as if to see around the corner. CJ was out of the barn right behind her, his curiosity getting the better of him. The trailer's solid swing door opened the opposite way, so they didn't see what was being led out of the trailer until they cleared the length of the door.

Whinnies came from one of the hungry horses in the barn and that was followed by a response from behind the door.

For a second, CJ checked himself, froze in place, his heart stopped, and his eyes went wide. He didn't remember dashing around the back of the trailer or Carson and she wasn't offended when he almost body blocked her to the ground in his haste.

Rio stepped carefully out of the three-horse slant load as CJ rounded the door. The reporter's camera fired away. CJ's face was a mixture of every emotion one could feel. Rio pulled at the loose rope around his neck to get to him.

A strangled cry from somewhere deep inside him preceded CJ's face finding an undamaged part of Rio and hiding it there. What followed was a silence that was pierced only by the sounds from a broken heart.

Carson moved over next to CJ and the girl handed her the rope. Carson touched CJ's back and felt a shudder. He pressed his forehead against Rio's face where the thick riot of red forelock used to be, and was overcome. His mouth was open, gasping as there was no air in the outside world. What air there was swirled like a twister around the man and his horse.

The reporter felt intrusive but it was the story she had come to tell. They had come all this way, Rio's journey and CJ's the farthest of all. Reluctantly, she backed off when Janine gently touched her arm and they withdrew to a discreet distance so CJ could have some space. Carson found his hand and slid the rope into it. Out of the corner of her eye, she saw her mother come around the corner of the barn.

Kitzie stopped when she saw what was happening. Her hand went up and covered her mouth and she started to cry at what she witnessed. The reporter continued to do her job, getting shots of everything as she wiped away tears. She took photos of mother and daughter hugging and crying, and Kitzie grabbing Janine in a bear hug. There was a cute shot of the three women, Carson, Janine, and Kitzie. Then she stepped to where she could snap some frames of CJ as he and Rio stood together at the trailer.

The day sparkled around them, the air cleansed. Rio planted his forehead into CJ's chest and both had their eyes closed. As CJ lifted his chin to the heavens, he mouthed, *Thank you...*

Goosebumps ran over the reporter's skin in little waves as she captured an indelible moment for an amazing story.

Chapter 73

Rio would take a long time to heal and Janine spent the afternoon conferring with CJ and the Collins women. They learned how Janine had met Rio, how she had done things she didn't know she could do to stabilize him, and that her father was very proud of how she had managed a difficult situation.

That evening, Kitzie retired early to the trailer, and when she awoke a few hours later, she noticed that Carson hadn't come in and she didn't see her until the next morning. There was a definite glow on her daughter and Kitzie knew that something special was happening. But Kitzie was distracted and upset. Her heart and mind had been arguing for days. Every time she walked around the home she would soon live in, she felt confused and bewildered. She missed him, which added kindling to the fire that gnawed at her belly. At times, she was so upset, her hands shook and she gripped them together to still them.

There was a stool in the open-floor-plan kitchen and great room area and Kitzie found herself there at the end of the day wondering what had happened. The more she wandered around the house, the more she felt it needed him to finish it. The roofers had come and knocked that out quickly, in a couple of days. Gutters…she had to get gutters, or so she had been told. But she didn't care about gutters. She cared about him.

The roofers had offered a referral and she was grateful, but there was still more to do inside before the winter set in, and they were running out of time.

She and Carson had talked about finding another contractor but there were none available. Everyone was booked months, if not years, out. And Kitzie had grown accustomed to a certain level of quality. Where would they find someone who cared like that? Stiles had been gone for less than a week but it felt like much longer.

After dinner, Carson helped her mother wade through more paperwork. Kitzie's organizational behavior left a little to be desired and Carson attempted to sort it out. She had her organization system spread out on the stove. The gas range had a stainless-steel top that fit over the burners and it made for a clean workspace, complete with its own little light.

"I wish I understood why he just left without saying anything," Kitzie blurted, then punched a key on the laptop keyboard, frustrated over something not happening on the screen.

"Hey, it doesn't like that. Be patient," Carson said with her back to her mother.

"Shit. You sound like me, say, a dozen years ago…" Kitzie's voice trailed off.

Carson turned to see why there was silence behind her. Kitzie had her face in her hands and was trying not to cry. She looked up and there was an ocean in her eyes.

"Hey, hey…" Carson put the sheaf of papers down and went over to her. "What's eating at you?"

Kitzie's frustration was etched into her face and she wiped a tear away. "It's hard to explain. I've been trying to get it, you know?"

Her frustration with Stiles was genuine but Carson got a

whiff that it might be something more.

Kitzie rested her chin on her fist. "It's like when you lose someone, it changes how you look at the world. I felt that need for someone had left me..." She looked embarrassed. "Certain...I was certain it was done. I didn't expect that it would find me again." She acted like she shouldn't have said it and tried to brush it off as silly. "I thought I would be alone. I never thought of it any other way."

Carson shared with Kitzie about Stiles and his daughter. Kitzie listened quietly. She was curious about what had sparked that conversation and asked Carson about it.

Carson said, "The painting..." She shrugged. The secret was out. "We wanted to surprise you. Come on, I'll show you."

They left the trailer and headed for the house. Carson flipped on an overhead light and motioned for Kitzie to wait in the kitchen area, then crossed the room to a stack of sheetrock leaning against the far wall. Kitzie watched Carson slide a wrapped bundle out from behind it and raised her eyebrows as Carson carried it to the kitchen and leaned it against the island. As Carson unwrapped it and the painting was revealed, Kitzie was silent, her hand over her mouth, stunned. Her mind played with memories.

It was Carson's turn to feel awkward. "We ran out of time, I guess. I showed this to him so he could hang it as a surprise for you." She hesitated. "He was doing a wall especially for it...said something about light and lighting..." She looked around the room. "Anyway, we had a moment and he talked about her."

Kitzie was quiet for a moment as she stared at the painting. Then she smiled. "Let's try to figure out which wall he was thinking of..."

A few days later, Kitzie sat on a stool in her new kitchen, looking out the window at the mountains beyond. She rested her forehead on the coolness of the counter. The silence of the house was strange to her, although she wasn't sure what sounds she imagined would fill it. She had been so overwhelmed that the feel of it as a home hadn't begun to develop. Kitzie lifted her head and slouched, elbow on the counter and her head propped up with it. She imagined that her posture was awful, yet she didn't have the will to straighten up. She decided that gravity was winning.

Annoyed with her wallowing, Kitzie pushed herself off of the stool and thought it was time to go. She turned and saw him standing in the open doorway. She never heard a footfall on the porch. Light from the setting sun glanced against the side of her face, still as a picture and as unreal as a midnight dream. She was both furious and relieved instantaneously, and her lips moved without sound until exasperation won out and she angrily exclaimed, "What the hell happened to you?"

Stiles hesitated. A shade of fear crossed his face and he looked down to momentarily find relief from her stare. Then he removed his hat, inhaled, and his gaze rose to meet hers.

"You," he answered plainly.

That wasn't the answer Kitzie expected and she stared at him for a moment.

Stiles stepped inside and went to the window. In the distance, huge mountains held the weight of the sky. He reached to the molding and ran his hand along the seamless joints. It had turned out exactly as he wanted it to. The air in the room was still and he felt her eyes on his back. He knew that he had to tell her everything, hold nothing back, and with a leaden feeling, Stiles knew things would change between them as suddenly as the wind when he did.

He held there. "If what I have to tell you alters how you feel, I will accept it and won't trouble you again." He turned and faced her. "Have you ever felt like your entire life has been distilled into a few short moments?" He looked toward the door. "Please say no."

Kitzie started to say something, shook her head instead, and said abruptly, "I can't."

He pointed her back to the stool. She took it, then looked down at her hands clasped tightly in her lap. She felt him close, saw the tips of his dusty boots near hers. His fingers tipped her chin up and without hesitation, he kissed her beautiful mouth.

"We shouldn't..." she tried, and he kissed her again.

His face close to hers, their eyes locked together, and he replied, "We both can't." His eyes smiled and Kitzie softened. "The time is now. It's maybe our last chance. How much of it do we take?"

She slid off the edge of the stool to her feet and put her arms around his neck. "All of it."

His hat fell to the hardwood floor and stayed there.

Their passion was intense and at the edge of the sensual cliff they were on, both were willing to leap off. Stiles held her body close to his and smelled her hair, felt her skin beneath his fingers.

"Wait," he said. "Oh, God, please forgive me." He took a gentle hold of her shoulders. He didn't want this to go too far before he told her what he had come back to say.

Kitzie's eyes were cloudy and unfocused. She was

absolutely beautiful and he didn't regret coming back. He wished he wasn't who he was, that he hadn't done the things he had done. But he forged ahead anyway. He had to and whatever came of it, he would make peace with his past as best he could. It would start right there.

"Why did you come back?" she whispered.

Eyes closed, he put his forehead to hers and whispered back, "To spend another hour in your eyes." He straightened, then half turned away, obviously in distress with himself. After a long pause, Stiles made the decision and said, "I have to tell you that I'm hopelessly in love with you. Whatever happens," and he turned his head and looked into her eyes again, "that will never change."

She withdrew into silence and sat back down as he paced before her…and told him everything.

Carson had Wyatt and was heading to the house. She saw her mother through the window, sitting at the kitchen island. The angle changed and she froze. She called Wyatt back to her side, took a few steps backward, then stopped, her eyes glued to the other figure in the room. Visible in one window, then the next, back and forth, he paced. At times, Stiles looked like a coiled spring unloading something heavy. Then he would stop, put his hand to his forehead, and rub his eyes as if he wanted to erase something if he could. Carson wanted to retreat and leave them to their privacy.

"Do you think you've seen enough?"

Carson jumped and Wyatt wiggled around CJ's legs.

"Shit!" She bent over to still her racing heart. "Gawd, don't do that."

CJ laughed and winced. "Come on, whatever that is..." He nodded toward the house. "...it's private. Let's go."

"But..." Carson looked back toward the house.

"No buts. Walk this way," CJ insisted gently.

Chapter 74

Rain had chased her, overrun her, and she had just gotten used to it. Rae arrived late morning with her truck and trailer and the sun came out. Three other rigs were already on-site with a veterinarian, who was evaluating horses. It was controlled chaos. She located the vet and the vice president of the group, Mary, near the trailers and they were working on a sedated horse. The survivors of the shooting party were being treated as best as everyone could manage. They were working on a stud colt that had deep, infected lacerations and the story of getting him settled to work on him was colorful. Not only had they sedated him but they hobbled him as well. Mary showed Rae an angry swelling on her shin.

"Jesus! It's not broken, is it?" Rae asked her.

From the other side of the colt, a head popped up and Rae smiled broadly at the vet—a handsome, younger man with a wild shock of red hair protruding from under his baseball cap, which had the rescue group's logo on it. He had surgical gloves on and was holding suture materials as he prepared to sew up one of the colt's lacerations.

"Nope," he joked. "But it's gonna be hella sore."

Mary shrugged. "It's far from my heart and I think I'll live."

He grinned. "Got some juicy maggots over here. Hungry, Rae?"

Rae made a face and stuck out her tongue. "Thanks, but I

already ate."

Mary added, "The things we do for horses."

"No shit," Rae replied. "Nice hat," she said to the vet.

He nodded. "Show Rae our oddball," he added without looking up.

"Oh, yeah. This'll blow your mind." Mary led the way around the four-horse fifth-wheel rigs to an area of portable panel paddocks.

"Good God…they were gonna shoot all of these?" Rae asked incredulously.

"Seems so. Your dad was around here earlier and said he'd be back."

The mustangs were easily discernable as wild stock and there were mares, foals, and yearlings in the one paddock. Rae scanned for the stallion and looked at Mary questioningly.

"He was too severely injured. His leg." Mary bent her index finger to indicate that the leg was broken. "Amazing that he was still protecting his herd, hurt like that. He was dead when we arrived. I think it was your dad who put him down. He's a good shot, your dad."

"He always was," Rae replied.

From the back of the group, Rae spied a horse that was noticeably taller than the others and definitely was not a mustang.

"Holy shit," Rae blurted. "What is that?"

They walked around the pen to the side where he was. His big, dark eyes followed them and as Rae took in the full measure of him, she noted how thin and emaciated he was. His feet were terrible and his coat was dull and worn down to raw skin in places. There was no mistaking it though, this was a Thoroughbred. The dusky dirt on his coat made one guess that he was dark-colored, maybe black, and he towered over his reluctant companions. He stood as separate from them as he could, and they pinned their ears at him, so the feeling was mutual.

Rae and Mary leaned against the panel and he took a couple of steps toward them. He was off in front. Rae guessed front left.

"Abscess?" she asked.

Mary replied, "We think so. We were waiting for you. He's not like the others."

Rae laughed.

Mary handed Rae a halter and Rae went into the pen and approached the gelding. He smelled her hand and she moved to his left side slowly but confidently. The other horses shied and bunched as far away from her as they could get. Still, Mary watched Rae's back as Rae slipped the right side of the halter around the horse's neck and flipped the strap over. She applied a soft but steady pressure and the gelding released and lowered his head. *Yes*, Rae thought, *he has history.*

She fastened the halter and felt to make sure it wasn't too snug. She stroked the side of his face. His head stayed low and his eyes half-closed, then he leaned gently against her. It was as if he was saying, "Thank you, I need your help."

Rae moved forward and the gelding came with her easily, despite the fact that he was tender-footed. It was an uneventful, limpy walk out of the pen and over to where the vet was.

Rae examined him more than the vet did. They were side by side so she conferred with him as she applied pressure with the hoof testers. The tenderness confirmed her suspicion of an abscess and Rae used her cell to call the farrier. They agreed that she should bring the horse to the barn where she kept Docket, and he'd meet her there. To make the trailer ride more comfortable, the vet administered a mild pain killer in a dose approximate to the drive.

The gelding loaded into Rae's trailer and was secured for the ride. There were hugs and fond farewells and Mary followed her and closed the driver's side door. The window was open and Mary leaned on the sill.

"What an amazing day this has been."

Rae nodded and smiled. "I've got this. And with what we know, I'll start working on everything tomorrow."

"You're not going back to the firm?" Mary asked.

"Hell no. The mustangs need a lawyer."

"I don't think you have that quite right."

"Close enough. We'll give those bastards a good fight."

Mary gently slapped her palms on the sill and smiled her thank you. "God bless." There was a moistness in her eyes as she stepped back from the truck and Rae put it into gear.

Rae started off gently and as she approached the highway, did the same with a slow stop. The gelding didn't scramble or kick. She negotiated the turn and listened to the sound of the V8 motor propel the rig smoothly to speed while she shifted through the gears.

Rae thought of her father and how he'd taught her how to drive a manual because no one needed a lesson to drive an automatic. She slipped it into fifth gear and hit her high beams, keeping an eye out for the reflection of eyeshine in the dark. Aside from the soothing hum of the motor, there were no other sounds but the wind. Rae was aware of the sky and stars that shone brightly in the pitch black, and calculated that it might be a later night than she had anticipated when this day had started.

There was a soft look of satisfaction on Rae's face. She

pondered that the work she embraced somehow gave her a new mission, a new passion. That was it—her passion was back. She hadn't noticed she had lost it. She was ready to fight for something important, not a hobby or some frivolous cause. The legal battle would save lives and require new strategies. She'd have to research legal positions, and most importantly, find the funding to carry this adventure to success. This invigorated Rae's thinking in ways she hadn't considered since law school. She felt her cleverness shake itself from the dark recesses and dispel her melancholy.

When she made the last turn into the barn and saw the parking lights of her shoer's dually, there was a bold new Rae inside ready for a fight.

Once they were set up, Rae medicated the gelding so that relieving the hoof abscess wouldn't bother him. The farrier went to work and when he was done, the black gelding's head hung low and the lead rope was swung over his back. The farrier told Rae that with some care, this would be a very nice horse.

Rae adored her shoer. They'd been friends for years and Docket loved him. He made every horse he worked on better. She told him the story and he shook his head and said something about weird small worlds.

"How the hell did he end up there?" He put his tools away and closed the back of his rig. "I didn't look, but is he tattooed?"

They looked inside the horse's upper lip and Rae scribbled the number on a scrap of something she found and put it in her pocket.

The gelding managed the drunk walk to a box stall Rae made ready for him and entered it as if he'd been there his whole life. The large wrap on his foot was finished with a child's disposable diaper, held together with duct tape, and would stay on until it was time for Rae to change it out for a new one. It would take a while for the hoof the farrier had dug out to grow back and Rae knew what to do for the best outcome, so he skipped the instructions. After all, this wasn't her first rodeo.

They watched the gelding through the metal bars of the sliding stall door.

"What a story he must have," the farrier said as he turned and headed to the truck with a goodnight wave.

Rae hung with the gelding for a little longer, the stall's light the only illumination in the long breezeway. She decided to sleep in the quarters of her fifth-wheel trailer. It was already set up and quite comfy. She would be up early to check on him and feed the whole barn. She texted the barn's owner and informed him so that everyone could sleep in in the morning.

Rae had no trouble falling asleep curled up and cozy in the trailer but sometime in the middle of the night, she awoke with a start. It took a minute to get her bearings. Sweat beaded her forehead and she edged herself out of the bed and climbed down to the floor. She used her bathroom and instead of climbing back up to bed, stopped at the door and opened it, leaving the screen door ajar to share its cool air with her. She sat on the sofa and looked out into the night and heard coyotes calling off in the distance. The ranch where she kept Docket was framed by low hills and the coyotes were calling to each other from opposite sides.

There was a sense of a shadow of the dream she'd been having when she awoke. It was uncomfortable. She had this scene in her mind of a horse trailer, one she didn't know, driving away. She was a little girl and was running down a rough gravel road, crying, screaming at it to stop, and watching it disappear. Tears of grief rolled down her cheeks as she pictured the beloved horse that had mysteriously disappeared a lifetime ago. The dream represented an unanswered prayer—the gnawing angst of no answers, no explanations, and her first experience of doing everything right and still losing.

She leaned her head back against the sofa and clenched the rest of the tears from her eyes. She opened them slowly and stared up at the light fixture above her head. She frowned and slowly sat up as a memory dawned on her.

Holy shit, she thought. *What if...* Rae shook off the thought with a rational, "No...it couldn't be." Then she sat up straight on the edge of the sofa. *But...what if?* She stood, wide awake, and searched her mind for where she had stashed the files that she had taken with her when she left.

"Oh, my God," she said out loud. "They're here..."

She slid a door aside to reveal the boxes in a storage area under the step up to her bed. The file boxes barely fit and they were wicked to her fingers to squeeze them out.

"Where...where is it..." she muttered as she shuffled through the boxes.

Dawn glowed on the paneled wood of the kitchenette. Rae had just about given up finding the file and she needed to go feed as she had promised. The files were scattered all over and would take some time to make right but she didn't care. In no time, she was in her boots and jeans and feeding the barn. When she got to the gelding, his kind, dark eyes followed her every move and he nickered softly as she slid the bolt to the feeder door and he walked the short span to the grass hay she placed in the rack. She would double-check the information from the file and compare it to the tattoo on his upper lip. But she'd seen the pictures and the warmth of recognition flushed over her, and she called him by his name.

Chapter 75

Early morning frost glittered on the fence posts. A blurry moon threw blue shadows on the pastures and fall leaves heralded the change in seasons.

It was a time of accumulating knowledge for Carson. Time to learn the business of the ranch, to understand how to gamble with nature, maybe break even, and maybe win. It was a time of change, of possibilities; time to make plans and to forge a way into the future. A time of learning and growing, and of team-building.

The weather worsened. Breaths puffed white in the icy air. Cold wind and snow flurries swirled in the warm light of the window. Inside Kitzie's new house, a beautiful Christmas tree could be seen and smiling faces enjoyed holiday meals. The gray, wintry wind beat the windows and cast a muted light on a large painting of a young girl and her horse on the great room wall. Soft, recessed lighting accented the room and glistened on the granite counter island, and the pellet stove radiated warmth.

Winter melted into the spring thaw, which poured across Three Corner country and its thunderstorms and changing weather swept over the ranch. A winter hare hopped through the rain and hurried to a den. Grasses renewed by the ash, encouraged by the moisture of rain and snow, found new sky to reach for. The earth replenished with the enthusiasm of renewal, spring calvings, and all manner of things made new.

The strongly built wraparound porch provided shade from the summer's heat. Outdoor furniture graced the side of the house with plump cushions that invited one to linger and enjoy the view. A tree had been given a place in the center of the parking area, along with a bit of grass, some pavers, a couple of Adirondack chairs, and a table tucked nearby. The promise of years could see the tree grow to considerable size that would cast a cooling pool of shade underneath. An owl called and another responded like an echo—the sounds of a summer's evening.

Carson found herself liking her life at the Three Bit more than she ever had. Kitzie appreciated that her daughter had qualities that had come late…but only too late for one of her parents. They found themselves united in a dream. His dream was theirs now. The Three Bit had survived economic threats, fire, and they were united in its continuity. They did more than understand each other, they shared common goals.

As Carson and Kitzie sat together in the kitchen, Carson looked at her mother and thanked her for loving her when she felt unlovable. Silently, she wondered how she had ever paused to question that. Talking about the past was seamed with memories as mother and daughter spent quiet time together getting ready, doing each other's hair.

Delicate local wildflowers scattered a pattern on the kitchen table after a night's work fashioning the wedding flowers. There were flowers in their hair. There was music playing—Carson's McGraw and Hill selections. The women didn't talk much. They didn't need to.

Carson finished the touches on her mother's hair and rested her hands on Kitzie's shoulders. Mother and daughter looked at each other in the mirror. Kitzie reached up and placed her hand on her daughter's.

"I'm so glad you came back. I've been afraid to tell you in case you were leaving again." She paused and smiled up at her in the mirror and Carson smiled back as she leaned down and hugged her mom.

Kitzie added, "Your father would be so proud of you."

"Argh, Mom! Don't make me cry." Carson looked up at the ceiling and fanned her hands to quell the urge. It didn't work. Then she saw tears in her mother's eyes. "Guess we both have to fix our mascara," she said and handed Kitzie a tissue.

Kitzie laughed. "I'm so glad you're here. I hardly know how to anymore."

Carson straightened. "OK, 'nough of that. We have to go." She took the towel off her mother's shoulders to reveal a lovely, cream-colored Western-cut shirt embellished with subtle flowers and sparkling rhinestones. It matched her complexion beautifully. The shirt was tucked into dark-brown, bootcut riding jeans and her fancy white Dan Post boots peeked out from underneath. Kitzie checked her delicate diamond earrings in the mirror.

"Are those the ones Dad gave you?" Carson asked.

Kitzie nodded. "I haven't worn them in years, and I don't want to lose one out there. Would you please check that I have them on securely?"

Carson checked them and nodded that they were OK.

Her mother hugged her and whispered in her ear, "It's going to be a beautiful day."

They walked to the barn, where the horses were saddled and waiting. Both were snoozing, their back legs cocked in a relaxed way. Carson had thoroughly groomed them the night before and even put a sheet on both to keep them clean. Sleep had eluded her and she had gone down early and braided ribbons and flowers into manes and tails. She was quite gifted at this and they looked amazing.

They mounted up and rode out together. As they went through the big pasture, they made a brief detour to the place where the stud was buried and Tuff's ashes had been scattered. It was awash in flowers and Kitzie audibly gasped when she saw it.

"How did *that* happen?" she said, mostly to herself.

Carson reached over and took her mother's hand. "It was Larry's idea...and I helped."

Kitzie was speechless. She dismounted, handed the reins to her daughter, and stepped to the place where she had scattered the ashes, now a riot of color. She needed a moment to do something she hadn't done since the day she'd said "I do" to the man she'd loved with all her being. She knelt, her back to her daughter. Carson felt her eyes well up. Then Kitzie stood. She spied something in the flowers and bent down to pick it up. It was a package wrapped in a kerchief. She unfolded it and found a brand-new paperback dictionary inside.

She looked at Carson and said, "What an odd thing..."

A note was tucked inside. Kitzie unfolded it, read it, and smiled. She thumbed through the pages and looked up at Carson, covered her mouth, and held back the emotion that would have smudged her make-up. She handed it up to Carson, who held it for her as Kitzie took the reins and mounted her horse.

Carson opened the cover and read the note. She leafed through the entire dictionary and saw lots of yellow highlights. She re-read the handwritten note. *"The things I will always do, with love, for you,"* she read aloud softly. "Wow."

They sat side by side and the horses stood quietly. Kitzie bowed her head, then cast a sideways glance at her daughter. Carson did the same. They sat on their horses and enjoyed a moment of silent reflection.

An Oregon swallowtail lit on a flower and from its vantage point, long tails brushed the high grass after hooved feet had parted it. The flowers braided into their tails moved to the rhythm of motion and a path of strewn petals showed them the way.

Carson looked back at the memorial. She wished she could talk to him, ask his advice, and confer with him. She had withheld a bit of information from everyone. She needed more time to adjust to her new financial realities before she revealed her secret.

They rode at a walk for many minutes, a gentle stroll not unlike many trail rides they had taken before and would no doubt take again. The farther from the grave the horses walked, the more the past fell away as they approached a different future. Kitzie and Carson looked around at the new growth. The carbon of the burnt material had impassioned the high desert in a way not seen in generations. For some, those on the proverbial fence about whether to stay or go, their tardiness at deciding was rewarded. Stories told around holiday tables would invariably mention the rebirth of the open range—the revival of commitment to the land and to each other.

Kitzie had taken time to work out the fractured pieces of their world. It came down to a moment of courage or a lifetime of regret, and love had conjured courage out of thin air. She knew she would regret a life without love.

Carson rode next to her mother and was awestruck by her beauty. Her strength had carried them all through the worst time of their lives.

The footfalls of the hooves were the soundtrack as they rode on a cow path that led to a bluff with a fantastic view of the Three Bit. The morning was soft, warm enough, and there was no breeze. The late spring air was alive with the sounds of birds.

The first person they saw was Lyle Martin. He had on a pair of smooth, beige leather chinks with finely tooled leather at the waist and tooled, triple-scalloped pieces on the side of each thigh with small conchos on each part. The long fringe fell from a matching leather border to midcalf. He wore a light-blue shirt and his favorite straw hat as he sat astride his big bay gelding. He smiled broadly at them and Carson complimented him.

"Well, don't you clean up good!" She rode up to him, leaned over, and reached for his hand to squeeze it.

"So do you," he replied as he squeezed hers back.

"Thank you." And she added, "For everything."

"Your family makes it easy," he said, looking at her. "You look radiant today."

"A far cry from that first night, huh?"

"A far cry," he said, smiling.

Kitzie pulled up next to him and he turned to her and they exchanged a few quiet words. Carson rode toward the lovely setting that had been created for the ceremony. The judge was near the straw bale altar, which consisted of four bales—two down flat and two symmetrically set at an angle. Flowers had been set all around them and a path of petals led to them. Carson wondered who had gone to this exquisite effort. She spotted Jorge's dogs and then saw him near the ATV. There was a small trailer hooked up to it and she surmised that was how the tables and benches had arrived. *Must have been a bumpy ride*, she thought.

Her eyes followed her heart, looking for CJ. He was down a bit farther, past Jorge and the ATV, bent over a couple of large boxes. A big ice chest was on the ground next to him. *Someone made more than one trip,* she thought. *I wonder if the cake made it…*

The judge was mounted on a handsome gray to perform the ceremony. He was a circuit court judge, now retired, and wore his black robe, which flowed off the back of his saddle onto the dappled-gray rump of his horse. The reins rested on the neck of his stoic mount and he thumbed through a slightly larger than palm-sized, well-worn leather-bound book. There were pieces of paper interspersed throughout it and he lifted one from the back, unfolded it, and checked that the words on it were correct. He then slid the book back into his saddlebag and nodded at Carson. She turned her horse back to her mother and they moved closer to him, not quite lined up, to begin. When it was time, four horses would be in a row in front of him.

Carson looked around again and saw CJ mounted up. She watched him straighten a new Stetson cowboy hat. He was taking his time and she smiled because he looked nervous. Lyle had loaned him one of his favorite horses and Carson watched CJ run a hand along its neck, then past the saddle and onto its flank. She looked over at her mother's profile. If she was nervous, she didn't show it. Kitzie smiled at her daughter and they reached toward each other to hold hands.

Over Carson's left shoulder she heard music. It was supposed to be "Canon in D" by Brian Crane from an iPhone, through a small speaker. It was one of those tiny but powerful ones and it should have been playing a special selection of music for the event. But that wasn't what she heard and it confused her. Instead, she heard a violin—a real one—and she looked around, bewildered. She saw a man she hadn't noticed before, standing well apart from everyone else. He must have walked in from the lee side of the bluff and he was playing beautifully.

Lyle rode his horse into her line of sight and she gave him a quizzical look. He winked at her and mouthed, *"A friend of mine."*

What a lovely gesture, Carson thought as she watched the violinist play.

The horses all turned their heads to the sound of other riders approaching up the track. Tammy ran ahead and was excited. She was starting to show some age and Wyker watched her to be sure she didn't overtire. Wyker was on Johnny, and he wore a nice Western-cut jacket and his best hat. Carson saw the love on his face as Tammy dashed over to Jorge's dogs in greeting.

From the rim, riding up the track of the bluff, came Larry Stiles, well mounted, again thanks to Lyle. Carson barely recognized him. Gruffly handsome, he was clean-shaven with the notable exception of his meticulously trimmed, white-gray mustache. There was a shining anticipation in his eyes under the brim of a beige felt Stetson. His crisp white shirt was buttoned close at the collar, complemented by a simple leather belt, khaki riding pants, and new, soft-brushed boots.

Carson felt someone ride up next to her and CJ appeared. His eyes betrayed him. She looked beautiful, and he smiled at her and she smiled back. He stared at her for a moment and Carson saw a whole world of bewilderment and desire. He couldn't think of anything more he needed now that Rio was back home and growing stronger.

Carson leaned in and whispered something to him. He looked away, then at his saddle horn, considering his answer. She waited with a closed-mouth smile as he struggled with it.

"OK," he finally said. "Today you should know. And," he added, "you can't laugh."

Carson crossed her heart and held up a Girl Scout salute.

The handsome face tilted a sideways look at her and her heart melted.

"You were never a Girl Scout," he said.

She feigned a pout.

CJ motioned with his index finger for her to come closer. He spoke a name softly. "Creighton James. Creighton James Burke."

Her eyes widened and she didn't laugh. "I like it…"

Then they both looked straight ahead and she heard him say, "You'd better."

Without looking at each other, they grinned. CJ reached for her hand and she gave it imperceptibly—the first link in a wonderful chain.

It was time for the ceremony to begin. Stiles' head was bowed and turned toward Wyker in a way that Carson couldn't see his face clearly, so there was no chance of lip-reading. Her brows knitted as she wondered what they were talking about.

Moments felt like hours, then Wyker looked over at them and something changed in his expression. It wasn't quite a smile that found the edges of his mouth as he looked at Kitzie, it was more of a realization, as if the planets had aligned in the span of words. Time stopped, the air stilled, and even the bugs went silent as if in a prolonged inhalation. Then Wyker smiled and turned to Stiles, extending an open hand. The stress of the conversation left Larry's body feeling like water had flowed to a dappled creek bed and washed away. Carson watched as he relaxed and smiled—as much as she had ever seen him smile—as they moved their horses forward together.

Stiles rode up and settled his horse. The judge said good morning to everyone and asked if they were ready to begin. The violin had moved off some, so that the music was more hushed, until the musician got the cue from the judge to stop.

The judge's message and tone were spot-on and marvelous. He talked about trials by the elements and human frailty. He spoke of relationships and the tenuousness of everyone's time on this earth. He wasn't overly wordy and spoke plainly. He spoke from the heart, of loss and redemption, and how finding forgiveness and love in this life superseded all other concerns. He paused and asked if either of them had something to say and Larry Stiles did. He turned and looked at Kitzie.

"To remember love after a long sleep, to remember what I once thought life could hold…it's like my heart has flexed its wings and you are the reason to try the air again."

Weeks later, Rae's trailer was again on the road with the black gelding settled in back. This was a much longer drive but it was well worth it. Rae liked long hauls. After she took the last exit and found the charming, tree-lined country road, she slowed and put her turn signal on out of habit, even though there was no one behind her.

The driveway was long and lined with even, white-washed,

three-rail fencing. Lush green pastures and long paddocks lined out vertically in almost perfect symmetry. Through the trees, a stately, elegant house stood off to the right, but Rae took the left turn and headed to the matching expanse of barn and arenas. She stopped the trailer in the shade of an enormous tree with an inviting seating area beneath it. She shut the truck off and looked around, in complete bliss. If Rae could choose a Heaven to wake up in, it would look an awful lot like this.

She exited the truck and smelled flowered air. *Honeysuckle?* she wondered as she inhaled. She heard a dog's eager feet approaching from the direction of the house. Two fine black Labs bounded toward her in delirious greeting. A woman followed. She looked smaller and her hair more gray, but Rae recognized her.

Rae didn't wait. It was the moment she had hoped for all these weeks. She walked swiftly to the back of the trailer and slipped in the door. She moved the partition over and secured it, and went to undo the black gelding from the metal loop. His whole being seemed to breathe in and he swelled like a loaf of dough. His head whipped toward Rae's and had she not been ready for it, she would have had a shiner by day's end.

"Easy," she said to him. She undid the quick-release knot and turned him to the left to exit the trailer. He froze just before stepping out, his nostrils huge as they sucked in the familiar smells of long ago. With no warning, he let out an ear-piercing call. It was only seconds before a reply came back.

Rae didn't have time to step away before he launched out. She let the long lead rope feed out and when it was good, she turned him and he stopped. His head was high and his eyes so alive, she thought they'd explode out of his head. He was almost uncontainable and when Rae stepped down from the trailer, she moved with him to clear the back, then sent him around her as his head whipped from side to side, taking everything in.

A choked sound came from behind Rae as the woman ran around the back of the trailer. Her mouth was open in disbelief. She didn't care that there was a ball of fire at the end of the lead rope. She flung herself at him and wrapped her arms around his neck, sobbing. Then Nairobi did the darnedest thing Rae had ever seen. He completely let down and stood four-square still, his head over her shoulder as her tears of joy wet the smooth black hair of his neck.

The woman reached up and undid the rope halter knot at the side of his face and dropped it to the ground. He hooked on to her and they slowly walked together toward an immaculate, huge barn. It was one of the nicest ones Rae had ever seen, and that was saying something.

An elderly man joined them, clearly overcome with emotion. Rae could see that he was a strong, proud man, who silently nodded to Rae and then stepped toward her, took her hand in his, and bowed his head to her. He had no words and neither did she. Together they watched the woman and the horse go into the barn side by side.

They followed and when they crossed the threshold, the man parted from Rae and vanished. She didn't really pay attention to where. The bond between Nairobi and this woman was so undeniable, so strong, it seemed to Rae that there had never been a doubt that he would find his way home.

The woman opened the door to a massive stall—probably a foaling stall of some kind, at least twelve by thirty if it was a dime—and Nairobi didn't hesitate a stride. He walked right in. It was as if he had never been gone at all. There was a thick pile of shavings in the center and he walked to it, through it, back over it, and circled in it. His back legs began to fold and his front end followed. He grunted as he eased himself down, then he moaned as he rolled in them. After a minute or so, he stretched out on top of the mussed-up pile, his neck laid flat on a shavings pillow, and his head close to his owner's feet. He looked up at her with one eye, and if Rae could swear to it, she would—he smiled.

The owner's tears flowed from a place of joy. She fell to her knees in the shavings and Nairobi nosed her. She stretched out next to him, expensive designer clothes be damned, her body alongside his back, her arm over his neck, and her face in his mane. The two lay there together. It was astonishing.

Rae stepped back, a little embarrassed to intrude on such a vulnerable, raw moment. It overwhelmed her and she wiped her own tears away. Jasper, her dog, nudged her leg and she stroked his head.

"I'm OK, buddy, really," she said as they walked outside.

There was a bench flanked by lovingly tended topiaries and Rae realized she needed to sit for a second. She looked over at the rig and saw that it had been turned around. The driver's side window was down and a man's powerful, dark forearm rested on it. Rae smiled, shook her head, and smiled. She was in a fantasy, but it was real. She glanced around, partly in disbelief and partly with a certainty that after everything, she was right where she should be.

Movement out of the corner of her eye told her she wasn't alone and she looked over at the woman, who now stood before her, completely covered in shavings. Rae got up and helped her shed some of the debris.

"Well, at least its aromatic," the woman laughed, then

shook herself like a horse.

They sat together and Jasper lay down, placed his head on his paws, and closed his eyes.

"I don't have words..." the woman said to Rae. She turned and looked into Rae's eyes. "But you must stay, and we will make the time for you to tell me how this happened."

"Uh...yeah. I see...well.." Rae wasn't sure where to go from there.

"You have the guest house," the woman added, and she rose without asking if that was desirable.

Rae and Jasper were on their feet.

"This may sound awkward but..." The woman's laugh was light and deep at the same time. It was a melodic sound that rolled and built, and it reminded Rae of someone who had loved her once. She said over her shoulder, "It's two bedrooms, two en suite bathrooms, and bigger than it should be. Dinner's at the main house at six. The rig is fine where it is."

Rae stood rooted.

"We have a lot to talk about, you and I..." And the woman started toward the main house.

Rae wasn't expecting any of this and Jasper, who was now several feet ahead of her, stopped and looked over his shoulder at Rae. Rae didn't know what to do. Jasper looked to the retreating lady and followed her.

"Jasper," Rae whispered.

He stopped and looked at her again, then at the rig, then the lady, and continued to follow her.

"Unbelievable," Rae said to herself as she watched Jasper leave.

Rae walked to the driver's side window where another smile waited.

Harper turned his head and the light caught his deep-brown eyes with their mischievous sparkle. Rae looked down at her boot and kicked at a non-existent something and Harper waited. His silence, his ability to say nothing and yet say everything, was a revelation.

"Where's the dog?" he asked.

She laughed. "Traitor." And she looked in the general direction he'd gone off to. "Truly cannot explain that."

"Your feelings hurt?" he said.

She looked back at him, shrugged, then said, "Yeah, a little. Never had that happen before."

He opened the trucked door and she stepped back. "Looks like we're staying."

"Wha…I mean…" Rae was flustered and didn't know how to transition to whatever was next. She added a confession. "The underside of my good nature may not be altogether admirable."

"Of course, you're a lawyer," he sassed.

She shrugged and looked after her dog, who had disappeared through a set of enormous doors. Looking after him, she mused, "That's remarkable…"

Harper closed the door, leaned against the truck, and crossed his arms. "What else hasn't happened to you before?" he said with a brilliant smile, the likes of which lit the world.

He turned to her and put his arm around her shoulders. "We'll find out together," he said as they followed Jasper.

Epilogue

The couple had hiked and backpacked most of the West and were attracted to the romance of the Oregon high desert. They studied topography maps that included the Steens and Trout Creek Mountains, the Desert Trail, Lambert Rocks, and Rhinehart. It was now a question of where to go, as an immense range fire had swept the entire area, devastating the landscape. The recovery from the fires had created an opportunity for the two naturalists to observe the process, and they were curious to see what had been spared and what still struggled...like their relationship was starting to do.

On the edge of the next phase of their life, the man hadn't committed and the woman was growing uncertain it would ever happen. They were close to breaking up when they drove through Burns and out Hwy 78. They decided to explore with a day hike and stay overnight, then go back to the highway and on to another location...if they weren't done with each other by then.

To get along, a truce of sorts had settled on the couple. She was quiet in her thoughts and he struggled with his own. He had been selfish, he realized, and hoped it wasn't too late. He didn't want to lose her. With every step he took, he became more convinced that he wanted to go into the future with her by his side, yet he was at a loss about how to express his feelings and he wondered if she would believe him.

In more ways than one, it was getting late. Soon it was time to pick a spot and pitch camp. He followed her along a fire trail, and felt that one of his boots had loosened and he had a twig or something in it. He called to her and she stopped. She may have been mildly annoyed or disinterested, he wasn't sure. He had been in his own head, rehearsing the right things to say and how to change things up and move forward together.

He sat down and took the boot off and shook the offending bit free, then put the boot back on and knelt to tie it. He looked toward her as he fumbled with the laces. She had turned and he could see her looking at something off in the distance. He smiled at her beauty, the grace of her, and he couldn't imagine his life without her. He stood up and she looked at him. They locked eyes and she managed a smile.

The man shifted his pack to rebalance it when something in the dirt just ahead of him caught his eye—something that sparkled, maybe a piece of quartz or a pop-top from an aluminum can, he thought wryly. Curious, he stepped forward and cleared some dirt away with the toe of his boot. There was black ash mixed with it. After the great Three Corner fire was history, if you scratched the earth deep enough, you could still smell it.

He frowned and crouched. The pack slid forward and tapped the back of his head. He almost didn't reach for the object to free it from its ashen home, but he did. He picked it up and it wasn't a pop-top—it was a ring. He sucked in a sharp breath, hardly able to believe his eyes. There were diamond accent stones up both sides of the ring's shank and the main part curved to a point. There were two bifurcations on each side, like glistening tree branches supporting the prong, two nice side stones and a rather impressive center diamond, all set in what he guessed was white gold.

He blew on it to clear away bits of debris and twisted it in his fingertips. It was wonderful. *Nature* made this, he thought.

He watched her walking ahead of him, a backpack with

great legs. He tried to breathe normally to stop the dizzy feeling he had after standing up with the object in his hand. It was stunning. He slipped it into his vest pocket, felt that it was secure, and slowly, very carefully, zipped it up. As he walked toward her, his hand went to it and felt the outline to make sure it was real. It looked real and felt real.

He caught up to her and the late afternoon light touched her face. It was as if the sun only shone on her and he reached for her hand. She smiled, and the wind caught up a piece of her hair and it danced.

And…

An anonymous donor fully funded a foundation whose primary purpose was to defend America's wild mustangs. The mustangs indeed got a good lawyer. Several of them, in fact.

The foundation was called the Nairobi Trust.

GLOSSARY

Banamine: Available by prescription from a veterinarian, Banamine is a potent analgesic (relieves pain) with anti-inflammatory and fever-reducing capacity.

Boot Jack: Sometimes known as a boot pull, it aids in the removal of boots. A u-shaped mouth grips the heel of the boot, you stand on the back of the device with the other foot and pull the foot free.

Bridle: Headgear used to control a horse, consisting of buckled straps to which a bit and reins are attached.

Bridle Horse or Finished Bridle Horse: A horse developed far enough that he can be ridden and worked one-handed in a leverage curb or spade bit. The original vaqueros developed their methods and took lots of time to build true leadership, partnership, and refinement.

Bute: Phenylbutazone is an analgesic (relieves pain) and anti-inflammatory medication commonly used for the treatment of lameness and pain in horses.

Chaps: Sturdy coverings for the legs of the rider, consisting of leather leggings and a belt. They are buckled over jeans with the belt and they have no seat.

Chinks: Chinkaderos, Chingaderos, also called armitas, chivarras, or brush-poppers, are short, lightweight leggings that provide protection to the rider's legs.

Cinch: A strap that keeps the saddle in place on a horse, runs under the horse's belly and is attached to the saddle on both sides.

Dallied: Tied without a knot.

Easy Boot: A quick alternative to shoeing when a horse loses a shoe. A lightweight rubber boot that fits on the horse's foot with a semi-aggressive tread, and can be used over various terrains. Cable buckles and ice studs can be installed to provide extra traction.

Fender: The adjustable part of a saddle that serves as a barrier between your leg and the horse, keeping your leg from contacting the horse's sweat or creating friction. Attached to a stirrup leather.

Flag: Desensitizing tool to train a horse.

Headstall: The central piece of the bridle that goes behind the ears and has cheek pieces that attach to the bit on either side.

Heritage Roughstock boot: Square-toed boot built for working cowboys, durable enough for the range, and steeped in solid tradition. This is one of the best-loved boot styles that the Ariat Company manufactures.

Horn: The knob at the front of a Western saddle positioned on the pommel; rider can hold on to it to balance; also allows vaqueros to control cattle by wrapping a rope around it.

Gooseneck: A truck trailer for transporting livestock with a projecting front end designed to attach to the bed of a pick-up truck.

Lace-up Ropers: A boot with a rounded toe and flexible fit. Many are lace-up boots, which provide a great fit and ankle support. If thrown from a saddle and dragged, this type of boot poses an issue because the rider's foot will not slip out of the boot.

Mecate: A long rope, traditionally of horsehair, approximately 20-25 feet long and up to about ¾ inch in diameter. In this story, I use the variation sometimes called mecate reins or McCarty, which is used as a rein system for a bridle with a bit. This design, usually of nylon rope, has a single looped rein attached to either side of a snaffle bit with a lead rein coming off the bit ring in a manner similar to the lead rein of a traditional mecate. This set-up is most often seen today among some practitioners of the natural horsemanship movement.

Pannier: Rectangular boxes typically made of canvas, leather, or wicker. For horse packing, they are supported by a pack saddle to distribute weight more evenly across the back of an animal.

Previcox: Chewable tablets used for the control of pain and inflammation associated with osteoarthritis and for the control of post-operative pain and inflammation associated with soft tissue and orthopedic surgery for dogs. In recent years, owners of aging horses and horses with lameness issues have used this product when long-term consistent use of bute is undesirable. It is an off-label usage and against regulations, but many horse owners use it successfully.

Reata: A long, noosed rope used to catch animals.

Rope Halter: A device made of rope that fits around the head of an animal and is used to lead or secure the animal. The ones described in this book have no metal components and the placement of the tied knots on the halter affect pressure points for refined training.

Stirrup: Holds the foot of the rider and is attached to most saddles by adjustable stirrup leathers to fit both the size of the rider. They are used to remain in correct position over the horse's center of balance.

Tie Line: Also called a high line or a picket line, this is a line stretched between two trees to which you tie your horse.

Vaquero: A horse-mounted livestock herder of a tradition that originated on the Iberian Peninsula. A cowboy, or more common in the West, a buckaroo. A cattle driver.

Worlds: Final scores from shows for the year are calculated in various show divisions, and the total qualifies a horse and rider to go. There are Open, Non-Pro, and Amateur divisions, and riders have to qualify for a limited number of slots to join the World Competition, which is referred to as "the Worlds."

Also Available...

Three Corner Rustlers (Available on Amazon.com)

Three Corner Rustlers Audio Book

Three Corner Fire Audio Book

(Available for download at iTunes and Amazon)

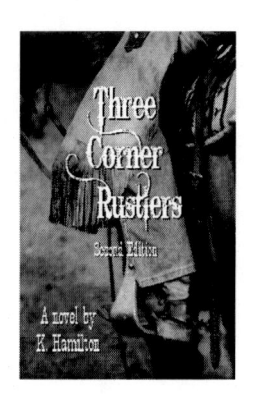

and

Three Corner Rustlers CD Box Set

Includes bonus music CD
"Three Corner Blues" by Lorin Rowan

Available only at www.kimvogee.com

Made in United States
North Haven, CT
13 February 2024